THE
APPEAL

Also by John Grisham

A Time to Kill
The Firm
The Pelican Brief
The Client
The Chamber
The Rainmaker
The Runaway Jury
The Partner
The Street Lawyer
The Testament
The Brethren
A Painted House
Skipping Christmas
The Summons
The King of Torts
Bleachers
The Last Juror
The Broker
The Innocent Man
Playing for Pizza

JOHN
GRISHAM

THE
APPEAL

DOUBLEDAY LARGE PRINT HOME LIBRARY EDITION

DOUBLEDAY

New York London Toronto Sydney Auckland

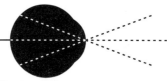

This Large Print Book carries the Seal of Approval of N.A.V.H.

TO PROFESSOR ROBERT C. KHAYAT

THE
APPEAL

PART ONE

THE
VERDICT

CHAPTER 1

The jury was ready.

After forty-two hours of deliberations that followed seventy-one days of trial that included 530 hours of testimony from four dozen witnesses, and after a lifetime of sitting silently as the lawyers haggled and the judge lectured and the spectators watched like hawks for telltale signs, the jury was ready. Locked away in the jury room, secluded and secure, ten of them proudly signed their names to the verdict while the other two pouted in their corners, detached and miserable in their dissension. There were hugs and smiles and no small measure of self-congratulation because they had survived this little war and could now march proudly back into the arena with a decision they had rescued through sheer determination and the dogged pursuit of compromise. Their ordeal was over; their civic duty complete. They had served above and beyond. They were ready.

The foreman knocked on the door and rustled Uncle Joe from his slumbers. Uncle Joe, the ancient bailiff, had guarded them while he also arranged their meals, heard their complaints, and quietly slipped their messages to the judge. In his younger years, back when his hearing was better, Uncle Joe was rumored to also eavesdrop on his juries through a flimsy pine door he and he alone had selected and installed. But his listening days were over, and, as he had confided to no one but his wife, after the ordeal of this particular trial he might just hang up his old pistol once and for all. The strain of controlling justice was wearing him down.

He smiled and said, "That's great. I'll get the judge," as if the judge were somewhere in the bowels of the courthouse just waiting for a call from Uncle Joe. Instead, by custom, he found a clerk and passed along the wonderful news. It was truly exciting. The old courthouse had never seen a trial so large and so long. To end it with no decision at all would have been a shame.

The clerk tapped lightly on the judge's door, then took a step inside and proudly announced, "We have a verdict," as if she had personally labored through the negotiations and now was presenting the result as a gift.

The judge closed his eyes and let loose a deep, satisfying sigh. He smiled a happy, nervous smile of enormous relief, almost disbelief, and finally said, "Round up the lawyers."

After almost five days of deliberations, Judge Harrison had resigned himself to the likelihood of a hung jury, his worst nightmare. After four years of bare-knuckle litigation and four months of a hotly contested trial, the prospect of a draw made him ill. He couldn't begin to imagine the prospect of doing it all again.

He stuck his feet into his old penny loafers, jumped from the chair grinning like a little boy, and reached for his robe. It was finally over, the longest trial of his extremely colorful career.

The clerk's first call went to the firm of Payton & Payton, a local husband-and-wife team now operating out of an abandoned dime store in a lesser part of town. A paralegal picked up the phone, listened for a few seconds, hung up, then shouted, "The jury has a verdict!" His voice echoed through the cavernous maze of small, temporary workrooms and jolted his colleagues.

He shouted it again as he ran to The Pit, where the rest of the firm was frantically gathering. Wes Payton was already there, and when his wife, Mary Grace, rushed in, their eyes met in a split second of unbridled fear and bewilderment. Two paralegals, two secretaries, and a bookkeeper gathered at the long, cluttered worktable, where they suddenly froze and gawked at one another, all waiting for someone else to speak.

Could it really be over? After they had waited for an eternity, could it end so suddenly? So abruptly? With just a phone call?

"How about a moment of silent prayer," Wes said, and they held hands in a tight circle and prayed as they had never prayed before. All manner of petitions were lifted up to God Almighty, but the common plea was for victory. Please, dear Lord, after all this time and effort and money and fear and doubt, please, oh please, grant us a divine victory. And deliver us from humiliation, ruin, bankruptcy, and a host of other evils that a bad verdict will bring.

The clerk's second call was to the cell phone of Jared Kurtin, the architect of the defense. Mr. Kurtin was lounging peacefully on a rented leather sofa in his temporary office on Front Street in downtown Hattiesburg, three blocks from the courthouse. He was reading a biography and watching the hours pass at $750 per. He listened calmly, slapped the phone shut, and said, "Let's go. The jury is ready." His dark-suited soldiers snapped to attention and lined up to escort him down the street in the direction of another crushing victory. They marched away without comment, without prayer.

Other calls went to other lawyers, then to the reporters, and within minutes the word was on the street and spreading rapidly.

———

Somewhere near the top of a tall building in lower Manhattan, a panic-stricken young man barged into a serious meeting and whispered the urgent news to Mr. Carl Trudeau, who immediately lost interest in the issues on the table, stood abruptly, and said, "Looks like the jury has reached a verdict." He marched out of the room and down the hall to a vast corner suite, where he removed his jacket, loosened his tie, walked to a window, and gazed through the early darkness at the Hudson River in the distance. He waited, and as usual asked himself how, exactly, so much of his empire could rest upon the combined wisdom of twelve average people in backwater Mississippi.

For a man who knew so much, that answer was still elusive.

———

People were hurrying into the courthouse from all directions when the Paytons parked on the street behind it. They stayed in the car for a moment, still holding hands. For four months they had tried not to touch each other anywhere near the courthouse. Someone was always watching. Maybe a juror or a reporter. It was important to be as professional as possible. The novelty of a married legal team surprised people, and the Paytons tried to treat each other as attorneys and not as spouses.

And, during the trial, there had been precious little touching away from the courthouse or anywhere else.

"What are you thinking?" Wes asked without looking at his wife. His heart was racing and his forehead was wet. He still gripped the wheel with his left hand, and he kept telling himself to relax.

Relax. What a joke.

"I have never been so afraid," Mary Grace said.

"Neither have I."

A long pause as they breathed deeply and watched a television van almost slaughter a pedestrian.

"Can we survive a loss?" she said. "That's the question."

"We have to survive; we have no choice. But we're not going to lose."

"Attaboy. Let's go."

They joined the rest of their little firm and entered the courthouse together. Waiting in her usual spot on the first floor by the soft drink machines was their client, the plaintiff, Jeannette Baker, and when she saw her lawyers, she immediately began to cry. Wes took one arm, Mary Grace the other, and they escorted Jeannette up the stairs to the main courtroom on the second floor. They could've carried her. She weighed less than a hundred pounds and had aged five years during the trial. She was depressed, at times delusional, and though not anorexic, she simply didn't eat. At thirty-four, she had already buried a child and a husband and was now at the end of a horrible trial she secretly wished she had never pursued.

The courtroom was in a state of high alert, as if bombs were coming and the sirens were wailing. Dozens of people milled about, or looked for seats, or chatted nervously with their eyes darting around. When Jared Kurtin and the defense army entered from a side door, everyone gawked as if he might know something they didn't. Day after day for the past four months he had proven that he could see around corners, but at that moment his face revealed nothing. He huddled gravely with his subordinates.

Across the room, just a few feet away, the Paytons and Jeannette settled into their chairs at the plaintiff's table. Same chairs, same positions, same deliberate strategy to impress upon the jurors that this poor widow and her two lonely lawyers were taking on a giant corporation with unlimited resources. Wes Payton glanced at Jared Kurtin, their eyes met, and each offered a polite nod. The miracle of the trial was that the two men were still able to treat each other with a modest dose of civility, even converse when absolutely necessary. It had become a matter of pride. Regardless of how nasty the situation, and there had been so many nasty ones, each was determined to rise above the gutter and offer a hand.

Mary Grace did not look over, and if she had, she would not have nodded or smiled. And it was a good thing that she did not carry a handgun in her purse, or half of the dark suits on the other side wouldn't be there. She arranged a clean legal pad on the table before her, wrote the date, then her name, then could not think of anything else to log in. In seventy-one days of trial she had filled sixty-six legal pads, all the same size and color and now filed in perfect order in a secondhand metal cabinet in The Pit. She handed a tissue to Jeannette. Though she counted virtually everything, Mary Grace had not kept a running tally on the number of tissue boxes Jeannette had used during the trial. Several dozen at least.

The woman cried almost nonstop, and while Mary Grace was profoundly sympathetic, she was also tired of all the damned crying. She was tired of everything—the exhaustion, the stress, the sleepless nights, the scrutiny, the time away from her children, their run-down apartment, the mountain of unpaid bills, the neglected clients, the cold Chinese food at midnight, the challenge of doing her face and hair every morning so she could be somewhat attractive in front of the jury. It was expected of her.

Stepping into a major trial is like plunging with a weighted belt into a dark and weedy pond. You manage to scramble up for air, but the rest of the world doesn't matter. And you always think you're drowning.

A few rows behind the Paytons, at the end of a bench that was quickly becoming crowded, the Paytons' banker chewed his nails while trying to appear calm. His name was Tom Huff, or Huffy to everyone who knew him. Huffy had dropped in from time to time to watch the trial and offer a silent prayer of his own. The Paytons owed Huffy's bank $400,000, and the only collateral was a tract of farmland in Cary County owned by Mary Grace's father. On a good day it might fetch $100,000, leaving, obviously, a substantial chunk of unsecured debt. If the Paytons lost the case, then Huffy's once promising career as a banker would be over. The bank president had long since stopped yelling at him. Now all the threats were by e-mail.

What had begun innocently enough with a simple $90,000 second-mortgage loan against their lovely suburban home had progressed into a gaping hellhole of red ink and foolish spending. Foolish at least in Huffy's opinion. But the nice home was gone, as was the nice downtown office, and the imported cars, and everything else. The Paytons were risking it all, and Huffy had to admire them. A big verdict, and he was a genius. The wrong verdict, and he'd stand in line behind them at the bankruptcy court.

The moneymen on the other side of the courtroom were not chewing their nails and were not particularly worried about bankruptcy, though it had been discussed. Krane

Chemical had plenty of cash and profits and assets, but it also had hundreds of potential plaintiffs waiting like vultures to hear what the world was about to hear. A crazy verdict, and the lawsuits would fly.

But they were a confident bunch at that moment. Jared Kurtin was the best defense lawyer money could buy. The company's stock had dipped only slightly. Mr. Trudeau, up in New York, seemed to be satisfied.

They couldn't wait to get home.

Thank God the markets had closed for the day.

Uncle Joe yelled, "Keep your seats," and Judge Harrison entered through the door behind his bench. He had long since cut out the silly routine of requiring everyone to stand just so he could assume his throne.

"Good afternoon," he said quickly. It was almost 5:00 p.m. "I have been informed by the jury that a verdict has been reached." He was looking around, making sure the players were present. "I expect decorum at all times. No outbursts. No one leaves until I dismiss the jury. Any questions? Any additional frivolous motions from the defense?"

Jared Kurtin never flinched. He did not acknowledge the judge in any way, but just kept doodling on his legal pad as if he were painting a masterpiece. If Krane Chemical lost, it would appeal with a vengeance, and the cornerstone of its appeal would be the obvious bias of the Honorable Thomas Alsobrook Harrison IV, a former trial lawyer with a proven dislike for all big corporations in general and, now, Krane Chemical in particular.

"Mr. Bailiff, bring in the jury."

The door next to the jury box opened, and somewhere a giant unseen vacuum sucked every ounce of air from the courtroom. Hearts froze. Bodies stiffened. Eyes found objects to fixate on. The only sound was that of the jurors' feet shuffling across well-worn carpet.

Jared Kurtin continued his methodical scribbling. His routine was to never look at the faces of the jurors when they returned with a verdict. After a hundred trials he knew they were impossible to read. And why bother? Their decision would be announced in a matter of seconds anyway. His team had strict instructions to ignore the jurors and show no reaction whatsoever to the verdict.

Of course Jared Kurtin wasn't facing financial and professional ruin. Wes Payton certainly was, and he could not keep his eyes from the eyes of the jurors as they settled into their seats. The dairy operator looked away, a bad sign. The schoolteacher stared right through Wes, another bad sign. As the foreman handed an envelope to the clerk, the minister's wife glanced at Wes with a look of pity, but then she had been offering the same sad face since the opening statements.

Mary Grace caught the sign, and she wasn't even looking for it. As she handed another tissue to Jeannette Baker, who was practically sobbing now, Mary Grace stole a look at juror number six, the one closest to her, Dr. Leona Rocha, a retired English professor at the university. Dr. Rocha, behind red-framed reading glasses, gave the quickest, prettiest, most sensational wink Mary Grace would ever receive.

"Have you reached a verdict?" Judge Harrison was asking.

"Yes, Your Honor, we have," the foreman said.

"Is it unanimous?"

"No, sir, it is not."

"Do at least nine of you agree on the verdict?"

"Yes, sir. The vote is 10 to 2."

"That's all that matters."

Mary Grace scribbled a note about the wink, but in the fury of the moment she could not read her own handwriting. Try to appear calm, she kept telling herself.

Judge Harrison took the envelope from the clerk, removed a sheet of paper, and began reviewing the verdict—heavy wrinkles burrowing into his forehead, eyes frowning as he pinched the bridge of his nose. After an eternity he said, "It appears to be in order." Not one single twitch or grin or widening of the eyes, nothing to indicate what was written on the sheet of paper.

He looked down and nodded at his court reporter and cleared his throat, thoroughly relishing the moment. Then the wrinkles softened around his eyes, the jaw muscles loosened, the shoulders sagged a bit, and, to Wes anyway, there was suddenly hope that the jury had scorched the defendant.

In a slow, loud voice, Judge Harrison read: "Question number one: 'Do you find, by a preponderance of the evidence, that the groundwater at issue was contaminated by Krane Chemical Corporation?' " After a treacherous pause that lasted no more than five seconds, he continued, "The answer is 'Yes.' "

One side of the courtroom managed to breathe while the other side began to turn blue.

"Question number two: 'Do you find, by a preponderance of the evidence, that the contamination was the proximate cause of the death or deaths of (a) Chad Baker and/or (b) Pete Baker?' Answer: 'Yes, for both.' "

Mary Grace managed to pluck tissues from a box and hand them over with her left hand while writing furiously with her right. Wes managed to steal a glance at juror number four, who happened to be glancing at him with a humorous grin that seemed to say, "Now for the good part."

"Question number three: 'For Chad Baker, what amount of money do you award to his mother, Jeannette Baker, as damages for his wrongful death?' Answer: 'Five hundred thousand dollars.' "

Dead children aren't worth much, because they earn nothing, but Chad's impressive award rang like an alarm because it gave a quick preview of what was to come. Wes stared at the clock above the judge and thanked God that bankruptcy had been averted.

"Question number four: 'For Pete Baker, what amount of money do you award to his widow, Jeannette Baker, as damages for his wrongful death?' Answer: 'Two and a half million dollars.' "

There was a rustle from the money boys in the front row behind Jared Kurtin. Krane could certainly handle a $3 million hit, but it was the ripple effect that suddenly terrified them. For his part, Mr. Kurtin had yet to flinch.

Not yet.

Jeannette Baker began to slide out of her chair. She was caught by both of her lawyers, who pulled her up, wrapped arms around her frail shoulders, and whispered to her. She was sobbing, out of control.

There were six questions on the list that the lawyers had hammered out, and if the jury answered yes to number five, then the whole world would go crazy. Judge Harrison was at that point, reading it slowly, clearing his throat, studying the answer. Then he revealed his mean streak. He did so with a smile. He glanced up a few inches, just above the sheet of paper he was holding, just over the cheap reading glasses perched on his nose, and he looked directly at Wes Payton. The grin was tight, conspiratorial, yet filled with gleeful satisfaction.

"Question number five: 'Do you find, by a preponderance of the evidence, that the actions of Krane Chemical Corporation were either intentional or so grossly negligent as to justify the imposition of punitive damages?' Answer: 'Yes.' "

Mary Grace stopped writing and looked over the bobbing head of her client to her husband, whose gaze was frozen upon her. They had won, and that alone was an exhilarating, almost indescribable rush of euphoria. But how large was their victory? At that crucial split second, both knew it was indeed a landslide.

"Question number six: 'What is the amount of punitive damages?' Answer: 'Thirty-eight million dollars.' "

There were gasps and coughs and soft whistles as the shock waves rattled around the courtroom. Jared Kurtin and his gang were busy writing everything down and trying to appear unfazed by the bomb blast. The honchos from Krane in the front row were trying to recover and breathe normally. Most glared at the jurors and thought vile thoughts that ran along the lines of ignorant people, backwater stupidity, and so on.

Mr. and Mrs. Payton were again both reaching for their client, who was overcome by the sheer weight of the verdict and trying pitifully to sit up. Wes whispered reassurances to Jeannette while repeating to himself the numbers he had just heard. Somehow, he managed to keep his face serious and avoid a goofy smile.

Huffy the banker stopped crunching his nails. In less than thirty seconds he had gone from a disgraced, bankrupt former bank vice president to a rising star with designs on a bigger salary and office. He even felt smarter. Oh, what a marvelous entrance into the bank's boardroom he would choreograph first thing in the morning. The judge was going on about formalities and thanking the jurors, but Huffy didn't care. He had heard all he needed to hear.

The jurors stood and filed out as Uncle Joe held the door and nodded with approval. He would later tell his wife that he had predicted such a verdict, though she had no memory of it. He claimed he hadn't missed a verdict in the many decades he had worked as a bailiff. When the jurors were gone, Jared Kurtin stood and, with perfect composure, rattled off the usual post-verdict inquiries, which Judge Harrison took with great compassion now that the blood was on the floor. Mary Grace had no response. Mary Grace didn't care. She had what she wanted.

Wes was thinking about the $41 million and fighting his emotions. The firm would survive, as would their marriage, their reputations, everything.

When Judge Harrison finally announced, "We are adjourned," a mob raced from the courtroom. Everyone grabbed a cell phone.

———

Mr. Trudeau was still standing at the window, watching the last of the sun set far beyond New Jersey. Across the wide room Stu the assistant took the call and ventured forward a few steps before mustering the nerve to say, "Sir, that was from Hattiesburg. Three million in actual damages, thirty-eight in punitive."

From the rear, there was a slight dip in the boss's shoulder, a quiet exhaling in frustration, then a mumbling of obscenities.

Mr. Trudeau slowly turned around and glared at the assistant as if he just might shoot the messenger. "You sure you heard that right?" he asked, and Stu desperately wished he had not.

"Yes, sir."

Behind him the door was open. Bobby Ratzlaff appeared in a rush, out of breath, shocked and scared and looking for Mr. Trudeau. Ratzlaff was the chief in-house lawyer, and his neck would be the first on the chopping block. He was already sweating.

"Get your boys here in five minutes," Mr. Trudeau growled, then turned back to his window.

———

The press conference materialized on the first floor of the courthouse. In two small groups, Wes and Mary Grace chatted patiently with reporters. Both gave the same answers to the same questions. No, the verdict was not a record for the state of Mississippi. Yes, they felt it was justified. No, it was not expected, not an award that large anyway. Certainly it would be appealed. Wes had great respect for Jared Kurtin, but not for his client. Their firm currently represented thirty other plaintiffs who were suing Krane Chemical. No, they did not expect to settle those cases.

Yes, they were exhausted.

After half an hour they finally begged off, and walked from the Forrest County Circuit Court building hand in hand, each lugging a heavy briefcase. They were photographed getting into their car and driving away.

Alone, they said nothing. Four blocks, five, six. Ten minutes passed without a word. The car, a battered Ford Taurus with a million miles, at least one low tire, and the constant click of a sticking valve, drifted through the streets around the university.

Wes spoke first. "What's one-third of forty-one million?"

"Don't even think about it."

"I'm not thinking about it. Just a joke."

"Just drive."

"Anyplace in particular?"

"No."

The Taurus ventured into the suburbs, going nowhere but certainly not going back to the office. They stayed far away from the neighborhood with the lovely home they had once owned.

Reality slowly settled in as the numbness began to fade. A lawsuit they had reluctantly filed four years earlier had now been decided in a most dramatic fashion. An excruciating marathon was over, and though they had a temporary victory, the costs had been great. The wounds were raw, the battle scars still very fresh.

The gas gauge showed less than a quarter of a tank, something that Wes would have barely noticed two years earlier. Now it was a much more serious matter. Back then he drove a BMW—Mary Grace had a Jaguar—and when he needed fuel, he simply pulled in to his favorite station and filled the tank with a credit card. He never saw the bills; they were handled by his bookkeeper. Now the credit cards were gone, as were the BMW and the Jaguar, and the same bookkeeper was working at half salary and doling out a few dollars in cash to keep the Payton firm just above the waterline.

Mary Grace glanced at the gauge, too, a recently acquired habit. She noticed and remembered the price of everything—a gallon of gas, a loaf of bread, a half gallon of milk. She was the saver and he was the spender, but not too many years ago, when the clients were calling and the cases were settling, she had relaxed a bit too much and enjoyed their success. Saving and investing had not been a priority. They were young, the firm was growing, the future had no limits.

Whatever she had managed to put into mutual funds had long since been devoured by the *Baker* case.

An hour earlier they had been broke, on paper, with ruinous debts far outweighing whatever flimsy assets they might list. Now things were different. The liabilities had not gone away, but the black side of their balance sheet had certainly improved.

Or had it?

When might they see some or all of this wonderful verdict? Might Krane now offer a settlement? How long would the appeal take? How much time could they now devote to the rest of their practice?

Neither wanted to ponder the questions that were haunting both of them. They were simply too tired and too relieved. For an eternity they had talked of little else, and now they talked about nothing. Tomorrow or the next day they could begin the debriefing.

"We're almost out of gas," she said.

No retort came to his weary mind, so Wes said, "What about dinner?"

"Macaroni and cheese with the kids."

The trial had not only drained them of their energy and assets; it had also burned away any excess weight they might have been carrying at the outset. Wes was down at least fifteen pounds, though he didn't know for sure because he hadn't stepped on the scale in months. Nor was he about to inquire into this delicate matter with his wife, but it was obvious she needed to eat. They had skipped many meals—breakfasts when they were scrambling to dress the kids and get them to school, lunches when one argued motions in Harrison's office while the other prepared for the next cross-examination, dinners when they worked until midnight and simply forgot to eat. Power-Bars and energy drinks had kept them going.

"Sounds great," he said, and turned left onto a street that would take them home.

———

Ratzlaff and two other lawyers took their seats at the sleek leather table in a corner of Mr. Trudeau's office suite. The walls were all glass and provided magnificent views of skyscrapers packed into the financial district, though no one was in the mood for scenery. Mr. Trudeau was on the phone across the room behind his chrome desk. The lawyers waited nervously. They had talked nonstop to the eyewitnesses down in Mississippi but still had few answers.

The boss finished his phone conversation and strode purposefully across the room. "What happened?" he snapped. "An hour ago you guys were downright cocky. Now we got our asses handed to us. What happened?" He sat down and glared at Ratzlaff.

"Trial by jury. It's full of risks," Ratzlaff said.

"I've been through trials, plenty of them, and I usually win. I thought we were paying the best shysters in the business. The best mouthpieces money can buy. We spared no expense, right?"

"Oh yes. We paid dearly. Still paying."

Mr. Trudeau slapped the table and barked, "What went wrong?!"

Well, Ratzlaff thought to himself and wanted to say aloud except that he very much treasured his job, let's start with the fact that our company built a pesticide plant in Podunk, Mississippi, because the land and labor were dirt cheap, then we spent the next thirty years dumping chemicals and waste into the ground and into the rivers, quite illegally of course, and we contaminated the drinking water until it tasted like spoiled milk, which, as bad as it was, wasn't the worst part, because then people started dying of cancer and leukemia.

That, Mr. Boss and Mr. CEO and Mr. Corporate Raider, is exactly what went wrong.

"The lawyers feel good about the appeal," Ratzlaff said instead, without much conviction.

"Oh, that's just super. Right now I really trust these lawyers. Where did you find these clowns?"

"They're the best, okay?"

"Sure. And let's just explain to the press that we're ecstatic about our appeal and perhaps our stock won't crash tomorrow. Is that what you're saying?"

"We can spin it," Ratzlaff said. The other two lawyers were glancing at the glass walls. Who wanted to be the first to jump?

One of Mr. Trudeau's cell phones rang and he snatched it off the table. "Hi, honey," he said as he stood and walked away. It was (the third) Mrs. Trudeau, the latest trophy, a deadly young woman whom Ratzlaff and everyone else at the company avoided at all costs. Her husband was whispering, then said goodbye.

He walked to a window near the lawyers and gazed at the sparkling towers around him. "Bobby," he said without looking, "do you have any idea where the jury got the figure of thirty-eight million for punitive damages?"

"Not right offhand."

"Of course you don't. For the first nine months of this year, Krane has averaged thirty-eight million a month in profits. A bunch of ignorant rednecks who collectively couldn't earn a hundred grand a year, and they sit there like gods taking from the rich and giving to the poor."

"We still have the money, Carl," Ratzlaff

said. "It'll be years before a dime changes hands, if, in fact, that ever happens."

"Great! Spin that to the wolves tomorrow while our stock goes down the drain."

Ratzlaff shut up and slumped in his chair. The other two lawyers were not about to utter a sound.

Mr. Trudeau was pacing dramatically. "Forty-one million dollars. And there are how many other cases out there, Bobby? Did someone say two hundred, three hundred? Well, if there were three hundred this morning, there will be three thousand tomorrow morning. Every redneck in south Mississippi with a fever blister will now claim to have sipped the magic brew from Bowmore. Every two-bit ambulance chaser with a law degree is driving there now to sign up clients. This wasn't supposed to happen, Bobby. You assured me."

Ratzlaff had a memo under lock and key. It was eight years old and had been prepared under his supervision. It ran for a hundred pages and described in gruesome detail the company's illegal dumping of toxic waste at the Bowmore plant. It summarized the company's elaborate efforts to hide the dumping, to dupe the Environmental Protection Agency, and to buy off the politicians at the local, state, and federal level. It recommended a clandestine but effective cleanup of the waste site, at a cost of some $50 million. It begged anyone who read it to stop the dumping.

And, most important at this critical moment, it predicted a bad verdict someday in a courtroom.

Only luck and a flagrant disregard for the rules of civil procedure had allowed Ratzlaff to keep the memo a secret.

Mr. Trudeau had been given a copy of it eight years earlier, though he now denied he'd ever seen it. Ratzlaff was tempted to dust it off now and read a few selected passages, but, again, he treasured his job.

Mr. Trudeau walked to the table, placed both palms flat on the Italian leather, glared at Bobby Ratzlaff, and said, "I swear to you, it will never happen. Not one dime of our hard-earned profits will ever get into the hands of those trailer park peasants."

The three lawyers stared at their boss, whose eyes were narrow and glowing. He was breathing fire, and finished by saying, "If I have to bankrupt it or break it into fifteen pieces, I swear to you on my mother's grave that not one dime of Krane's money will ever be touched by those ignorant people."

And with that promise, he walked across the Persian rug, lifted his jacket from a rack, and left the office.

CHAPTER 2

Jeannette Baker was taken by her relatives back to Bowmore, her hometown twenty miles from the courthouse. She was weak from shock and sedated as usual, and she did not want to see a crowd and pretend to celebrate. The numbers represented a victory, but the verdict was also the end of a long, arduous journey. And her husband and little boy were still quite dead.

She lived in an old trailer with Bette, her stepsister, on a gravel road in a forlorn Bowmore neighborhood known as Pine Grove. Other trailers were scattered along other unpaved streets. Most of the cars and trucks parked around the trailers were decades old, unpainted and dented. There were a few homes of the permanent variety, immobile, anchored on slabs fifty years earlier, but they, too, were aging badly and showed signs of obvious neglect. There were few jobs in Bowmore and even fewer in Pine Grove, and a quick stroll along Jeannette's street would depress any visitor.

The news arrived before she did, and a small crowd was gathering when she got home. They put her to bed, then they sat in the cramped den and whispered about the verdict and speculated about what it all meant.

Forty-one million dollars? How would it affect the other lawsuits? Would Krane be forced to clean up its mess? When could she expect to see some of the money? They were cautious not to dwell on this last question, but it was the dominant thought.

More friends arrived and the crowd spilled out of the trailer and onto a shaky wooden deck, where they pulled up lawn chairs and sat and talked in the cool air of the early evening. They drank bottled water and soft drinks. For a long-suffering people, the victory was sweet. Finally, they had won. Something. They had struck back at Krane, a company they hated with every ounce of energy they could muster, and they had finally landed a retaliatory blow. Maybe the tide was turning. Somewhere out there beyond Bowmore someone had finally listened.

They talked about lawyers and depositions and the Environmental Protection Agency and the latest toxicology and geological reports. Though they were not well educated, they were fluent in the lingo of toxic waste and groundwater contamination and cancer clusters. They were living the nightmare.

Jeannette was awake in her dark bedroom, listening to the muffled conversations around her. She felt secure. These were her people, friends and family and fellow victims. The bonds were tight, the suffering shared. And the money would be, too. If she ever saw a dime, she planned to spread it around.

As she stared at the dark ceiling, she was not overwhelmed by the verdict. Her relief at being finished with the ordeal of the trial far outweighed the thrill of winning. She wanted to sleep for a week and wake up in a brand-new world with her little family intact and everyone happy and healthy. But, for the first time since she heard the verdict, she asked herself what, exactly, she might purchase with the award.

Dignity. A dignified place to live and a dignified place to work. Somewhere else of course. She would move away from Bowmore and Cary County and its polluted rivers and streams and aquifers. Not far, though, because everyone she loved lived nearby. But she dreamed of a new life in a new house with clean water running through it, water that did not stink and stain and cause sickness and death.

She heard another car door slam shut, and she was grateful for her friends. Perhaps she should fix her hair and venture out to say hello. She stepped into the tiny bathroom next to her bed, turned on the light, turned on the faucet at the sink, then sat on the edge of the tub and stared at the stream of grayish water running into the dark stains of the fake-porcelain bowl.

It was fit for flushing human waste, nothing else. The pumping station that produced the water was owned by the City of Bowmore, and the city itself prohibited the drinking of its own water. Three years earlier the council had passed a resolution urging the citizens to use it only for flushing. Warning signs were posted in every public restroom. "DON'T DRINK THE WATER, by Order of the City Council." Clean water was trucked in from Hattiesburg, and every home in Bowmore, mobile and otherwise, had a five-gallon tank and dispenser. Those who could afford it had hundred-gallon reservoirs mounted on stilts near their back porches. And the nicest homes had cisterns for rainwater.

Water was a daily challenge in Bowmore. Every cup was contemplated, fussed over, and used sparingly because the supply was uncertain. And every drop that entered or touched a human body came from a bottle that came from a source that had been inspected and certified. Drinking and cooking were easy compared with bathing and cleaning. Hygiene was a struggle, and most of the women of Bowmore wore their hair short. Many of the men wore beards.

The water was legendary. Ten years earlier, the city installed an irrigation system for its youth baseball field, only to watch the grass turn brown and die. The city swimming pool was closed when a consultant tried treating the water with massive amounts of chlorine, only to watch it turn brackish and reek like a sewage pit. When the Methodist church burned, the firemen realized, during a losing battle, that the water, pumped from an untreated supply, was having an incendiary effect. Years before that, some residents of Bowmore suspected the water caused tiny cracks in the paint of their automobiles after a few wash jobs.

And we drank the stuff for years, Jeannette said to herself. We drank it when it started to stink. We drank it when it changed colors. We drank it while we complained bitterly to the city. We drank it after it was tested and the city assured us it was safe. We drank it after we boiled it. We drank it in our coffee and tea, certain the heat would cure it. And when we stopped drinking it, we showered and bathed in it and inhaled its steam.

What were we supposed to do? Gather at the well each morning like the ancient Egyptians and carry it home in pots on our heads? Sink our own wells at $2,000 a hole and find the same putrid mix the city had found? Drive to Hattiesburg and find a spare tap and haul it back in buckets?

She could hear the denials—those from long ago when the experts pointed at their charts and lectured the city council and the mob packed into a crowded boardroom, telling them over and over that the water had been tested and was just fine if properly cleansed with massive doses of chlorine. She could hear the fancy experts Krane Chemical had brought in at trial to tell the jury that, yes, there may have been some minor "leakage" over the years at the Bowmore plant, but not to worry because bichloronylene and other "unauthorized" substances had actually been absorbed by the soil and eventually carried away in an underground stream that posed no threat whatsoever to the town's drinking water. She could hear the government scientists with their lofty vocabularies talk down to the people and assure them that the water they could barely stand to smell was fine to drink.

Denials all around as the body count rose. Cancer struck everywhere in Bowmore, on every street, in almost every family. Four times the national average. Then six times, then ten. At her trial, an expert hired by the Paytons explained to the jury that for the geographical area as defined by the Bowmore city limits, the rate of cancer was fifteen times the national average.

There was so much cancer that they got themselves studied by all manner of public and private researchers. The term "cancer cluster" became common around town, and Bowmore was radioactive. A clever magazine journalist labeled Cary County as Cancer County, U.S.A., and the nickname stuck.

Cancer County, U.S.A. The water placed quite a strain on the Bowmore Chamber of Commerce. Economic development disappeared, and the town began a rapid decline.

Jeannette turned off the tap, but the water was still there, unseen in the pipes that ran unseen through the walls and into the ground somewhere underneath her. It was always there, waiting like a stalker with unlimited patience. Quiet and deadly, pumped from the earth so polluted by Krane Chemical.

She often lay awake at night listening for the water somewhere in the walls.

A dripping faucet was treated like an armed prowler.

She brushed her hair with little purpose, once again tried not to look at herself too long in the mirror, then brushed her teeth with water from a jug that was always on the sink. She flipped on the light to her room, opened the door, forced a smile, then stepped into the cramped den, where her friends were packed around the walls.

It was time for church.

―――――

Mr. Trudeau's car was a black Bentley with a black chauffeur named Toliver who claimed to be Jamaican, though his immigration documents were as suspicious as his affected Caribbean accent. Toliver had been driving the great man for a decade and could read his moods. This was a bad one, Toliver determined quickly as they fought the traffic along the FDR toward midtown. The first signal had been clearly delivered when Mr. Trudeau slammed the right rear door himself before a lunging Toliver could fulfill his duties.

His boss, he had read, could have nerves of cold steel in the boardroom. Unflappable, decisive, calculating, and so on. But in the solitude of the backseat, even with the privacy window rolled up as tightly as possible, his real character often emerged. The man was a hothead with a massive ego who hated to lose.

And he had definitely lost this one. He was on the phone back there, not yelling but certainly not whispering. The stock would crash. The lawyers were fools. Everyone had lied to him. Damage control. Toliver caught only pieces of what was being said, but it was obvious whatever happened down there in Mississippi had been disastrous.

His boss was sixty-one years old and, according to *Forbes*, had a net worth of almost $2 billion. Toliver often wondered, how much was enough? What would he do with another billion, then another? Why work so hard when he had more than he could ever spend? Homes, jets, wives, boats, Bentleys, all the toys a real white man could ever want.

But Toliver knew the truth. No amount of money could ever satisfy Mr. Trudeau. There were bigger men in town, and he was running hard to catch them.

Toliver turned west on Sixty-third and inched his way to Fifth, where he turned suddenly and faced a set of thick iron gates that quickly swung back. The Bentley disappeared underground, where it stopped and a security guard stood waiting. He opened the rear door. "We'll leave in an hour," Mr. Trudeau barked in Toliver's general direction, then disappeared, carrying two thick briefcases.

The elevator raced up sixteen levels to the top, where Mr. and Mrs. Trudeau lived in lavish splendor. Their penthouse rambled over the top two floors and looked out from its many giant windows at Central Park. They had purchased the place for $28 million shortly after their momentous wedding six years earlier, then spent another $10 million or so bringing it up to designer-magazine quality. The overhead included two maids, a chef, a butler, his and hers valets, at least one nanny, and of course the obligatory personal assistant to keep Mrs. Trudeau properly organized and at lunch on time.

A valet took his briefcases and overcoat as he flung them off. He bounded up the stairs to the master suite, looking for his wife. He had no real desire to see her at the moment, but their little rituals were expected. She was in her dressing room, a hairdresser on each side, both working feverishly on her straight blond hair.

"Hello, darling," he said dutifully, more for the benefit of the hairdressers, both young males who seemed not the least bit affected by the fact that she was practically nude.

"Do you like my hair?" Brianna asked, glaring at the mirror as the boys stroked and fussed, all four hands doing something. Not, "How was your day?" Not, "Hello, dear." Not, "What happened with the trial?" Just simply, "Do you like my hair?"

"It's lovely," he said, already backing away. Ritual complete, he was free to go and leave her with her handlers. He stopped at their massive bed and looked at her evening gown—"Valentino," she had already advised him. It was bright red with a plunging neckline that might or might not adequately cover her fantastic new breasts. It was short, almost sheer, probably weighed less than two ounces, and probably cost at least $25,000. It was a size 2, which meant it would sufficiently drape and hang on her emaciated body so the other anorexics at the party would drool in mock admiration at how "fit" she looked. Frankly, Carl was growing weary of her obsessive routines: an hour a day with a trainer ($300 per), an hour of one-on-one yoga ($300 per), an hour a day with a nutritionist ($200 per), all in an effort to burn off every last fat cell in her body and keep her weight between ninety and ninety-five pounds. She was always ready for sex—that was part of the deal—but now he sometimes worried about getting poked with a hip bone or simply crushing her in the pile. She was only thirty-one, but he had noticed a wrinkle or two just above her nose. Surgery could fix the problems, but wasn't she paying a price for all this aggressive starvation?

He had more important things to worry about. A young, gorgeous wife was just one part of his magnificent persona, and Brianna Trudeau could still stop traffic.

They had a child, one that Carl could easily have forgone. He already had six, plenty, he reasoned. Three were older than Brianna. But she insisted, and for obvious reasons. A child was security, and since she was married to a man who loved ladies and adored the institution of marriage, the child meant family and ties and roots and, left unsaid, legal complications in the event things unraveled. A child was the protection every trophy wife needed.

Brianna delivered a girl and selected the hideous name of Sadler MacGregor Trudeau, MacGregor being Brianna's maiden name and Sadler being pulled from the air. She at first claimed Sadler had been a roguish Scottish relative of some variety, but abandoned that little fiction when Carl stumbled across a book of baby names. He really didn't care. The child was his by DNA only. He had already tried the father bit with prior families and had failed miserably.

Sadler was now five and had virtually been abandoned by both parents. Brianna, once so heroic in her efforts to become a mother, had quickly lost interest in things maternal and had delegated her duties to a series of nannies. The current one was a thick young woman from Russia whose papers were as dubious as Toliver's. Carl could not, at that moment, remember her name. Brianna hired her and was thrilled because she spoke Russian and could perhaps pass on the language to Sadler.

"What language did you expect her to speak?" Carl had asked.

But Brianna had no response.

He stepped into the playroom, swooped up the child as if he couldn't wait to see her, exchanged hugs and kisses, asked how her day had been, and within minutes managed a graceful escape to his office, where he grabbed a phone and began yelling at Bobby Ratzlaff.

After a few fruitless calls, he showered, dried his perfectly dyed hair, half-gray, and got himself into his newest Armani tux. The waistband was a bit snug, probably a 34, up an inch from the early days when Brianna stalked him around the penthouse. As he dressed himself, he cursed the evening ahead and the party and the people he would see there. They would know. At that very moment, the news was racing around the financial world. Phones were buzzing as his rivals roared with laughter and gloated over Krane's misfortune. The Internet was bursting with the latest from Mississippi.

For any other party, he, the great Carl Trudeau, would simply call in sick. Every day of his life he did whatever he damned well pleased, and if he decided to rudely skip a party at the last minute, what the hell? But this was not just any event.

Brianna had wormed her way onto the

board of the Museum of Abstract Art, and tonight was their biggest blowout. There would be designer gowns, tummy tucks and stout new breasts, new chins and perfect tans, diamonds, champagne, foie gras, caviar, dinner by a celebrity chef, a silent auction for the pinch hitters and a live auction for the sluggers. And, most important, there would be cameras on top of cameras, enough to convince the elite guests that they and only they were the center of the world. Oscar night, eat your heart out.

The highlight of the evening, at least for some, would be the auctioning of a work of art. Each year the committee commissioned an "emerging" painter or sculptor to create something just for the event, and usually forked over a million bucks or so for the result. Last year's painting had been a bewildering rendering of a human brain after a gunshot, and it went for six mill. This year's item was a depressing pile of black clay with bronze rods rising into the vague outline of a young girl. It bore the mystifying title *Abused Imelda* and would have sat neglected in a gallery in Duluth if not for the sculptor, a tortured Argentine genius rumored to be on the verge of suicide, a sad fate that would instantly double the value of his creations, something that was not lost on savvy New York art investors. Brianna had left brochures around the penthouse and had dropped several hints to the effect that *Abused Imelda* would be stunning in their foyer, just off the elevator entrance.

Carl knew he was expected to buy the damned thing and was hoping there would not be a frenzy. And if he became its owner, he was already hoping for a quick suicide.

She and Valentino appeared from the dressing room. The hair boys were gone, and she had managed to get into the gown and the jewelry all by herself. "Fabulous," Carl said, and it was indeed true. In spite of the bones and ribs, she was still a beautiful woman. The hair very much resembled what he had seen at six that morning when he kissed her goodbye as she sipped her coffee. Now, a thousand dollars later, he could tell little difference.

Oh, well. He knew very well the price of trophies. The prenuptial gave her $100,000 a month to play with while married and twenty million when they split. She also got Sadler with liberal visitation for the father, if he so chose.

In the Bentley, they hurried from beneath the apartment building and were onto Fifth Avenue when Brianna said, "Oh, my, I forgot to kiss Sadler. What kind of mother am I?"

"She's fine," Carl said, who likewise had failed to say good night to the child.

"I feel awful," Brianna said, feigning disgust. Her full-length black Prada coat was split so that the backseat was dominated by her amazing legs. Legs from the floor up to her armpits. Legs unadorned by hosiery or clothing or anything whatsoever. Legs for Carl to see and admire and touch and fondle and she really didn't care if Toliver had a good look, either. She was on display, as always.

Carl rubbed them because they felt nice, but he wanted to say something like "These things are beginning to resemble broomsticks."

He let it pass.

"Any word from the trial?" she finally asked.

"The jury nailed us," he said.

"I'm so sorry."

"We're fine."

"How much?"

"Forty-one million."

"Those ignorant people."

Carl told her little about the complicated and mysterious world of the Trudeau Group. She had her charities and causes and lunches and trainers, and that kept her busy. He didn't want and didn't tolerate too many questions.

Brianna had checked online and knew exactly what the jury decided. She knew what the lawyers were saying about the appeal, and she knew Krane's stock would take a major hit early the next morning. She did her research and kept her secret notes. She was gorgeous and thin, but she was not stupid. Carl was on the phone.

The MuAb building was a few blocks south, between Fifth and Madison. As the traffic inched closer, they could see the popping flashes of a hundred cameras. Brianna perked up, crunched her perfect abs, brought her new additions to attention, and said, "God, I hate those people."

"Who?"

"All those photographers."

He snickered at the obvious lie. The car stopped and an attendant in a tuxedo opened the door as the cameras swung to the black Bentley. The great Carl Trudeau popped out without a smile, then the legs followed. Brianna knew precisely how to give the photographers, and thus the gossip pages and maybe, just maybe, a fashion magazine or two, what they wanted—miles of sensuous flesh without revealing everything. The right foot landed first, shoed with Jimmy Choo at a hundred bucks per toe, and as she expertly swung around, the coat opened and Valentino cooperated upward and the whole world saw the real benefit of being a billionaire and owning a trophy.

Arm in arm they glided across the red carpet, waving at the photographers and ignoring the handful of reporters, one of whom had the audacity to yell, "Hey, Carl, any comment on the verdict in Mississippi?" Carl of course did not hear, or pretended not to. But his pace quickened slightly and they were soon inside, on somewhat safer turf. He hoped. They were greeted by paid greeters; coats were taken; smiles were offered; friendly cameras appeared; old pals materialized; and they were soon lost in the warm cluster of seriously rich people pretending to enjoy one another's company.

Brianna found her soul mate, another

anorexic trophy with the same unusual body—everything superbly starved but the ridiculous breasts. Carl went straight for the bar, and almost made it before he was practically tackled by the one jerk he hoped to avoid. "Carl, ole boy, bad news down south I hear," the man boomed as loudly as possible.

"Yes, very bad," Carl said in a much lower voice as he grabbed a champagne flute and began to drain it.

Pete Flint was number 228 on the *Forbes* list of the 400 richest Americans. Carl was number 310, and each man knew exactly where the other fit on the roster. Numbers 87 and 141 were also in the crowd, along with a host of unranked contenders.

"Thought your boys had things under control," Flint pressed on, slurping a tall glass full of either scotch or bourbon. He somehow managed a frown while working hard to conceal his delight.

"Yes, we thought so, too," Carl said, wishing he could slap the fat jowls twelve inches away.

"What about the appeal?" Flint asked gravely.

"We're in great shape."

At last year's auction, Flint had valiantly hung on to the frenzied end and walked away with the *Brain After Gunshot*, a $6 million artistic waste but one that launched the MuAb's current capital campaign. No doubt he would be in the hunt for tonight's grand prize.

"Good thing we shorted Krane last week," he said.

Carl started to curse him but kept his cool. Flint ran a hedge fund famous for its daring. Had he really shorted Krane Chemical in anticipation of a bad verdict? Carl's puzzled glare concealed nothing.

"Oh yes," Flint went on, pulling on his glass and smacking his lips. "Our man down there said you were screwed."

"We'll never pay a dime," Carl said gamely.

"You'll pay in the morning, ole boy. We're betting Krane's stock drops 20 percent." And with that he turned and walked away, leaving Carl to finish off his drink and lunge for another. Twenty percent? Carl's laser-quick mind did the math. He owned 45 percent of the outstanding common shares of

Krane Chemical, a company with a market value of $3.2 billion, based on the day's closing price. A 20 percent decline would cost him $280 million, on paper. No real cash losses, of course, but still a rough day around the office.

Ten percent was more like it, he thought. The boys in finance agreed with him.

Could Flint's hedge fund short a significant chunk of Krane's stock without Carl knowing about it? He stared at a confused bartender and pondered the question. Yes, it was possible, but not likely. Flint was simply rubbing a little salt.

The museum's director appeared from nowhere, and Carl was delighted to see him. He would never mention the verdict, if he in fact knew about it. He would say only nice things to Carl, and of course he would comment on how fabulous Brianna looked. He would ask about Sadler and inquire into the renovation of their home in the Hamptons.

They chatted about such things as they carried their drinks through the crowded lobby, dodging little pockets of dangerous conversations, and settled themselves before *Abused Imelda*. "Magnificent, isn't it?" the director mused.

"Beautiful," Carl said, glancing to his left as number 141 happened by. "What will it go for?"

"We've been debating that all day around here. Who knows with this crowd. I say at least five million."

"And what's it worth?"

The director smiled as a photographer snapped their picture. "Now, that's an entirely different issue, isn't it? The sculptor's last major work was sold to a Japanese gentleman for around two million. Of course, the Japanese gentleman was not donating large sums of money to our little museum."

Carl took another sip and acknowledged the game. MuAb's campaign goal was $100 million over five years. According to Brianna, they were about halfway there and needed a big boost from the evening's auction.

An art critic with the *Times* introduced himself and joined their conversation. Wonder if he knows about the verdict, Carl thought. The critic and the director discussed the Argentine sculptor and his mental problems as Carl studied *Imelda* and asked himself if he really wanted it permanently situated in the foyer of his luxurious penthouse.

His wife certainly did.

CHAPTER 3

The Paytons' temporary home was a three-bedroom apartment on the second level of an old complex near the university. Wes had lived nearby in his college days and still found it hard to believe he was back in the neighborhood. But there had been so many drastic changes it was difficult to dwell on just one.

How temporary? That was the great question between husband and wife, though the issue hadn't been discussed in weeks, nor would it be discussed now. Maybe in a day or two, when the fatigue and the shock wore off and they could steal a quiet moment and talk about the future. Wes eased the car through the parking lot, passing an overfilled Dumpster with debris littered around it. Mainly beer cans and broken bottles. The college boys humored themselves by hurling their empties from the upper floors, across the lot, above the cars, in the general direction of the Dumpster. When the bottles crashed, the noise boomed through the complex and the students were amused. Others were not. For the two sleep-deprived Paytons, the racket was at times unbearable.

The owner, an old client, was widely considered the worst slumlord in town, by the students anyway. He offered the place to the Paytons, and their handshake deal called for a thousand bucks a month in rent. They had lived there for seven months, paid for three, and the landlord insisted he was not worried. He was patiently waiting in line with many other creditors. The law firm of Payton & Payton had once proven it could attract clients and generate fees, and its two partners were certainly capable of a dramatic comeback.

Try this comeback, Wes thought as he turned in to a parking place. Is a verdict of

$41 million drama enough? For a moment he felt feisty, then he was tired again.

Slaves to a dreadful habit, both got out of the car and grabbed their briefcases in the rear seat. "No," Mary Grace announced suddenly. "We are not working tonight. Leave these in the car."

"Yes, ma'am."

They hustled up the stairs, loud raunchy rap spilling from a window nearby. Mary Grace rattled the keys and unlocked the door, and suddenly they were inside, where both children were watching television with Ramona, their Honduran nanny. Liza, the nine-year-old, rushed forth yelling, "Mommy, we won, we won!" Mary Grace lifted her in the air and clutched her tightly.

"Yes, dear, we won."

"Forty billion!"

"Millions, dear, not billions."

Mack, the five-year-old, ran to his father, who yanked him up, and for a long moment they stood in the narrow foyer and squeezed their children. For the first time since the verdict, Wes saw tears in his wife's eyes.

"We saw you on TV," Liza was saying.

"You looked tired," Mack said.

"I am tired," Wes said.

Ramona watched from a distance, a tight smile barely visible. She wasn't sure what the verdict meant, but she understood enough to be pleased with the news.

Overcoats and shoes were removed, and the little Payton family fell onto the sofa, a very nice thick leather one, where they hugged and tickled and talked about school. Wes and Mary Grace had managed to keep most of their furnishings, and the shabby apartment was decorated with fine things that not only reminded them of the past but, more important, reminded them of the future. This was just a stop, an unexpected layover.

The den floor was covered with notebooks and papers, clear evidence that the homework had been done before the television was turned on.

"I'm starving," Mack announced as he tried in vain to undo his father's tie.

"Mom says we're having macaroni and cheese," Wes said.

"All right!" Both kids voiced their approval, and Ramona eased into the kitchen.

"Does this mean we get a new house?" Liza asked.

"I thought you liked this place," Wes said.

"I do, but we're still looking for a new house, right?"

"Of course we are."

They had been careful with the children. They had explained the basics of the lawsuit to Liza—a bad company polluted water that harmed many people—and she quickly declared that she didn't like the company, either. And if the family had to move into an apartment to fight the company, then she was all for it.

But leaving their fine new home had been traumatic. Liza's last bedroom was pink and white and had everything a little girl could want. Now she shared a smaller room with her brother, and though she didn't complain, she was curious about how long the arrangement might last. Mack was generally too preoccupied with full-day kindergarten to worry about living quarters.

Both kids missed the old neighborhood, where the homes were large and the backyards had pools and gym sets. Friends were next door or just around the corner. The school was private and secure. Church was a block away and they knew everyone there.

Now they attended a city elementary school where there were far more black faces than white, and they worshipped in a downtown Episcopal church that welcomed everyone.

"We won't move anytime soon," Mary Grace said. "But maybe we can start looking."

"I'm starving," Mack said again.

The topic of housing was routinely avoided when one of the kids raised it, and Mary Grace finally rose to her feet. "Let's go cook," she said to Liza. Wes found the remote and said to Mack, "Let's watch *SportsCenter*." Anything but local news.

"Sure."

Ramona was boiling water and dicing a tomato. Mary Grace hugged her quickly and said, "A good day?" Yes, a good day, she agreed. No problems at school. Homework was already finished. Liza drifted off to her bedroom. She had yet to show any interest in kitchen matters.

"A good day for you?" Ramona asked.

"Yes, very good. Let's use the white cheddar." She found a block of it in the fridge and began grating it.

"You can relax now?" Ramona asked.

"Yes, for a few days anyway." Through a friend at church, they had found Ramona hiding and half-starved in a shelter in Baton Rouge, sleeping on a cot and eating boxed food sent south for hurricane victims. She had survived a harrowing three-month journey from Central America, through Mexico, then Texas, and on to Louisiana, where none of the things she had been promised materialized. No job, no host family, no paperwork, no one to take care of her.

Under normal circumstances, hiring an illegal and unnaturalized nanny had never occurred to the Paytons. They quickly adopted her, taught her to drive but only on a few selected streets, taught her the basics of the cell phone, computer, and kitchen appliances, and pressed her to learn English. She had a good foundation from a Catholic school back home, and she spent her daytime hours holed up in the apartment cleaning and mimicking the voices on television. In eight months, her progress was impressive. She preferred to listen, though, especially to Mary Grace, who needed someone to unload on. During the past four months, on the rare nights when Mary Grace prepared dinner, she chatted nonstop while

Ramona absorbed every word. It was wonderful therapy, especially after a brutal day in a courtroom crowded with high-strung men.

"No trouble with the car?" Mary Grace asked the same question every night. Their second car was an old Honda Accord that Ramona had yet to damage. For many good reasons, they were terrified of turning loose on the streets of Hattiesburg an illegal, unlicensed, and quite uninsured alien in a Honda with a zillion miles and their two happy little children in the rear seat. They had trained Ramona to travel a memorized route through the backstreets, to the school, to the grocery, and, if necessary, to their office. If the police stopped her, they planned to beg the cops, the prosecutor, and the judge. They knew them well.

Wes knew for a fact that the presiding city judge had his own illegal pulling his weeds and cutting his grass.

"A good day," Ramona said. "No problem. Everything is fine."

A good day indeed, Mary Grace thought to herself as she began melting cheese.

The phone rang and Wes reluctantly picked up the receiver. The number was unlisted because a crackpot had made threats. They used their cell phones for virtually everything. He listened, said something, hung up, and walked to the stove to disrupt the cooking.

"Who was it?" Mary Grace asked with concern. Every call to the apartment was greeted with suspicion.

"Sherman, at the office. Says there are some reporters hanging around, looking for the stars." Sherman was one of the paralegals.

"Why is he at the office?" Mary Grace asked.

"Just can't get enough, I guess. Do we have any olives for the salad?"

"No. What did you tell him?"

"I told him to shoot at one of them and the rest'll disappear."

"Toss the salad, please," she said to Ramona.

They huddled over a card table wedged in a corner of the kitchen, all five of them. They held hands as Wes prayed and gave thanks for the good things of life, for family and friends and school. And for the food. He was also thankful for a wise and generous jury and a fantastic result, but he would save that for later. The salad was passed first, then the macaroni and cheese.

"Hey, Dad, can we camp out?" Mack blurted, after he'd swallowed.

"Of course!" Wes said, his back suddenly aching. Camping out in the apartment meant layering the den floor with blankets and quilts and pillows and sleeping there, usually with the television on late at night, usually on Friday nights. It worked only if Mom and Dad joined the fun. Ramona was always invited but wisely declined.

"Same bedtime, though," Mary Grace said. "This is a school night."

"Ten o'clock," said Liza, the negotiator.

"Nine," said Mary Grace, a thirty-minute add-on that made both kids smile.

Mary Grace was knee to knee with her children, savoring the moment and happy that the fatigue might soon be over. Maybe she could rest now, and take them to school, visit their classes, and eat lunch with them. She longed to be a mother, nothing more, and it would be a gloomy day when she was forced to reenter a courtroom.

Wednesday night meant potluck casseroles at the Pine Grove Church, and the turnout was always impressive. The busy church was located in the middle of the neighborhood, and many worshippers simply walked a block or two on Sundays and Wednesdays. The doors were open eighteen hours a day, and the pastor, who lived in a parsonage behind the church, was always there, waiting to minister to his people.

They ate in the fellowship hall, an ugly metal addition stuck to the side of the chapel, where folding tables were covered with all manner of home-cooked recipes. There was a basket of white dinner rolls, a large dispenser of sweet tea, and, of course, lots of bottled water. The crowd would be even larger tonight, and they hoped Jeannette would be there. A celebration was in order.

Pine Grove Church was fiercely independent with not the slightest link to any denomination, a source of quiet pride for its founder, Pastor Denny Ott. It had been built by Baptists decades earlier, then dried up like the rest of Bowmore. By the time Ott arrived, the congregation consisted of only a few badly scarred souls. Years of infighting had decimated its membership. Ott cleaned out the rest, opened the doors to the community, and reached out to the people.

He had not been immediately accepted, primarily because he was from "up north" and spoke with such a clean, clipped accent. He had met a Bowmore girl at a Bible college in Nebraska, and she brought him south. Through a series of misadventures he found himself as the interim pastor of Second Baptist Church. He wasn't really a Baptist, but with so few young preachers in the area the church could not afford to be selective. Six months later all the Baptists were gone and the church had a new name.

He wore a beard and often preached in flannel shirts and hiking boots. Neckties were not forbidden but were certainly frowned upon. It was the people's church, a place where anyone could find peace and solace with no worries about wearing the Sunday best. Pastor Ott got rid of King James and the old hymnal. He had little use for the mournful anthems written by ancient pilgrims. Worship services were loosened up, modernized with guitars and slide shows. He believed and taught that poverty and injustice were more important social issues than abortion and gay rights, but he was careful with his politics.

The church grew and prospered, though he cared nothing about money. A friend from seminary ran a mission in Chicago, and through this connection Ott maintained a large inventory of used but very usable clothing in the church's "closet." He badgered the larger congregations in Hattiesburg and Jackson and with their contributions kept a well-stocked food bank at one end of the fellowship hall. He pestered drug companies for their leftovers, and the church's "pharmacy" was filled with over-the-counter medications.

Denny Ott considered all of Bowmore to be his mission, and no one would go hungry or homeless or sick if he could possibly prevent it. Not on his watch, and his watch never ended.

He had conducted sixteen funerals of his own people killed by Krane Chemical, a company he detested so bitterly that he constantly prayed for forgiveness. He didn't hate the nameless and faceless people who owned Krane, to do so would compromise his faith, but he most certainly hated the corporation itself. Was it a sin to hate a corporation? That furious debate raged in his soul every day, and to be on the safe side, he kept praying.

All sixteen were buried in the small cemetery behind the church. When the weather was warm, he cut the grass around the headstones, and when it was cold, he painted the white picket fence that surrounded the cemetery and kept the deer away. Though he had not planned it, his church had become the hub of anti-Krane activity in Cary County. Almost all of its members had been touched by the illness or death of someone harmed by the company.

His wife's older sister finished Bowmore High with Mary Grace Shelby. Pastor Ott and the Paytons were extremely close. Legal advice was often dispensed in the pastor's study with the door closed and one of the Paytons on the phone. Dozens of depositions had been taken in the fellowship hall, packed with lawyers from big cities. Ott disliked the corporate lawyers almost as much as the corporation itself.

Mary Grace had phoned Pastor Ott often during the trial and had always warned him not to be optimistic. He certainly was not.

When she called two hours earlier with the astounding news, Ott grabbed his wife and they danced through the house yelling and laughing. Krane had been nailed, humbled, exposed, brought to justice. Finally.

He was greeting his flock when he saw Jeannette enter with her stepsister Bette and the rest of her entourage. She was immediately engulfed by those who loved her, those who wanted to share in this great moment and offer a quiet word. They sat her in the rear of the room, near an old piano, and a receiving line materialized. She managed to smile a few times and even say thanks, but she looked so weak and frail.

With the casseroles growing colder by the minute, and with a full house, Pastor Ott finally called things to order and launched into a windy prayer of thanks. He finished with a flourish and said, "Let us eat."

As always, the children and old folks lined up first, and dinner was served. Ott made his way to the back and was soon sitting next to Jeannette. As the attention shifted away from her and to the food, she whispered to her pastor, "I'd like to go to the cemetery."

He led her through a side door, onto a

narrow gravel drive that dipped behind the church and ran for fifty yards to the small graveyard. They walked slowly, silently, in the dark. Ott opened the wooden gate, and they stepped into the cemetery, neat and tidy and well tended to. The headstones were small. These were working people, no monuments or crypts or gaudy tributes to great ones.

Four rows down on the right, Jeannette knelt between two graves. One was Chad's, a sickly child who'd lived only six years before tumors choked him. The other held the remains of Pete, her husband of eight years. Father and son, resting side by side forever. She visited them at least once a week and never failed to wish she could join them. She rubbed both headstones at the same time, then began talking softly. "Hello, boys, it's Mom. You won't believe what happened today."

Pastor Ott slipped away, leaving her alone with her tears and thoughts and quiet words that he did not want to hear. He waited by the gate, and as the minutes passed, he watched the shadows move through the rows of headstones as the moonlight shifted through the clouds. He had already buried Chad and Pete. Sixteen in all, and counting. Sixteen silent victims who perhaps were not so silent anymore. From within the little picket-fenced cemetery at the Pine Grove Church a voice had finally been heard. A loud angry voice that begged to be heard and was demanding justice.

He could see her shadow and hear her talking.

He had prayed with Pete in the minutes before he finally slipped away, and he had kissed the forehead of little Chad in his final hour. He had scraped together money for their caskets and funerals. Then he and two of his deacons had dug the graves. Their burials were eight months apart.

She stood, said her farewells, and began moving. "We need to go inside," Ott said.

"Yes, thank you," she said, wiping her cheeks.

———

Mr. Trudeau's table cost him $50,000, and since he wrote the check, he could damned well control who sat with him. To his left was Brianna, and next to her was her close friend Sandy, another skeleton who'd just been contractually released from her last marriage and was on the prowl for husband number three. To his right was a retired banker friend and his wife, pleasant folks who preferred to chat about the arts. Carl's urologist sat directly across from him. He and his wife were invited because they said little. The odd man out was a lesser executive at Trudeau Group who simply drew the short straw and was there by coercion.

The celebrity chef had whipped up a tasting menu that began with caviar and champagne, then moved on to a lobster bisque, a splash of sautéed foie gras with trimmings, fresh Scottish game hen for the carnivores, and a seaweed bouquet for the veggies. Dessert was a gorgeous layered gelato creation. Each round required a different wine, including dessert.

Carl cleaned every plate put before him and drank heavily. He spoke only to the banker because the banker had heard the news from down south and appeared to be sympathetic. Brianna and Sandy whispered rudely and, in the course of dinner, hammered every other social climber in the crowd. They managed to push the food around their plates while eating virtually none of it. Carl, half-drunk, almost said something to his wife while she tinkered with her seaweed. "Do you know how much that damned food cost?" he wanted to say, but there was no sense starting a fight.

The celebrity chef, one Carl had never heard of, was introduced and got a standing ovation from the four hundred guests, virtually all of them still hungry after five courses. But the evening wasn't about food. It was about money.

Two quick speeches brought the auctioneer to the front. *Abused Imelda* was rolled into the atrium, hanging dramatically from a small mobile crane, and left to hover twenty feet off the floor for all to see clearly. Concert-style spotlights made it even more exotic. The crowd grew quiet as the tables were cleared by an army of illegal immigrants in black coats and ties.

The auctioneer rambled on about *Imelda*, and the crowd listened. Then he talked about the artist, and the crowd really listened. Was he truly crazy? Insane? Close to suicide? They wanted details, but the auctioneer held the high ground. He was British and very proper, which would add at least a million bucks to the winning bid.

"I suggest we start the bidding at five million," he said through his nose, and the crowd gasped.

Brianna was suddenly bored with Sandy. She moved closer to Carl, fluttered her eyelashes at him, and placed a hand on his thigh. Carl responded by nodding at the nearest floor assistant, a man he'd already spoken to. The assistant flashed a sign to the podium, and *Imelda* came to life.

"And we have five million," the auctioneer announced. Thunderous applause. "A nice place to start, thank you. And now onward to six."

Six, seven, eight, nine, and Carl nodded at ten. He kept a smile on his face, but his stomach was churning. How much would this abomination cost him? There were at least six billionaires in the room and several more in the making. No shortage of enormous egos, no shortage of cash, but at that moment none of the others needed a headline as desperately as Carl Trudeau.

And Pete Flint understood this.

Two bidders dropped out on the way to eleven million. "How many are left?" Carl whispered to the banker, who was watching the crowd and searching for the competition.

"It's Pete Flint, maybe one more."

That son of a bitch. When Carl nodded at twelve, Brianna practically had her tongue in his ear.

"We have twelve million." The crowd exploded with applause and hoorays, and the auctioneer wisely said, "Let's catch our breath here." Everyone took a sip of something. Carl gulped more wine. Pete Flint was behind him, two tables back, but Carl didn't dare turn around and acknowledge their little battle.

If Flint had really shorted Krane's stock, then he would reap millions from the verdict. Carl, obviously, had just lost millions because of it. It was all on paper, but then wasn't everything?

Imelda was not. It was real, tangible, a work of art that Carl could not lose, not to Pete Flint anyway.

Rounds 13, 14, and 15 were dragged out beautifully by the auctioneer, each ending in rapturous applause. Word had spread quickly, and everyone knew it was Carl Trudeau and Pete Flint. When the applause died, the two heavyweights settled in for more. Carl nodded at sixteen million, then accepted the applause.

"Do we have seventeen million?" boomed the auctioneer, quite excited himself.

A long pause. The tension was electric. "Very well, we have sixteen. Going once, going twice, ah yes—we have seventeen million."

Carl had been making and breaking vows throughout the ordeal, but he was determined not to exceed seventeen million bucks. As the roar died down, he settled back in his seat, cool as any corporate raider with billions in play. He was finished, and quite happy about it. Flint was bluffing, and now Flint was stuck with the old girl for $17 million.

"Dare I ask for eighteen?" More applause. More time for Carl to think. If he was willing to pay seventeen, why not eighteen? And if he jumped at eighteen, then Flint would realize that he, Carl, was staying to the bloody end.

It was worth a try.

"Eighteen?" asked the auctioneer.

"Yes," Carl said, loud enough for many to hear. The strategy worked. Pete Flint retreated to the safety of his unspent cash and watched in amusement as the great Carl Trudeau finished off a lousy deal.

"Sold for eighteen million, to Mr. Carl Trudeau," roared the auctioneer, and the crowd leaped to its feet.

They lowered *Imelda* so her new owners could pose with her. Many others, both envious and proud, gawked at the Trudeaus and their new addition. A band cranked up and it was time to dance. Brianna was in heat—the money had sent her into a frenzy—and halfway through the first dance Carl gently shoved her back a step. She was hot and lewd and flashing as much skin as possible. Folks were watching and that was fine with her.

"Let's get out of here," Carl said after the second dance.

CHAPTER 4

During the night, Wes had somehow managed to gain the sofa, a much softer resting place, and when he awoke before daylight, Mack was wedged tightly by his side. Mary Grace and Liza were sprawled on the floor beneath them, wrapped in blankets and dead to the world. They had watched television until both kids dropped off, then quietly opened and finished a bottle of cheap champagne they had been saving. The alcohol and the fatigue knocked them out, and they vowed to sleep forever.

Five hours later Wes opened his eyes and could not close them. He was back in the courtroom, sweating and nervous, watching the jurors file in, praying, searching for a sign, then hearing the majestic words of Judge Harrison. Words that would ring in his ears forever.

Today would be a fine day, and Wes couldn't waste any more of it on the sofa.

He eased away from Mack, covered him with a blanket, and moved silently to their cluttered bedroom, where he slipped into his running shorts and shoes and a sweat-shirt. During the trial, he tried to run every day, often at midnight, often at five in the morning. A month earlier, he'd found him-self six miles from home at 3:00 a.m. The running cleared his mind and relieved the stress. He plotted strategy, cross-examined witnesses, argued with Jared Kurtin, ap-pealed to the jurors, did a dozen tasks as he pounded the asphalt in the dark.

Perhaps on this run he might concentrate on something, anything, other than the trial. Maybe a vacation. A beach. But the appeal was already bugging him.

Mary Grace did not move as he eased from the apartment and locked the door be-hind him. It was 5:15.

Without stretching, he took off and was

soon on Hardy Street, headed for the campus of the University of Southern Mississippi. He liked the safety of the place. He circled around the dorms where he once lived, around the football stadium where he once played, and after half an hour pulled into Java Werks, his favorite coffee shop, across the street from the campus. He placed four quarters on the counter and took a small cup of the house blend. Four quarters. He almost laughed as he counted them out. He had to plan his coffee and was always looking for quarters.

At the end of the counter was a collection of morning newspapers. The front-page headline of the *Hattiesburg American* screamed: "Krane Chemical Nailed for $41 Million." There was a large, splendid photo of him and Mary Grace leaving the courthouse, tired but happy. And a smaller photo of Jeannette Baker, still crying. Lots of quotes from the lawyers, a few from the jurors, including a windy little speech by Dr. Leona Rocha, who, evidently, had been a force in the jury room. She was quoted as saying, among other gems, "We were angered by Krane's arrogant and calculated abuse of the land, by their disregard for safety, and then their deceit in trying to conceal it."

Wes loved that woman. He devoured the long article while ignoring his coffee. The state's largest paper was the *Clarion-Ledger*, out of Jackson, and its headline was somewhat more restrained, though still impressive: "Jury Faults Krane Chemical—Huge Verdict." More photos, quotes, details of the trial, and after a few minutes Wes caught himself skimming. The *Sun Herald* from Biloxi had the best line so far: "Jury to Krane—Fork It Over."

Front-page news and photos in the big dailies. Not a bad day for the little law firm of Payton & Payton. The comeback was under way, and Wes was ready. The office phones would start ringing with potential clients in need of divorces and bankruptcies and a hundred other nuisances that Wes had no stomach for. He would politely send them away, to other small-timers, of which there was an endless supply, and he would check the nets each morning and look for the big ones. A massive verdict, photos in the paper, the talk of the town, and business was about to increase substantially.

He drained his coffee and hit the street.

Carl Trudeau also left home before sunrise. He could hide in his penthouse all day and let his communications people deal with the disaster. He could hide behind his lawyers. He could hop on his jet and fly away to his villa on Anguilla or his mansion in Palm Beach. But not Carl. He had never run from a brawl, and he wouldn't start now.

Plus, he wanted to get away from his wife. She'd cost him a fortune last night and he was resenting it.

"Good morning," he said abruptly to Toliver as he scampered into the rear seat of the Bentley.

"Good morning, sir." Toliver wasn't about to ask something stupid, such as "How are you doing, sir?" It was 5:30, not an unusual hour for Mr. Trudeau, but not a customary one, either. They normally left the penthouse an hour later.

"Let's push it," the boss said, and Toliver roared down Fifth Avenue. Twenty minutes later, Carl was in his private elevator with Stu, an assistant whose only job was to be on call 24/7 in case the great man needed something. Stu had been alerted an hour earlier and given instructions: Fix the coffee, toast a wheat bagel, squeeze the orange juice. He was given a list of six newspapers to arrange on Mr. Trudeau's desk, and was in the midst of an Internet search for stories about the verdict. Carl barely acknowledged his presence.

In his office, Stu took his jacket, poured his coffee, and was told to hurry along with the bagel and juice.

Carl settled into his aerodynamic designer chair, cracked his knuckles, rolled himself up to his desk, took a deep breath, and picked up the *New York Times*. Front page, left column. Not front page of the Business section, but the front page of the whole damned paper!! Right up there with a bad war, a scandal in Congress, dead bodies in Gaza.

The front page. "Krane Chemical Held Liable in Toxic Deaths," read the headline, and Carl's clenched jaw began to slacken. Byline, Hattiesburg, Mississippi: "A state court jury awarded a young widow $3 million in actual damages and $38 million in punitive damages in her wrongful-death claims against Krane Chemical." Carl read quickly—he knew the wretched details. The

Times got most of them right. Every quote from the lawyers was so predictable. Blah, blah, blah.

But why the front page?

He took it as a cheap shot, and was soon hit with another on page 2 of Business, where an analyst of some variety held forth on Krane's other legal problems, to wit, hundreds of potential lawsuits claiming pretty much the same thing Jeannette Baker had claimed. According to the expert, a name Carl had never seen, which was unusual, Krane's exposure could be "several billion" in cash, and since Krane, with its "questionable policies regarding liability insurance," was practically "naked," such exposure could be "catastrophic."

Carl was cursing when Stu hurried in with juice and a bagel. "Anything else, sir?" he asked.

"No, now close the door."

Carl rallied briefly in the Arts section. On the front page beneath the fold there was a story about last night's MuAb event, the highlight of which had been a spirited bidding war, and so on. In the bottom right-hand corner was a decent-sized color photo of Mr. and Mrs. Carl Trudeau posing with their newest acquisition. Brianna, ever photogenic, as she damned well should be, emanated glamour. Carl looked rich, thin, and young, he thought, and *Imelda* was as baffling in print as she was in person. Was she really a work of art? Or was she just a hodgepodge of bronze and cement thrown together by some confused soul working hard to appear tortured?

The latter, according to a *Times* art critic, the same pleasant gentleman Carl had chatted with before dinner. When asked by the reporter if Mr. Trudeau's $18 million purchase was a prudent investment, the critic answered, "No, but it is certainly a boost for the museum's capital campaign." He then went on to explain that the market for abstract sculpture had been stagnant for over a decade and wasn't likely to improve, at least in his opinion. He saw little future for *Imelda*. The story concluded on page 7 with two paragraphs and a photo of the sculptor, Pablo, smiling at the camera and looking very much alive and, well, sane.

Nevertheless, Carl was pleased, if only for a moment. The story was positive. He appeared unfazed by the verdict, resilient, in command of his universe. The good press was worth something, though he knew its value was somewhere far south of $18 million. He crunched the bagel without tasting it.

Back to the carnage. It was splashed across the front pages of the *Wall Street Journal*, the *Financial Times*, and *USA Today*. After four newspapers, he was tired of reading the same quotes from the lawyers and the same predictions from the experts. He rolled back from his desk, sipped his coffee, and reminded himself of exactly how much he loathed reporters. But he was still alive. The battering by the press was brutal, and it would continue, but he, the great Carl Trudeau, was taking their best shots and still on his feet.

This would be the worst day of his professional life, but tomorrow would be better.

It was 7:00 a.m. The market opened at 9:30. Krane's stock closed at $52.50 the day before, up $1.25 because the jury was taking forever and appeared to be hung. The morning's experts were predicting panic selling, but their damage estimates were all over the board.

He took a call from his communications director and explained that he would not talk to any reporters, journalists, analysts, whatever they called themselves and regardless of how many were calling or camped out in the lobby. Just stick to the company line—"We are planning a vigorous appeal and expect to prevail." Do not deviate one word.

At 7:15, Bobby Ratzlaff arrived with Felix Bard, the chief financial officer. Neither had slept more than two hours, and both were amazed that their boss had found the time to go partying. They unpacked their thick files, made the obligatory terse greetings, then huddled around the conference table. They would be there for the next twelve hours. There was much to discuss, but the real reason for the meeting was that Mr. Trudeau wanted some company in his bunker when the market opened and all hell broke loose.

Ratzlaff went first. A truckload of post-trial motions would be filed, nothing would change, and the case would move on to the Mississippi Supreme Court. "The court has a history of being plaintiff-friendly, but that's changing. We have reviewed the rulings in big tort cases over the past two years, and the court usually splits 5 to 4 in favor of the plaintiff, but not always."

"How long before the final appeal is over?" Carl asked.

"Eighteen to twenty-four months."

Ratzlaff moved on. A hundred and forty lawsuits were on file against Krane because of the Bowmore mess, about a third of them being death cases. According to an exhaustive and ongoing study by Ratzlaff, his staff, and their lawyers in New York, Atlanta, and Mississippi, there were probably another three hundred to four hundred cases with "legitimate" potential, meaning that they involved either death, probable death, or moderate to severe illness. There could be thousands of cases in which the claimants suffered minor ailments such as skin rashes, lesions, and nagging coughs, but for the time being, these were classified as frivolous.

Because of the difficulty and cost of proving liability, and linking it with an illness, most of the cases on file had not been pushed aggressively. This, of course, was about to change. "I'm sure the plaintiff's lawyers down there are quite hungover this morning," Ratzlaff said, but Carl did not crack a smile. He never did. He was always reading, never looking at the person with the floor, and missed nothing.

"How many cases do the Paytons have?" he asked.

"Around thirty. We're not sure, because they have not actually filed suit in all of them. There's a lot of waiting here."

"One article said that the *Baker* case almost bankrupted them."

"True. They hocked everything."

"Bank loans?"

"Yes, that's the rumor."

"Do we know which banks?"

"I'm not sure if we know that."

"Find out. I want the loan numbers, terms, everything."

"Got it."

There were no good options, Ratzlaff said, working from his outline. The dam has cracked, the flood is coming. The lawyers will attack with a vengeance, and defense costs would quadruple to $100 million a year, easily. The nearest case could be ready for trial in eight months, same courtroom, same judge. Another big verdict, and, well, who knows.

Carl glanced at his watch and mumbled

something about making a call. He left the table again, paced around the office, then stopped at the windows looking south. The Trump Building caught his attention. Its address was 40 Wall Street, very near the New York Stock Exchange, where before long the common shares of Krane Chemical would be the talk of the day as investors jumped ship and speculators gawked at the roadkill. How cruel, how ironic, that he, the great Carl Trudeau, a man who had so often watched happily from above as some unfortunate company flamed out, would now be fighting off the vultures. How many times had he engineered the collapse of a stock's price so he could swoop down and buy it for pennies? His legend had been built with such ruthless tactics.

How bad would it be? That was the great question, always followed soon by number two: How long would it last?

He waited.

CHAPTER 5

Tom Huff put on his darkest and finest suit, and after much debate decided to arrive at work at the Second State Bank a few minutes later than usual. An earlier entry would seem too predictable, perhaps a little too cocky. And, more important, he wanted everyone in place when he arrived—the old tellers on the main floor, the cute secretaries on the second, and the vice somethings, his rivals, on the third floor. Huffy wanted a triumphant arrival with as big an audience as possible. He'd gambled bravely with the Paytons, and the moment belonged to him.

What he got instead was an overall dismissal by the tellers, a collective cold shoulder from the secretaries, and enough devious grins from his rivals to make him suspicious. On his desk he found a message marked "Urgent" to see Mr. Kirkhead. Something was up, and Huffy began to feel considerably less cocky. So much for a dramatic entrance. What was the problem?

Mr. Kirkhead was in his office, waiting, with the door open, always a bad sign. The boss hated open doors, and in fact boasted of a closed-door management style. He was caustic, rude, cynical, and afraid of his shadow, and closed doors served him well.

"Sit down," he barked, with no thought of a "Good morning" or a "Hello" or, heaven forbid, a "Congratulations." He was camped behind his pretentious desk, fat hairless head bent low as if he sniffed the spreadsheets as he read them.

"And how are you, Mr. Kirkhead?" Huffy chirped. How badly he wanted to say "Prickhead" because he said it every other time he referred to his boss. Even the old gals on the main floor sometimes used the substitution.

"Swell. Did you bring the Payton file?"

"No, sir. I wasn't asked to bring the Payton file. Something the matter?"

"Two things, actually, now that you mention it. First, we have this disastrous loan to these people, over $400,000, past due of course and horribly under-collateralized. By far the worst loan in the bank's portfolio."

He said "these people" as if Wes and Mary Grace were credit card thieves.

"This is nothing new, sir."

"Mind if I finish? And now we have this obscene jury award, which, as the banker holding the paper, I guess I'm supposed to feel good about, but as a commercial lender and business leader in this community, I think it really sucks. What kind of message do we send to prospective industrial clients with verdicts like this?"

"Don't dump toxic waste in our state?"

Prickhead's fat jowls turned red as he swept away Huffy's retort with the wave of a hand. He cleared his throat, almost gargling with his own saliva.

"This is bad for our business climate," he said. "Front page all over the world this morning. I'm getting phone calls from the home office. A very bad day."

Lots of bad days over in Bowmore, too,

Huffy thought. Especially with all those funerals.

"Forty-one million bucks," Prickhead went on. "For a poor woman who lives in a trailer."

"Nothing wrong with trailers, Mr. Kirkhead. Lots of good folks live in them around here. We make the loans."

"You miss the point. It's an obscene amount of money. The whole system has gone crazy. And why here? Why is Mississippi known as a judicial hellhole? Why do trial lawyers love our little state? Just look at some of the surveys. It's bad for business, Huff, for our business."

"Yes, sir, but you must feel better about the Payton loan this morning."

"I want it repaid, and soon."

"So do I."

"Give me a schedule. Get with these people and put together a repayment plan, one that I will approve only when it looks sensible. And do it now."

"Yes, sir, but it might take a few months for them to get back on their feet. They've practically shut down—"

"I don't care about them, Huff. I just want this damned thing off the books."

"Yes, sir. Is that all?"

"Yes. And no more litigation loans, you understand?"

"Don't worry."

———

Three doors down from the bank, the Honorable Jared Kurtin made a final inspection of the troops before heading back to Atlanta and the icy reception waiting there. Headquarters was a recently renovated old building on Front Street. The well-heeled defense of Krane Chemical had leased it two years earlier, then retrofitted it with an impressive collection of technology and personnel.

The mood was somber, as might be expected, though many of the locals were not troubled by the verdict. After months of working under Kurtin and his arrogant henchmen from Atlanta, they felt a quiet satisfaction in watching them retreat in defeat. And they would be back. The verdict guaranteed new enthusiasm from the victims, more lawsuits, trials, and so on.

On hand to witness the farewell was Frank Sully, local counsel and partner in a Hattiesburg defense firm first hired by Krane and later demoted in favor of a "big firm" from Atlanta. Sully had been given a seat at the rather crowded defense table and had suffered the indignity of sitting through a four-month trial without saying a word in open court. Sully had disagreed with virtually every tactic and strategy employed by Kurtin. So deep was his dislike and distrust of the Atlanta lawyers that he had circulated a secret memo to his partners in which he predicted a huge punitive award. Now he gloated privately.

But he was a professional. He served his client as well as his client would allow, and he never failed to do what Kurtin instructed him to do. And he would gladly do it all over again because Krane Chemical had paid his little firm over a million dollars to date.

He and Kurtin shook hands at the front door. Both knew they would speak by phone before the day was over. Both were quietly thrilled by the departure. Two leased vans hauled Kurtin and ten others to the airport, where a handsome little jet was waiting for the seventy-minute flight, though they were in no hurry. They missed their homes and families, but what could be more humiliating than limping back from Podunk with their tails between their legs?

———

Carl remained safely tucked away on the forty-fifth floor, while on the Street the rumors raged. At 9:15, his banker from Goldman Sachs called, for the third time that morning, and delivered the bad news that the exchange might not open trading with Krane's common shares. It was too volatile. There was too much pressure to sell.

"Looks like a fire sale," he said bluntly, and Carl wanted to curse him.

The market opened at 9:30 a.m., and Krane's trading was delayed. Carl, Ratzlaff, and Felix Bard were at the conference table, exhausted, sleeves rolled up, elbows deep in papers and debris, phones in each hand, all conversations frantic. The bomb finally landed just after 10:00 a.m., when Krane began trading at $40.00 a share. There were no buyers, and none at $35.00. The plunge was temporarily reversed at $29.50 when speculators entered the fray and began buying. Up and down it went for the next hour. At noon, it was at $27.25 in heavy trading, and to make matters worse, Krane was the big business story of the morning. For their market updates, the cable shows happily switched to their Wall Street analysts, all of whom gushed about the stunning meltdown of Krane Chemical.

Then back to the headlines. Body count from Iraq. The monthly natural disaster. And Krane Chemical.

Bobby Ratzlaff asked permission to run to his office. He took the stairs, one flight down, and barely made it to the men's room. The stalls were empty. He went to the far one, raised the lid, and vomited violently.

His ninety thousand shares of Krane common had just decreased in value from about $4.5 million to around $2.5 million, and the collapse wasn't over. He used the stock as collateral for all his toys—the small house in the Hamptons, the Porsche Carrera, half interest in a sailboat. Not to mention overhead items such as private school tuition and golf club memberships. Bobby was now unofficially bankrupt.

For the first time in his career, he understood why they jumped from buildings in 1929.

The Paytons had planned to drive to Bowmore together, but a last-minute visit to their office by their banker changed things. Wes decided to stay behind and deal with Huffy. Mary Grace took the Taurus and drove to her hometown.

She went to Pine Grove, then to the church, where Jeannette Baker was waiting along with Pastor Denny Ott and a crowd of other victims represented by the Payton firm. They met privately in the fellowship hall and lunched on sandwiches, one of which was eaten by Jeannette herself, a rarity. She was composed, rested, happy to be away from the courthouse and all its proceedings.

The shock of the verdict was beginning to wear off. The possibility of money changing hands lightened the mood, and it also prompted a flood of questions. Mary Grace was careful to downplay expectations. She detailed the arduous appeals ahead for the *Baker* verdict. She was not optimistic about a settlement, or a cleanup, or even the next trial. Frankly, she and Wes did not have the funds, nor the energy, to take on Krane in another long trial, though she did not share this with the group.

She was confident and reassuring. Her

clients were at the right place; she and Wes had certainly proved that. There would soon be many lawyers sniffing around Bowmore, looking for Krane victims, making promises, offering money perhaps. And not just local lawyers, but the national tort boys who chased cases from coast to coast and often arrived at the crash sites before the fire trucks. Trust no one, she said softly but sternly. Krane will flood the area with investigators, snitches, informants, all looking for things that might be used against you one day in court. Don't talk to reporters, because something said in jest could sound quite different in a trial. Don't sign anything unless it's first reviewed by the Paytons. Don't talk to other lawyers.

She gave them hope. The verdict was echoing through the judicial system. Government regulators had to take note. The chemical industry could no longer ignore them. Krane's stock was crashing at that very moment, and when the stockholders lost enough money, they would demand changes.

When she finished, Denny Ott led them in prayer. Mary Grace hugged her clients, wished them well, promised to see them again in a few days, then walked with Ott to the front of the church for her next appointment.

The journalist's name was Tip Shepard. He had arrived about a month earlier, and after many attempts had gained the confidence of Pastor Ott, who then introduced him to Wes and Mary Grace. Shepard was a freelancer with impressive credentials, several books to his credit, and a Texas twang that neutralized some of Bowmore's distrust of the media. The Paytons had refused to talk to him during the trial, for many reasons. Now that it was over, Mary Grace would do the first interview. If it went well, there might be another.

———

"Mr. Kirkhead wants his money," Huffy was saying. He was in Wes's office, a makeshift room with unpainted Sheetrock walls, stained concrete floor, and Army-surplus furniture.

"I'm sure he does," Wes shot back. He was already irritated that his banker would arrive just hours after the verdict with signs of attitude. "Tell him to get in line."

"We're way past due here, Wes, come on."

"Is Kirkhead stupid? Does he think that the jury gives an award one day and the defendant writes a check the next?"

"Yes, he's stupid, but not that stupid."

"He sent you over here?"

"Yes. He jumped me first thing this morning, and I expect to get jumped for many days to come."

"Couldn't you wait a day, two days, maybe a week? Let us breathe a little, maybe enjoy the moment?"

"He wants a plan. Something in writing. Repayments, stuff like that."

"I'll give him a plan," Wes said, his words trailing off. He did not want to fight with Huffy. Though not exactly friends, they were certainly friendly and enjoyed each other's company. Wes was extremely grateful for Huffy's willingness to roll the dice. Huffy admired the Paytons for losing it all as they risked it all. He had spent hours with them as they surrendered their home, office, cars, retirement accounts.

"Let's talk about the next three months," Huffy said. The four legs of his folding chair were uneven and he rocked slightly as he talked.

Wes took a deep breath, gave a roll of the eyes. He suddenly felt very tired. "Once upon a time, we were grossing fifty thousand a month, clearing thirty, before taxes. Life was good, you remember. It'll take a year to crank up that treadmill, but we can do it. We have no choice. We'll survive until the appeals run their course. If the verdict stands, Kirkhead can take his money and take a hike. We'll retire, time for the sailboat. If the verdict is reversed, we'll go bankrupt and start advertising for quickie divorces."

"Surely the verdict will attract clients."

"Of course, but most of it'll be junk."

By using the word "bankrupt," Wes had gently placed Huffy back in his box, along with old Prickhead and the bank. The verdict could not be classified as an asset, and without it the Paytons' balance sheet looked as bleak as it did a day earlier. They had lost virtually everything already, and to be adjudged bankrupt was a further indignity they were willing to endure. Pile it on.

They would be back.

"I'm not giving you a plan, Huffy. Thanks for asking. Come back in thirty days and we'll talk. Right now I've got clients who've been ignored for months."

"So what do I tell Mr. Prickhead?"

"Simple. Push just a little bit harder, and he can use the paper to wipe with. Ease off, give us some time, and we'll satisfy the debt."

"I'll pass it along."

———

At Babe's Coffee Shop on Main Street, Mary Grace and Tip Shepard sat in a booth near the front windows and talked about the town. She remembered Main Street as a busy place where people shopped and gathered. Bowmore was too small for the large discount stores, so the downtown merchants survived. When she was a kid, traffic was often heavy, parking hard to find. Now half the storefronts were covered with plywood, and the other half were desperate for business.

A teenager with an apron brought two cups of black coffee and left without a word. Mary Grace added sugar while Shepard watched her carefully. "Are you sure the coffee is safe?" he asked.

"Of course. The city finally passed an ordinance forbidding the use of its water in restaurants. Plus, I've known Babe for thirty years. She was one of the first to buy her water."

Shepard took a cautious sip, then arranged his tape recorder and notebook.

"Why did you take the cases?" he asked.

She smiled and shook her head and kept stirring. "I've asked myself that a thousand times, but the answer is really simple. Pete, Jeannette's husband, worked for my uncle. I knew several of the victims. It's a small town, and when so many people became ill, it was obvious there had to be a reason. The cancer came in waves, and there was so much suffering. After attending the first three or four funerals, I realized something had to be done."

He took notes and ignored the pause.

She continued. "Krane was the biggest employer, and for years there had been rumors of dumping around the plant. A lot of folks who worked there got sick. I remember coming home from college after my sophomore year and hearing people talk about how bad the water was. We lived a mile outside of town and had our own well, so it was never a problem for us. But things got worse in town. Over the years, the rumors of dumping grew and grew until everyone came to believe them. At the same time, the water turned into a putrid liquid that was undrinkable. Then the cancer hit—liver, kidney, urinary tract, stomach, bladder, lots of leukemia. I was in church one Sunday with my parents, and I could see four slick, shiny bald heads. Chemo. I thought I was in a horror movie."

"Have you regretted the litigation?"

"No, never. We've lost a lot, but then so has my hometown. Hopefully, the losing is over now. Wes and I are young; we'll survive. But many of these folks are either dead or deathly ill."

"Do you think about the money?"

"What money? The appeal will take eighteen months, and right now that seems like an eternity. You have to see the big picture."

"Which is?"

"Five years from now. In five years, the toxic dump will be cleaned up and gone forever and no one will ever be hurt by it again. There will be a settlement, one big massive settlement where Krane Chemical, and its insurers, are finally brought to the table with their very deep pockets and are forced to compensate the families they have ruined. Everybody gets their share of damages."

"Including the lawyers."

"Absolutely. If not for the lawyers, Krane would still be here manufacturing pillamar 5 and dumping its by-products in the pits behind the plant, and no one could hold them accountable."

"Instead, they are now in Mexico—"

"Oh yes, manufacturing pillamar 5 and dumping its by-products in the pits behind the plants. And nobody gives a damn. They don't have these trials down there."

"What are your chances on appeal?"

She sipped the stale and heavily sugared coffee and was about to answer when an insurance agent stopped by, shook her hand, hugged her, said thanks several times, and appeared to be on the verge of tears when he walked away. Then Mr. Greenwood, her junior high principal, now retired, spotted her as he entered and practically crushed her in a bear hug. He ignored Shepard while rambling on about how proud he was of her. He thanked her, promised to keep praying for her, asked about her family, and so on.

As he withdrew in a windy farewell, Babe, the owner, came over for a hug and another lengthy round of congratulations.

Shepard finally stood and eased out the door. A few minutes later, Mary Grace made her exit. "Sorry about that," she said. "It's a big moment for the town."

"They are very proud."

"Let's go see the plant."

The Krane Chemical Bowmore Plant Number Two, as it was officially known, was in an abandoned industrial park on the east side of the city limits. The plant was a series of flat-roofed cinder-block buildings, connected by massive piping and conveyors. Water towers and storage silos rose behind the buildings. Everything was overgrown with kudzu and weeds. Because of the litigation, the company had secured the facility with miles of twelve-foot chain-link fencing, topped with glistening razor wire. Heavy gates were chained and padlocked. Like a prison, where bad things happened, the plant shut out the world and kept its secrets buried within.

Mary Grace had visited the plant at least a dozen times during the litigation, but always with a mob—other lawyers, engineers, former Krane employees, security guards, even Judge Harrison. The last visit had been two months earlier when the jurors were given a tour.

She and Shepard stopped at the main gate and examined the padlocks. A large, decaying sign identified the plant and its owner. As they stared through the chain-link fence, Mary Grace said, "Six years ago, when it became apparent that litigation was inevitable, Krane fled to Mexico. The employees were given three days' notice and $500 in severance pay; many of them had worked here for thirty years. It was an incredibly stupid way to leave town, because some of their former workers were our best witnesses during the trial. The bitterness was, and is, astounding. If Krane had any friends in Bowmore, it lost every one of them when it screwed its employees."

A photographer working with Shepard met them at the front gate and began snapping away. They strolled along the fence, with Mary Grace directing the brief tour. "For years, this place was unlocked. It was routinely vandalized. Teenagers hung out here, drinking and doing drugs. Now people stay as far away as possible. The gates and fences are really not needed. No one wants to get near this place."

From the north side, a long row of thick metal cylinders was visible in the midst of the plant. Mary Grace pointed and explained, "That's known as Extraction Unit Two. The bichloronylene was reduced as a by-product and stored in those tanks. From there, some was shipped away for a proper disposal, but most was taken into the woods there, farther back on the property, and simply dumped into a ravine."

"Proctor's Pit?"

"Yes, Mr. Proctor was the supervisor in charge of disposal. He died of cancer before we could subpoena him." They walked twenty yards along the fence. "We really can't see from here, but there are three ravines in there, deep in the woods, where they simply hauled the tanks and covered them with dirt and mud. Over the years, they began to leak—they were not even sealed properly—and the chemicals soaked into the earth. This went on for years, tons and tons of bichloronylene and cartolyx and aklar and other proven carcinogens. If you can believe our experts, and the jury evidently did, the poisons finally contaminated the aquifer from which Bowmore pumps its water."

A security detail in a golf cart approached on the other side of the fence. Two overweight guards with guns stopped and stared. "Just ignore them," Mary Grace whispered.

"What're you lookin' for?" a guard asked.

"We're on the right side of the fence," she answered.

"What're you lookin' for?" he repeated.

"I'm Mary Grace Payton, one of the attorneys. You boys move along."

Both nodded at once, and then slowly drove away.

She glanced at her watch. "I really need to be going."

"When can we meet again?"

"We'll see. No promises. Things are quite hectic right now."

They drove back to the Pine Grove Church and said goodbye. When Shepard was gone, Mary Grace walked three blocks to Jeannette's trailer. Bette was at work, the place was quiet. For an hour, she sat with her client under a small tree and drank bottled lemonade. No tears, no tissues, just girl talk about life and families and the past four months together in that awful courtroom.

CHAPTER 6

With an hour to go before trading closed, Krane bottomed at $18 a share, then began a rather feeble rally, if it could be called that. It nibbled around $20 a share for half an hour before finding some traction at that price.

To add to the catastrophe, investors for some reason chose to exact revenge on the rest of Carl's empire. His Trudeau Group owned 45 percent of Krane and smaller chunks of six other public companies— three chemical companies, an oil exploration firm, an auto parts maker, and a chain of hotels. Shortly after lunch, the common shares of the other six began slipping as well. It made no sense whatsoever, but then the market often cannot be explained. Misery is contagious on Wall Street. Panic is common and rarely understood.

Mr. Trudeau did not see the chain reaction coming, nor did Felix Bard, his savvy financial wizard. As the minutes dragged by, they watched in horror as a billion dollars in market value slipped away from the Trudeau Group.

Blame was rampant. Obviously, it all went back to the verdict in Mississippi. But many analysts, especially the babbling experts on cable, made much of the fact that Krane Chemical had for years chosen to go brazenly forward without the benefit of full liability insurance. The company had saved a fortune in premiums, but was now giving it back in spades. Bobby Ratzlaff was listening to one such analyst on a television in a corner when Carl snapped, "Turn that thing off!"

It was almost 4:00 p.m., the magic hour when the exchange closed and the bloodshed ended. Carl was at his desk, phone stuck to his head. Bard was at the conference table watching two monitors and recording the latest stock prices. Ratzlaff was pale and sick and even more bankrupt than before, and he went from window to window as if selecting the one for his final flight.

The other six stocks rallied at the final buzzer, and though they were down significantly, the damage was not ruinous. The companies were solid performers, and their stocks would readjust themselves in due course. Krane, on the other hand, was a train wreck. It closed at $21.25, a full $31.25 collapse since the day before. Its market value had shrunk from $3.2 billion to $1.3 billion. Mr. Trudeau's 45 percent share of the misery was about $850 million. Bard quickly added the declines from the other six companies and computed a one-day loss for his boss at $1.1 billion. Not a record, but probably enough to land Carl on someone's Top Ten list.

After a review of the closing numbers, Carl ordered Bard and Ratzlaff to put on their jackets, straighten their ties, and follow him.

Four floors below, in the corporate offices of Krane Chemical, its top executives were hunkered down in a small dining room reserved exclusively for themselves. The food was notoriously bland, but the view was impressive. Lunch had not been important that day; no one had an appetite. They had been waiting for an hour, shell-shocked and expecting an explosion from above. A mass funeral would have been a livelier event. But Mr. Trudeau managed to brighten up the room. He marched purposefully in, his two minions in tow—Bard with a plastic grin, Ratzlaff green at the gills—and, instead of yelling, thanked the men (all boys) for their hard work and commitment to the company.

A wide smile, and Carl said, "Gentlemen, this is not a very good day. One which I'm sure we'll remember for a long time." His voice was pleasant, just another friendly little drop-in from the man at the top.

"But today is now over, thankfully, and we are still standing. Tomorrow, we start kicking ass."

A few nervous looks, maybe a smile or two. Most were expecting to be sacked on the spot.

He continued: "I want you to remember three things that I'm about to say on this historic occasion. First, no one in this room is losing his job. Second, Krane Chemical will survive this miscarriage of justice. And third, I do not intend to lose this fight."

He was the epitome of the confident leader, the captain rallying his troops in their foxholes. A victory sign and long cigar and he could've been Churchill in his finest hour. He ordered chins up, backs to the wall, and so on.

Even Bobby Ratzlaff began to feel better.

————

Two hours later, Ratzlaff and Bard were finally dismissed and sent home. Carl wanted time to reflect, to lick his wounds, to clear his head. To help matters, he fixed himself a scotch and took off his shoes. The sun was setting somewhere beyond New Jersey, and he said good riddance to such an unforgettable day.

He glanced at his computer and checked the day's phone calls. Brianna had called four times, nothing urgent. If she had an important matter, Carl's secretary logged it as "Your Wife" and not "Brianna." He'd call her later. He was in no mood for the summary of her daily workouts.

There were over forty calls, and number

twenty-eight caught his attention. Senator Grott had checked in from Washington. Carl barely knew him personally, but every serious corporate player knew of The Senator. Grott had served three terms in the U.S. Senate from New York before he retired, voluntarily, and joined a powerful law firm to make his fortune. He was Mr. Washington, the ultimate insider, the seasoned counselor and adviser with offices on Wall Street, Pennsylvania Avenue, and anywhere else he chose. Senator Grott had more contacts than anyone, often golfed with whoever happened to occupy the White House, traveled the world in search of more contacts, offered advice only to the powerful, and was generally regarded as the top connection between big corporate America and big government. If The Senator called, you called him back, even though you'd just lost a billion dollars. The Senator knew exactly how much you had lost and was concerned about it.

Carl dialed the private number. After eight rings a gruff voice said, "Grott."

"Senator Grott, Carl Trudeau here," Carl said politely. He was deferential to very few people, but The Senator demanded and deserved respect.

"Oh yes, Carl," came the reply, as if they had played golf many times. Just a couple of old pals. Carl heard the voice and thought of the countless times he'd seen The Senator on the news. "How is Amos?" he asked.

The contact, the name that linked both men to this call. "Great. Had lunch with him last month." A lie. Amos was the managing partner of the corporate law firm Carl had been using for a decade. Not The Senator's firm, not even close. But Amos was a substantial person, certainly big enough to be mentioned by The Senator.

"Give him my regards."

"Certainly." Now get on with it, Carl was thinking.

"Listen, I know it's been a long day, so I won't keep you." A pause. "There is a man in Boca Raton that you should see, name is Rinehart, Barry Rinehart. He's a consultant of sorts, though you'll never find him in the phone book. His firm specializes in elections."

A long pause, and Carl had to say something. So he said, "Okay. I'm listening."

"He is extremely competent, smart, discreet, successful, and expensive. And if anyone can fix this verdict, Mr. Rinehart is your man."

"Fix this verdict," Carl repeated.

The Senator continued: "If you're interested, I'll give him a call, open the door."

"Well, yes, I'd certainly be interested."

Fix this verdict. It was music.

"Good, I'll be in touch."

"Thank you."

And with that the conversation was over. So typical of The Senator. A favor here, the payback there. All contacts running to and fro, everybody's back getting properly scratched. The call was free, but one day The Senator would be paid.

Carl stirred his scotch with a finger and looked at the rest of his calls. Nothing but misery.

Fix this verdict, he kept repeating.

In the center of his immaculate desk was a memo marked "CONFIDENTIAL." Weren't all of his memos confidential? On the cover sheet someone had scrawled with a black marker the name "PAYTON." Carl picked it up, arranged both feet on his desk, and flipped through it. There were photos, the first from yesterday's trial when Mr. and Mrs. Payton were leaving the courthouse, walking hand in hand in glorious triumph. There was an earlier one of Mary Grace from a bar publication, with a quick bio. Born in Bowmore, college at Millsaps, law school at Ole Miss, two years in a federal clerkship, two in a public defender's office, past president of the county bar association, certified trial lawyer, school board, member of the state Democratic Party and a few tree-hugger groups.

From the same publication, a photo and bio of James Wesley Payton. Born in Monroe, Louisiana, lettered in football at Southern Miss, law school at Tulane, three years as an assistant prosecutor, member of all the available trial lawyer groups, Rotary Club, Civitan, and so on.

Two backwater ambulance chasers who had just orchestrated Carl's exit from the Forbes 400 list of the richest Americans.

Two children, an illegal nanny, public schools, Episcopal church, near foreclosures on both home and office, near repossessions of two automobiles, a law practice (no other partners, just support staff) that was now ten years old and was once fairly profitable (by small-town standards) but now sought refuge in an abandoned dime store where the rent was at least three months in arrears. And then the good part— heavy debts, at least $400,000 to Second State Bank on a line of credit that is basically unsecured. No payments, not even on the interest, in five months. Second State Bank was a local outfit with ten offices in south Mississippi. Four hundred thousand dollars borrowed for the sole purpose of financing the lawsuit against Krane Chemical.

"Four hundred thousand dollars," Carl mumbled. So far he'd paid almost $14 million to defend the damned thing.

Bank accounts are empty. Credit cards no longer in use. Other clients (non-Bowmore variety) rumored to be frustrated by lack of attention.

No other substantial verdicts to speak of. Nothing close to $1 million.

Summary: These people are heavily in debt and hanging on by their fingernails. A little push, and they're over the edge. Strategy: Drag out the appeals, delay, delay. Crank up pressure from the bank. Possible buyout of Second State, then call the loan.

Bankruptcy would be the only course. Huge distraction as appeals rage on. Also, Paytons would be unable to pursue their other thirty (or so) cases versus Krane and would probably decline more clients.

Bottom line: this little law firm can be destroyed.

The memo was unsigned, which was no surprise, but Carl knew it was written by one of two hatchet men working in Ratzlaff's office. He'd find out which one and give the boy a raise. Good work.

The great Carl Trudeau had dismantled large conglomerates, taken over hostile boards of directors, fired celebrity CEOs, upset entire industries, fleeced bankers, manipulated stock prices, and destroyed the careers of dozens of his enemies.

He could certainly ruin a garden-variety mom-and-pop law firm in Hattiesburg, Mississippi.

————

Toliver delivered him home shortly after 9:00 p.m., a time selected by Carl because Sadler would be in bed and he would not be forced to dote on a child he had no interest in. The other child could not be avoided.

Brianna was waiting, dutifully, for him. They would dine by the fire.

When he walked through the door, he came face-to-face with *Imelda*, already permanently ensconced in the foyer and looking more abused than the night before. He couldn't help but gawk at the sculpture. Did the pile of brass rods really resemble a young girl? Where was the torso? Where were the limbs? Where was her head? Had he really paid that much money for such an abstract mess?

And how long might she haunt him in his own penthouse?

As his valet took his coat and briefcase, Carl stared sadly at his masterpiece, then heard the dreaded words "Hello, darling." Brianna swept into the room, a flowing red gown trailing after her. They pecked cheeks.

"Isn't it stunning?" she gushed, flopping an arm at *Imelda*.

"Stunning is the word," he said.

He looked at Brianna, then he looked at *Imelda*, and he wanted to choke both of them. But the moment passed. He could never admit defeat.

"Dinner is ready, darling," she cooed.

"I'm not hungry. Let's have a drink."

"But Claudelle has fixed your favorite—grilled sole."

"No appetite, dear," he said, yanking off his tie and tossing it to his valet.

"Today was awful, I know," she said. "A scotch?"

"Yes."

"Will you tell me about it?" she asked.

"I'd love to."

Brianna's private money manager, a woman unknown to Carl, had called throughout the day with updates on the collapse. Brianna knew the numbers, and she had heard the reports that her husband was down a billion or so.

She dismissed the kitchen staff, then changed into a much more revealing nightgown. They met by the fire and chatted until he fell asleep.

CHAPTER 7

At 10:00 a.m. Friday, two days post-verdict, the Payton firm met in The Pit, a large open space with unpainted Sheetrock walls lined with homemade bookshelves and cluttered with a heavy collage of aerial photos, medical summaries, juror profiles, expert-witness reports, and a hundred other trial documents and exhibits. In the center of the room was a table of sorts—four large pieces of inch-thick plywood mounted on sawhorses and surrounded with a sad collection of metal and wooden chairs, almost all of which were missing a piece or two. The table had obviously been the center of the storm for the past four months, with piles of papers and stacks of law books. Sherman, a paralegal, had spent most of the previous day hauling out coffee cups, pizza boxes, Chinese food containers, and empty water bottles. He'd also swept the concrete floors, though no one could tell.

Their previous office, a three-story building on Main Street, had been beautifully decorated, well-appointed, and spruced up each night by a cleaning service. Appearance and neatness were important back then.

Now they were just trying to survive.

In spite of the dismal surroundings, the mood was light, and for obvious reasons. The marathon was over. The incredible verdict was still hard to believe. United by sweat and hardship, the tight-knit little firm had taken on the beast and won a big one for the good guys.

Mary Grace called the meeting to order. The phones were put on hold because Tabby, the receptionist, was very much a part of the firm and was expected to participate in the discussion. Thankfully, the phones were beginning to ring again.

Sherman and Rusty, the other paralegal,

wore jeans, sweatshirts, no socks. Working in what was once a dime store, who could care about a dress code? Tabby and Vicky, the other receptionist, had abandoned nice clothes when both snagged dresses on the hand-me-down furniture. Only Olivia, the matronly bookkeeper, turned herself out each day in proper office attire.

They sat around the plywood table, sipping the same bad coffee they were now addicted to, and listened with smiles as Mary Grace did her recap. "There will be the usual post-trial motions," she was saying. "Judge Harrison has scheduled a hearing in thirty days, but we expect no surprises."

"Here's to Judge Harrison," Sherman said, and they toasted him with their coffee.

It had become a very democratic firm. Everyone present felt like an equal. Anyone could speak whenever he or she felt like it. Only first names were used. Poverty is a great equalizer.

Mary Grace continued: "For the next few months, Sherman and I will handle the *Baker* case as it moves forward, and we will keep the other Bowmore cases current. Wes and Rusty will take everything else and start generating some cash."

Applause.

"Here's to cash," Sherman said, another toast. He possessed a law degree from a night school but had not been able to pass the bar exam. He was now in his mid-forties, a career paralegal who knew more law than most lawyers. Rusty was twenty years younger and contemplating med school.

"While we're on the subject," Mary Grace continued, "Olivia has given me the latest red-ink summary. Always a pleasure." She picked up a sheet of paper and looked at the numbers. "We are now officially three months behind in rent, for a total of $4,500."

"Oh, please evict us," Rusty said.

"But the landlord is still our client and he's not worried. All other bills are at least two months past due, except, of course, the phones and electricity. Salaries have not been paid in four weeks—"

"Five," Sherman said.

"Are you sure?" she asked.

"As of today. Today is payday, or at least it used to be."

"Sorry, five weeks past due. We should have some cash in a week if we can settle the *Raney* case. We'll try to catch up."

"We're surviving," Tabby said. She was

the only single person in the firm. All others had spouses with jobs. Though budgets were painfully tight, they were determined to survive.

"How about the Payton family?" Vicky asked.

"We're fine," Wes said. "I know you're concerned, thank you, but we're getting by just like you. I've said this a hundred times, but I'll say it again. Mary Grace and I will pay you as soon as we possibly can. Things are about to improve."

"We're more concerned about you," Mary Grace added.

No one was leaving. No one was threatening.

A deal had been struck long ago, though it was not in writing. If and when the Bowmore cases paid off, the money would be shared by the entire firm. Maybe not equally, but everyone present knew they would be rewarded.

"How about the bank?" Rusty asked. There were no secrets now. They knew Huffy had stopped by the day before, and they knew how much Second State Bank was owed.

"I stiff-armed the bank," Wes said. "If they

push a little more, then we'll file Chapter 11 and screw 'em."

"I vote to screw the bank," Sherman said.

It seemed to be unanimous around the room that the bank should get screwed, though everyone knew the truth. The lawsuit would not have been possible without Huffy's lobbying on their behalf and convincing Mr. Prickhead to raise the line of credit. They also knew that the Paytons would not rest until the bank was paid.

"We should clear twelve thousand from the *Raney* case," Mary Grace said. "And another ten thousand from the dog bite."

"Maybe fifteen," Wes said.

"Then what? Where is the next settlement?" Mary Grace threw this on the table for all to consider.

"Geeter," Sherman said. It was more of a suggestion.

Wes looked at Mary Grace. Both gave blank looks to Sherman. "Who's Geeter?"

"Geeter happens to be a client. Slip and fall at the Kroger store. Came in about eight months ago." There were some odd glances around the table. It was obvious that the two lawyers had forgotten one of their clients.

"I don't recall that one," Wes admitted.

"What's the potential?" Mary Grace asked.

"Not much. Shaky liability. Maybe twenty thousand. I'll review the file with you on Monday."

"Good idea," Mary Grace said and quickly moved on to something else. "I know the phones are ringing, and we are definitely broke, but we are not about to start taking a bunch of junk. No real estate or bankruptcies. No criminal cases unless they can pay the freight. No contested divorces—we'll do the quickies for a thousand bucks, but everything must be agreed on. This is a personal injury firm, and if we get loaded down with the small stuff, we won't have time for the good cases. Any questions?"

"There's a lot of weird stuff coming in by phone," Tabby said. "And from all over the country."

"Just stick to the basics," Wes said. "We can't handle cases in Florida or Seattle. We need quick settlements here at home, at least for the next twelve months."

"How long will the appeals take?" Vicky asked.

"Eighteen to twenty-four months," Mary Grace answered. "And there's not much we can do to push things along. It's a process, and that's why it's important to hunker down now and generate some fees elsewhere."

"Which brings up another point," Wes said. "The verdict changes the landscape dramatically. First, expectations are through the roof right now, and our other Bowmore clients will soon be pestering us. They want their day in court, their big verdict. We must be patient, but we can't let these people drive us crazy. Second, the vultures are descending on Bowmore. Lawyers will be chasing one another looking for clients. It will be a free-for-all. Any contact from another attorney is to be reported immediately. Third, the verdict places even greater pressure on Krane. Their dirty tricks will get even dirtier. They have people watching us. Trust no one. Speak to no one. Nothing leaves this office. All papers are shredded. As soon as we can afford it, we'll hire nighttime security. Bottom line—watch everyone and watch your backs."

"This is fun," Vicky said. "Like a movie."

"Any questions?"

"Yes," Rusty said. "Can Sherman and I start chasing ambulances again? It's been four months, you know, since the beginning of the trial. I really miss the excitement."

"I haven't seen the inside of an ER in weeks," Sherman added. "And I miss the sounds of the sirens."

It wasn't clear if they were joking or not, but the moment was humorous and good for a laugh. Mary Grace finally said, "I really don't care what you do; I just don't want to know everything."

"Meeting adjourned," Wes said. "And it's Friday. Everyone has to leave at noon. We're locking the doors. See you Monday."

———

They picked up Mack and Liza from school, and after fast food for lunch they headed south through the countryside for an hour, until they saw the first sign for Lake Garland. The roads narrowed before finally turning to gravel. The cabin was at the dead end of a dirt trail, perched above the water on stilts and wedged into a tight spot where the woods met the shoreline. A short pier ran from the porch into the water, and beyond it the vast lake seemed to stretch for miles. There was no other sign of human activity, either on the lake or anywhere around it.

The cabin was owned by a lawyer friend in Hattiesburg, a man Wes had once worked for and who had declined to get involved in the Bowmore mess. That decision had seemed a wise one, until about forty-eight hours ago. Now there was considerable doubt.

The original idea had been to drive a few more hours to Destin and have a long weekend on the beach. But they simply couldn't afford it.

They unloaded the car as they roamed through the spacious cabin, an A-frame with a huge loft, which Mack surveyed and declared perfect for another night of "camping out."

"We'll see," Wes said. There were three small bedrooms on the main level, and he planned to find a comfortable bed. Serious sleep was the goal for the weekend. Sleep and time with the kids.

As promised, the fishing gear was in a storage room under the porch. The boat was winched at the end of the pier, and the children watched with anticipation as Wes lowered it into the water. Mary Grace fiddled with the life jackets and made sure both kids were properly secured. An hour after they arrived, she was tucked away comfortably under a quilt in a lounge chair on the porch, book in hand, watching the rest of her family inch across the blue horizon of Lake Garland, three small silhouettes in search of bream and crappie.

It was mid-November, and red and yellow leaves were falling, twisting in the breeze, and covering the cabin, the pier, and the water around it. There were no sounds. The small boat motor was too far away. The wind was too soft. The birds and wildlife were elsewhere for the moment. Perfect stillness, a rare event in any life but one that she especially treasured now. She closed the book, closed her eyes, and tried to think of something unrelated to the past few months.

Where would they be in five years? She concentrated on the future because the past was thoroughly consumed by the *Baker* case. They would certainly be in a house, though never again would they hock their future with a fat mortgage on a showy little castle in the suburbs. She wanted a home, nothing more. She no longer cared about imported cars and an expensive office and all the other toys that once seemed so important. She wanted to be a mother to her children, and she wanted a home to raise them in.

Family and assets aside, she wanted more lawyers. Their firm would be larger and full of smart and talented lawyers who did nothing but pursue the creators of toxic dumps and bad drugs and defective products. One day Payton & Payton would be known not for the cases it won but for the crooks it hauled into court for judgment.

She was forty-one years old, and she was tired. But the fatigue would pass. The old dreams of full-time motherhood and a cushy retirement were forever forgotten. Krane Chemical had converted her into a radical and a crusader. After the last four months, she would never be the same.

Enough. Her eyes were wide open.

Every thought took her back to the case, to Jeannette Baker, the trial, Krane Chemical. She would not spend this quiet and lovely weekend dwelling on such matters. She opened her book and started to read.

———

For dinner, they roasted hot dogs and marshmallows over a stone pit near the water, then sat on the pier in the darkness and watched the stars. The air was clear and cool, and they huddled together under a quilt. A distant light flickered on the horizon, and after some discussion it was agreed upon that it was just a boat.

"Dad, tell us a story," Mack said. He was squeezed between his sister and his mother.

"What kind of story?"

"A ghost story. A scary one."

His first thought was about the dogs of Bowmore. For years a pack of stray dogs had roamed the outskirts of the town. Often, in the dead of night, they shrieked and yelped and made more noise than a pack of coyotes. Legend held that the dogs were rabid and had been driven crazy because they drank the water.

But he'd had enough of Bowmore. He remembered one about a ghost who walked on water in the night, looking for his beloved wife, who'd drowned. He began to tell it, and the children squeezed closer to their parents.

CHAPTER 8

A uniformed guard opened the gates to the mansion, then nodded smartly to the driver as the long black Mercedes rushed by, in a hurry as always. Mr. Carl Trudeau had the rear seat, alone, already lost in the morning's papers. It was 7:30 a.m., too early for golf or tennis and too early for Saturday morning traffic in Palm Beach. Within minutes, the car was on Interstate 95, racing south.

Carl ignored the market reports. Thank God the week was finally over. Krane closed at $19.50 the day before and showed no signs of finding a permanent floor. Though he would be forever known as one of the very few men who'd lost a billion dollars in a day, he was already plotting his next legend. Give him a year and he'd have his billion back. In two years, he'd double all of it.

Forty minutes later he was in Boca Raton, crossing the waterway, headed for the clusters of high-rise condos and hotels packed along the beach. The office building was a shiny glass cylinder ten floors tall with a gate and a guard and not one word posted on a sign of any type. The Mercedes was waved through and stopped under a portico. A stern-faced young man in a black suit opened the rear door and said, "Good morning, Mr. Trudeau."

"Good morning," Carl said, climbing out.

"This way, sir."

———

According to Carl's hasty research, the firm of Troy-Hogan worked very hard at not being seen. It had no Web site, brochure, advertisements, listed phone number, or anything else that might attract clients. It was not a law firm, because it was not registered with the State of Florida, or any other state for that matter. It had no registered lobbyists. It was a corporation, not a limited partnership or some other variety of association. It was unclear where the name originated because there was no record of anyone named Troy or Hogan. The firm was known to provide marketing and consulting services, but there was no clue as to the nature of this business. It was domiciled in Bermuda and had been registered in Florida for eight years. Its domestic agent was a law firm in Miami. It was privately owned, and no one knew who owned it.

The less Carl learned about the firm, the more he admired it.

The principal was one Barry Rinehart, and here the trail grew somewhat warmer. According to friends and contacts in Washington, Rinehart had passed through D.C. twenty years earlier without leaving a fingerprint. He had worked for a congressman, the Pentagon, and a couple of midsized lobbying outfits—the typical résumé of a million others. He left town for no apparent reason in 1990 and surfaced in Minnesota, where he ran the successful campaign of a political unknown who got elected to Congress. Then he went to Oregon, where he worked his magic in a Senate race. As his reputation began to rise, he abruptly quit doing campaigns and disappeared altogether. End of trail.

Rinehart was forty-eight years old, married and divorced twice, no children, no criminal record, no professional associations, no civic clubs. He had a degree in political science from the University of Maryland and a law degree from the University of Nevada.

No one seemed to know what he was doing now, but he was certainly doing it well. His suite on the top floor of the cylinder was beautifully decorated with minimalist contemporary art and furniture. Carl, who spared no expense with his own office, was impressed.

Barry was waiting at the door of his office. The two shook hands and exchanged the usual pleasantries as they took in the details of the other's suit, shirt, tie, shoes. Nothing off-the-rack. No detail left undone, even though it was a Saturday morning in south Florida. Impressions were crucial, especially to Barry, who was thrilled at the prospect of snaring a new and substantial client.

Carl had half-expected a slick car salesman with a bad suit, but he was pleasantly surprised. Mr. Rinehart was dignified, soft-spoken, well-groomed, and very much at ease in the presence of such a powerful man. He was certainly not an equal, but he seemed to be comfortable with this.

A secretary asked about coffee as they stepped inside and met the ocean. From the tenth floor, beachside, the Atlantic stretched forever. Carl, who gazed at the Hudson River several times a day, was envious. "Beautiful," he said, staring from the row of ten-foot glass windows.

"Not a bad place to work," Barry said.

They settled into beige leather chairs as the coffee arrived. The secretary closed the door behind her, giving the place a nice secure feel.

"I appreciate you meeting me on a Saturday morning and with such short notice," Carl said.

"The pleasure is mine," Barry said. "It's been a rough week."

"I've had better. I take it you've spoken personally with Senator Grott."

"Oh yes. We chat occasionally."

"He was very vague about your firm and what you do."

Barry laughed and crossed his legs. "We

do campaigns. Have a look." He picked up a remote and pushed the button, and a large white screen dropped from the ceiling and covered most of a wall, then the entire nation appeared. Most of the states were in green, the rest were in a soft yellow. "Thirty-one states elect their appellate and supreme court judges. They are in green. The yellow ones have the good sense to appoint their courts. We make our living in the green ones."

"Judicial elections."

"Yes. That's all we do, and we do it very quietly. When our clients need help, we target a supreme court justice who is not particularly friendly, and we take him, or her, out of the picture."

"Just like that."

"Just like that."

"Who are your clients?"

"I can't give you the names, but they're all on your side of the street. Big companies in energy, insurance, pharmaceuticals, chemicals, timber, all types of manufacturers, plus doctors, hospitals, nursing homes, banks. We raise tons of money and hire the people on the ground to run aggressive campaigns."

"Have you worked in Mississippi?"

"Not yet." Barry punched another button and America was back. The green states slowly turned black. "The darker states are the ones we've worked in. As you can see, they're coast-to-coast. We maintain a presence in all thirty-nine."

Carl took some coffee, and nodded as if he wanted Barry to keep talking.

"We employ about fifty people here, the entire building is ours, and we accumulate enormous amounts of data. Information is power, and we know everything. We review every appellate decision in the green states. We know every appellate judge, their backgrounds, families, prior careers, divorces, bankruptcies, all the dirt. We review every decision and can predict the outcome of almost every case on appeal. We track every legislature and keep up with bills that might affect civil justice. We also monitor important civil trials."

"How about the one in Hattiesburg?"

"Oh yes. We were not at all surprised at the verdict."

"Then why were my lawyers surprised?"

"Your lawyers were good but not great. Plus, the plaintiff has a better case. I've studied a lot of toxic dumps, and Bowmore is one of the worst."

"So we'll lose again?"

"That's my prediction. The flood is coming."

Carl glanced at the ocean and drank some more coffee. "What happens on appeal?"

"Depends on who's on the Mississippi Supreme Court. Right now, there's a very good chance the verdict will be affirmed in a 5-to-4 decision. The state has been notoriously sympathetic to plaintiffs for the past two decades and, as you probably know, has a well-earned reputation as a hotbed of litigation. Asbestos, tobacco, fen-phen, all sorts of crazy class actions. Tort lawyers love the place."

"So I'll lose by one vote?"

"More or less. The court is not entirely predictable, but, yes, it's usually a 5-to-4 split."

"So all we need is a friendly judge?"

"Yes."

Carl placed his cup on a table and shot to his feet. He slid out of his jacket, hung it over a chair, then walked to the windows and stared at the ocean. A cargo ship inched along a mile out, and he watched it for several minutes. Barry slowly sipped his coffee.

"Do you have a judge in mind?" Carl finally asked.

Barry hit the remote. The screen went blank, then disappeared into the ceiling. He stretched as if he had a sore back, then said, "Perhaps we should talk business first."

Carl nodded and took his chair. "Let's hear it."

"Our proposal goes something like this. You hire our firm, the money gets wired into the proper accounts, then I will give you a plan for restructuring the Supreme Court of Mississippi."

"How much?"

"There are two fees. First, a million as a retainer. This is all properly reported. You officially become our client, and we provide consulting services in the area of government relations, a wonderfully vague term that covers just about anything. The second fee is seven million bucks, and we take it offshore. Some of this will be used to fund the campaign, but most will be preserved. Only the first fee goes on the books."

Carl was nodding, understanding. "For eight million, I can buy myself a supreme court justice."

"That's the plan."

"And this judge earns how much a year?"

"Hundred and ten thousand."

"A hundred and ten thousand dollars," Carl repeated.

"It's all relative. Your mayor in New York City spent seventy-five million to get elected to a job that pays a tiny fraction of that. It's politics."

"Politics," Carl said as if he wanted to spit. He sighed heavily and slumped an inch or two in his chair. "I guess it's cheaper than a verdict."

"Much cheaper, and there will be more verdicts. Eight million is a bargain."

"You make it sound so easy."

"It's not. These are bruising campaigns, but we know how to win them."

"I want to know how the money is spent. I want the basic plan."

Barry walked over and replenished his coffee from a silver thermos. Then he walked to his magnificent windows and gazed out at the Atlantic. Carl glanced at his watch. He had a 12:30 tee time at the Palm

Beach Country Club; not that it mattered that much. He was a social golfer who played because he was expected to play.

Rinehart drained his cup and returned to his chair. "The truth, Mr. Trudeau, is that you really don't want to know how the money is spent. You want to win. You want a friendly face on the supreme court so that when *Baker versus Krane Chemical* is decided in eighteen months, you'll be certain of the outcome. That's what you want. That's what we deliver."

"For eight million bucks I would certainly hope so."

You blew eighteen on a bad piece of sculpture three nights ago, Barry thought but wouldn't dare say. You have three jets that cost forty million each. Your "renovation" in the Hamptons will set you back at least ten million. And these are just a few of your toys. We're talking business here, not toys. Barry's file on Carl was much thicker than Carl's file on Barry. But then, in fairness, Mr. Rinehart worked hard to avoid attention, while Mr. Trudeau worked even harder to attract it.

It was time to close the deal, so Barry quietly pressed on. "Mississippi has its judicial elections a year from now, next November. We have plenty of time, but none to waste. Your timing is convenient and lucky. As we slug it out through the election next year, the case plods along through the appellate process. Our new man will take office a year from January, and about four months later will come face-to-face with *Baker versus Krane Chemical*."

For the first time, Carl saw a flash of the car salesman, and it didn't bother him at all. Politics was a dirty business where the winners were not always the cleanest guys in town. One had to be a bit of a thug to survive.

"My name cannot be at risk," he said sternly.

Barry knew he had just collected another handsome fee. "It's impossible," he said with a fake smile. "We have fire walls everywhere. If one of our operatives gets out of line, does something wrong, we make sure another guy takes the fall. Troy-Hogan has never been even remotely tarnished. And if they can't catch us, they damned sure can't find you."

"No paperwork."

"Only for the initial fee. We are, after all, a

legitimate consulting and government relations firm. We will have an official rela-
tionship with you: consulting, marketing,
communications—all those wonderfully nebulous words that hide everything else. But
the offshore arrangement is completely confidential."

Carl thought for a long time, then smiled
and said, "I like it. I like it a lot."

CHAPTER 9

The law office of F. Clyde Hardin & Associates had no associates. It was just Clyde and Miriam, his feeble secretary who outranked him because she had been there for over forty years, far longer than Clyde. She had typed deeds and wills for his father, who came home from the Second War without a leg and was famous for removing his wooden one in front of juries to distract them. The old man was gone now, long gone, and he had bequeathed his old office and old furniture and old secretary to his only child, Clyde, who was fifty-four and very old himself.

The Hardin law office had been a fixture on Main Street in Bowmore for over sixty years. It had survived wars, depressions, recessions, sit-ins, boycotts, and desegregation, but Clyde wasn't so sure it could survive Krane Chemical. The town was drying up around him. The nickname Cancer County was simply too much to overcome. From his ringside seat, he had watched merchants and cafés and country lawyers and country doctors throw in the towel and abandon the town.

Clyde never wanted to be a lawyer, but his father gave him no choice. And though he survived on deeds and wills and divorces, and though he managed to appear reasonably happy and colorful with his seersucker suits, paisley bow ties, and straw hats, he silently loathed the law and the small-town practice of it. He despised the daily grind of dealing with people too poor to pay him, of hassling with other deadbeat lawyers trying to steal said clients, of bickering with judges and clerks and just about everybody else who crossed his path. There were only six lawyers left in Bowmore, and Clyde was the youngest. He dreamed of retiring to a lake or a beach, anywhere, but those dreams would never come true.

Clyde had sugared coffee and one fried egg at 8:30 every morning at Babe's, seven doors to the right of his office, and a grilled cheese and iced tea every noon at Bob's Burgers, seven doors to the left. At five every afternoon, as soon as Miriam tidied up her desk and said goodbye, Clyde pulled out the office bottle and had a vodka on the rocks. He normally did this alone, in the solitude of the day, his finest hour. He cherished the stillness of his own little happy hour. Often the only sounds were the swishing of a ceiling fan and the rattling of his ice cubes.

He'd had two sips, gulps really, and the booze was beginning to glow somewhere in his brain when there was a rather aggressive knock on his door. No one was expected. Downtown was deserted by five every afternoon, but there was the occasional client looking for a lawyer. Clyde was too broke to ignore the traffic. He placed his tumbler on a bookshelf and walked to the front. A well-dressed gentleman was waiting. He introduced himself as Sterling Bitch or something of that order. Clyde looked at his business card. Bintz. Sterling Bintz. Attorney-at-Law. From Philadelphia, PA.

Mr. Bintz was about forty years old, short and thin, intense, with the smugness that Yankees can't help but exude when they venture into decaying towns of the Deep South.

How could anyone live like this? their smirks seemed to ask.

Clyde disliked him immediately, but he also wanted to return to his vodka, so he offered Sterling a cocktail. Sure, why not?

They settled around Clyde's desk and began to drink. After a few minutes of boring chitchat, Clyde said, "Why don't you get to the point?"

"Certainly." The accent was sharp and crisp and oh so grating. "My firm specializes in class actions for mass torts. That's all we do."

"And you're suddenly interested in our little town. What a surprise."

"Yes, we are interested. Our research tells us that there may be over a thousand potential cases around here, and we'd like to sign up as many as possible. But we need local counsel."

"You're a bit late, bud. The ambulance

chasers have been combing this place for the past five years."

"Yes, I understand that most of the death cases have been secured, but there are many other types. We'd like to find those victims with liver and kidney problems, stomach lesions, colon trouble, skin diseases, as many as a dozen other afflictions, all caused, of course, by Krane Chemical. We screen them with our doctors, and when we have a few dozen, we hit Krane with a class action. This is our specialty. We do it all the time. The settlement could be huge."

Clyde was listening but pretending to be bored. "Go on," he said.

"Krane's been kicked in the crotch. They cannot continue to litigate, so they'll eventually be forced to settle. If we have the first class action, we're in the driver's seat."

"We?"

"Yes. My firm would like to associate with your firm."

"You're looking at my firm."

"We'll do all the work. We need your name as local counsel, and your contacts and presence here in Bowmore."

"How much?" Clyde was known to be

rather blunt. No sense mincing words with this little shyster from up north.

"Five hundred bucks per client, then 5 percent of the fees when we settle. Again, we do all the work."

Clyde rattled his ice cubes and tried to do the math.

Sterling pressed on. "The building next door is vacant. I—"

"Oh yes, there are many vacant buildings here in Bowmore."

"Who owns the one next door?"

"I do. It's part of this building. My grandfather bought it a thousand years ago. And I got one across the street, too. Empty."

"The office next door is the perfect place for a screening clinic. We fix it up, give it a medical ambience, bring in our doctors, then advertise like hell for anyone who thinks he or she might be sick. They'll flock in. We sign them up, get the numbers, then file a massive action in federal court."

It had the distinct ring of something fraudulent, but Clyde had heard enough about mass torts to know that Sterling here knew what he was talking about. Five hundred clients, at $500 a pop, plus 5 percent when they won the lottery. He reached for the office bottle and refilled both glasses.

"Intriguing," Clyde said.

"It could be very profitable."

"But I don't work in federal court."

Sterling sipped the near-lethal serving and offered a smile. He knew perfectly well the limitations of this small-town blowhard. Clyde would have trouble defending a shoplifting case in city court. "Like I said. We do all the work. We're hardball litigators."

"Nothing unethical or illegal," Clyde said.

"Of course not. We've been winning class action in mass tort cases for twenty years. Check us out."

"I'll do that."

"And do it quick. This verdict is attracting attention. From now on, it's a race to find the clients and file the first class action."

———

After he left, Clyde had a third vodka, his limit, and near the end of it found the courage to tell all the locals to go to hell. Oh, how they would love to criticize him! Advertising for victims/clients in the county's weekly paper, turning his office into a cheap clinic for assembly-line diagnoses, crawling into bed with some slimy lawyers from up north, profiting from the misery of his people. The list would be long and the gossip would consume Bowmore, and the more he drank, the more determined he became to throw caution to the wind and, for once, try to make some money.

For a character with such a blustery personality, Clyde was secretly afraid of the courtroom. He had faced a few juries years earlier and had been so stricken with fear that he could hardly talk. He had settled into a safe and comfortable office practice that paid the bills but kept him away from the frightening battles where the real money was made and lost.

For once, why not take a chance?

And wouldn't he be helping his people? Every dime taken from Krane Chemical and deposited somewhere in Bowmore was a victory. He poured a fourth drink, swore it was the last, and decided that, yes, damn it, he would hold hands with Sterling and his gang of class action thieves and strike a mighty blow for justice.

Two days later, a subcontractor Clyde

had represented in at least three divorces arrived early with a crew of carpenters, painters, and gofers, all desperate for work, and began a quick renovation of the office next door.

Twice a month Clyde played poker with the owner of the *Bowmore News*, the county's only paper. Like the town itself, the weekly was declining and trying to hang on. In its next edition, the front page was dominated by news about the verdict over in Hattiesburg, but there was also a generous story about Lawyer Hardin's association with a major national law firm from Philadelphia. Inside was a full-page ad that practically begged every citizen of Cary County to drop by the new "diagnostic facility" on Main Street for screening that was absolutely free.

Clyde enjoyed the crowd and the attention and was already counting his money.

———

It was 4:00 a.m., cold and dark with a threat of rain, when Buck Burleson parked his truck in the small employees' lot at the Hattiesburg pumping station. He collected his thermos of coffee, a cold biscuit with ham, and a 9-millimeter automatic pistol and carried it all to an eighteen-wheel rig with unmarked doors and a ten-thousand-gallon tanker as its payload. He started the engine and checked the gauges, tires, and fuel.

The night supervisor heard the diesel and walked out of the second-floor monitoring room. "Hello, Buck," he called down.

"Mornin', Jake," Buck said with a nod. "She loaded?"

"Ready to go."

That part of the conversation had not changed in five years. There was usually an exchange about the weather, then a farewell. But on this morning, Jake decided to add a wrinkle to their dialogue, one he'd been contemplating for a few days. "Those folks any happier over in Bowmore?"

"Damned if I know. I don't hang around."

And that was it. Buck opened the driver's door, gave his usual "See you later," and closed himself inside. Jake watched the tanker ease along the drive, turn left at the street, and finally disappear, the only vehicle moving at that lonesome hour.

On the highway, Buck carefully poured coffee from the thermos into its plastic screw-on cup. He glanced at his pistol on the passenger's seat. He decided to wait on the biscuit. When he saw the sign announcing Cary County, he glanced at his gun again.

He made the trip three times a day, four days a week. Another driver handled the other three days. They swapped up frequently to cover vacations and holidays. It was not the career Buck had envisioned. For seventeen years he'd been a foreman at Krane Chemical in Bowmore, earning three times what they now paid him to haul water to his old town.

It was ironic that one of the men who'd done so much to pollute Bowmore's water now hauled in fresh supplies of it. But irony was lost on Buck. He was bitter at the company for fleeing and taking his job with it. And he hated Bowmore because Bowmore hated him.

Buck was a liar. This had been proven several times, but never in a more spectacular fashion than during a brutal cross-examination a month earlier. Mary Grace Payton had gently fed him enough rope, then watched him hang himself in front of the jury.

For years, Buck and most of the supervisors at Krane had flatly denied any chemical dumping whatsoever. They were ordered to do so by their bosses. They denied it in company memos. They denied it when talking to company lawyers. They denied it in affidavits. And they certainly denied it when the plant was investigated by the Environmental Protection Agency and the U.S. Attorney's Office. Then the litigation began. After denying it for so long and so fervently, how could they suddenly flip their stories and tell the truth? Krane, after fiercely promoting the lying for so long, vanished. It escaped one weekend and found a new home in Mexico. No doubt some tortilla-eating jackass down there was doing Buck's job for $5 a day. He swore as he sipped his coffee.

A few of the managers came clean and told the truth. Most clung to their lies. It didn't matter, really, because they all looked like fools at trial, at least those who testified. Some tried to hide. Earl Crouch, perhaps the biggest liar of all, had been relocated to a Krane plant near Galveston. There was a rumor that he had disappeared under mysterious circumstances.

Buck again glanced at the 9-millimeter.

So far, he had received only one threatening phone call. He wasn't sure about the other managers. All had left Bowmore, and they did not keep in touch.

Mary Grace Payton. If he'd had the pistol during his cross-examination, he might have shot her, her husband, and a few of the lawyers for Krane, and he would have saved one bullet for himself. For four devastating hours, she had exposed one lie after another. Some of the lies were safe, he'd been told. Some were hidden away in memos and affidavits that Krane kept buried. But Ms. Payton had all the memos and all the affidavits and much more.

When the ordeal was almost over, when Buck was bleeding and the jury was furious and Judge Harrison was saying something about perjury, Buck almost snapped. He was exhausted, humiliated, half-delirious, and he almost jumped to his feet, looked at the jurors, and said, "You want the truth, I'll give it to you. We dumped so much shit into those ravines it's a wonder the whole town didn't explode. We dumped gallons every day—BCL and cartolyx and aklar, all class-1 carcinogens—hundreds of gallons of toxic stuff directly into the ground. We dumped it from vats and buckets and barrels and drums. We dumped it at night and in broad daylight. Oh sure, we stored a lot of it in sealed green drums and paid a fortune to a specialty firm to haul it away. Krane complied with the law. They kissed the EPA's ass. You've seen the paperwork, everything nice and proper. Real legal like. While the starched shirts in the front office were filling out forms, we were out back in the pits burying the poison. It was much easier and much cheaper to dump it. And you know what? Those same assholes up front knew exactly what we were doing out back." Here he would point a deadly finger at the Krane executives and their lawyers. "They covered it up! And they're lying to you now. Everybody's lying."

Buck gave this speech out loud as he drove, though not every morning. It was oddly comforting to do so, to think about what he should have said instead of what he did. A piece of his soul and most of his manhood had been left behind in that courtroom. Lashing out in the privacy of his big truck was therapeutic.

Driving to Bowmore, however, was not. He was not from there and had never liked the town. When he lost his job, he had no choice but to leave.

As the highway became Main Street, he turned right and drove for four blocks. The distribution point had been given the nickname the "city tank." It was directly below the old water tower, an unused and decayed relic whose metal panels had been eaten from the inside by the city's water. A large aluminum reservoir now served the town. Buck pulled his tanker onto an elevated platform, killed the engine, stuffed the pistol into his pocket, and got out of the truck. He went about his business of unloading his cargo into the reservoir, a discharge that took thirty minutes.

From the reservoir, the water would go to the town's schools, businesses, and churches, and though it was safe enough to drink in Hattiesburg, it was still greatly feared in Bowmore. The pipes that carried it along were, for the most part, the same pipes that had supplied the old water.

Throughout the day, a constant stream of traffic arrived at the reservoir. The people pulled out all manner of plastic jugs and metal cans and small drums, filled them, then took them home.

Those who could afford to contracted with private suppliers. Water was a daily challenge in Bowmore.

It was still dark as Buck waited for his tank to empty. He sat in the cab with the heater on, door locked, pistol close by. There were two families in Pine Grove that he thought about each morning as he waited. Tough families, with men who'd served time. Big families with uncles and cousins. Each had lost a kid to leukemia. Each was now suing.

And Buck was a well-known liar.

———

Eight days before Christmas, the combatants gathered for the last time in Judge Harrison's courtroom. The hearing was to wrap up all loose ends, and especially to argue the post-trial motions.

Jared Kurtin looked fit and tanned after two weeks of golf in Mexico. He greeted Wes warmly and even managed to smile at Mary Grace. She ignored him by talking to Jeannette, who still looked gaunt and worried but at least wasn't crying.

Kurtin's pack of subordinates shuffled papers at hundreds of dollars an hour each, while Frank Sully, the local counsel, watched them smugly. It was all for show. Harrison wasn't about to grant any relief to Krane Chemical, and everybody knew it.

Others were watching. Huffy held his usual spot, curious as always, still worried about the loan and his future. There were several reporters, and even a courtroom artist, the same one who'd covered the trial and sketched faces that no one could recognize. Several plaintiffs' lawyers were there to observe and to monitor the progress of the case. They were dreaming of a massive settlement that would allow them to become rich while avoiding the type of brutal trial the Paytons had just endured.

Judge Harrison called things to order and charged ahead. "So nice to see everyone again," he said drily. "There are a total of fourteen motions that have been filed— twelve by the defense, two by the plaintiff— and we are going to dispose of all of them before noon." He glared at Jared Kurtin, as if daring him to utter one superfluous word.

He continued: "I've read all the motions and all the briefs, so please don't tell me anything that you've already put in writing. Mr. Kurtin, you may proceed."

The first motion was for a new trial. Kurtin quickly went through all the reasons his client got screwed, beginning with a couple of jurors he wanted to bounce, but Harrison refused. Kurtin's team had conjured up a total of twenty-two errors they deemed grave enough to complain about, but Harrison felt otherwise. After listening to the lawyers argue for an hour, the judge ruled against the motion for a new trial.

Jared Kurtin would have been shocked at any other ruling. These were routine matters now, the battle had been lost, but not the war.

The other motions followed. After a few minutes of uninspired argument on each one, Judge Harrison said, "Overruled."

When the lawyers finished talking, and as papers were being gathered and briefcases were being closed, Jared Kurtin addressed the court and said, "Your Honor, it's been a pleasure. I'm sure we'll do the whole thing over in about three years."

"Court's adjourned," His Honor said rudely, then rapped his gavel loudly.

Two days after Christmas, late on a raw, windy afternoon, Jeannette Baker walked from her trailer through Pine Grove to the church and to the cemetery behind it. She kissed the small headstone at Chad's grave, then sat down and leaned against her husband Pete's. This was the day he died, five years earlier.

In five years she had learned to dwell on the good memories, though she couldn't get rid of the bad ones. Pete, a big man, down to 120 pounds, unable to eat, finally unable to force water through the tumors in his throat and esophagus. Pete, thirty years old and as gaunt and pale as a dying man twice that age. Pete, the tough guy, crying at the unrelenting pain and begging her for more morphine. Pete, the big talker and spinner of big tales, unable to emit anything but a pitiful groan. Pete, begging her to help him end it all.

Chad's final days had been relatively calm. Pete's had been horrific. She had seen so much.

Enough of the bad memories. She was there to talk about their life together, their

romance, their first apartment in Hattiesburg, the birth of Chad, the plans for more
children and a larger house, and all the
dreams they once laughed about. Little
Chad with a fishing pole and an impressive
string of bream from her uncle's pond. Little
Chad in his first T-ball uniform with Coach
Pete by his side. Christmas and Thanksgiv-
ing, a vacation at Disney World when they
were both sick and dying.

She stayed until after dark, as she always
did.

Denny Ott watched her from the kitchen
window of the parsonage. The little cemetery he maintained so carefully was getting
more than its share of traffic these days.

CHAPTER 10

The New Year began with another funeral. Miss Inez Perdue died after a lengthy and painful deterioration of her kidneys. She was sixty-one years old, a widow, with two adult children who'd luckily left Bowmore as soon as they were old enough. Uninsured, she died in her small home on the outskirts of town, surrounded by friends and her pastor, Denny Ott. After he left her, Pastor Ott went to the cemetery behind the Pine Grove Church and, with the help of another deacon, began digging her grave, number seventeen.

As soon as the crowd thinned, the body

of Miss Inez was loaded into an ambulance and taken directly to the morgue at the Forrest County Medical Center in Hattiesburg. There, a doctor hired by the Payton law firm spent three hours removing tissue and blood and conducting an autopsy. Miss Inez had agreed to this somber procedure when she signed a contract with the Paytons a year earlier. A probe of her organs and an examination of her tissue might produce evidence that one day would be crucial in court.

Eight hours after her death, she was back in Bowmore, in a cheap casket tucked away for the night in the sanctuary of the Pine Grove Church.

Pastor Ott had long since convinced his flock that once the body is dead and the spirit ascends into heaven, the earthly rituals are silly and of little significance. Funerals, wakes, embalming, flowers, expensive caskets—all were a waste of time and money. Ashes to ashes, dust to dust. God sent us into the world naked and that's how we should leave.

The following day he conducted Miss Inez's service before a full house that included Wes and Mary Grace, as well as a couple of other lawyers looking on with curiosity. During these services, and he was certainly becoming accomplished, Pastor Ott strove to make the occasion uplifting, at times even humorous. Miss Inez was the backup piano player for the church, and though she played with heavy hands and great enthusiasm, she usually missed about half the notes. And since she was practically deaf, she had no idea how bad she sounded. Recollections of her performances lightened the mood.

It would be easy to bash Krane Chemical and its multitude of sins, but Pastor Ott never mentioned the company. She was dead and nothing could change that. Everybody knew who killed her.

After a one-hour service, the pallbearers lifted her wooden casket onto Mr. Earl Mangram's authentic buckboard, the only one left in the county. Mr. Mangram had been an early victim of Krane, burial number three in Denny Ott's career, and he specifically requested that his casket be hauled away from the church and to the cemetery on his grandfather's buckboard with his ancient mare, Blaze, under tack. The short procession had been such a hit that it became an instant tradition at Pine Grove.

When Miss Inez's casket was placed on the carriage, Pastor Ott, standing next to Blaze, pulled her bridle and the old quarter horse began lumbering along, leading the little parade away from the front of the church, down the side road, and back to the cemetery.

———

Holding fast to the southern tradition, her farewell was followed by a potluck get-together in the fellowship hall. For a people so accustomed to dying, the post-burial meal allowed the mourners to lean on one another and share their tears. Pastor Ott made the rounds, chatting with everyone, praying with some.

The great question at these dark moments was, who was next? In many ways, they felt like prisoners. Isolated, suffering, not sure which one would be chosen by the executioner. Rory Walker was a fourteen-year-old who was losing ground fast in his decadelong battle with leukemia. He was probably next. He was at school and missed the Perdue service, but his mother and grandmother were there.

The Paytons huddled in a corner with Jeannette Baker and talked about everything but the case. Over paper plates sparsely covered with a broccoli-and-cheese casserole, they learned that she was now working as a night clerk in a convenience store and had her eye on a nicer trailer. She and Bette were fighting. Bette had a new boyfriend who slept over often and seemed much too interested in Jeannette's legal situation.

Jeannette looked stronger and her mind was sharper. She had gained a few pounds and said she was no longer taking all those antidepressants. People were treating her differently. She explained in a very low voice as she watched the others: "For a while these people were really proud. We struck back. We won. Finally, somebody on the outside had listened to us, all these poor little people in this poor little town. Everybody circled around me and said sweet things. They cooked for me, cleaned the trailer, somebody was always stopping by. Anything for poor little Jeannette. But as the days went by, I started hearing the money talk. How long will the appeal take? When will the money come in? What was I planning to do with it? And on and on. Bette's younger brother stayed over one night, drank too much, and tried to borrow a thousand dollars. We got into a fight and he said everybody in town knew that I'd already received some of the money. I was shocked. People were talking. All kinds of rumors. Twenty million this and twenty million that. How much will I give away? What kind of new car am I going to get? Where will I build my big new house? They watch everything I buy now, which isn't much. And the men—every tomcat in four counties is calling, wanting to stop by and say hello or take me to the movies. I know for a fact that two of them are not even divorced yet. Bette knows their cousins. I couldn't care less about men."

Wes glanced away.

"Are you talking to Denny?" Mary Grace asked.

"Some. And he's wonderful. He tells me to keep praying for those who gossip about me. I pray for them all right. I really do. But I get the feeling that they're praying harder for me and the money." She looked around suspiciously.

Dessert was banana pudding. It was also an excuse to drift away from Jeannette. The Paytons had several other clients present, and each needed to be given some attention. When Pastor Ott and his wife began clearing the tables, the mourners finally headed for the door.

Wes and Mary Grace met with Denny in his study next to the sanctuary. It was time for the post-burial legal update. Who had fallen ill? What were the new diagnoses? Who in Pine Grove had hired another law firm?

"This Clyde Hardin thing is out of control," Denny said. "They're advertising on the radio and once a week in the paper, full page. They're almost guaranteeing money. People are flocking in."

———

Wes and Mary Grace had walked down Main Street prior to the service for Miss Inez. They wanted to see firsthand the new screening clinic next to F. Clyde's office. On the sidewalk, there were two large coolers filled with bottled water and packed with ice. A teenager with a Bintz & Bintz T-shirt handed them a bottle each. The label read: "Pure Spring Water. Compliments of Bintz & Bintz, Attorneys." There was a toll-free number.

"Where does the water come from?" Wes had asked the kid.

"Not from Bowmore," came the quick retort.

As Mary Grace chatted up the boy, Wes stepped inside, where he joined three other potential clients who were waiting to get themselves screened. None gave any indication of being ill. Wes was greeted by a comely young lady of no more than eighteen, who handed him a brochure, a form on a clipboard, and a pen and instructed him to fill out both front and back. The brochure was professionally done and gave the basics of the allegations against Krane Chemical, a company now "proven in court" to have contaminated the drinking water of Bowmore and Cary County. All inquiries were directed to the firm of Bintz & Bintz in Philadelphia, Pennsylvania. The questions on the form were all background and medical, except for the last two: (1) Who referred you to this office? and (2) Do you know anyone else who might be a potential victim of Krane Chemical? If so, list names and phone numbers. As Wes was scribbling on the form, the doctor entered the waiting room from somewhere in the rear and called for the next patient. He wore a white physician's office jacket, complete with a stethoscope around his neck. He was either Indian or Pakistani and looked no older than thirty.

After a few minutes inside, Wes excused himself and left.

———

"It's small-time stuff," Wes said to Denny. "They'll sign up a few hundred cases, most of them frivolous. Then they'll file a class action in federal court. If they're lucky, it'll be settled years from now for a few thousand bucks each. The lawyers will skim off some nice fees. But there's a better chance that Krane will never settle, and if that happens, then all those new clients get nothing and Clyde Hardin will be forced to go back to drafting deeds."

"How many from your church have signed up?" Mary Grace asked.

"I don't know. They don't tell me everything."

"We're not worried about it," Wes said. "Frankly, we have enough of these cases to keep us busy for a long time."

"Did I see a couple of spies at the service today?" Mary Grace asked.

"Yes. One was a lawyer named Crandell, from Jackson. He's been hanging around since the trial. He's actually stopped by here to say hello. Just a hustler."

"I've heard of him," Wes said. "Has he hooked any cases?"

"Not from this church."

They discussed the lawyers for a while, then had their usual conversation about Jeannette and the new pressures she was facing. Ott was spending time with her and was confident she was listening to him.

After an hour they wrapped up their meeting. The Paytons drove back to Hattiesburg, another client in the ground, another injury case now converted into a wrongful-death suit.

———

The preliminary paperwork arrived at the Mississippi Supreme Court in the first week of January. The trial transcript, 16,200 pages, was finalized by the court reporters, and copies were sent to the clerk of the court and to the lawyers. An order was entered giving Krane Chemical, the appellant, ninety days to file its brief. Sixty days after that, the Paytons would file their rebuttal.

In Atlanta, Jared Kurtin passed the file to the firm's appellate unit, the "eggheads," as they were known, brilliant legal scholars who functioned poorly in normal circles and were best kept in the library. Two partners, four associates, and four paralegals were already hard at work on the appeal when the massive transcript arrived and they had their first look at every word that was recorded at trial. They would dissect it and find dozens of reasons for a reversal.

In a lesser section of Hattiesburg, the transcript was plopped on the plywood table in The Pit. Mary Grace and Sherman gawked at it in disbelief, almost afraid to touch it. Mary Grace had once tried a case that went on for ten full days. Its transcript had been twelve hundred pages long, and she read it so many times that the sight of it made her ill. Now this.

If they had an advantage, it was because

they had been in the courtroom throughout the entire trial and knew most of what was in the transcript. Indeed, Mary Grace appeared on more pages than any other participant.

But it would be read many times, and procrastination was not an option. The trial and its verdict would be cleverly and savagely attacked by Krane's lawyers. Jeannette Baker's lawyers had to match them argument for argument, word for word.

In the heady days after the verdict, the plan had been for Mary Grace to concentrate on the Bowmore cases while Wes worked the other files to generate income. The publicity had been priceless; the phones rang incessantly. Every nutcase in the Southeast suddenly needed the Paytons. Lawyers mired in hopeless lawsuits called for help. Family members who'd lost loved ones to cancer saw the verdict as a hopeful sign. And the usual assortment of criminal defendants, divorcing spouses, battered women, bankrupt businesses, slip-and-fall hustlers, and fired employees called or even stopped by in pursuit of these famous lawyers. Very few could pay a decent fee.

Legitimate personal injury cases, however, had proven scarce. The "Big One," the perfect case with clear liability and a defendant with deep pockets, the case upon which retirement dreams often rest, had not yet found its way to the Payton law firm. There were a few more car wrecks and workers' compensation cases, but nothing worth a trial.

Wes worked feverishly to close as many files as possible, and with some success. The rent was now current, at least at the office. All past-due wages had been paid. Huffy and the bank were still on edge but afraid to push harder. No payments had been made, either on principal or on interest.

CHAPTER 11

They settled on a man named Ron Fisk, a lawyer unknown outside of his small town of Brookhaven, Mississippi, an hour south of Jackson, two hours west of Hattiesburg, and fifty miles north of the Louisiana state line. He was selected from a pool of similar résumés, though none of those considered had the slightest hint that their names and backgrounds were being so carefully evaluated. Young white male, one marriage, three children, reasonably handsome, reasonably well dressed, conservative, devout Baptist, Ole Miss law school, no ethical glitches in the law career, not a hint of criminal trouble beyond a speeding ticket, no affiliation with any trial lawyer group, no controversial cases, no experience whatsoever on the bench.

There was no reason anyone outside of Brookhaven would ever have heard the name of Ron Fisk, and that was exactly what made him their ideal candidate. They picked Fisk because he was just old enough to cross their low threshold of legal experience, but still young enough to have ambitions.

He was thirty-nine years old, a junior partner in a five-man firm that specialized in defending lawsuits involving car wrecks, arson, injured workers, and a myriad of other routine liability claims. The firm's clients were insurance companies who paid by the hour, thus allowing the five partners to earn comfortable but not lucrative salaries. As a junior partner, Fisk made $92,000 the year before. A far cry from Wall Street but not bad money in small-town Mississippi.

A supreme court justice was currently earning $110,000.

Fisk's wife, Doreen, earned $41,000 as the assistant director of a privately owned mental health clinic. Everything was mortgaged—home, both cars, even some furniture. But the Fisks had a perfect credit rating. They vacationed once a year with their children in Florida, where they rented a condo in a high-rise for a thousand bucks a week. There were no trust funds and nothing significant to be expected from their parents' estates.

The Fisks were squeaky-clean. There was nothing to dig up in the heat of a nasty campaign. Absolutely nothing, they were certain of that.

———

Tony Zachary entered the building at five minutes before 2:00 p.m. and stated his business. "I have an appointment with Mr. Fisk," he said politely, and a secretary disappeared. As he waited, he examined the place. Sagging bookshelves laden with dusty tomes. Worn carpet. The musty smell of a fine old building in need of some work. A door opened, and a handsome young man stuck out a hand. "Mr. Zachary, Ron Fisk," he said warmly, as he probably did to all new clients.

"A pleasure."

"This is my office," Fisk said, sweeping

his hand at the door. They walked through it, closed it, then settled around a large busy desk. Zachary declined coffee, water, a soda. "I'm fine, thanks," he said.

Fisk had his sleeves rolled up and his tie loosened, as if he'd been performing manual labor. Zachary liked the image immediately. Nice teeth, just a touch of gray above the ears, strong chin. This guy was definitely marketable.

They played Who-do-you-know? for a few minutes, with Zachary claiming to be a longtime resident of Jackson, where he'd spent most of his career in government relations, whatever that meant. Since he knew that Fisk had no history of political involvement, he had little fear of being exposed. In truth, he'd lived in Jackson less than three years and until very recently had worked as a lobbyist for an association of asphalt contractors. There was a state senator from Brookhaven they both knew, and they chatted about him for a few minutes, anything to pass the time.

When things were comfortable, Zachary said, "Let me apologize, I'm really not a new client. I'm here on some much more important business."

Fisk frowned and nodded. Keep talking, sir.

"Have you ever heard of a group called Judicial Vision?"

"No."

Few people had. In the murky world of lobbying and consulting, Judicial Vision was a newcomer.

Zachary moved on. "I'm the executive director for the state of Mississippi. It's a national group. Our sole purpose is to elect quality people to the appellate courts. By quality, I mean conservative, business oriented, temperate, highly moral, intelligent, and ambitious young judges who can literally, Mr. Fisk, and this is the core of what we believe, change the judicial landscape of this country. And if we can do that, then we can protect the rights of the unborn, restrict the cultural garbage that is consumed by our children, honor the sanctity of marriage, keep homosexuals out of our classrooms, fight off the gun-control advocates, seal our borders, and protect the true American way of life."

Both took a deep breath.

Fisk wasn't sure where he fit into this raging war, but his pulse was definitely up ten beats per minute. "Yes, well, sounds like an interesting group," he said.

"We're committed," Zachary said firmly. "And we're also determined to bring sanity back to our civil litigation system. Runaway verdicts and hungry trial lawyers are robbing us of economic advancement. We're scaring companies away from Mississippi, not attracting them."

"There's no doubt about that," Fisk said, and Zachary wanted to shout for joy.

"You see all the frivolous stuff they file. We work hand in hand with the national tort-reform groups."

"That's good. And why are you in Brookhaven?"

"Are you politically ambitious, Mr. Fisk? Ever thought about tossing your hat in the ring for elective office?"

"Not really."

"Well, we've done our research, and we think you'd be an excellent candidate for the supreme court."

Fisk instinctively laughed at such foolishness, but it was the sort of nervous laugh that leads you to believe that whatever is supposed to be humorous is really not. It's serious. It can be pursued.

"Research?" he said.

"Oh yes. We spend a lot of time looking for candidates who (*a*) we like and (*b*) can win. We study the opponents, the races, the demographics, the politics, everything, really. Our data bank is unmatched, as is our ability to generate serious funds. Care to hear more?"

Fisk kicked back in his reclining rocker, put his feet on his desk and his hands behind his head, and said, "Sure. Tell me why you're here."

"I'm here to recruit you to run against Justice Sheila McCarthy this November in the southern district of Mississippi," he announced confidently. "She is very beatable. We don't like her or her record. We have analyzed every decision she's made in her nine years on the bench, and we think she's a raging liberal who manages to hide her true colors, most of the time. Do you know her?"

Fisk was almost afraid to say yes. "We met once, just in passing. I don't really know her."

Actually, according to their research, Justice McCarthy had participated in three rulings in cases involving Ron Fisk's law firm, and each time she had ruled the other way. Fisk had argued one of the cases, a hotly disputed arson mess involving a warehouse. His client lost on a 5-to-4 vote. It was quite likely that he had little use for Mississippi's only female justice.

"She is very vulnerable," Zachary said.

"What makes you think I can beat her?"

"Because you are a clean-cut conservative who believes in family values. Because of our expertise in running blitzkrieg campaigns. Because we have the money."

"We do?"

"Oh yes. Unlimited. We partner with some powerful people, Mr. Fisk."

"Please call me Ron."

It'll be Ronny Boy before you know it. "Yes, Ron, we coordinate the fund-raising with groups that represent banks, insurance companies, energy companies, big business, I'm talking serious cash here, Ron. Then we expand the umbrella to include the groups that are dearest to us—the conservative Christian folks, who, by the way, can produce huge sums of money in the heat of a campaign. Plus, they turn out the vote."

"You make it sound easy."

"It's never easy, Ron, but we seldom lose.

We've honed our skills in a dozen or so races around the country, and we're making a habit of pulling off victories that surprise a lot of people."

"I've never sat on the bench."

"We know that, and that's why we like you. Sitting judges make tough decisions. Tough decisions are sometimes controversial. They leave trails, records that opponents can use against them. The best candidates, we have learned, are bright young guys like yourself who don't carry the baggage of prior decisions."

Inexperience had never sounded so good.

There was a long pause as Fisk tried to gather his thoughts. Zachary stood and walked to the Wall of Respect, this one covered in diplomas, Rotary Club citations, golfing photos, and lots of candid shots of the family. Lovely wife Doreen. Ten-year-old Josh in a baseball uniform. Seven-year-old Zeke with a fish almost as big as himself. Five-year-old Clarissa dressed for soccer. "Beautiful family," Zachary said, as if he knew nothing about them.

"Thanks," Fisk said, truly beaming.

"Gorgeous kids."

"Good genes from their mother."

"First wife?" Zachary asked, offhanded and innocent.

"Oh yes. Met her in college."

Zachary knew that, and much more. He returned to his seat and resumed his position.

"I haven't checked recently," Fisk said, somewhat awkwardly, "but what does the job pay now?"

"One ten," Tony said and suppressed a smile. He was making more progress than he realized.

Fisk grimaced slightly as if he couldn't afford such a drastic cut in pay. His mind was racing, though, dizzy with the possibilities. "So you're recruiting candidates for the supreme court," he said, almost in a daze.

"Not for every seat. We have some good judges here, and we'll support them if they draw opponents. But McCarthy has got to go. She is a feminist who's soft on crime. We're going to take her out. I hope it's with you."

"And if I say no?"

"Then we'll go to the next name on our list. You're number one."

Fisk shook his head, bewildered. "I don't

know," he said. "It would be hard to leave my firm."

But at least he was thinking about leaving the firm. The bait was in the water, and the fish was watching it. Zachary nodded in agreement. Completely sympathetic. The firm was a collection of worn-out paper pushers who spent their time deposing drunk drivers and settling fender benders the day before trial. For fourteen years, Fisk had been doing the same thing over and over. Each file was the same.

———

They took a booth in a pastry shop and ordered ice cream sundaes. "What is a blitzkrieg campaign?" Fisk asked. They were alone. All other booths were empty.

"It's basically an ambush," Zachary replied, warming up to his favorite subject. "Right now Judge McCarthy has no idea she has an opponent. She's thinking, hoping, actually confident, that no one will challenge her. She has six thousand bucks in her campaign account, and she won't raise another dime if she doesn't have to. Let's say you decide to run. The qualifying deadline is four months away, and we'll wait until the last minute to announce your candidacy. However, we get busy right now. We put your team together. We get the money in the bank. We print all the yard signs, bumper stickers, brochures, direct mail materials. We cut your television ads, hire the consultants, pollsters, and the like. When you announce, we flood the district with direct mail. The first wave is the friendly stuff—you, your family, your minister, Rotary Club, Boy Scouts. The second wave is a hard but honest look at her record. You start campaigning like a madman. Ten speeches a day, every day, all over the district. We'll buzz you around in private planes. She won't know where to begin. She will be overwhelmed from the first day. On June 30, you'll report a million bucks in your campaign fund. She won't have ten thousand. The trial lawyers will scramble and raise some money for her, but it'll be a drop in the bucket. After Labor Day, we start hitting hard with television ads. She's soft on crime. Soft on gays. Soft on guns. Against the death penalty. She'll never recover."

The sundaes arrived and they began eating. "How much will this cost?" Fisk asked.

"Three million bucks."

"Three million bucks! For a supreme court race?"

"Only if you want to win."

"And you can raise that much money?"

"Judicial Vision already has the commitments. And if we need more, we'll get more."

Ron took a mouthful of ice cream and, for the first time, asked himself why an organization was willing to spend a fortune to unseat a supreme court justice who had little impact on the social issues of the day. The Mississippi courts rarely were drawn into cases involving abortion, gay rights, guns, immigration. They dealt with the death penalty all the time, but were never expected to abolish it. The weightier matters were always in federal court.

Perhaps the social issues were important, but something else was at work here. "This is about liability, isn't it?" Fisk asked.

"It's a package, Ron, with several elements. But, yes, limiting liability is a huge priority of our organization and its affiliated groups. We're going to find a horse for this race—hope it's you, but if not, then we'll go to the next guy—and when we find our man, we will expect a firm commitment to limit liability in civil litigation. The trial lawyers must be stopped."

———

Doreen brewed decaf coffee late that night. The kids were asleep, but the adults definitely were not. Nor would they be anytime soon. Ron had called her from the office after Mr. Zachary left, and since then they had thought of nothing but the supreme court.

Issue number one: They had three young children. Jackson, home of the supreme court, was an hour away, and the family was not leaving Brookhaven. Ron thought he would need to spend only two nights a week in Jackson, at most. He could commute; it was an easy drive. And he could work from home. Secretly, to him, the idea of getting away from Brookhaven for a couple of nights each week was not altogether unappealing. Secretly, to her, the idea of having the house to herself occasionally was refreshing.

Issue number two: The campaign. How could he play politics for the rest of the year while continuing to practice law? His firm would be supportive, he thought, but it would not be easy. But then, nothing worth-while is without sacrifice.

Issue number three: Money, though this was not a significant concern. The increase in pay was obvious. His net from the law firm's profits rose slightly each year, but no big bonuses were likely. Judicial salaries in Mississippi were increased periodically by the legislature. Plus, the state had a better retirement plan and health coverage.

Issue number four: His career. After four-teen years of doing the same thing, with no break in sight, he found the idea of a sud-den career change exhilarating. The mere thought of leaving the ranks of thousands to become only one of nine was thrilling. Jumping from the county courthouse to the pinnacle of the state's legal system in one boisterous somersault was so exciting that it made him laugh. Doreen was not laugh-ing, though she was very amused and en-gaged.

Issue number five: Failure. What if he lost? In a landslide? Would they be humili-ated? This was a humbling thought, but he kept repeating what Tony Zachary had said. "Three million bucks will win the race, and we'll get the money."

Which brought up the rather large issue of who exactly was Tony Zachary, and could they believe him? Ron had spent an hour online tracking down Judicial Vision and Mr. Zachary. Everything looked legitimate. He called a friend from law school, a career man with the attorney general's office in Jackson, and, without revealing his motives, nibbled around the edges of Judicial Vision. The friend had heard of them, he thought, but didn't know much about them. And besides, he dealt with offshore oil rights and stayed away from politics.

Ron had called the Judicial Vision office in Jackson and was routed through a maze back to Mr. Zachary's secretary, who informed him that her boss was traveling in south Mississippi. After she hung up, she called Tony and reported the contact.

———

The Fisks met Tony for lunch the following day at the Dixie Springs Café, a small restaurant near a lake ten miles south of Brookhaven, far away from potential eavesdroppers in the town's restaurants.

For the occasion, Zachary adopted a slightly different posture. Today he was the

man with other options. Here's the deal—
take it or leave it because my list is long and
I have other young white Protestant male
lawyers to talk to. He was gentle and perfectly charming, especially to Doreen, who
began the lunch with suspicion but was
soon won over.

At some point during the sleepless night,
both Mr. and Mrs. Fisk had independently
arrived at the same conclusion. Life would
be much fuller, much richer in their little
town if Lawyer Fisk became Justice Fisk.
Their status would be elevated magnifi-
cently. No one could touch them, and while
they didn't seek power or notoriety, the al-
lure was irresistible.

"What's your principal concern?" Tony
asked after fifteen minutes of worthless
chatter.

"Well, it's January," Ron began. "And for
the next eleven months I will do little else
but plan and execute the campaign. Natu-
rally, I'm worried about my law practice."

"Here's one solution," Tony said without
hesitation. He had solutions for everything.
"Judicial Vision is a well-coordinated and
concerted effort. We have lots of friends
and supporters. We can arrange for some

legal work to be shifted to your firm. Timber, energy, natural gas, big clients with interests in this part of the state. Your firm might want to add a lawyer or two to handle things while you're busy elsewhere, but that should ease the strain. If you choose to run, you will not suffer financially. Quite the opposite."

The Fisks couldn't help but look at each other. Tony buttered a saltine and took a large bite.

"Legitimate clients?" Doreen asked, then wished she'd kept her mouth shut.

Tony frowned as he chewed, then when he could speak he said, rather sternly, "Everything we do, Doreen, is legitimate. We are completely ethical to begin with— our ultimate mission is to clean up the court, not trash it. And everything we do will be scrutinized. This race will become heated and attract a lot of attention. We do not stumble."

Chastised, she lifted her knife and went for a roll.

Tony continued: "No one can question legitimate legal work and fair fees paid by clients, whether big or small."

"Of course," Ron said. He was already

thinking about the wonderful conversation with his partners as they anticipated this infusion of new business.

"I can't see myself as a political wife," Doreen said. "You know, out on the campaign trail giving speeches. I've never even thought about it."

Tony smiled and exuded charm. He even offered a quick laugh. "You can do as much or as little as you like. With three young children, I would guess that you'll be pretty busy on the home front."

Over catfish and hush puppies, they agreed to meet again in a few days when Tony was passing through. They would have another lunch, and a final decision would be made. November was far away, but there was so much work to do.

CHAPTER 12

She once laughed at herself when she went through the dreaded ritual of crawling onto her stationary bike at dawn and pedaling away, going nowhere as the sun crept up and lightened her little gym. For a woman whose public veneer was a somber face behind an intimidating black robe, she was amused at what people would think if they could see her on the bike, in old sweats, hair a mess, eyes swollen, face unadorned with cosmetics. But that was a long time ago. Now she just went through the routine with little thought of how she looked or what anyone might think. Of particular concern now was the fact that she had gained five pounds over the holidays, eleven since her divorce. The gaining had to be stopped before the losing could commence. At fifty-one, the pounds were clinging now, refusing to burn away as quickly as when she was younger.

Sheila McCarthy was not a morning person. She hated mornings, hated getting out of bed before her sleep was finished, hated the cheery voices on television, hated the traffic on the way to the office. She didn't eat breakfast, because she hated breakfast food. She hated coffee. She had always secretly loathed those who reveled in their early morning exploits—the joggers, yoga nuts, workaholics, hyperactive soccer moms. As a young circuit court judge in Biloxi, she had often scheduled trials for 10:00 a.m., a scandalous hour. But it was her court and she made the rules.

Now she was one of nine, and the tribunal on which she served clung desperately to its traditions. On certain days she could roll in at noon and work until midnight, her preferred schedule, but most of the time she was expected by 9:00 a.m.

She was sweating after one mile. Eighty-four calories burned. Less than a cup of Häagen-Dazs chocolate chip mint, her most serious temptation. A television hung from a rack above the bike, and she watched and listened as the locals gushed over the latest car wrecks and murders. Then the weatherman was back for the third time in twelve minutes, clucking on about snow in the Rockies because there wasn't a single cloud at home to analyze.

After two miles, and down 161 calories, Sheila stopped for water and a towel, then crawled onto the treadmill for more work. She switched to CNN for a quick review of the national gossip. When she had burned 250 calories, Sheila quit and went to the shower. An hour later, she left her two-story condo on the reservoir, got into her bright red BMW convertible sports car, and headed to work.

———

The Mississippi Supreme Court is divided into three neat districts—northern, central, and southern—with three justices elected from each. A term is eight years, with no limit. Judicial elections take place in the off years, those quiet ones in which there are no races for local, legislative, or other state-wide positions. Once obtained, a seat on the court lasts for a long time, usually until death or voluntary retirement.

The elections are nonpartisan, with all candidates running as independents. Campaign finance laws limit contributions from individuals at $5,000 each, and $2,500 from organizations, including political action committees and corporations.

Sheila McCarthy was appointed to the bench nine years earlier by a friendly governor, following the death of her predecessor. She ran unopposed once and was certainly planning on another easy victory. There was not the faintest whiff of a rumor that someone out there had designs on her seat.

With nine years' experience, she out-ranked only three others, and was still considered by most members of the state bar to be a relative newcomer. Tracking her written opinions and her voting record baffled liberals and conservatives alike. She was a moderate, a consensus builder, neither a strict constructionist nor a judicial activist, but more or less a practical fence straddler who, some said, decided the best outcome first, then found enough law to support it.

As such, she was an influential member of the court. She could broker a deal between the hard right-wingers, of which there were always automatically four in number, and the liberals, of which there were two on most days and none on others. Four on the right and two on the left meant Sheila had two comrades in the center, though this simplistic analysis had burned many a lawyer trying to predict an outcome. Most cases on the docket defied categorization. Where's the liberal or conservative side in a big messy divorce, or a boundary line dispute between two timber companies? Many cases were decided 9–0.

The supreme court does its work in the Carroll Gartin Justice Building in downtown Jackson, across the street from the state capitol. Sheila parked in her reserved space underneath the building. She rode the elevator to the fourth floor alone and stepped into her suite at exactly 8:45. Paul, her chief clerk, a strikingly handsome twenty-eight-year-old single straight male of whom she was extremely fond, walked into her office seconds after she did.

"Good morning," Paul said. He had long dark curly hair and a small diamond in his ear, and he somehow managed to maintain a perfect growth of three days' worth of stubble. Hazel eyes. She often expected to see Paul modeling Armani suits in the fashion magazines stacked around her condo. Paul had more to do with her gym time than she cared to admit.

"Good morning," she said coolly, as if she had barely noticed him.

"You have the *Sturdivant* hearing at nine."

"I know that," she said, glancing at his rear end as he walked across her office. Faded jeans. The ass of a model.

He walked out, her eyes following every step.

Her secretary took his place. She locked the door and pulled out a small makeup kit, and when Justice McCarthy was ready, the touch-up was done quickly. The hair— short, almost above the ear, half sandy blond and half gray, and now carefully colored twice a month at $400 a pop—was fussed into place, then sprayed.

"What are my chances with Paul?" Sheila asked with her eyes closed.

"A bit young, don't you think?"

The secretary was older than her boss

and had been doing the touch-ups for almost nine years. She kept powdering.

"Of course he's young. That's the point."

"I don't know. I hear he's awfully busy with that redhead in Albritton's office."

Sheila had heard the rumors, too. A gorgeous new clerk from Stanford was getting plenty of attention down the hall, and Paul usually had his pick.

"Have you read the *Sturdivant* briefs?" Sheila asked, standing as she prepared to be robed.

"Yes." The secretary carefully draped the black robe over her shoulders. The zipper ran down the front. Both ladies tugged and fussed until the bulky garment was perfect.

"Who killed the cop?" Sheila asked, gently pulling the zipper.

"It wasn't Sturdivant."

"I agree." She stepped before a full-length mirror, and both ladies inspected the presentation. "Can you tell I've gained weight?" Sheila asked.

"No." Same answer to the same question.

"Well, I have. And that's why I love these things. They can hide twenty pounds."

"You love it for another reason, dear, and we both know it. You're the only girl out there with eight boys, and none of them are as tough or as smart as you."

"And sexy. Don't forget sexy."

The secretary laughed at the idea. "No competition, dear. Those old goats can only dream about sex."

And they went off, out of the office, down the hall, where they met Paul again. He rattled off some key points in the *Sturdivant* case as they rode the elevator to the third floor, where the courtroom was located. One lawyer might argue this, and the other might possibly argue that. Here are some questions to trip both of them.

Three blocks away from where Justice McCarthy assumed her position on the bench, a group of rather intense men and (two) women gathered to discuss her demise. They met in a windowless conference room in a nondescript building, one of many clustered near the state capitol where countless civil servants and lobbyists ground out the work of running Mississippi.

The meeting was hosted by Tony Zachary and Judicial Vision. The guests were the directors of other like-minded "government relations" firms, some with vague names that deflected categorization—Freedom Network, Market Partnership, Commerce Council, Enterprise Advocacy. Other names got right to the point—Citizens Opposed to Lawsuit Tyranny (COLT), Fair Litigation Association, Jury Watch, Tort Reform Committee of Mississippi. And the old guard was there, the associations representing the interests of banks, insurance, oil, medicine, manufacturing, retail, commerce, trade, and the best of our American way of life.

In the murky world of legislative manipulation, where loyalties shift overnight and a friend can become an enemy by noon, the people in the room were known, at least to Tony Zachary, to be worthy of trust.

"Ladies and gentlemen," Tony began, standing with a half-eaten croissant on the plate before him, "the purpose of this meeting is to inform you that we will remove Sheila McCarthy from the supreme court in November and her replacement will be a young justice committed to economic growth and limited liability."

There was light applause around the table. Everyone else was seated, all curious and listening. No one was certain who was behind Judicial Vision. Zachary had been around a few years and had a fair reputation, but he had no personal money. Nor did his group have much of a membership. Nor had he ever shown much interest in the civil justice system. His newfound passion for changing liability laws seemed to spring from nowhere.

But there was no doubt that Zachary and Judicial Vision were well funded. And in their game, that meant everything.

"We have the initial financing on the table, with more committed down the road," he said proudly. "More, of course, will be needed from you. We have a campaign plan, a strategy, and we, Judicial Vision, will be running the show."

More applause. The biggest obstacle was always coordination. There were so many groups, so many issues, so many egos. Raising the money was easy, from their side of the street anyway, but spending it wisely was often the challenge. The fact that Tony had, rather aggressively, assumed control was wonderful news. The rest of them were more than content to write the checks and turn out the voters.

"What about a candidate?" someone asked.

Tony smiled and said, "You'll love him. Can't give you his name right now, but you'll love him. Made for television." Ron Fisk had not yet said yes to the campaign, but Tony knew that he would. And if, for some reason, he did not, there were more names on the list. They would indeed have themselves a candidate, and soon, even if it took sackfuls of cash.

"Shall we talk money?" Tony asked, then plunged headlong into the issue before anyone could respond. "We have a million bucks on the table. I want to spend more than both candidates spent in the last contested race. That was two years ago, and I don't need to remind you that your boy in that race came up short. My boy in this race will not lose. To guarantee this, I need two million from you and your members."

Three million for such a race was a shock. In the last governor's race, a race that covered all eighty-two counties and not just a third of them, the winner spent $7 million and the loser spent half that. And a good governor's race was always a major spectacle, the centerpiece of state politics. Passions were high, turnouts even higher.

A race for a seat on the supreme court, when one did occur, seldom drew more than a third of the registered voters.

"How do you plan to spend $3 million?" someone asked. It was telling that the question was not about raising so much money. It was assumed they had access to pockets deep enough.

"Television, television, television," Tony responded. This was partly true. Tony would never reveal his entire strategy. He and Mr. Rinehart planned to spend a lot more than three million, but many of their expenditures would be either in cash or carefully hidden out of state.

An assistant popped up and began passing around thick folders. "This is what we've done in other states," Tony was saying. "Please take it with you and read it at your leisure."

There were questions about his plan, and more about his candidate. Tony revealed little, but continually emphasized his need for their financial commitments, the sooner the better. The only blip in the meeting came when the director of COLT informed them that his group had been actively recruiting candidates to run against McCarthy and that he himself had a plan to take her out. COLT advertised eight thousand members, though that number was dubious. Most of its activists were ex-litigants who'd been burned in a lawsuit of some variety. The organization had credibility, but it did not have a million dollars. After a brief but tense flare-up, Tony invited the COLT guy to go run his own campaign, at which time he backed down quickly and rejoined ranks.

Before adjourning, Tony urged secrecy, a vital element of the campaign. "If the trial lawyers find out now that we have a horse in the race, they will crank up their fund-raising machine. They beat you the last time."

They were irked by this second reference to "their" loss in the last race, as if they would've won if only they'd had Tony. But everyone let it pass. The mere mention of the trial lawyers immediately refocused their attention.

They were too excited about the race to bicker.

The class action claimed to include "over three hundred" victims injured in various ways by the gross negligence of Krane Chemical at its Bowmore plant. Only twenty were named as plaintiffs, and of these twenty perhaps half had significant afflictions. Whether their ailments were linked to polluted groundwater would be a question for another day.

It was filed in Hattiesburg at the federal courthouse, a good stone's throw from the Forrest County Circuit Court building, where Dr. Leona Rocha and her jury had rendered its verdict barely two months earlier. Lawyers Sterling Bintz of Philadelphia and F. Clyde Hardin of Bowmore were on hand to do the filing, and also to chat with any reporters who'd responded to their prefiling press alert. Sadly, there were no television cameras, only a couple of green print reporters. At least for F. Clyde, though, it was an adventure. He hadn't been near a federal courthouse in over thirty years.

For Mr. Bintz, the pathetic lack of recognition was appalling. He had dreamed of huge headlines and long stories with splendid photographs. He had filed many important class actions and had usually managed to get them adequately covered by the media. What was wrong with the rural Mississippians?

F. Clyde hurried back to Bowmore, to his office, where Miriam was lingering to see how things went. "What channel?" she asked.

"None."

"What?" It was without a doubt the biggest day in the history of the firm of F. Clyde Hardin & Associates, and Miriam couldn't wait to watch it all on television.

"We decided not to deal with those reporters. Can't trust them," F. Clyde explained as he glanced at his watch. It was a quarter after five, past time for Miriam to leave the office. "No need to stick around," he said, flinging his jacket. "I've got things under control here."

She quickly left, disappointed, and F. Clyde went straight for the office bottle. The chilled, thick vodka soothed him immediately, and he began to replay his big day. With a bit of luck, the Hattiesburg paper would include his photo.

Bintz was claiming three hundred clients. At $500 each, F. Clyde was due a nice referral fee. So far he'd been paid only $3,500, most of which he used for back taxes.

He poured a second drink and said what the hell. Bintz wouldn't screw him, because he needed him. He, F. Clyde Hardin, was now an attorney of record in one of the most important class action cases in the country. All roads ran through Bowmore, and F. Clyde was the man.

CHAPTER 13

It was explained to his firm that Mr. Fisk would be in Jackson for the entire day, something to do with personal business. In other words, don't ask. As a partner he had earned the right to come and go as he pleased, though Fisk was so disciplined and organized that anyone in the firm could usually find him within five minutes.

He left Doreen on the front steps at dawn. She was invited to make the trip, but with a job and three kids it simply wasn't possible, not with such short notice. Ron left the house without breakfast, not that time was a factor. Tony Zachary had said, "We'll eat on the plane," and this was enough to entice Ron to skip his bran flakes.

The Brookhaven airstrip was too small for the jet, so Ron happily agreed to rush off to the airport in Jackson. He had never been within a hundred yards of a private jet, and had never given much thought to flying on one. Tony Zachary was waiting at the general aviation terminal with a hearty handshake and a vigorous "Good morning, Your Honor." They walked purposefully across the tarmac, past a few old turboprops and pistons—smaller, inferior vessels. Waiting in the distance was a magnificent carrier, as sleek and exotic as a spaceship. Its navigation lights were flickering. Its handsome stairway was extended down, a splendid invitation to its special passengers. Ron followed Tony up the steps to the landing, where a pretty flight attendant in a short skirt welcomed them aboard, took their jackets, and showed them their selection of seats.

"Ever been on a Gulfstream before?" Tony asked as they settled in. One of the pilots said hello as he pushed a button to retract the stairway.

"No," Ron said, gawking at the polished

mahogany and soft leather and gold trimmings.

"This is a G5, the Mercedes of private
jets. This one could take us to Paris, nonstop."

Then let's go to Paris instead of Washington, Ron thought as he leaned into the aisle
to absorb the length and size of the airplane. A quick count revealed seating for at
least a dozen pampered folks. "It's beautiful," he said. He wanted to ask who owned
it. Who was paying for the trip? Who was
behind this gold-plated recruitment? But to
inquire would be rude, he told himself. Just
relax, enjoy the trip, enjoy the day, and remember all the details because Doreen will
want to hear them.

The flight attendant was back. She explained emergency procedures, then asked
what they might like for breakfast. Tony
wanted scrambled eggs, bacon, and hash
browns. Ron ordered the same.

"Bathroom and kitchen are in the back,"
Tony said, as if he traveled by G5 every day.
"The sofa pulls out if you need a nap." Cof-
fee arrived as they began to taxi. The flight
attendant offered a variety of newspapers.
Tony grabbed one, yanked it open, waited a

few seconds, then asked, "You keeping up with that Bowmore litigation?"

Ron pretended to look at a newspaper as he continued to soak in the luxury of the jet. "Somewhat," he said.

"They filed a class action yesterday," Tony said in disgust. "One of those national tort firms out of Philadelphia. I guess the vultures have arrived." It was his first comment to Ron on the subject, but it definitely would not be his last.

The G5 took off. It was one of three owned by various entities controlled by the Trudeau Group, and leased through a separate charter company that made it impossible to track the true owner. Ron watched the city of Jackson disappear below him. Minutes later, when they leveled off at forty-one thousand feet, he could smell the rich aroma of bacon in the skillet.

———

At Dulles general aviation, they were whisked into the rear of a long black limo, and forty minutes later they were in the District, on K Street. Tony explained en route that they had a 10:00 a.m. meeting with one group of potential backers, then a quiet lunch, then a 2:00 p.m. meeting with another group. Ron would be home in time for dinner. He was almost dizzy from the excitement of such luxurious travel and feeling so important.

On the seventh floor of a new building, they stepped into the rather plain lobby of the American Family Alliance and spoke to an even plainer receptionist. Tony's summary on the jet had been: "This group is perhaps the most powerful of all the conservative Christian advocates. Lots of members, lots of cash, lots of clout. The Washington politicians love them and fear them. Run by a man named Walter Utley, a former congressman who got fed up with all the liberals in Congress and left to form his own group."

Fisk had heard of Walter Utley and his American Family Alliance.

They were escorted into a large conference room where Mr. Utley himself was waiting with a warm smile and handshake and several introductions to other men, all of whom had been included in Tony's briefing on the jet. They represented such groups as Prayer Partnership, Global Light, Family Roundtable, Evangelical Initiative, and a few others. All significant players in national politics, according to Tony.

They settled around the table, behind notepads and briefing papers, as if they were about to place Mr. Fisk under oath and take his deposition. Tony led off with a summary of the Supreme Court of Mississippi and kept his comments generally positive. Most of the judges were good men with solid voting records. But, of course, there was the matter of Justice Sheila McCarthy and her closet liberalism. She couldn't be trusted on the issues. She was divorced. She was rumored to have loose morals, but Tony stopped without going into specifics.

To challenge her, they needed Ron here to step forward and answer the bell. Tony ran through a quick biography of their man and, in doing so, did not offer a single fact that was not already known by those present. He handed off to Ron, who cleared his throat and thanked them for the invitation. He began talking about his life, education, upbringing, parents, wife, and kids. He was a devout Christian, a deacon in St. Luke's Baptist Church, a Sunday school teacher. Rotary Club, Ducks Unlimited, youth league baseball coach. He stretched his résumé as far as he could, then shrugged as if to say, "There's nothing else."

He and his wife had been praying about this decision. They had even met with their pastor for yet more prayer, hopefully at a higher level. They were comfortable. They were ready.

Everyone was still warm, friendly, delighted he was there. They asked about his background—was there anything back there that could haunt him? An affair, a DUI, a stupid fraternity prank in college? Any ethics complaints? First and only marriage? Yes, good, we thought so. Any claims of sexual harassment from your staff? Anything like that? Anything whatsoever to do with sex because sex is the killer in a hot campaign? And while they were on the subject, what about gays? Gay marriage? Absolutely not! Civil unions? No, sir, not in Mississippi. Gays adopting children? No, sir.

Abortion? Opposed. All abortions? Opposed.

Death penalty? Very much in favor.

No one seemed to grasp the contradiction between the two.

Guns, the Second Amendment, the right to bear arms, and so on? Ron loved his guns, but was curious for a second about why these religious men were concerned about weapons. Then it hit him—it's all about politics and getting elected. His life-time of hunting pleased them mightily, and he dragged it out as much as possible. No animal seemed safe.

Then the squeaky-voiced director of the Family Roundtable pursued a line of questions dealing with the separation of church and state, and everybody seemed to nod off. Ron held his ground, answering thoughtfully, and seemed to satisfy those few who were listening. He also began to realize that it was all a show. Their minds had been made up long before he left Brookhaven that morning. He was their man, and at the moment he was simply preaching to the choir.

The next round of questions dealt with freedom of speech, especially religious speech. "Should a small-town judge be al-lowed to hang the Ten Commandments in his courtroom?" was the question. Ron sensed that this issue intrigued them, and he was at first inclined to be perfectly hon-est and say no. The U.S. Supreme Court has ruled that it's a violation of the separation of church and state, and Ron happened to agree. He did not, however, want to upset the party, so he said, "One of my heroes is my local circuit court judge in Brookhaven." He began to bob and weave. "A great man. He's had the Ten Commandments hanging on his wall for thirty years, and I've always admired him."

A slick nonanswer that they recognized for what it was. They also recognized that it was a fine example of slickness that could help Mr. Fisk survive a heated campaign. So there was no follow-up, no objection. They were, after all, battle-tested political operatives, and they could appreciate a savvy nonresponse when they heard one.

After an hour, Walter Utley glanced at his watch and announced that he was a bit behind schedule. The day held many more important meetings. He concluded the little meet and greet with a declaration that he was very impressed with Ron Fisk and saw no reason why his American Family Alliance could not only endorse him but hit the ground running down there and get some votes. Everyone nodded around the table, and Tony Zachary seemed as proud as a new father.

———

"There's been a change in our lunch plans," he said when they were once again tucked away in the limo. "Senator Rudd would like to see you."

"Senator Rudd?" Fisk asked in disbelief.

"You got it," Tony said proudly.

Myers Rudd was halfway through his seventh term (thirty-nine years) in the U.S. Senate, and for at least the last three elections he had scared away all opposition. He was despised by at least 40 percent of the people and loved by at least 60 percent, and he had perfected the art of helping those on his side of the street and dismissing all others. He was a legend in Mississippi politics, the fixer, the inveterate meddler in local races, the king who picked his candidates, the assassin who slaughtered those who ran against his candidates, the bank who could finance any race and funnel hoards of cash, the wise old man who led his party, and the thug who destroyed the others.

"Senator Rudd has an interest in this case?" Fisk asked, so innocently.

Tony gave him a wary look. How naive can one be? "Of course he does. Senator

Rudd is very close to those folks you just met. He maintains a perfect voting record in their score books. Perfect, mind you. Not 95 percent, but perfect. One of only three in the Senate, and the other two are rookies."

What will Doreen say about this? Ron thought to himself. Lunch with Senator Rudd, in Washington! They were somewhere near the Capitol when the limo ducked into a one-way street. "Let's jump out here," Tony said before the driver could get out. They headed for a narrow door next to an old hotel called the Mercury. An ancient doorman in a green uniform frowned as they approached. "To see Senator Rudd," Tony said abruptly, and the frown lessened somewhat. Inside, they were led along the edge of an empty and gloomy dining room and down a passageway. "It's The Senator's private quarters," Tony said quietly. Ron was greatly impressed. Ron was noticing the worn carpet and peeling paint, but the old building had a strong dose of shabby elegance. It had a history. How many deals have been put together inside these walls? he asked himself.

At the end of the hallway, they walked into a small private dining room where all man-

ner of serious power was on display. Senator Rudd was seated at the small table, cell
phone stuck to his head. Ron had never met
him, but he certainly looked familiar. Dark
suit, red tie, thick shiny gray hair plastered
to the left and held in place with no small
amount of spray, large round face that
seemed to grow thicker each year. No fewer
than four of his minders and handlers were
hovering like bees, all engaged in urgent cell
phone chats, probably with one another.

Tony and Fisk waited, watching the show.
Government in action.

Suddenly The Senator slapped his phone
shut, and the other four conversations were
instantly concluded. "Clear out," the great
man grunted, and his minions fled like mice.
"How are you, Zachary?" he said, standing
behind the table. Introductions were made,
small talk pursued for a moment. Rudd
seemed to know everyone back home in
Brookhaven, an aunt once lived there, and
he was honored to meet this Mr. Fisk that
he'd heard so much about. At some prede-
termined point, Tony said, "I'll be back in an
hour," and vanished. He was replaced by a
waiter in a tuxedo.

"Sit down," Rudd insisted. "The food's

not much, but the privacy is great. I eat here five times a week." The waiter ignored the comment and handed over menus.

"It's lovely," Ron said, looking around at the walls lined with books that had been neither read nor dusted in a hundred years. They were dining in a small library. No wonder it's so private. They ordered soup and grilled swordfish. The waiter closed the door when he left.

"I have a meeting at one," Rudd said, "so let's talk fast." He began pouring sugar into his iced tea and stirring it with a soupspoon.

"Certainly."

"You can win this race, Ron, and God knows we need you."

Words from the king, and hours later Ron would quote them over and over to Doreen. It was a guarantee from a man who'd never lost, and from that opening volley Ron Fisk was a candidate.

"As you know," Rudd continued because he really wasn't accustomed to listening, especially in conversations with small-time politicians from back home, "I don't get involved in local races." Fisk's first impulse was to laugh, and loudly, but he quickly realized that The Senator was dead serious.

"However, this race is too important. I'll do what I can, which is nothing to sneeze at, you know?"

"Of course."

"I've made some powerful friends in this business, and they will be happy to support your campaign. Just takes a phone call from me."

Ron was nodding politely. Two months earlier, *Newsweek* ran a cover story on the mountains of special-interest cash in Washington and the politicians who took it. Rudd topped the list. He had over $11 million in his campaign war chest, yet had no foreseeable race. The notion of a viable opponent was too ridiculous to even consider. Big business owned him—banks, insurance, oil, coal, media, defense, pharmaceuticals—no segment of corporate America had escaped the tentacles of his fundraising machine.

"Thank you," Ron said because he felt obligated.

"My folks can put together a lot of money. Plus, I know the people in the trenches. The governor, the legislators, the mayors. Ever hear of Willie Tate Ferris?"

"No, sir."

"He's a supervisor, beat four, Adams County, in your district. I kept his brother out of prison, twice. Willie Tate will walk the streets for me. And he is the most powerful politician in those parts. One phone call from me, and you got Adams County." He snapped his fingers. Just like that the votes were falling in place.

"Ever hear of Link Kyzer? Sheriff in Wayne County?"

"Maybe."

"Link's an old friend. Two years ago he needed new patrol cars, new radios, new bulletproof vests and guns and everything. County wouldn't give him crap, so he calls me. I go to Homeland Security, talk to some friends, twist some arms, and Wayne County suddenly gets six million bucks to fight terrorism. They got more patrol cars than they got cops to drive them. Their radio system is better than the navy's. And, lo and behold, the terrorists have decided to stay the hell out of Wayne County." He laughed at his own punch line, and Ron was obliged to guffaw along with him. Nothing like wasting a few more million tax dollars.

"You need Link, you got Link, and Wayne

County," Rudd promised as he slugged down some tea.

With two counties under his belt, Ron began contemplating the other twenty-five in the southern district. Would the next hour be spent listening to war stories from all of them? He rather hoped not. The soup arrived.

"This gal, McCarthy," Rudd said between slurps. "She's never been on board." Which Ron took as an indictment on the grounds of not supporting Senator Rudd. "She's too liberal, plus, between us boys, she just ain't cut out for the black robe. Know what I mean?"

Ron nodded slightly as he studied his soup. Little wonder The Senator preferred dining in private. He doesn't know her first name, Ron said to himself. He knows very little about her, except that she is indeed female and, in his opinion, out of place.

To ease things away from the good ole white boy talk, Ron decided to interject a semi-intelligent question. "What about the Gulf Coast? I have very few contacts down there."

Predictably, Rudd scoffed at the question. No problem. "My wife's from Bay St.

Louis," he said, as if that alone could guarantee a landslide for his chosen one. "You got those defense contractors, naval shipyards, NASA, hell, I own those people."

And they probably own you, Ron thought. Sort of a joint ownership.

A cell phone hummed next to The Senator's tea glass. He glanced at it, frowned, and said, "Gotta take this. It's the White House." He gave the impression of being quite irritated.

"Should I step outside?" Ron asked, at once impressed beyond words but also horrified that he might eavesdrop on some crucial matter.

"No, no," Rudd said as he waved him down. Fisk tried to concentrate on his soup, and tea, and roll, and though it was a lunch he would never forget, he suddenly wished it would quickly come to an end. The phone call did not. Rudd grunted and mumbled and gave no clue as to which crisis he was averting. The waiter returned with the swordfish, which sizzled a bit at first but soon cooled off. The white beets beside it were swimming in a large pool of butter.

When the world was safe again, Rudd hung up and stuck a fork into the center of his swordfish. "Sorry about that," he said. "Damned Russians. Anyway, I want you to run, Ron. It's important to the state. We have got to get our court in line."

"Yes, sir, but—"

"And you have my complete support. Nothing public, mind you, but I'll work my ass off in the background. I'll raise serious cash. I'll crack the whip, break some arms, the usual routine down there. It's my game, son, trust me."

"What if—"

"No one beats me in Mississippi. Just ask the governor. He was twenty points down with two months to go, and was trying to do it himself. Didn't need my help. I flew down, had a prayer meeting, the boy got converted, and he won in a landslide. I don't like to get involved down there, but I will. And this race is that important. Can you do it?"

"I think so."

"Don't be silly, Ron. This is a onetime chance to do something great. Think of it, you, at the age of, uh—"

"Thirty-nine."

"Thirty-nine, damned young, but you're on the Supreme Court of Mississippi. And once we get you there, you'll never leave. Just think about it."

"I'm thinking very hard, sir."

"Good."

The phone hummed again, probably the president. "Sorry," Rudd said as he stuck it in his ear and took a huge bite of fish.

———

The third and final stop on the tour was at the office of the Tort Reform Network on Connecticut Avenue. With Tony back in charge, they blitzed through the introductions and short speeches. Fisk answered a few benign questions, much lighter fare than what had been served up by the religious boys that morning. Once again, he was overwhelmed by the impression that everyone was going through the motions. It was important for them to touch and hear their candidate, but there seemed to be little interest in a serious evaluation. They were relying on Tony, and since he'd found his man, then so had they.

Unknown to Ron Fisk, the entire forty-minute meeting was captured by a hidden camera and sent upstairs to a small media room where Barry Rinehart was watching carefully. He had a thick file on Fisk, one with photos and various summaries, but he was anxious to hear his voice, watch his eyes and hands, listen to his answers. Was he photogenic, telegenic, well dressed, handsome enough? Was his voice reassuring, trustworthy? Did he sound intelligent or dull? Was he nervous in front of such a group, or calm and confident? Could he be packaged and properly marketed?

After fifteen minutes, Barry was convinced. The only negative was a hint of nervousness, but then that was to be expected. Yank a man out of Brookhaven and thrust him before a strange crowd in a strange city and he's likely to stutter a few times. Nice voice, nice face, decent suit. Barry had certainly worked with less.

He would never meet Ron Fisk, and, as in all of Barry's campaigns, the candidate would never have the slightest clue about who was pulling the strings.

———

Flying home, Tony ordered a whiskey sour and tried to force a drink on Ron, who declined and stuck with coffee. It was the perfect setting for a drink—aboard a luxurious jet, with a gorgeous young lady as the bartender, at the end of a long and stressful day, with no one in the world watching and knowing.

"Just coffee," Ron said. Regardless of the setting, he knew he was still being evaluated. Plus, he was a teetotaler anyway. The decision was easy.

Not that Tony was much of a drinker. He took a few sips of his cocktail, loosened his tie, settled deep into his seat, and eventually said, "Rumor has it that this McCarthy gal hits the booze pretty hard."

Ron simply shrugged. The rumor had not made its way to Brookhaven. He figured that at least 50 percent of the people there couldn't name any of the three justices from the southern district, let alone their habits, good or bad.

Another sip, and Tony kept going. "Both of her parents were heavy drinkers. Of course, they're from the Coast, so that's not unexpected. Her favorite hangout is a club called Tuesday's, near the reservoir. Ever hear of it?"

"No."

"Kind of a meat market for the middle-aged swingers, so I hear. Never been there myself."

Fisk refused to take the bait. Such low gossip seemed to bore him. This didn't bother Tony. In fact, he found it admirable. Let the candidate keep the high ground. The mud would be slung by others.

"How long have you known Senator Rudd?" Fisk asked, changing the subject.

"A long time." And for the remainder of the short trip they talked about their great senator and his colorful career.

———

Ron raced home, still floating from such a heady encounter with power and its trappings. Doreen was waiting for the details. They ate warmed-up spaghetti while the kids finished homework and prepared for bed.

She had many questions, and Ron struggled with some of the answers. Why were so many diverse groups willing to spend so much on an unknown and thoroughly inexperienced politician? Because they were committed. Because they preferred bright, clean-cut young men with the right beliefs and without the baggage of prior service.

And if Ron said no, they would find another candidate just like him. They were determined to win, to clean up the court. It was a national movement, and a critical one.

The fact that her husband had dined alone with Senator Myers Rudd was the clincher. They would take a dramatic plunge into the unknown world of politics, and they would conquer.

CHAPTER 14

Barry Rinehart took the shuttle to La-Guardia, and from there a private car to the Mercer hotel in SoHo. He checked in, showered, and changed into a heavier wool suit because snow was expected. He picked up a fax at the front desk, then walked eight blocks to a tiny Vietnamese restaurant near the Village, one that had yet to appear in the travel guides. Mr. Trudeau preferred it for discreet meetings. It was empty and he was early, so Barry settled himself onto a bar stool and ordered a drink.

F. Clyde Hardin's cheap class action may have been small news in Mississippi, but it was a far better story in New York. The daily financial publications ran with it, and the battered shares of Krane's common stock took another drubbing.

Mr. Trudeau had spent the day working the phones and yelling at Bobby Ratzlaff. Krane's stock had been trading between $18.00 and $20.00, but the class action knocked it back a few bucks. It closed at $14.50, a new low, and Carl pretended to be upset. Ratzlaff, who had borrowed a million bucks from his retirement fund, seemed even more depressed.

The lower the better. Carl wanted the stock to fall as far as possible. He'd already lost a billion on paper and he could lose more, because one day it would all come roaring back. Unknown to anyone, except two bankers in Zurich, Carl was already buying Krane's stock through a wonderfully nebulous company in Panama. He was carefully gathering shares in small lots so that his buying would not upset the downward trend. Five thousand shares on a slow day and twenty thousand on a busy one, but nothing that would draw attention.

Fourth-quarter earnings were due soon, and Carl had been cooking the books since Christmas. The stock would continue to slide. Carl would continue to buy.

He sent Ratzlaff away after dark, then returned a few calls. At seven, he crawled into the backseat of his Bentley and Toliver drove him to the Vietnamese place.

Carl had not seen Rinehart since their first meeting in Boca Raton, back in November, three days after the verdict. They did not use regular mail, e-mail, faxes, overnight parcels, landlines, or standard cell phones. Each had a secure smart phone that was linked solely to the other, and once a week, when Carl had the time, he called for an update.

They were led through a bamboo curtain to a dimly lit side room with one table. A waiter brought drinks. Carl was going through the motions of cursing class actions and the lawyers who bring them. "We're down to nosebleeds and skin rashes," he said. "Every redneck who ever drove by the plant down there is suddenly a plaintiff. No one remembers the good old days when we paid the highest wages in south Mississippi. Now the lawyers have created a stampede and it's a race to the courthouse."

"It could get worse," Barry said. "We know of another group of lawyers who are rounding up clients. If they file, then their class will be added to the first one. I wouldn't sweat it."

"You wouldn't sweat it? You're not burning cash in legal fees."

"You're going to get it back, Carl. Relax." It was now Carl and Barry, first names and lots of familiarity.

"Relax. Krane closed today at $14.50. If you owned twenty-five million shares, you might find it hard to relax."

"I would be relaxed, and I would be buying."

Carl knocked back his scotch. "You're getting pretty cocky."

"I saw our boy today. He made the rounds in Washington. Nice-looking fella, so clean-cut it's frightening. Smart, good speaker, handles himself well. Everybody was impressed."

"Has he signed on?"

"He will tomorrow. He had lunch with Senator Rudd, and the ole boy knows how to twist arms."

"Myers Rudd," Carl said, shaking his head. "What a fool."

"Indeed, but he can always be bought."

"They can all be bought. I spent over four million last year in Washington. Sprinkled it around like Christmas candy."

"And I'm sure Rudd got his share. You and I know he's a moron, but the people in Mississippi don't. He's the king and they worship him down there. If he wants our boy to run, then the race is on."

Carl squirmed out of his jacket and flung it across a chair. He removed his cuff links, rolled up his sleeves, and, with no one to watch, loosened his tie and slouched in his chair. He sipped his scotch. "Do you know the story about Senator Rudd and the EPA?" he asked, with full knowledge that fewer than five people knew the details.

"No," Barry said, tugging at his own tie.

"Seven, maybe eight years ago, before the lawsuits started, the EPA came to Bowmore and started their mischief. The locals there had been complaining for years, but EPA is not known for swift action. They poked around, ran some tests, became somewhat alarmed, then got pretty agitated. We were watching all this very closely. We had people all over the place. Hell, we have people inside the EPA. Maybe we cut some corners with our waste, I don't know, but the bureaucrats really became aggressive. They were talking about criminal investigations, calling in the U.S. attorney, bad stuff, but still kept internal. They were on the verge of going public with all sorts of demands—a zillion-dollar cleanup, horrendous fines, maybe even a shutdown. A man named Gabbard was CEO of Krane at the time; he's gone now, but a decent sort who knew how to persuade. I sent Gabbard to Washington with a blank check. Several blank checks. He got with our lobbyists and set up a new PAC, another one that supposedly worked to further the interests of chemical and plastics manufacturers. They mapped out a plan, the key to which was getting Senator Rudd on our side. They're scared of him down there, and if he wants the EPA to get lost, then you can forget the EPA. Rudd's been on the Appropriations Committee for a hundred years, and if EPA threatens to buck him, then he simply threatens to cut their funding. It's complicated, but it's also very simple. Plus, this is Mississippi, Rudd's backyard, and he had more contacts and clout than anyone else. So our boys at the new PAC wined and dined Rudd, and he knew exactly what was happening. He's a simpleton, but he's played the game for so long he's written most of the rules."

Platters of shrimp and noodles arrived and were casually ignored. Another round of drinks.

"Rudd finally decided that he needed a million bucks for his campaign account, and we agreed to route it through all the dummy corporations and fronts that you guys use to hide it. Congress has made it legal, but it would otherwise be known as bribery. Then Rudd wanted something else. Turns out he's got this slightly retarded grandson who has some weird fixation on elephants. Kid loves elephants. Got pictures all over his walls. Watches wildlife videos. And so on. And what The Senator would really like is one of those first-class, four-star African safaris so he can take his grandson to see a bunch of elephants. No problem. Then he decides that the entire family would enjoy such a trip, so our lobbyists arrange the damned thing. Twenty-eight people, two private jets, fifteen days in the African bush drinking Dom Pérignon, eating lobster and steak, and, of course, gawking at a thousand elephants. The bill was close to three hundred grand and he never had a clue it was paid for by me."

"A bargain."

"An absolute bargain. He buried the EPA and they fled Bowmore. They couldn't touch us. And, as a side benefit, Senator Rudd is now an expert on all issues dealing with Africa. AIDS, genocide, famine, human rights abuses—you name it and he's an expert because he spent two weeks in the Kenyan outback watching wild game from the back of a Land Rover."

They shared a laugh and made the first advance upon the noodles. "Did you ever contact him when the lawsuits started?" Barry asked.

"No. The lawyers took over with a vengeance. I remember one conversation with Gabbard about Rudd, but it was the combined wisdom back then that politics would not mix with the litigation. We were pretty confident. How wrong we were."

They ate for a few minutes, but neither seemed thrilled with the food.

"Our boy's name is Ron Fisk," Barry said

as he handed over a large manila envelope. "Here are the basics. Some photos, a background check, no more than eight pages, at your request."

"Fisk?"

"That's him."

———

Brianna's mother was in the area, her twice-yearly drop-in, and for such visits Carl insisted that they use the mansion in the Hamptons and leave him alone in the city. Her mother was two years younger than Carl and fancied herself attractive enough to catch his eye. He spent less than an hour a year in her presence, and each time caught himself practically praying that Brianna had a different set of genes. He loathed the woman. The mother of a trophy wife is not automatically a trophy mother-in-law, and she is usually much too enamored with the topic of money. Carl had loathed each of his mothers-in-law. He detested the very notion that he had a mother-in-law in the first place.

So they were gone. The Fifth Avenue penthouse was all his. Brianna had loaded up Sadler MacGregor, the Russian nanny, her assistant, her nutritionist, and a maid or two and headed out in a small caravan to the island, where she could invade their fine home up there and abuse the staff.

Carl stepped from his private elevator, came face-to-face with *Abused Imelda*, cursed at the sight of her, ignored his valet, dismissed the rest of the staff, and when he was finally alone in the wonderful privacy of his bedroom, he put on his pajamas, a bathrobe, and heavy wool socks. He found a cigar, poured a single malt, and stepped out onto the small terrace overlooking Fifth Avenue and Central Park. The air was raw and windy, perfect.

Rinehart had cautioned him against fretting the details of the campaign. "You don't want to know everything," he said more than once. "Trust me. This is my profession, and I'm very good at what I do."

But Rinehart had never lost a billion dollars. According to one newspaper article, about Carl no less, only six other men had ever lost a billion dollars in one day. Barry would never know the humiliation of falling so fast and so hard in this city. Friends become harder to find. Carl's jokes were not funny. Certain portions of the social circuit seemed to be closed (though he knew this was ever so temporary). Even his wife seemed a bit colder and less fawning. Not to mention the cold shoulders from those who really mattered—the bankers, fund managers, investment gurus, the elite of Wall Street.

As the wind reddened his cheeks, he looked slowly around at the buildings up and down Fifth Avenue. Billionaires everywhere. Did anyone feel sorry for him, or were they delighted at his fall? He knew the answer because he had taken so much delight when others had stumbled.

Keep laughing, boys, he said with a long pull on the malt. Laugh your asses off, because I, Carl Trudeau, now have a new secret weapon. His name is Ron Fisk, a nice, gullible young man purchased (offshore) by me for chump change.

Three blocks to the north, at the top of a building Carl could barely see, was the penthouse of Pete Flint, one of his many enemies. Two weeks earlier, Pete had made the cover of *Hedge Fund Reports*, dressed in an ill-fitting designer suit. He was obviously gaining weight. The story raved about Pete and his fund and, in particular, a spectacular final quarter last year, thanks almost solely to his shrewd shorting of Krane Chemical. Pete claimed to have made a half-billion dollars on Krane because of his brilliant prediction that the trial would end badly. Carl's name wasn't mentioned; it wasn't necessary. It was common knowledge that he'd lost a billion, and there was Pete Flint claiming to have raked in half of it. The humiliation was beyond painful.

Mr. Flint knew nothing about Mr. Fisk. By the time he heard his name, it would be too late and Carl would have his money back. Plus a lot more.

CHAPTER 15

The winter meeting of the Mississippi Trial Advocates (MTA) was held each year in Jackson, in early February while the legislature was still in session. It was usually a weekend affair with speeches, seminars, political updates, and the like. Because the Paytons currently had the hottest verdict in the state, the trial lawyers wanted to hear from them. Mary Grace demurred. She was an active member, but it wasn't her scene. The gatherings typically included long cocktail hours and war stories from the trenches. Girls were not excluded, but they didn't exactly fit in, either. And someone needed to stay home with Mack and Liza.

Wes reluctantly volunteered. He, too, was an active member, but the winter meetings were usually boring. The summer conventions at the beach were more fun and family oriented, and the Payton clan had attended two of them.

Wes drove to Jackson on a Saturday morning and found the mini-convention at a downtown hotel. He parked far away so none of his fellow trial lawyers would see what he was driving these days. They were noted for their flashy cars and other toys, and Wes, at the moment, was embarrassed by the ragged Taurus that had survived the trip from Hattiesburg. He would not spend the night, because he could not afford a hundred bucks for a room. It could be argued that he was a millionaire, in someone's calculation, but three months after the verdict he was still squeezing every dime. Any payday from the Bowmore mess was a distant dream. Even with the verdict, he still questioned his sanity in getting involved with the litigation.

Lunch was in the grand ballroom with seating for two hundred, an impressive crowd. As the preliminaries dragged on, Wes, from his seat on the dais, studied the crowd.

Trial lawyers, always a colorful and eclectic bunch. Cowboys, rogues, radicals, longhairs, corporate suits, flamboyant mavericks, bikers, deacons, good ole boys, street hustlers, pure ambulance chasers, faces from billboards and yellow pages and early morning television. They were anything but boring. They fought among themselves like a violent family, yet they had the ability to stop bickering, circle the wagons, and attack their enemies. They came from the cities, where they feuded over cases and clients, and they came from the small towns, where they honed their skills before simple jurors reluctant to part with anyone's money. Some had jets and buzzed around the country piecing together the latest class action in the latest mass tort. Others were repulsed by the mass tort game and clung proudly to the tradition of trying legitimate cases one at a time. The new breed were entrepreneurs who filed cases in bulk and settled them that way, rarely facing a jury. Others lived for the thrill of the courtroom. A few did their work in firms where they pooled money and talent, but firms of trial lawyers were notoriously difficult to keep together. Most were lone gunmen too eccentric to keep much of a staff. Some made millions each year, others scraped by, most were in the $250,000 range. A few were broke at the moment. Many were up one year and down the next, always on the roller coaster and always willing to roll the dice.

If they shared anything, it was a streak of fierce independence and the thrill of representing David against Goliath.

On the political right, there is the establishment, the money, and big business and the myriad groups it finances. On the left, there are the minorities, labor unions, schoolteachers, and the trial lawyers. Only the trial lawyers have money, and it's pocket change compared with big business.

Though there were times when Wes wanted to choke them as a whole, he felt at home here. These were his colleagues, his fellow warriors, and he admired them. They could be arrogant, bullish, dogmatic, and they were often their own worst enemies. But no one fought as hard for the little guy.

As they lunched on cold chicken and even colder broccoli, the chairman of the legislative affairs committee delivered a rather bleak update on various bills that were still alive over at the capitol. The tort reformers were back and pushing hard to enact measures designed to curtail liability and close courthouse doors. He was followed by the chairman of political affairs, who was more upbeat. Judicial elections were in November, and though it was too early in the year to be sure, it appeared as though their "good" judges at both the trial and the appellate levels would not draw serious opposition.

After frozen pie and coffee, Wes Payton was introduced and received a rousing welcome. He began by apologizing for the absence of his co-counsel, the real brains behind the Bowmore litigation. She hated to miss the event but believed she was needed more at home with the kids. Wes then launched into a long recap of the *Baker* trial, the verdict, and the current state of other lawsuits against Krane Chemical. Among such a crowd, a $41 million verdict was a much-revered trophy, and they could have listened for hours to the man who obtained it. Only a few had felt firsthand the thrill of such a victory, and all of them had swallowed the bitter pill of a bad verdict.

When he finished, there was another round of boisterous applause, then an impromptu question-and-answer session. Which experts had been effective? How much were the litigation expenses? (Wes politely refused to give the amount. Even in a room of big spenders, the sum was too painful to discuss.) What was the status of settlement talks, if any? How would the class action affect the defendant? What about the appeal? Wes could have talked for hours and kept his audience.

Later that afternoon, during an early cocktail hour, he held court again, answering more questions, deflecting more gossip. A group that was circling a toxic dump in the northern part of the state descended on him and wheedled advice. Would he take a look at their file? Recommend some experts? Come visit the site? He finally escaped by going to the bar, and there he bumped into Barbara Mellinger, the savvy and battle-weary executive director of the MTA and its chief lobbyist.

"Got a minute?" she asked, and they retreated to a corner where no one could hear them.

"I've picked up a frightening rumor," she

said, sipping gin and watching the crowd. Mellinger had spent twenty years in the halls of the capitol and could read the terrain like no other. And she was not prone to gossip. She heard more than anyone, but when she passed along a rumor, it was usually more than just that.

"They're coming after McCarthy," she said.

"They?" Wes was standing next to her, also watching the crowd.

"The usual suspects—Commerce Council and that group of thugs."

"They can't beat McCarthy."

"Well, they can certainly try."

"Does she know it?" Wes had lost interest in his diet soda.

"I don't think so. No one knows it."

"Do they have a candidate?"

"If they do, I don't know who it is. But they have a knack for finding people to run."

What, exactly, was Wes supposed to say or do? Campaign funding was the only defense, and he couldn't contribute a dime.

"Do these guys know?" he asked, nodding at the little pockets of conversation.

"Not yet. We're lying low right now, waiting. McCarthy, typically, has no money in the bank. The Supremes think they're invincible, above politics and all that, and by the time an opponent pops up, they've been lulled to sleep."

"You got a plan?"

"No. It's wait and see for now. And pray that it's only a rumor. Two years ago, in the McElwayne race, they waited until the last minute to announce, and by then they had a million plus in the bank."

"But we won that race."

"Indeed. But tell me you were not terrified."

"Beyond terrified."

An aging hippie with a ponytail lurched forward and boomed, "Y'all kicked their asses down there." His opening gave every impression that he would consume at least the next half hour of Wes's life. Barbara began her escape. "To be continued," she whispered.

Driving home, Wes savored the occasion for a few miles, then slipped into a dark funk over the McCarthy rumor. He kept nothing from Mary Grace, and after dinner that night they slipped out of the apartment and went for a long walk. Ramona and the children were watching an old movie.

Like all good lawyers, they had always watched the supreme court carefully. They read and discussed every opinion, a habit they started when their partnership began and one they clung to with conviction. In the old days, membership on the court changed little. Openings were created by deaths, and the temporary appointments usually became permanent. Over the years, the governors had wisely chosen the fill-ins, and the court was respected. Noisy campaigns were unheard-of. The court took pride in keeping politics out of its agenda and rulings. But the genteel days were changing.

"But we beat them with McElwayne," she said more than once.

"By three thousand votes."

"It's a win."

Two years earlier, when Justice Jimmy McElwayne got himself ambushed, the Paytons had been too mired in the Bowmore litigation to contribute financially. Instead, they had devoted what little spare time they had to a local committee. They had even worked the polls on Election Day.

"We've won the trial, Wes, and we're not losing the appeal," she said.

"Agreed."

"It's probably just a rumor."

———

The following Monday afternoon, Ron and Doreen Fisk sneaked away from Brookhaven and drove to Jackson for a late meeting with Tony Zachary. There were some people they needed to meet.

It had been agreed that Tony would serve as the official director of the campaign. The first person he brought into the conference room was the proposed director of finance, a sharply dressed young man with a long history of statewide campaigns, in a dozen states no less. His name was Vancona, and he quickly, and confidently, laid out the basic structure of their financial plan. He used a laptop and a projector and everything was flashed against a white screen, in vivid color. On the income side, the coalition of supporters would contribute $2.5 million. Many of these were the folks Ron had met in Washington, and for good measure Vancona presented a long list of groups. The names were a blur, but the sheer number was impressive. They could expect another $500,000 from individual donors around the district, moneys that would be generated when Ron hit the stump and began to win friends and impress folks.

"I know how to raise the money," Vancona said more than once, but without being offensive. Three million dollars was the magic number, and it virtually guaranteed a win. Ron and Doreen were overwhelmed.

Tony watched them carefully. They weren't stupid. They were just as easily misled as anyone else would be under the circumstances. They asked a few questions, but only because they had to.

On the expense side, Vancona had all the numbers. Television, radio, and newspaper ads, direct mail, travel, salaries (his would be $90,000 for the venture), office rental, all the way down to bumper stickers, yard signs, billboards, and rental cars. His grand total was $2.8 million, which left some wiggle room.

Tony slid over two thick binders, each majestically labeled: "SUPREME COURT, SOUTHERN DISTRICT, RON FISK VERSUS SHEILA MCCARTHY. CONFIDENTIAL."

"It's all in there," he said.

Ron flipped some pages, asked a few benign questions.

Tony nodded gravely as if his boy had genuine insight.

The next visitor—Vancona stayed in the room, a member of the team now—was a saucy sixty-year-old woman from D.C. whose specialty was advertising. She introduced herself as Kat something or other. Ron had to glance at his notebook to confirm—Broussard. Next to her name was her title: Director of Advertising.

Where had Tony found all these people?

Kat was filled with big-city hyperactivity. Her firm specialized in state races and had worked in over a hundred.

What's your winning percentage? Ron wanted to ask, but Kat left few openings for questions. She adored his face and voice and felt confident they would put together the "visuals" that would adequately convey his depth and sincerity. Wisely, she spent most of her time looking at Doreen as she talked, and the girls connected. Kat took a seat.

Communications would be handled by a Jackson firm. Its boss was another fast-talking lady named Candace Grume, and, not surprisingly, she had vast experience in these matters. She explained that a successful campaign must coordinate in communications at all times. "Loose lips sink ships," she chirped. "They also lose elections." The current governor was a client, and she saved the best for last. Her firm had represented Senator Rudd for over a decade. Enough said.

She yielded the floor to the pollster, a brainy statistician named Tedford who managed to claim, in less than five minutes, that he had correctly predicted the outcome of virtually every race in recent history. He was from Atlanta. If you're from the big city of Atlanta and you find yourself in the outback, then it's important to remind everyone there that you are indeed from Atlanta. After twenty minutes they were tired of Tedford.

The field coordinator was not from Atlanta but from Jackson. His name was Hobbs, and Hobbs looked vaguely familiar, at least to Ron. He boasted that he had been running successful campaigns in the state—sometimes out front, sometimes in the background—for fifteen years. He threw out the names of his winners without a thought of mentioning his losers. He preached about the necessity of local organization, grassroots democracy, knocking on doors, turning out the vote, and so on. He had an oily voice, and at times his eyes glowed with the fervor of a street preacher. Ron disliked him immediately. Later, Doreen would admit she found him charming.

Two hours after the parade began, Doreen was almost catatonic, and Ron's notepad was bristling with the drivel he wrote in an effort to remain engaged.

The team was now complete. Five well-paid professionals. Six including Tony, but his salary would be covered by Judicial Vision. Ron, poring through his notebook while Hobbs was ranting, found the column that projected "professional salaries" at $200,000 and "consultants" at $175,000. He made a note to quiz Tony about these amounts later. They seemed much too high, but then what did he know about the ins and outs of a high-powered campaign?

They broke for coffee, and Tony herded the others out of the room. They left with warm farewells, excitement about the thrilling race ahead, and promises to meet again as soon as possible.

When Tony was alone again with his

clients, he suddenly looked tired. "Look, I know this is a lot. Forgive me, but everybody is busy and time is crucial. I thought one big meeting would work better than a bunch of smaller ones."

"No problem," Ron managed to say. The coffee was working.

"Remember, this is your campaign," Tony continued, straight-faced.

"Are you sure about that?" Doreen asked. "Doesn't really feel like it."

"Oh yes, Doreen. I've assembled the best team available, but you can cut any one of them right now. Just say the word, and I'll be on the phone finding a replacement. Someone you don't like?"

"No, it's just that—"

"It's overwhelming," Ron admitted. "That's all."

"Of course it is. It's a major campaign."

"Major campaigns don't have to be overwhelming. I realize I'm a novice here, but I'm not naive. Two years ago in the McElwayne race, the challenger raised and spent about two million dollars and ran a great race. Now we're tossing around numbers that are far more than that. Where is the money coming from?"

Tony snapped on his reading glasses and reached for a binder. "Well, I thought we covered that," he said. "Vancona went over the numbers."

"I can read, Tony," Ron shot across the table. "I see the names and amounts. That's not the question. I want to know why these people are willing to pony up three million bucks to support someone they've never heard of."

Tony slowly peeled off his reading glasses with an air of exasperation. "Ron, haven't we covered this a dozen times? Last year, Judicial Vision spent almost four million to elect a guy in Illinois. We spent close to six million in Texas. These numbers are outrageous, but winning has become very expensive. Who's writing the checks? The folks you met in Washington. The economic development movement. The conservative Christians. Doctors who are being abused by the system. These are people who are demanding change, and they are willing to pay for it."

Ron drank some more coffee and looked at Doreen. A long, silent moment passed.

Tony re-shifted, cleared his throat, and

said softly, "Look, if you want out, then just say the word. It's not too late."

"I'm not quitting, Tony," Ron said. "But this is too much for one day. All these professional consultants and—"

"I'll handle these people. That's my job. Yours is to hit the stump and convince the voters you're the man. The voters, Ron and Doreen, will never see these people. They will never see me, thank God. You are the candidate. It's your face, your ideas, your youth and enthusiasm that will convince them. Not me. Not a bunch of staff members."

Fatigue overcame them and the conversation lagged. Ron and Doreen gathered up the bulky notebooks and said their good-byes. The drive home was quiet, but not unpleasant. By the time they drove through an empty downtown Brookhaven, they were once again excited by the challenge.

The Honorable Ronald M. Fisk, Justice, Mississippi Supreme Court.

CHAPTER 16

Justice McCarthy eased into her office late Saturday morning and found it deserted. She flipped through her mail as she turned on her computer. Online, at her official e-mail address, there was the usual court business. At her personal address, there was a note from her daughter confirming dinner that night at her home in Biloxi. There were notes from two men, one she'd been dating and one who was still a possibility.

She wore jeans, sneakers, and a brown tweed riding jacket her ex-husband gave her many years ago. There was no weekend dress code at the supreme court because only the clerks showed up.

Her chief clerk, Paul, materialized without a sound and said, "Good morning."

"What are you doing here?" she asked.

"The usual. Reading briefs."

"Anything of interest?"

"No." He tossed a magazine on her desk and said, "This one is on the way. Could be fun."

"What is it?"

"The big verdict from Cancer County. Forty-one million dollars. Bowmore."

"Oh yes," she said, picking up the magazine. Every lawyer and judge in the state claimed to know someone who knew something about the *Baker* verdict. The coverage had been extensive, during the trial and especially afterward. It was often discussed by Paul and the other clerks. They were already watching it, anticipating the arrival in a few months of the appellate briefs.

The article covered all aspects of the Bowmore waste site and the litigation it created. There were photos of the town, desolate and boarded up; photos of Mary Grace peering at the razor wire outside the Krane plant and sitting with Jeannette

Baker under a shade tree, each holding a bottle of water; photos of twenty of the alleged victims—blacks, whites, kids, and old folks. The central character, though, was Mary Grace, and her importance grew as the paragraphs flew by. It was her case, her cause. Bowmore was her town and her friends were dying.

Sheila finished the article and was suddenly bored with the office. The drive to Biloxi would take three hours. She left without seeing another person and headed south, in no particular hurry. She stopped for gas in Hattiesburg and, on a whim, turned east, suddenly curious about Cancer County.

———

When she presided over trials, Judge McCarthy often sneaked to the scene of the dispute for a furtive firsthand look at the site. The murky details of a tanker collision on a busy bridge became much clearer after she spent an hour on the bridge, alone, at night, at the precise moment of the accident. In a murder case, the defendant's claim of self-defense was discounted by her after she ventured into the alleyway where the body was found. A light from a warehouse window glared down, illuminating the spot. During the trial of a wrongful death at a railroad crossing, she drove the street night and day, twice stopping for trains, and became convinced the driver was at fault. She kept these opinions to herself, of course. The jury was the trier of fact, not the judge, but a strange curiosity often attracted her to the scene. She wanted to know the truth.

Bowmore was as bleak as the article said. She parked behind a church two blocks from Main Street and took a walk. It was unlikely that she would see another red BMW convertible in the town, and the last thing she wanted was attention.

Even for a Saturday, traffic and commerce were slow. Half the storefronts were boarded up, and only a few of the survivors were open. A pharmacy, a discount store, a few other retail merchants. She paused at the office of F. Clyde Hardin & Associates. He was mentioned in the article.

As was Babe's Coffee Shop, where Sheila took a stool at the counter in anticipation of learning something about the case. She would not be disappointed.

It was almost 2:00 p.m. and no one else was at the counter. Two mechanics from the Chevrolet place were having a late lunch in a front booth. The diner was quiet, dusty, in need of paint and refinished floors, and apparently hadn't changed much in decades. The walls were covered with football schedules dating back to 1961, class pictures, old newspaper articles, anything anybody wanted to display. A large sign announced: "We Use Only Bottled Water."

Babe appeared across the counter and began with a friendly "What would you like, dear?" She wore a starched white uniform, spotless burgundy apron with "Babe" embroidered in pink, white hose, and white shoes, and could have stepped from a 1950s movie. She had probably been around that long, though her teased hair was still aggressively colored. It almost matched her apron. She had the wrinkled eyes of a smoker, but the wrinkles were no match for the thick layer of foundation Babe caulked on every morning.

"Just some water," Sheila said. She was curious about the water.

Babe performed most of her tasks while gazing forlornly at the street through the large windows. She grabbed a bottle and said, "You're not from around here."

"Just passing through," Sheila said. "I have some kinfolks over in Jones County." And it was true. A distant aunt, one she thought might still be alive, had always lived next door in Jones County.

In front of her, Babe placed a six-ounce bottle of water with the simple label "Bottled for Bowmore." She explained that she, too, had kinfolks in Jones County. Before they went too far down the genealogical road, Sheila hastily changed subjects. In Mississippi, sooner or later, everyone is related.

"What's this?" she asked, holding the bottle.

"Water," Babe said with a puzzled look.

Sheila held it closer, allowing Babe to take charge of the conversation. "All our water here in Bowmore is bottled. Trucked in from Hattiesburg. Can't drink the stuff they pump here. It's contaminated. Where you from?"

"The Coast."

"You ain't heard about the Bowmore water?"

"Sorry." Sheila unscrewed the cap and took a swig. "Tastes like water," she said.

"You oughta taste the other stuff."

"What's wrong with it?"

"Good Lord, honey," Babe said and glanced around to see if anyone else had heard this shocking question. There was no one else, so Babe popped the top on a diet soda and sidled up the counter. "You ever heard of Cancer County?"

"No."

Another look of disbelief. "That's us. This county has the highest rate of cancer in the country because the drinking water is polluted. There used to be a chemical plant here, Krane Chemical, buncha smart boys from New York. For many years—twenty, thirty, forty, depending on who you believe—they dumped all kinds of toxic crap—pardon my language—into some ravines behind the plant. Barrels and barrels, drums and drums, tons and tons of the crap went into the pit, and it eventually filtered into an underground aquifer that the city—run by some real dunces, mind you— built a pump over back in the late eighties. The drinking water went from clear to light gray to light yellow. Now it's brown. It began smelling funny, then it began stinking. We fought with the city for years to clean it up, but they stonewalled us. Boy, did they ever. Anyway, the water became a huge fight, and then, honey, the bad stuff started. Folks started dying. Cancer hit like the plague around here. Folks were dying right and left. Still are. Inez Perdue succumbed in January. I think she was number sixty-five. Something like that. It all came out in the trial." She paused to examine two pedestrians who were strolling along the sidewalk.

Sheila carefully sipped the water. "There was a trial?" she asked.

"You ain't heard of the trial either?"

Sheila gave an innocent shrug and said again, "I'm from the Coast."

"Oh, boy." Babe switched elbows and leaned on the right one. "For years there was talk about lawsuits. I get all the lawyers in here for their little coffee chats and no one taught those boys how to whisper. I heard it all. Still hearing it. Big talk for a long time. They're gonna sue Krane Chemical for this and for that, but nothing happened. I think that the suit was just too big, plus you're taking on a big chemical company with lots of money and lots of slick lawyers. The talk died down, but the cancer didn't. Kids were dying of leukemia. Folks with tumors in their kidneys, liver, bladder, stomach, and, honey, it's been awful. Krane made a fortune off a pesticide called pillamar 5, which was outlawed twenty years ago. Outlawed here, but not down in Guatemala and places like that. So they kept making pillamar 5 here, shipping it off to the banana republics, where they sprayed it on their fruits and vegetables and then shipped 'em all back here for us to eat. That came out in the trial, too, and they tell me it really ticked off the jury. Something sure ticked 'em off."

"Where was the trial?"

"You sure you don't have any kinfolks here?"

"I'm sure."

"Any friends here in Bowmore?"

"None."

"And you ain't no reporter, are you?"

"Nope. I'm just passing through."

Satisfied with her audience, Babe took a deep breath and plunged on. "They moved it out of Bowmore, which was a smart move because any jury here would've handed down a death penalty for Krane and the crooks who run it, and they tried the case over in Hattiesburg. Judge Harrison, one of my favorites. Cary County is in his district, and he's been eating here for many years. He likes the ladies, but that's okay. I like the men. Anyway, for a long time the lawyers just talked, but no one would dare take on Krane. Then a local girl, a young woman, mind you, one of our own, said to hell with it and filed a massive suit. Mary Grace Payton, grew up a mile out of town. Bowmore High School class valedictorian. I remember when she was a kid. Her daddy, Mr. Truman Shelby, still comes in from time to time. I love that girl. Her husband is a lawyer, too, they practice together in Hattiesburg. They sued for Jeannette Baker, sweet girl, whose husband and little boy died of cancer eight months apart. Krane fought like hell, had a hundred lawyers, according to the traffic. The trial lasted for months and damned near broke the Paytons, from what I hear. But they won. Jury threw the book at Krane. Forty-one million dollars. I can't believe you missed it. How could anyone miss it? It put Bowmore on the map. You want something to eat, honey?"

"How about a grilled cheese?"

"You got it." Babe threw two pieces of white bread on the grill without missing a beat. "Case is on appeal, and I pray every night that the Paytons'll win. And the lawyers are back, sniffing around, looking for new victims. Ever hear of Clyde Hardin?"

"Never met him."

"He's seven doors down, on the left, been here forever. A member of my eight-thirty coffee club, a bunch of blowhards. He's okay, but his wife's a snot. Clyde is afraid of the courtroom, so he hooked up with some real shysters from Philadelphia—Pennsylvania, not Mississippi—and they've filed a class action on behalf of a bunch of deadbeats who are trying to join the parade. Rumor has it that some of their so-called clients don't even live here. They're just looking for a check." She unwrapped two slices of processed cheddar and placed them on the hot bread. "Mayonnaise?"

"No."

"How about some fries?"

"No thanks."

"Anyway, the town's split worse than ever. The folks who are really sick are angry at these new victims who are just claiming to be. Funny what money does to some folks. Always looking for a handout. Some of the lawyers think Krane'll finally give in and make a big settlement. Folks'll get rich. Lawyers'll get even richer. But others are convinced Krane will never admit any wrongdoing. They never have. Six years ago, when the lawsuit talk was hot, they simply folded up one weekend and fled to Mexico, where I'm sure they're free to dump and pollute all they want to. Probably killing Mexicans right and left. It's criminal what that company did. It killed this town."

When the bread was almost black, she put the sandwich together, sliced it in two, and served it with a slice of dill pickle.

"What happened to the Krane employees?"

"Got screwed. No surprises there. A lot of them left the area to find work. Ain't much in the way of jobs around here. Some were nice folks, others knew what was happening and kept quiet. If they squealed, they'd get fired. Mary Grace found some of them and hauled them back for the trial. Some told the truth. Some lied, and Mary Grace ripped them to pieces, according to what I hear. I never watched the trial, but I got reports almost daily. The whole town was on pins and needles. There was a man named Earl Crouch who ran the plant for many years. Made good money, and rumor has it that Krane bought him off when they tucked tail. Crouch knew all about the dumping, but during his deposition he denied everything. Lied like a dog. That was two years ago. They say that Crouch has disappeared under mysterious circumstances. Mary Grace couldn't find him to come testify at trial. He's gone. AWOL. Not even Krane could find him."

She let this rich little nugget hang in the air for a moment as she sauntered over to check on the Chevrolet mechanics. Sheila chewed on the first bite of the sandwich and pretended to have little interest in the story.

"How's the grilled cheese?" Babe asked when she was back.

"Great." Sheila took a sip of water and waited for the narrative to continue. Babe leaned in closer and lowered her voice.

"There's a family over in Pine Grove, the Stones. Tough bunch. In and out of prison for stealing cars and such. Not the kinda folks you'd want to start a fight with. Four, maybe five years ago, one of the little Stone boys caught cancer and died quick. They hired the Paytons and their suit is still pending. What I hear is that the Stones found Mr. Earl Crouch somewhere out in Texas and got their revenge. Just a rumor, and folks here ain't talking about it. Wouldn't surprise me, though. Nobody messes with the Stones. Feelings are raw, very raw. You mention Krane Chemical around here people want to fight."

Sheila wasn't about to mention it. Nor was she about to pry much deeper. The mechanics stood, stretched, went for the toothpicks, and headed for the cash register. Babe met them there and insulted them as she took their money, about $4 each. Why were they working on a Saturday? What did their boss think he was accomplishing? Sheila managed to choke down half the sandwich.

"You want another one?" Babe asked when she returned to her stool.

"No thanks. I need to be going." Two teenagers ambled in and settled at a table.

Sheila paid her bill, thanked Babe for the conversation, promised to stop in again. She walked to her car, then spent half an hour crisscrossing the town. The magazine article mentioned Pine Grove and Pastor Denny Ott. She drove slowly through the neighborhood around the church and was struck by its depressed state. The article had been kind. She found the abandoned industrial park, then the Krane plant, gloomy and haunted but protected behind the razor wire.

After two hours in Bowmore, Sheila left, hopefully never to return. She understood the anger that led to the verdict, but judicial reasoning must exclude all emotions. There was little doubt Krane Chemical had done bad things, but the issue was whether their waste actually caused the cancers. The jury certainly thought so.

It would soon be the job of Justice McCarthy and her eight colleagues to settle the matter.

———

They tracked her movements to the Coast, to her home three blocks off the Bay of Biloxi. She was there for sixty-five minutes, then drove a mile to her daughter's home on Howard Street. After a long dinner with her daughter, son-in-law, and two small grandchildren, she returned to her home and spent the night, apparently alone. At ten on Sunday morning, she had brunch at the Grand Casino with a female acquaintance. A quick check of license plates revealed this person to be a well-known local divorce lawyer, probably an old friend. After brunch, McCarthy returned to her home, changed into blue jeans, and left with her overnight bag. She drove nonstop to her condo in north Jackson, arriving at 4:10. Three hours later, a man by the name of Keith Christian (white male, age forty-four, divorced, history professor) showed up with what appeared to be a generous supply of take-out Chinese food. He did not leave the McCarthy condo until seven the following morning.

Tony Zachary summarized these reports himself, pecking away at a laptop he still despised. He'd been a terrible typist long before the Internet, and his skills had improved only marginally. But the details could be trusted to no one—no assistant, no secretary. The matter demanded the utmost secrecy. Nor could his summaries be e-mailed or faxed. Mr. Rinehart insisted that they be sent by overnight letter via Federal Express.

PART TWO

THE
CAMPAIGN

CHAPTER 17

In the old town of Natchez there is a slice of land below a bluff, near the river, known as Under-the-Hill. It has a long and colorful history that begins with the earliest days of steamboat traffic on the Mississippi. It attracted all the characters—the merchants, traders, boat captains, speculators, and gamblers—headed to New Orleans. Because money was changing hands, it also attracted ruffians, vagabonds, swindlers, bootleggers, gunrunners, whores, and every imaginable misfit from the underworld. Natchez was rich with cotton, most of which was shipped and traded through its port, Under-the-Hill. Easy money created the need for bars, gambling dens, brothels, and flophouses. A young Mark Twain was a regular during his days as a steamboat pilot. Then the Civil War killed river traffic. It also wiped out the fortunes in Natchez, and most of its nightlife. Under-the-Hill suffered a long period of decline.

In 1990, the Mississippi legislature approved a bill that allowed riverboat gambling, the idea being that a handful of fake paddle wheelers would churn up and down the river while their cargo of retirees played bingo and blackjack. Along the Mississippi River, businessmen rushed to establish these floating casinos. Remarkably, once the legislation was actually read and analyzed, it was discovered that the boats would not be required to physically leave the shore. Nor were they required to be equipped with any type of engine to propel them. As long as they touched the river, or any of its chutes, sloughs, oxbow lakes, man-made canals, or backwaters, the structures qualified as riverboats under the legislation. Under-the-Hill made a brief comeback.

Unfortunately, upon further analysis, the

legislation accidentally approved full-fledged Vegas-style casino gambling, and within a few years this roaring new industry had settled itself along the Gulf Coast and in Tunica County, near Memphis. Natchez and the other river towns missed the boom, but did manage to hang on to a few of their engineless, stationary casinos.

———

One such establishment was the Lucky Jack. There, at his favorite blackjack table with his favorite dealer, Clete Coley sat hunched over a stack of $25 chips and sipped a rum and soda. He was up $1,800 and it was time to quit. He watched the door, waiting on his appointment.

Coley was a member of the bar. He had a degree, a license, a name in the yellow pages, an office with the word "Attorney" on the door, a secretary who answered the occasional phone call with an unenthusiastic "Law Office," and business cards with all the necessary data. But Clete Coley wasn't a real lawyer. He had few clients to speak of. He wouldn't draft a will, or a deed, or a contract, at gunpoint. He didn't hang around the courthouse, and he disliked most of the other lawyers in Natchez. Clete was simply a rogue, a big, loud, hard-drinking rogue of a lawyer who made more money at the casinos than he did at the office. He'd once dabbled in politics, and barely missed an indictment. He'd dabbled in government contracts, and dodged another one. In his early years, after college, he'd done some pot smuggling, but abruptly abandoned that career when a partner was found dead. In fact, his conversion was so complete that he became an undercover narcotics officer. He went to law school at night and finally passed the bar exam on his fourth attempt.

He doubled-down on an eight and a three, drew a jack, and collected another $100. His favorite cocktail waitress brought him another drink. No one spent as much time in the Lucky Jack as Mr. Coley. Anything for Mr. Coley. He watched the door, checked his watch, and kept gambling.

"You expecting someone?" asked Ivan, the dealer.

"Would I tell you?"

"Reckon not."

The man he was expecting had also escaped a few indictments. They went back almost twenty years, though they were anything but friends. This would be their second meeting. The first had gone well enough to lead to this one.

Ivan was showing fourteen when he drew a queen and went bust. Another $100 for Clete. He had his rules. When he won $2,000 he quit, and when he lost $500 he quit. Anything between those limits and he would play and drink all night. The IRS would never know it, but he was up eighty grand for the year. Plus, all the rum was free.

He flipped two chips to Ivan and began the elaborate task of freeing his massive body from the elevated chair.

"Thanks, Mr. Coley," Ivan said.

"Always a pleasure." Clete stuffed the rest of the chips into the pockets of his light brown suit. Always brown, always a suit, always with shiny Lucchese cowboy boots. At six feet four, he weighed at least 280, though no one knew for sure, but he was more thick than fat. He lumbered away toward the bar, where his appointment had arrived. Marlin was taking a seat at a corner table, one with a view of the floor. No greetings of any sort, no eye contact. Clete dropped into a chair and pulled out a pack of cigarettes. A waitress brought them drinks.

"I have the money," Marlin said, finally.

"How much?"

"Same deal, Clete. Nothing's changed. We're just waiting on you to say yes or no."

"And I'll ask you again. Who is 'we'?"

"It's not me. I'm an independent contractor, paid a fee for a job well done. I'm on no one's payroll. I've been hired to recruit you for the race, and if you say no, then I might be hired to recruit someone else."

"Who's paying you?"

"That's confidential, Clete. I explained this a dozen times last week."

"You did. Maybe I'm a little dense. Or maybe I'm just a little nervous. Perhaps I want answers. Otherwise, I'm not in."

Based on their first meeting, Marlin was doubtful that Clete Coley would eventually say no to $100,000 in cash in unmarked bills. Marlin had virtually put it on the table. A hundred grand to get in the race and stir things up. Coley would make a beautiful candidate—loud, outrageous, colorful, able to say anything with no concern about the fallout. An anti-politician the press would follow like ants.

"Here's what I can tell you," Marlin said, with a rare eyeball-to-eyeball glance at Clete. "Fifteen years ago, in a county far away from here, a young man and his young family returned home from church one night. They didn't know it, but two black punks were in the house, a very nice house, and they were burglarizing the hell out of it. The punks were hopped up on crack, pistols in every pocket, nasty characters. When the young family came home and surprised them, things got out of control. The girls got raped. Everybody got a bullet in the head, then the punks set the house on fire. Cops caught them the next day. Full confessions, DNA, the works. They've been on death row at Parchman ever since. Turns out the young man's family has serious money. His father had a nervous breakdown, went insane, poor guy. But he's back and he's pissed. He's furious that the punks are still alive. He's livid that his beloved state never executes anybody. He hates the judicial system, and he especially hates the nine honorable members of the supreme court. He, Clete, is where the money is coming from."

It was all a lie, but lying was a part of the job.

"I like that story," Clete said, nodding.

"The money is peanuts to him. It's yours if you jump in the race and talk about nothing but the death penalty. Hell, it's a natural. The people here love the death penalty. We got polls that show almost 70 percent believe in it and more than that are upset because we don't use it enough in Mississippi. You can blame it on the supreme court. It's a perfect issue."

Clete was still nodding. For a week he'd thought of little else. It was indeed the perfect issue, and the court was the perfect target. A race would be a hell of a lot of fun.

"You mentioned a couple of groups," he said, slugging his double rum.

"There are several, but two in particular. One is Victims Watching, a tough bunch who've lost loved ones and been chewed up by the system. They don't have a lot of members, but they are committed. Between me and you, Mr. X is also secretly funding this group. The other is the Law Enforcement Coalition, a very legitimate law-and-order group with some clout. Both of these will jump on board."

Clete was nodding, grinning, watching a cocktail waitress glide by with a tray loaded with drinks. "Such balance," he said, just loud enough to be heard.

"I really have nothing else to add," Marlin said without pushing.

"Where's the money?"

Marlin took a deep breath and couldn't conceal a smile. "In the trunk of my car. Half of it, fifty grand. Take that now, and the day you officially announce, you get the other fifty."

"Fair enough."

They shook hands, then both grabbed their drinks. Marlin pulled keys out of a pocket. "My car is a green Mustang with a black top, on your left when you leave. Take the keys, take the car, take the money, I don't want to see it. I'll sit here and play blackjack until you return."

Clete grabbed the keys, struggled to his feet, then strutted across the casino floor and out the door.

———

Marlin waited for fifteen minutes, then called the cell phone of Tony Zachary. "Looks like we've hooked us one," he said.

"He took the money?" Tony asked.

"The deal is going down now, but, yes, you'll never see that money again. I suspect that the Lucky Jack will get its share, but, regardless, he's in."

"Excellent."

"This guy is going to be a scream, you know? The cameras will love him."

"Let's hope so. I'll see you tomorrow."

Marlin found a spot at a $5 table and managed to lose a hundred bucks in half an hour.

Clete was back, grinning, the happiest man in Natchez. Marlin was certain that his trunk was now empty.

They returned to the bar and drank until midnight.

———

Two weeks later, Ron Fisk was leaving baseball practice when his cell phone rang. He was the head coach of his son Josh's Little League team, the Raiders, and the first game was a week away. Josh was in the backseat with two of his teammates, sweaty and dirty and very happy.

At first, Ron ignored the phone, then glanced at the caller ID. It was Tony

Zachary. They talked at least twice a day. "Hello, Tony," he said.

"Ron, you got a minute?" Tony always asked this, as if he were willing to call back later. Ron had learned that Tony was never willing to call back later. Every call was urgent.

"Sure."

"A bit of a wrinkle, I'm afraid. Looks like the race might be more crowded than we thought. Are you there?"

"Yes."

"Just got it from a good source that some crackpot named Clete Coley, from Natchez, I believe, will announce tomorrow that he is running against Judge McCarthy."

Ron took a deep breath, then pulled onto the street next to the city's baseball complex. "Okay, I'm listening."

"Ever heard of him?"

"No." Ron knew several lawyers in Natchez, but not this one.

"Me neither. We're doing a background check now. The preliminary stuff is not too impressive. Sole practitioner, not much of a reputation, at least as a lawyer. Got his license suspended eight years ago for six months, something to do with neglecting clients. Two divorces. No bankruptcies. One DUI but no other criminal record. That's about all we know, but we're digging."

"Where does this fit?"

"Don't know. Let's wait and see. I'll call when I hear more."

Ron dropped off Josh's friends, then rushed home to tell Doreen. They fretted over dinner, then stayed up late tossing around scenarios.

———

At ten the following morning, Clete Coley wheeled to a stop at the edge of High Street, directly in front of the Carroll Gartin Justice Building. Two rented vans were behind him. All three vehicles were parked illegally, but then their drivers were looking for trouble. A half-dozen volunteers quickly spilled out of the vans and began carrying large posters up a few steps to the sweeping concrete terrace that surrounded the building. Another volunteer hauled up a makeshift podium.

A capitol policeman noticed this activity and strolled over to inquire.

"I'm announcing my candidacy for the supreme court," Clete explained at full volume. He was flanked by two beefy young men in dark suits, one white, one black, both almost as large as Clete himself.

"You got a permit?" the officer asked.

"Yep. Got it from the attorney general's office."

The cop disappeared, in no particular hurry. The display was put together rapidly, and when it was complete, it stood twenty feet high, thirty feet long, and was nothing but faces. High school graduation portraits, candid snapshots, family photos, all enlarged and in color. The faces of the dead.

As the volunteers scurried about, the reporters began arriving. Cameras were mounted on tripods. Microphones were mounted on the podium. Photographers began snapping away, and Clete was ecstatic. More volunteers arrived, some with homemade posters with proclamations such as "Vote the Liberals Out," "Support the Death Penalty," and "Victims Have Voices."

The cop was back. "I can't seem to find anyone who knows anything about your permit," he said to Clete.

"Well, you found me, and I'm telling you that I have permission."

"From who?"

"One of those assistant attorney generals in there."

"You got a name?"

"Oswalt."

The cop left to go find Mr. Oswalt.

The commotion attracted the attention of those inside the building, and work came to a halt. Rumors flew, and when word reached the fourth floor that someone was about to announce a campaign for a seat on the court, three of its justices dropped everything and hustled to a window. The other six, those whose terms expired in later years, likewise ventured over out of curiosity.

Sheila McCarthy's office faced High Street, and it was soon filled with her clerks and staff, all suddenly alarmed. She whispered to Paul, "Why don't you go down there and see what's up?"

Others, from the court and from the attorney general's office, eased down, too, and Clete was thrilled with the mob that was quickly gathering in front of his podium. The cop returned with reinforcements, and just as Clete was about to give his speech, he was confronted by the officers. "Sir, we're gonna have to ask you to leave."

"Hang on, boys, I'll be through in ten minutes."

"No, sir. This is an illegal gathering. Disband it now, or else."

Clete stepped forward, chest to chest with the much smaller officer, and said, "Don't show your ass, okay? You got four television cameras watching everything. Just be cool, and I'll be outta here before you know it."

"Sorry."

With that, Clete strode to the podium, and a wall of volunteers closed ranks behind him. He smiled at the cameras and said, "Good morning, and thanks for coming. My name is Clete Coley. I'm a lawyer from Natchez, and I'm announcing my candidacy for the supreme court. My opponent is Judge Sheila McCarthy, without a doubt the most liberal member of this criminal-coddling, do-nothing supreme court." The volunteers roared with approval. The reporters smiled at their good fortune. A few almost laughed.

Paul swallowed hard at this unbelievable volley. The man was loud, fearless, and colorful and was loving every second of the attention.

And he was just warming up. "Behind me you see the faces of one hundred and eighty-three people. Black, white, grandmothers, babies, educated, illiterate, from all over the state and from all walks of life. All innocent, all dead, all murdered. Their killers are, as we speak, preparing for lunch up at Parchman, on death row. All duly convicted by juries in this state, all properly sent to death row to be executed." He paused and grandly waved at the faces of the innocents.

"In Mississippi, we have sixty-eight men and two women on death row. They're safe there, because this state refuses to execute them. Other states do not. Other states are serious about following their laws. Since 1978, Texas has executed 334 killers. Virginia, 81; Oklahoma, 76; Florida, 55; North Carolina, 41; Georgia, 37; Alabama, 32; and Arkansas, 24. Even northern states like Missouri, Ohio, and Indiana. Hell, Delaware has executed 14 killers. Where is Mississippi? Currently in nineteenth place. We have executed only 8 killers, and that, my friends, is why I'm running for the supreme court."

The capitol police now numbered almost a dozen, but they seemed content to watch and listen. Riot control was not a specialty, and besides, the man was sounding pretty good.

"Why don't we execute?" Clete yelled at the crowd. "I'll tell you why. It's because our supreme court pampers these thugs and allows their appeals to drag on forever. Bobby Ray Root killed two people in cold blood during the robbery of a liquor store. Twenty-seven years ago. He's still on death row, getting three meals a day, seeing his mother once a month, with no execution date in sight. Willis Briley murdered his four-year-old stepdaughter." He stopped and pointed to the photo of a little black girl at the top of the display. "That's her, cute little thing in the pink dress. She'd be thirty years old now. Her murderer, a man she trusted, has been on death row for twenty-four years. I could go on and on, but the point is well made. It's time to shake up this court and show all of those who have committed murder or who might do so that, in this state, we're serious about enforcing our laws."

He paused for another boisterous round

of applause, one that obviously inspired him.

"Justice Sheila McCarthy has voted to reverse more murder convictions than any other member of the court. Her opinions are filled with legalistic nit-pickings that warm the soul of every criminal defense lawyer in the state. The ACLU loves her. Her opinions drip with sympathy for these murderers. They give hope to the thugs on death row. It is time, ladies and gentlemen, to take away her robe, her pen, her vote, her power to trample the rights of the victims."

Paul considered scribbling down some of this, but he was too petrified to move. He wasn't sure his boss voted so often in favor of capital defendants, but he was certain that virtually all of their convictions were affirmed. Regardless of shoddy police work, racism, malice by prosecutors, stacked juries, and boneheaded rulings by presiding judges, regardless of how horribly defective the trial was, the supreme court rarely reversed a conviction. Paul found it sickening. The split was usually 6–3, with Sheila leading a vocal but overmatched minority. Two of the justices had never voted to reverse a capital conviction. One had never voted to reverse a criminal conviction.

Paul knew that privately his boss was opposed to capital punishment, but she was also committed to upholding the laws of the state. A great deal of her time was spent on death cases, and he had never once seen her substitute her personal beliefs for a strict following of the law. If the trial record was clean, she did not hesitate to join the majority and affirm a conviction.

Clete did not yield to the temptation of speaking too long. He'd made his points. His announcement was a fabulous success. He lowered his voice, grew more sincere, and finished by saying: "I urge all Mississippians who care about law and order, all who are sick of random, senseless crimes, to join with me in turning this court upside down. Thank you." More applause.

Two of the larger officers moved in close to the podium. The reporters began to throw questions. "Have you ever served as a judge? How much financial support do you have? Who are these volunteers? Do you have specific proposals to shorten the appeals?"

Clete was about to begin with his answers when an officer grabbed his arm and said, "That's it, sir. Party's over."

"Go to hell," Clete said as he yanked his arm away. The rest of the police contingent scurried forward, jostling through the volunteers, many of whom began yelling at them.

"Let's go, buddy," the officer said.

"Get lost." Then to the cameras he boomed, "Look at this. Soft on crime but to hell with the freedom of speech."

"You're under arrest."

"Arrest! You're arresting me because I'm making a speech." As he said this, he gently, and voluntarily, placed both hands behind his back.

"You don't have a permit, sir," one officer said as two more slapped on the handcuffs.

"Look at these supreme court guards, sent down from the fourth floor by the very people I'm running against."

"Let's go, sir."

As he moved from the podium, Clete kept yelling, "I won't be in jail long, and when I get out, I'll hit the streets telling the truth about these liberal bastards. You can count on that."

Sheila watched the spectacle from the safety of her window. Another clerk, standing near the reporters, relayed the news via cell phone.

That nut down there had chosen her.

———

Paul lingered until the display was removed and the crowd drifted away, then he raced up the steps to Sheila's office. She was at her desk, with the other clerk and Justice McElwayne. The air was heavy, the mood somber. They looked at Paul as if he might by chance have some good news.

"This guy's crazy," he said. They nodded their agreement.

"He doesn't appear to be a pawn for big business," McElwayne said.

"I've never heard of him," Sheila said softly. She appeared to be in shock. "I guess an easy year just became very complicated."

The idea of starting a campaign from scratch was overwhelming.

"How much did your race cost?" Paul asked. He had just joined the court two years earlier, when Justice McElwayne was under assault.

"One point four million."

Sheila grunted and laughed. "I have

$6,000 in my campaign account. It's been there for years."

"But I had a legitimate opponent," McElwayne added. "This guy is a nut."

"Nuts get elected."

———

Twenty minutes later, Tony Zachary watched the show in his locked office, four blocks away. Marlin had captured it all on video, and was more than pleased to see it again.

"We've created a monster," Tony said, laughing.

"He's good."

"Maybe too good."

"Anybody else you want in the race?"

"No, I think the ballot is complete at this point. Nice work."

Marlin left, and Tony punched the number for Ron Fisk. Not surprisingly, the busy lawyer answered after the first ring. "I'm afraid it's true," Tony said gravely, then recounted the announcement and the arrest.

"The guy must be crazy," Ron said.

"Definitely. My first impression is that this is not all bad. In fact, it could help us. This clown will generate a lot of coverage, and he seems perfectly willing to take a hatchet to McCarthy."

"Why do I have a knot in my stomach?"

"Politics is a rough game, Ron, something you're about to learn. I'm not worried, not right now. We stick to our game plan, nothing changes."

"It seems to me that a crowded field only helps the incumbent," Ron observed. And he was right, as a general rule.

"Not necessarily. There's no reason to panic. Besides, we can't do anything about others who jump in. Stay focused. Let's sleep on it and talk tomorrow."

CHAPTER 18

Clete Coley's colorful launch landed with perfect timing. There was not another interesting story throughout the entire state. The press seized Coley's announcement and beat it like a drum. And who could blame them? How often does the public get to see vivid footage of a lawyer getting handcuffed and dragged away while yelling about those "liberal bastards." And such a loud, large lawyer at that? His haunting display of dead faces was irresistible. His volunteers, especially the relatives of the victims, were more than happy to chat with the reporters and tell their stories. His gall in holding the rally directly under the noses of the supreme court was humorous, even admirable.

He was rushed downtown to central headquarters, and there he was booked, fingerprinted, and photographed. He assumed, correctly, that his mug shot would find its way to the press in short order, and so he had a few moments to think about its message. An angry scowl might confirm the suspicion that this guy was a bit off his rocker. A goofy smile might lead to questions about his sincerity—who smiles when he's just arrived at the jail? He settled on a simple blank face, with just a trace of a curious glare, as if to say, "Why are they picking on me?"

Procedures called for every inmate to strip, shower, and change into an orange jumpsuit, and this usually happened before the mug shot. But Clete would have none of it. The charge was simple trespass, with a maximum fine of $250. Bail was twice that, and Clete, his pockets bulging with $100 bills, flashed enough money around to let the authorities know he was on his way out of jail, not the other way around. So they skipped the shower and the jumpsuit, and Clete was photographed in his nicest brown suit, starched white shirt, paisley silk tie in a perfect knot. His long, graying hair was in place.

The process took less than an hour, and when he emerged a free man, he was thrilled to see that most of the reporters had followed him. On a city sidewalk, he answered their questions until they finally grew weary.

On the evening news, he was the lead story, with all the drama of the day. On the late night news, he was back. He watched it all on a wide-screen TV in a bikers' bar in south Jackson, where he was holed up for the night, buying drinks for everyone who could get in the door. His tab was over $1,400. A campaign expense.

The bikers loved him and promised to turn out in droves to get him elected. Of course, not a single one was a registered voter. When the bar closed, Clete was driven away in a bright red Cadillac Escalade, just leased by the campaign at a thousand dollars a month. Behind the wheel was one of his new bodyguards, the white one, a young man only slightly more sober than his boss. They made it to the motel without further arrest.

At the offices of the Mississippi Trial Advocates on State Street, Barbara Mellinger, executive director and chief lobbyist, met for an early round of coffee with her assistant, Skip Sanchez. For the first cup, they mulled over the morning newspapers. They had copies of four of the dailies from the southern district—Biloxi, Hattiesburg, Laurel, and Natchez—and Mr. Coley's face was on the front page of all four. The Jackson paper reported little else. The *Times-Picayune* out of New Orleans had a readership along the Coast, and it ran an AP story, with photo (handcuffs) on page 4.

"Perhaps we should advise all our candidates to get themselves arrested when they do their announcements," Barbara said drily and with no attempt at humor. She hadn't smiled in twenty-four hours. She drained her first cup and went for more.

"Who the hell is Clete Coley?" Sanchez asked, staring at the various photos of the man. Jackson and Biloxi had the mug shot—the look of a man who would throw a punch and ask questions after it landed.

"I called Walter last night, down in

Natchez," she was saying. "He says Coley has been around for years, always on the edge of something shady but smart enough not to get caught. He thinks that at one time he did oil and gas work. There was a bad deal with some small business loans. Now he fancies himself a gambler. Never been seen within six blocks of the courthouse. He's unknown."

"Not anymore."

Barbara got up and moved slowly around the office. She refilled the cups, then sat down and resumed her study of the newspapers.

"He's not a tort reformer," Skip said, though not without some doubt. "He doesn't fit their mold. He's got too much baggage for a hard campaign. There's at least one DUI, at least two divorces."

"I think I agree, but if he's never been involved before, then why is he suddenly screaming about the death penalty? Where does this conviction come from? This passion? Plus, his show yesterday was well organized. He's got people. Where do they come from?"

"Do we really care? Sheila McCarthy beats him two to one. We should be thrilled he is what he is—a buffoon who, we think, is not being financed by the Commerce Council and all the corporate boys. Why aren't we happy?"

"Because we're trial lawyers."

Skip turned gloomy again.

"Should we arrange a meeting with Judge McCarthy?" Barbara asked after a long, heavy pause.

"In a couple of days. Let the dust settle."

———

Judge McCarthy was up early, and why not? She certainly couldn't sleep. At 7:30 she was seen leaving her condo. She was trailed to the Belhaven section of Jackson, an older neighborhood. She parked in the driveway of the Honorable Justice James Henry McElwayne.

Tony was hardly surprised by this little get-together.

Mrs. McElwayne greeted her warmly and invited her inside, through the den and kitchen and all the way back to his study. Jimmy, as he was known to his friends, was just finishing the morning papers.

McElwayne and McCarthy. Big Mac and Little Mac, as they were sometimes referred to. They spent a few minutes chatting about Mr. Coley and his astounding press coverage, then got down to business.

"Last night, I went through my campaign files," McElwayne said as he handed over a folder an inch thick. "The first section is a list of contributors, beginning with the heavy hitters and going south. All the big checks were written by trial lawyers."

The next section summarized his campaign's expenses, numbers that Sheila found hard to believe. After that there were reports from consultants, sample ads, poll results, a dozen other campaign-related reports.

"This brings back bad memories," he said.

"Sorry. This is not what I wanted, believe me."

"You have my sympathy."

"Who's behind this guy?"

"I thought about it all night. He could be a decoy. He's definitely a nut. Whatever he is, you can't take him lightly. If he's your only opponent, sooner or later the bad guys will find their way into his camp. They'll bring their money. And this guy with a fat checkbook could really be frightening."

McElwayne had once been a state senator, then an elected chancery court judge. He'd fought the political wars. Two years earlier, Sheila watched helplessly as he was savaged and abused in a bitter campaign. At its lowest point, when his opponent's television ads (later known to be financed by the American Rifle Association) accused him of being in favor of gun control (there is no greater sin in Mississippi), she had told herself that she would never, under any circumstances, allow herself to be so degraded. It wasn't worth it. She would scamper back to Biloxi, open a little boutique firm, and see her grandchildren every other day. Someone else could have the job.

Now she wasn't so sure. She was angered by Coley's attacks. Her blood was not yet boiling, but it wouldn't take much more. At fifty-one, she was too young to quit and too old to start over.

They talked politics for over an hour. McElwayne spun yarns of old elections and colorful politicians, and Sheila gently nudged him back to the battles she now faced. His campaign had been expertly run by a young lawyer who took a leave of absence from a large Jackson firm. McElwayne promised to call him later in the day and check his pulse. He promised to call the big donors and the local operatives. He knew the editors of the newspapers. He would do whatever he could to protect her seat on the bench.

Sheila left at 9:14, drove nonstop to the Gartin building, and parked.

———

The Coley announcement was noted at Payton & Payton, but little was said. On April 18, the day after, three important events occurred, and the firm had no interest in other news. The first event was well received. The others were not.

The good news was that a young lawyer from the tiny town of Bogue Chitto stopped by and cut a deal with Wes. The lawyer, an office practitioner with no personal injury experience, had somehow managed to become the attorney for the survivors of a pulpwood cutter who'd been killed in a horrible accident on Interstate 55 near the Louisiana line. According to the highway patrol, the accident had been caused by the recklessness of the driver of an eighteen-wheeler owned by a large company. An eye-witness was already on record stating that the truck passed her in a wild rush, and she was doing "around" seventy miles per hour. The lawyer had a contingency agreement that would give him 30 percent of any recovery. He and Wes agreed to equally split it. The pulpwood cutter was thirty-six years old and earned about $40,000 a year. The math was easy. A million-dollar settlement was quite possible. Wes drew up a lawsuit in less than an hour and was ready to file. The case was especially gratifying because the young lawyer chose the Payton firm on account of its recent reputation. The *Baker* verdict had finally attracted a worthwhile client.

The depressing news was the arrival of Krane's appellant brief. It was 102 pages long—twice the limit—and gave every impression of being beautifully researched and written by an entire team of very bright lawyers. It was too long and two months late, but the concessions had been granted by the court. Jared Kurtin and his men had been very persuasive in their arguments for more time and more pages. It was, obviously, not a routine case.

Mary Grace would have sixty days to respond. After the brief was gawked at by the rest of the firm, she hauled it to her desk for the first reading. Krane was claiming a grand total of twenty-four errors at trial, each worthy of correction on appeal. It began pleasantly enough with an exhaustive review of all the comments and rulings by Judge Harrison that allegedly revealed his intense bias against the defendant. Then it challenged the selection of the jury. It attacked the experts called on behalf of Jeannette Baker: the toxicologist who testified as to the near-record levels of BCL and cartolyx and aklar in Bowmore's drinking water; the pathologist who described the highly carcinogenic nature of these chemicals; the medical researcher who described the record rate of cancer in and around Bowmore; the geologist who tracked the toxic wastes through the ground and into the aquifer under the town's well; the driller who drilled the test holes; the doctors who performed the autopsies on both Chad and Pete Baker; the scientist who studied pesticides and said ghastly things about pillamar 5; and the most crucial expert, the medical researcher who linked BCL and cartolyx to the cancerous cells found in the bodies. The

Paytons had used fourteen expert witnesses, and each was criticized at length and declared unqualified. Three were described as charlatans. Judge Harrison was wrong time and again for allowing them to testify. Their reports, entered into evidence after lengthy fights, were picked apart, condemned in scholarly language, and labeled as "junk science." The verdict itself was against the overwhelming weight of the evidence and a clear indication of undue sympathy on the part of the jury. Harsh but skillful words were used to attack the punitive element. The plaintiff fell far short in her efforts to prove that Krane had contaminated the drinking water either by gross negligence or by outright intent. Finally, the brief ended with a strident plea for a reversal and new trial, or, better yet, an outright dismissal by the supreme court. "This outrageous and unjustified verdict should be reversed and rendered," it read in closing. In other words, throw it out forever.

The brief was well written, well reasoned, and persuasive, and after two hours of nonstop reading Mary Grace finished it with a splitting headache. She took three Advil, then gave it to Sherman, who eyed it with all the caution he would have given a rattlesnake.

———

The third event, and the most alarming news, came in a phone call from Pastor Denny Ott. Wes took it after dark, then walked to his wife's office and closed the door.

"That was Denny," he said.

As Mary Grace looked at her husband's face, her first thought was that another client had passed away. There had been so many sad phone calls from Bowmore that she could almost anticipate one. "What is it?"

"He talked to the sheriff. Mr. Leon Gatewood is missing."

Though they had no affection whatsoever for the man, the news was still troubling. Gatewood was an industrial engineer who had worked at the Krane plant in Bowmore for thirty-four years. A company man to the core, he had retired when Krane fled to Mexico, and had admitted, in deposition and on cross-examination at trial, that the company had given him a termination package worth three years' salary, or about

$190,000. Krane was not known for such generosity. The Paytons had found no other employee with such a sweet deal.

Gatewood had retired to a little sheep farm in the southwest corner of Cary County, about as far from Bowmore and its water as one could possibly get and still reside in the county. During his three-day deposition, he steadfastly denied any dumping at the plant. At trial, with a stack of documents, Wes had grilled him without mercy. Gatewood called the other Krane employees liars. He refused to believe records that showed tons of toxic by-products had, in fact, not been hauled away from the plant, but had simply gone missing. He laughed at incriminating photographs of some of the six hundred decomposed BCL drums dug up from the ravine behind the plant. "You doctored those," he shot back at Wes. His testimony was so blatantly fabricated that Judge Harrison talked openly, in chambers, of perjury charges. Gatewood was arrogant, belligerent, and short-tempered and made the jury despise Krane Chemical. He was a powerful witness for the plaintiff, though he testified only after being dragged to court by a subpoena. Jared Kurtin could have choked him.

"When did this happen?" she asked.

"He went fishing alone two days ago. His wife is still waiting."

The disappearance of Earl Crouch in Texas two years earlier was still an unsolved mystery. Crouch had been Gatewood's boss. Both had vehemently defended Krane and denied what had become obvious. Both had complained of harassment, even death threats. And they weren't alone. Many of the people who worked there, who made the pesticides and dumped the poisons, had been threatened. Most had drifted away from Bowmore, to escape the drinking water, to look for other jobs, and to avoid getting sucked into the coming storm of litigation. At least four had died of cancer.

Others had testified and told the truth. Others, including Crouch, Gatewood, and Buck Burleson, had testified and lied. Each group hated the other, and collectively they were hated by the remainder of Cary County.

"I guess the Stones are at it again," Wes said.

"You don't know that."

"No one will ever know. I'm just happy they're our clients."

"Our clients are restless down there," she said. "It's time for a meeting."

"It's time for dinner. Who's cooking?"

"Ramona."

"Tortillas or enchiladas?"

"Spaghetti."

"Let's go find a bar and have a drink, just the two of us. We need to celebrate, dear. This little case from Bogue Chitto might just be a quick million-dollar settlement."

"I'll drink to that."

CHAPTER 19

After ten performances, Coley's Faces of the Dead Tour came to an end. It ran out of gas in Pascagoula, the last of the big towns in the southern district. Though he tried desperately along the way, Clete was unable to get himself arrested again. He did, however, manage to generate quite a buzz at every stop. The reporters loved him. Admirers grabbed his brochures and began writing checks, albeit small ones. The local cops watched his announcements with silent approval.

But after ten days, Clete needed a break. He returned to Natchez and was soon at the

Lucky Jack taking cards from Ivan. He had no real campaign strategy, no plan. He'd left nothing behind in the places he stopped, except for some fleeting publicity. There was no organization, except for a few volunteers that he would soon ignore. Frankly, he wasn't about to spend the time or the money necessary to rev up a campaign of respectable size. He wasn't about to touch the cash Marlin had given him, not for campaign expenses anyway. He would spend whatever contributions trickled in, but he had no plans to lose money on this adventure. The attention was addictive and he would show up when necessary to make a speech, attack his opponent, and attack liberal judges of all stripes, but his priority was gambling and drinking. Clete had no dreams of winning. Hell, he wouldn't take the job if they handed it to him. He had always hated those thick law books.

Tony Zachary flew to Boca Raton and was picked up by a chauffeur-driven car. He had been to Mr. Rinehart's office once before and looked forward to the return. They would spend most of the next two days together.

Over a splendid lunch with a beautiful view of the ocean, they had a great time reviewing the antics of their stooge, Clete Coley. Barry Rinehart had read every press clipping and seen every TV news report. They were quite pleased with their decoy.

Next, they analyzed the results of their first major poll. It covered five hundred registered voters in the twenty-seven counties of the southern district and had been conducted the day after Coley's tour ended. Not surprisingly, at least to Barry Rinehart, 66 percent could not name any of the three supreme court judges from the southern district. Sixty-nine percent were unaware that the voters actually elected the members of the supreme court.

"And this is a state where they elect highway commissioners, public service commissioners, the state treasurer, state commissioners of insurance and agriculture, county tax collectors, county coroners, everybody but the dogcatcher," Barry said.

"They vote every year," Tony said, peering over his reading glasses. He had stopped eating and was looking at some graphs.

"Every single year. Whether it's municipal, judicial, state and local, or federal, they go to the polls every year. Such a waste. Small wonder turnout is low. Hell, the voters are sick of politics."

Of the 34 percent who could name a supreme court justice, only half mentioned Sheila McCarthy. If the election were held today, 18 percent would vote for her, 15 percent would vote for Clete Coley, and the rest either were undecided or simply wouldn't vote because they didn't know anyone in the race.

After some initial straightforward questions, the poll began to reveal its slant. Would you vote for a supreme court candidate who is opposed to the death penalty? Seventy-three percent said they would not.

Would you vote for a candidate who supports the legal marriage of two homosexuals? Eighty-eight percent said no.

Would you vote for a candidate who is in favor of tougher gun-control laws? Eighty-five percent said no.

Do you own at least one gun? Ninety-six percent said yes.

The questions had multiple parts and follow-ups, and were obviously designed to walk the voter down a path lined with hot-button issues. No effort was made to explain that the supreme court was not a legislative body; it did not have the responsibility or jurisdiction to make laws dealing with these issues. No effort was made to keep the field level. Like many polls, Rinehart's skillfully shifted into a subtle attack.

Would you support a liberal candidate for the supreme court? Seventy percent would not.

Are you aware that Justice Sheila McCarthy is considered the most liberal member of the Mississippi Supreme Court? Eighty-four percent said no.

If she is the most liberal member of the court, will you vote for her? Sixty-five percent said no, but most of those being polled didn't like the question. If? Was she or wasn't she the most liberal? Anyway, Barry considered the question useless. The promising part was how little name recognition Sheila McCarthy had after nine years on the bench, though, in his experience, this was not unusual. He could argue with anyone, privately, that this was another perfect reason why state supreme court judges shouldn't be elected in the first place. They should not be politicians. Their names should not be well-known.

The poll then shifted away from the supreme court and settled onto the individual participants. There were questions about religious faith, belief in God, church attendance, financial support of the church, and so on. And there were questions about certain issues—where do you stand on abortion, stem cell research, et cetera?

The poll wrapped up with the basics—race, marital status, number of children, if any, approximate income status, and voting history.

The overall results confirmed what Barry suspected. The voters were conservative, middle-class, and white (78 percent) and could easily be turned against a liberal judge. The trick, of course, was to convert Sheila McCarthy from the sensible moderate she was into the raging liberal they needed her to be. Barry's researchers were analyzing every word she had ever written in a legal ruling, both at the circuit court level and on the supreme court. She could not escape her words; no judge could ever do that. And Barry planned to hang her with her own words.

After lunch, they moved to the conference table, where Barry had a display of the initial mock-ups of Ron Fisk's campaign literature. There were hundreds of new photographs of the Fisk family in all its wholesomeness—walking into church, on the front porch, at the baseball park, the parents together, alone, dripping with love and affection.

The first soft ads were still being edited, but Barry wanted to share them anyway. They had been filmed by a crew sent from Washington to Mississippi. The first was of Fisk standing by a Civil War monument at the Vicksburg battlefield, gazing off into the distance as if listening to distant cannons. His soft, richly accented voice played over: "I'm Ron Fisk. My great-great-grandfather was killed on this spot in July of 1863. He was a lawyer, a judge, and a member of the state legislature. His dream was to serve on the supreme court. That's my dream today. I am a seventh-generation Mississippian, and I ask for your support."

Tony was surprised. "The Civil War?"

"Oh yes. They love it."

"What about the black vote?"

"We'll get 30 percent of it, from the churches. That's all we need."

The next ad was shot in Ron's office.

Jacket off, sleeves rolled up, desk arranged in a careful clutter. Looking sincerely at the camera, Ron talked about his love of the law, the pursuit of truth, the demands of fairness from those who sit on the bench. It was a fairly bland effort, but it did convey warmth and intelligence.

There were a total of six ads. "Just the soft ones," Barry promised. A couple would not survive editing, and there was a good chance the camera crew would be sent back for more.

"What about the nasty ones?" Tony asked.

"Still in the writing stage. We won't need them until after Labor Day."

"How much have we spent so far?"

"Quarter of a million. A drop in the bucket."

They spent two hours with an Internet consultant whose firm did nothing but raise money for political races. So far, he had put together an e-mail bank with just over forty thousand names—individuals with a history of contributing, members of the associations and groups already on board, known political activists at the local level, and a smaller number of people outside of Mississippi who would feel sympathetic enough to send a check. He guessed that the list would grow by another ten thousand, and he projected total contributions at somewhere in the range of $500,000. Most important, his list was ready and waiting. When given the green light, he simply pushed a button, the solicitation flew out, and the checks started coming.

———

The green light was the principal topic over a long dinner that night. The deadline to qualify was a month away. Though there were the usual rumors, Tony firmly believed that the race would attract no one else. "There will be only three horses," he said. "And we own two of them."

"What's McCarthy doing?" Barry asked. He received daily updates on her movements, which so far had revealed little.

"Not much. She appears to be shell-shocked. One day she's unopposed; the next day she's got some crazy cowboy named Coley calling her a liberal convict lover and the newspapers are printing everything he says. I'm sure she's getting advice from McElwayne, her sidekick, but she has yet to put together a staff for the campaign."

"Is she raising money?"

"The trial lawyers issued one of their standard panic e-mails last week, begging for money from the membership. I have no idea how that's going."

"Sex?"

"Just the usual boyfriend. You've got the report. No real dirt yet."

Shortly after opening the second bottle of a fine Oregon pinot noir, they decided to launch Fisk in two weeks. The boy was ready, straining at the leash, desperate to hit the trail. Everything was in place. He was taking a six-month leave from his firm, and his partners were happy. And well they should be. They had just picked up five new clients—two large timber companies, a pipeline contractor from Houston, and two natural gas firms. The vast coalition of lobbying groups was on board, ready with cash and foot soldiers. McCarthy was afraid of her shadow and apparently hoping Clete Coley would simply go away or self-destruct.

They touched glasses and toasted the eve of an exciting campaign.

As always, the meeting was held in the fellowship hall of the Pine Grove Church. And as usual, several non-clients tried to wiggle their way in to hear the latest. They were politely escorted out by Pastor Ott, who explained that this was a very confidential meeting between the lawyers and their clients.

Other than the *Baker* case, the Paytons had thirty Bowmore cases. Eighteen involved people who were already dead. The other twelve involved people with cancer in various stages. Four years earlier, the Paytons had made the tactical decision to take their best case—Jeannette Baker's—and try it first. It would be far cheaper than trying all thirty-one at one time. Jeannette was the most sympathetic, having lost her entire family in the span of eight months. That decision now looked brilliant.

Wes and Mary Grace hated these meetings. A sadder, more tragic group of people could not be found anywhere. They had lost children, husbands, and wives. They were terminally ill and living with incredible pain. They asked questions that could not be answered, over and over, in slightly different variations because no two cases were identical. Some wanted to quit, and others wanted to fight forever. Some wanted money, and others just wanted Krane to be held accountable. There were always tears, and harsh words, and for this reason Pastor Ott was there as a calming influence.

Now, with the *Baker* verdict legendary, the Paytons knew the rest of their clients had much higher expectations. Six months after the verdict, the clients were more anxious than ever. They called the office more often. They sent more letters and e-mails.

The meeting had the extra tension caused by the funeral, three days earlier, of Leon Gatewood, a man they all despised. His body was found in a pile of brush three miles downriver from his capsized fishing boat. There was no evidence of foul play, but everyone suspected it. The sheriff was busy with an investigation.

All thirty families were represented. The notepad Wes passed around had sixty-two names on it, names he knew well, including that of Frank Stone, a caustic bricklayer who usually said little during these meetings. It was assumed, without a shred of evidence, that if Leon Gatewood's death had been caused by someone else, then Frank Stone knew something about it.

Mary Grace began with a warm hello. She thanked them for coming, and for their patience. She talked about the *Baker* appeal, and for a little dramatic effect she hoisted the thick brief filed by Krane's lawyers as evidence that many hours were being spent on the appellate front. All briefs would be in by September, then the supreme court would decide how to handle the case. It had the option of passing it off to a lower court, the court of appeals, for an initial review, or it could simply keep it. A case of this magnitude would eventually be decided by the supreme court, and she and Wes were of the opinion that it would bypass the lower court. If that happened, oral arguments would be scheduled for later in the year, or perhaps early next year. Her best guess was a final ruling in about a year.

If the court affirmed the verdict, there were several possible scenarios. Krane would be under enormous pressure to settle the remaining claims, which, of course, would be a highly favored result. If Krane refused to settle, she was of the opinion that

Judge Harrison would consolidate the other cases and try them in one huge trial. In that event, their firm would have the resources to fight on. She confided in the clients that they had spent borrowed funds in excess of $400,000 to get the *Baker* case to a jury, and they simply could not do it again unless the first verdict was upheld.

As poor as the clients were, they were not nearly as broke as their lawyers.

"What if the *Baker* verdict is rejected by the court?" asked Eileen Johnson. Her head was bare from chemo, and she weighed less than a hundred pounds. Her husband held her hand throughout the meeting.

"That's a possibility," Mary Grace admitted. "But we are confident it won't happen." She said this with more assurance than she possessed. The Paytons felt good about the appeal, but any rational lawyer would be nervous. "But if it happens, the court will send it back for another trial. It could be on all issues, or simply on damages. It's hard to predict."

She moved on, anxious to get away from more talk about losing. She assured them that their cases were still receiving the full attention of their firm. Hundreds of documents were being processed each week and filed away. Other experts were being sought. They were in a holding pattern, but still working hard.

"What about this class action?" asked Curtis Knight, the father of a teenage boy who'd died four years earlier. The question seemed to arouse the crowd. Others, less deserving, were encroaching on their territory.

"Forget about it," she said. "Those plaintiffs are at the bottom of the pile. They win only if there's a settlement, and any settlement must first satisfy your claims. We control the settlement. You are not competing with those people."

Her answer seemed good enough.

Wes took over with cautionary words. Because of the verdict, the pressure on Krane Chemical was greater than ever. They probably had investigators in the area, watching the plaintiffs, trying to gather information that might be damaging. Be careful who you talk to. Be wary of strangers. Report anything even remotely unusual.

For a long-suffering people, this was not welcome news. They had enough to worry about.

The questions continued and went on for over an hour. The Paytons worked hard to reassure, to show compassion and confidence, to give hope. But the tougher challenge was keeping a lid on expectations.

If anyone in the room was concerned about a supreme court race, it was never mentioned.

CHAPTER 20

When he stepped forward and gazed at the large congregation on Sunday morning, Ron Fisk had no idea how many pulpits he would visit over the next six months. Nor did he realize that the pulpit would become a symbol of his campaign.

He thanked his minister for the opportunity, then thanked his congregation, his fellow members of St. Luke's Baptist Church, for their indulgence. "Tomorrow, down the street at the Lincoln County Courthouse, I will announce my candidacy for the Mississippi Supreme Court. Doreen and I have been struggling with and praying about this for several months now. We have counseled with Pastor Rose. We have discussed it with our children, our families, and our friends. And we are finally at peace with our decision and want to share it with you before the announcement tomorrow."

He glanced at his notes, looked a little nervous, then continued.

"I have no background in politics. Frankly, I've never had the stomach for it. Doreen and I have established a happy life here in Brookhaven, raising our kids, worshipping here with you, taking part in our community. We are blessed, and we thank God every day for his goodness. We thank God for this church and for friends like you. You are our family."

Another nervous pause.

"I seek to serve on the supreme court because I cherish the values that we share. Values based on the Bible and our faith in Christ. The sanctity of the family—man and woman. The sanctity of life. The freedom to enjoy life without fear of crime and government intervention. Like you, I am frustrated by the erosion of our values. They are under attack by our society, by our depraved culture, and by many of our politicians. Yes, also by our courts. I offer my candidacy as one man's fight against liberal judges. With your help, I can win. Thank you."

Mercifully brief—another long-winded sermon was surely coming next—Ron's words were so well received that a polite round of applause rippled through the sanctuary as he returned to his seat and sat with his family.

Two hours later, while the white churchgoers in Brookhaven were having lunch and the black ones were just getting cranked up, Ron bounded up red-carpeted steps to the massive podium of the Mount Pisgah Church of God in Christ on the west side of town and delivered a lengthier version of the morning's comments. (He omitted the word "liberal.") Until two days earlier, he had never met the reverend of the town's largest black congregation. A friend pulled some strings and manipulated an invitation.

That night, in the middle of a rowdy Pentecostal holy hour, he grabbed the pulpit, waited for the racket to die down, then introduced himself and made his appeal. He ignored his notes and spoke longer. He went after the liberals again.

Driving home afterward, he was struck by

how few people he actually knew in his small town. His clients were insurance companies, not people. He rarely ventured outside the security of his neighborhood, his church, his social circle. Frankly, he preferred to stay there.

At nine Monday morning he gathered on the steps of the courthouse with Doreen and the kids, his law firm, a large group of friends, courthouse employees and regulars, and most of his Rotary Club, and he announced his candidacy to the rest of the state. It was not planned as a media event. Only a few reporters and cameras showed up.

Barry Rinehart subscribed to the strategy of peaking on Election Day, not when the announcement is made.

Ron delivered his carefully worded and rehearsed remarks for fifteen minutes, with lots of applause thrown in. He answered every question the reporters had, then moved inside to a small, empty courtroom, where he happily gave a thirty-minute exclusive to one of the political reporters for the Jackson newspaper.

The party then moved three blocks down the street, where Ron cut the ribbon across the door of his official campaign headquarters in an old building that had been freshly painted and covered with campaign propaganda. Over coffee and biscuits, he chatted with friends, posed for pictures, and sat for another interview, this one with a newspaper he'd never heard of. Tony Zachary was there, supervising the festivities and watching the clock.

Simultaneously, a press release of his announcement was sent to every newspaper in the state and to the major dailies throughout the Southeast. One was also e-mailed to each member of the supreme court, each member of the legislature, every other elected official in the state, every registered lobbyist, thousands of state employees, every doctor with a license, and every lawyer admitted to the bar. There were 390,000 registered voters in the southern district. Rinehart's Internet consultants had found e-mail addresses for about a fourth of them, and these lucky folks received the news online while Ron was still at the courthouse making his speech. A total of 120,000 e-mails went out in one blast.

Forty-two thousand solicitations for money were sent by e-mail, along with a message that touted the virtues of Ron Fisk while attacking the social evils caused by "liberal, left-leaning judges who substitute their own agendas for those of the people."

From a rented warehouse in south Jackson, a building Ron Fisk did not know about and would never lay eyes on, 390,000 stuffed envelopes were removed and taken to the central post office. Inside each was a campaign brochure with lots of endearing photos, a warm letter from Ron himself, a smaller envelope if one wished to send back a check, and a complimentary bumper sticker. The colors were red, white, and blue, and the artwork was obviously done by professionals. Every detail in the mailing was of the highest quality.

At 11:00 a.m., Tony moved the show south to McComb, the eleventh-largest city in the district. (Brookhaven ranked fourteenth with a population of 10,800.) Traveling in a newly leased Chevrolet Suburban, with a volunteer named Guy at the wheel, with his new but already indispensable first assistant, Monte, in the front seat and on the phone, and with Doreen sitting by his side on the rather spacious middle bench of the SUV, Ron Fisk smiled smugly at the countryside flying by him. It was a moment to be savored. His first foray into politics, and in such grand style. All those supporters, their enthusiasm, the press and the cameras, the heady challenge of the job ahead, the thrill of winning, all in just the first two hours of the campaign. The strong rush of adrenaline was only a sample of what was coming. He imagined a great victory in November. He could see himself springing from the mundane anonymity of a small-town law practice to the prestige of the supreme court. It all lay before him.

Tony followed closely behind, relaying a quick update to Barry Rinehart.

At the City Hall in McComb, Ron announced again. The crowd was small but loud. There were a few friends, but the rest were total strangers. After two quick interviews, with photos, he was driven to the McComb airstrip, where he boarded a Lear 55, a handsome little jet built like a rocket, although, as Ron couldn't help but notice, much smaller than the G5 that had whisked him to Washington. Doreen barely managed to suppress her excitement at her first encounter with a private jet. Tony joined the flight. Guy raced ahead with the SUV.

Fifteen minutes later they landed in Hattiesburg, population forty-eight thousand, the third-largest city in the district. At 1:00 p.m., Ron and Doreen were the guests at a Prayer Lunch thrown together by a loose coalition of fundamentalist pastors. The setting was an old Holiday Inn. Tony waited in the bar.

Over badly fried chicken and butter beans, Ron did more listening than talking. Several of the preachers, evidently still inspired by their Sunday labors, felt the need to bless him with their views on various issues and evils. Hollywood, rap music, celebrity culture, rampant pornography, the Internet, underage drinking, underage sex, and on and on. Ron nodded sincerely and was soon ready to escape. When he did say a few words, he chose all the right ones. He and Doreen had prayed about this race and felt the Lord's hand in it. Laws created by man should strive to emulate the laws of God. Only men of clear moral vision should judge the problems of others. And so on. He was unequivocally endorsed on the spot.

Freed from the meeting, Ron addressed a group of two dozen supporters outside the Forrest County Circuit Court building. The event was covered by the Hattiesburg TV station. After a few questions, he walked along Main Street, shaking hands with any and all, passing out his slick brochures, and ducking into every law office for a quick heyhowdy. At 3:30, the Lear 55 took off and headed to the Coast. At eight thousand feet and climbing, it flew over the southwest corner of Cancer County.

Guy was waiting with the Suburban at the Gulfport-Biloxi Regional Airport. Ron kissed Doreen goodbye, and the plane took her back to McComb. Another driver there would take her to Brookhaven. At the Harrison County Courthouse, Ron announced again, answered the same questions, then sat down for a long interview with the *Sun Herald.*

Biloxi was the home of Sheila McCarthy. It was adjacent to Gulfport, the largest city in the southern district, with a population of sixty-five thousand. Biloxi and Gulfport were the center of the Coast region, a three-county area along the Gulf with 60 percent of the votes. To the east was Ocean Springs, Gautier, Moss Point, Pascagoula, and then Mobile. To the west was Pass

Christian, Long Beach, Waveland, Bay St. Louis, then New Orleans.

Tony planned for Ron to spend at least half of his time there during the campaign. At 6:00 p.m., the candidate was introduced to his Coast office, a renovated fast-food franchise on Highway 90, the heavily traveled four-lane at the beach. Brightly colored campaign signs blanketed the area around the headquarters, and a large crowd gathered to hear and meet their candidate. Ron knew none of them. Nor did Tony. Virtually all were employees of some of the companies indirectly financing the campaign. Half worked in the regional office of a national auto insurance company. When Ron arrived and saw his headquarters, its decorations, and the crowd, he marveled at the organizational skills of Tony Zachary. This might be easier than he thought.

The Gulf Coast's economy is now fueled by casinos, so he throttled back his high moral comments and dwelled on his conservative approach to judicial thought. He talked about himself, his family, his son Josh's undefeated Little League team. And for the first time, he voiced concern over the state's crime rate and its seeming indifference to executing condemned killers.

Clete Coley would've been proud.

Dinner that night was a fancy fund-raiser at the Biloxi Yacht Club, a thousand dollars a plate. The crowd was a mix of corporate suits, bankers, doctors, and insurance defense lawyers. Tony counted eighty-four present.

Late that night, with Ron asleep in the room next door, Tony called Barry Rinehart with a summary of the great day. It wasn't as colorful as Clete's dramatic entrance, but it was far more productive. Their candidate had handled himself well.

———

Day two began with a 7:30 Prayer Breakfast at a hotel in the shadows of the casinos. It was sponsored by a newly organized group known as the Brotherhood Coalition. Most of those in attendance were fundamentalist pastors from a dozen strains of Christianity. Ron was quickly learning the strategy of adapting to his audience, and he felt at home talking about his faith and how it would shape his decisions on the supreme court. He emphasized his long service to the Lord as a deacon and Sunday school teacher, and almost choked up when he recalled the story of his son's baptism. Again, he was endorsed on the spot.

At least half the state awoke to morning newspapers with full-page ads for candidate Ron Fisk. The ad in Jackson's *Clarion-Ledger* had a handsome photograph above the bold caption "Judicial Reform." Smaller print gave Ron's pertinent biographical data, with emphasis on his membership in his church, civic organizations, and the American Rifle Association. Still smaller print listed an impressive collection of endorsements: family groups, conservative Christian activists, panels of ministers, and associations that seemed to represent the rest of humanity; doctors, nurses, hospitals, dentists, nursing homes, pharmacists, retail merchants, real estate agents, banks, savings and loans, finance companies, brokerage firms, mortgage banks, insurance companies (health, life, medical, fire, casualty, malpractice), highway contractors, architects, energy companies, natural gas producers, and three "legislative relations" groups that represented the manufacturers of virtually every product to be found in any store.

In other words, everyone who might get sued and therefore paid insurance premiums as protection. The list reeked of money and proclaimed that Ron Fisk, heretofore unknown, was now in the race as a serious player.

The ad cost $12,000 in the Jackson *Clarion-Ledger*, $9,000 in the Biloxi *Sun Herald*, and $5,000 in the *Hattiesburg American*.

The two-day cost of the Fisk rollout was roughly $450,000, which did not include travel expenses, the jet, and the Internet assault. The bulk of the money was spent on direct mail.

Ron spent the rest of Tuesday and Wednesday on the Coast, with every minute planned with precision. Campaigns habitually run late, but not with Tony in charge. They announced at the courthouses in Jackson and Hancock counties, prayed with preachers, stopped at dozens of law offices, worked a few busy streets handing out brochures, and shook hands. Ron even kissed his first baby. And it was all recorded by a film crew.

On Thursday, Ron made six more stops throughout south Mississippi, then hurried back to Brookhaven for a quick change of clothes. The game began at six. Doreen was already there with the kids. The Raiders were warming up, and Josh was pitching. The team was in the dugout listening to an assistant when Coach Fisk hustled in and took charge.

There was a nice crowd at the game. Ron already felt like a celebrity.

———

Rather than researching law, Sheila's two clerks spent the day collecting press accounts of the Ron Fisk rollout. They gathered copies of the full-page ads from the different newspapers. They tracked the news online. As the file grew thicker, their moods sank.

Sheila tried gamely to go about her job as if nothing was happening. The sky was falling, but she pretended to ignore it. Privately, and this usually meant a closed-door session with Big Mac, she was stunned and thoroughly overwhelmed. Fisk was spending what looked like a million dollars, and she had raised virtually nothing.

Clete Coley had convinced her she had light opposition. The Fisk ambush was so brilliantly executed she felt as though she'd been killed in battle.

———

The board of directors of the Mississippi Trial Advocates met in an emergency meeting late Thursday afternoon in Jackson. Its current president was Bobby Neal, a veteran trial lawyer with many verdicts under his belt and a long history of service to the MTA. Eighteen of the twenty directors were present, the highest number in many years.

The board, by its very nature, was a collection of high-strung and highly opinionated lawyers who worked by their own rules. Few had ever had a boss. Most had clawed their way up through the lower rungs of the profession to reach a level of great respectability, at least in their opinions. To them, no calling was higher than that of representing the poor, the injured, the unwanted, the troubled.

Typically, each gathering was long and loud and usually began with everyone present demanding the floor. And that was a normal meeting. Place the same group in an urgent setting with their backs pinned to the wall by the sudden and imminent threat of losing one of their most trusted allies on the supreme court, and all eighteen began arguing at once. Each had all the answers. Barbara Mellinger and Skip Sanchez sat in one corner, silent. No alcohol was being served. No caffeine. Only water.

After a raucous half hour, Bobby Neal managed to bring the meeting into some semblance of order. He got their attention when he informed them that he had spent an hour with Justice McCarthy earlier in the day. "She is in great spirits," he said with a smile, one of the few around the table that afternoon. "She is hard at work doing her job and really doesn't want to get sidetracked. However, she understands politics and said more than once that she will run a hard campaign and has every intention of winning. I promised our unwavering support."

He paused, shifted gears. "However, I found the meeting a bit discouraging. Clete Coley announced four weeks ago, and Sheila still doesn't even have a campaign manager. She has raised a few bucks, but she wouldn't say how much. I got the impression that she settled down after the Coley thing and convinced herself he was simply a nut with no credibility. She thought she could slide. Her thoughts have now changed dramatically. She's been asleep, and now she's running to catch up. As we know from experience, there is very little money on our side of the street, except ours."

"It'll take a million bucks to beat this guy," someone said, and the comment was rapidly drowned out in a wave of ridicule. A million wasn't close. The tort reformers spent two million against Judge McElwayne, and they lost by three thousand votes. They'll spend more than that this time around because they're better organized and really ticked off. And the guy who ran against McElwayne was a reprobate who'd never tried a lawsuit and had spent the last ten years teaching political science at a junior college. This guy Fisk is a real lawyer.

So they talked about Fisk for a while, at least four different conversations boiling at any given moment.

Tapping his water glass, Bobby Neal slowly dragged them back to his agenda. "There are twenty of us on this board. If we commit ten thousand each, right now, Sheila's campaign can at least get organized."

Instant silence. Deep breaths were taken. Water was gulped. Eyes darted here and there, searching for other eyes that might agree or disagree with this bold proposition.

Someone at the far end of the table barked, "That's ridiculous." The lights flickered. The AC vents went silent. Everyone gawked at Willy Benton, a fiery little Irish brawler from Biloxi. Benton rose slowly and spread his hands. They had heard his passionate summations before, and they settled in for another. Juries found him irresistible.

"Gentlemen, and lady, this is the beginning of the end. We can't fool ourselves. The forces of evil who want to slam the courthouse doors and deny our clients their rights, the same pro-business lobby that has slowly, methodically marched across this country and purchased one supreme court seat after another, that same bunch of assholes is here, banging on our door. You saw their names in those ads Fisk ran. It's a confederation of dunces, but they have the money. We have what I believe is a consistent one-vote majority on the supreme court, and here we sit, the only group who can fight these thugs, and we argue about how much we should give. I'll tell you what we should give. Everything! Because if we don't, then the practice of law as we know it will quickly fade away. We won't take cases anymore, because we won't be able to win them. The next generation of trial lawyers will not exist.

"I gave a hundred thousand dollars to Judge McElwayne, and it was a stretch. I'll do the same for Judge McCarthy. I don't have an airplane. I don't handle the mass torts and rake in outrageous fees. Y'all know me. I'm from the old school, one case at a time, one trial after another. But I'll sacrifice again. So should you. We all have our toys. If you can't pledge fifty thousand each, then get off this board and go home. You know you can afford it. Sell a condo, a car, a boat, skip a couple of vacations. Hock your wife's diamonds. You pay your secretaries fifty grand a year. Sheila McCarthy is far more important than any secretary or any associate."

"The limit is five thousand per person, Willy," someone said.

"Well aren't you a smart son of a bitch," he fired back. "I have a wife and four children. That's thirty grand right there. I also have two secretaries and some satisfied clients. I'll raise a hundred thousand bucks by the end of the week, and everyone here can do the same."

He sat down, his face red. After a long pause, Bobby Neal looked at Barbara Mellinger and asked, "How much did we give Judge McElwayne?"

"One point two, from about three hundred trial lawyers."

"How much did he raise?"

"One point four."

"How much would you guess McCarthy will need to win?"

It was a subject Barbara and Skip Sanchez had discussed for three days. "Two million," she said without hesitation.

Bobby Neal frowned and recalled the fund-raising efforts two years earlier on behalf of Jimmy McElwayne. Pulling teeth without anesthesia would have been easier.

"Then we have to raise two million bucks," he said with confidence. They nodded gravely and seemed to agree on that figure. They returned to the challenge on the table, and a fierce debate erupted about how much each should commit. The ones who earned a lot also spent a lot. Those who were struggling were afraid to commit. One admitted he'd lost his last three jury trials and was effectively broke at the moment. Another, a mass tort star with his own jet, promised $150,000.

They adjourned without agreeing on a fixed amount, which surprised no one.

CHAPTER 21

The qualifying deadline passed with no other fireworks. Justice Calligan from the central district and Justice Bateman from the northern escaped opposition and were safe for another eight years. Both had a history of showing little sympathy for accident victims, consumers, and criminal defendants, and thus were greatly admired by the business community. At the local level, only two of the state's circuit court judges drew opposition.

One, though, was Judge Thomas Alsobrook Harrison IV. An hour before the deadline passed, a Hattiesburg real estate lawyer named Joy Hoover filed the necessary papers and fired a few shots in a press release. She was a local political activist, well regarded and well-known in the county. Her husband was a popular pediatrician who operated a free clinic for poor mothers as a hobby.

Hoover was recruited by Tony Zachary and Judicial Vision. She was a gift from Barry Rinehart to Carl Trudeau, who, on several occasions in quiet conversations with Rinehart, had voiced his strong feelings against the judge who presided over the *Baker* trial. That judge now had his hands full and would be unable to meddle, as he was prone to do, in other races. For a mere $100,000, the legitimate, above-the-table commitment to Hoover, Judge Harrison now had much more serious matters on his hands.

Rinehart was scheming on several fronts. He picked a quiet day in late June to fire his next salvo.

Two gay men, Al Meyerchec and Billy Spano, had quietly arrived in Jackson three months earlier. They rented a small apartment near Millsaps College, registered to vote, and obtained Mississippi driver's licenses. Their old ones were from Illinois. They claimed to be self-employed illustrators who worked at home. They kept to themselves and met no one.

On June 24, they walked into the offices of the Hinds County Circuit Clerk and requested the necessary forms to apply for a license to be married. The clerk balked and attempted to explain that the laws under which she operated did not allow same-sex marriages. Things grew tense, heated words were offered by Meyerchec and Spano, and they finally left. They called a reporter from the *Clarion-Ledger* and gave their side of the story.

The following day, with the reporter and a photographer, they returned to the clerk's office and again requested the paperwork. When it was denied, they began shouting and threatening to sue. The next day the story was front-page news, complete with a photograph of the two men as they berated the hapless clerk. They retained a radical lawyer, paid him $10,000, and made good on their pledge to litigate the matter. The new lawsuit also made the front page.

It was shocking news. Stories of attempts by gay people to legally marry were common in places like New York, Massachusetts, and California but were unheard-of in Mississippi. What was the world coming to?

A follow-up story revealed that the two men were new to the area, were unknown in the gay community, and had no apparent ties to any business, any family, or anything else in the state. Graphic condemnations were offered by those who could be expected to say such things. A local state senator explained that these matters were governed by state laws and said laws were not about to be changed, not while he was running the legislature. Meyerchec and Spano were unavailable for comment. Their lawyer said they traveled extensively on business. In truth, they were back in Chicago, where one worked as an interior designer and the other owned a bar. They would retain their legal residence in Mississippi and return only when their lawsuit required it.

Jackson was then rocked by another brutal crime. Three gang members, all armed with assault weapons, invaded a rented duplex occupied by twenty or so illegal immigrants from Mexico. The Mexicans were known to work eighteen hours a day, save every dime, then send it all home once a month. Such home invasions were not uncommon in Jackson and other southern cities. In the chaos of the crime, with the Mexicans scrambling about pulling cash from floors and walls and shrieking hysterically in Spanish as the gunmen screamed in very plain English, one of the Mexicans produced a pistol and fired some shots, hitting no one. The gunfire was returned, and a frantic scene turned even more horrific. When the shooting stopped, four of the Mexicans were dead, three were injured, and the gang members had retreated into the night. Their haul was estimated at about $800, though the police would never be certain.

Barry Rinehart could not claim the event as one of his creations, but he was nonetheless pleased to hear about it.

A week later, at a forum sponsored by a law-enforcement association, Clete Coley seized the crime with zeal and hammered away at his usual themes of violence running unchecked and aided by a liberal court that was stifling executions in Mississippi.

He pointed at Sheila McCarthy, onstage next to Ron Fisk, and harshly blamed her for the court's unwillingness to use the death chamber up at Parchman. The crowd loved him.

Ron Fisk was not to be outdone. He railed against gangs and drugs and lawlessness, and he criticized the supreme court, though in softer language. He then unveiled a five-step plan to streamline capital murder appeals, and his staff handed out the specific proposals as he spoke. It was an impressive showing, and Tony, seated in the rear, was delighted at the performance.

By the time Justice McCarthy rose to speak, the crowd was ready to throw stones. She calmly explained the complexities of death penalty appeals and said that a great deal of the court's time was devoted solely to these difficult cases. She stressed the need to be careful and thorough and make sure each defendant's rights were properly guarded. The law knows no greater burden than protecting the legal rights of those society has decided to execute. She reminded the crowd that at least 120 men and women condemned to death row had later been completely exonerated, including two in Mississippi. Some of these people had spent twenty years waiting to die. In the nine years she had served on the court, she had participated in forty-eight death penalty cases. Of those, she had voted with the majority twenty-seven times to affirm the convictions, but only after being certain that fair trials had been conducted. In the other cases, she had voted to reverse the convictions and send the cases back for retrials. She did not regret a single vote. She did not consider herself a liberal, a conservative, or a moderate. She was a supreme court justice, sworn to fairly review her cases and uphold the law. Yes, she was personally opposed to the death penalty, but she had never substituted her convictions for the laws of the state.

When she finished, there was a scattering of light applause, but only of the polite variety. It was difficult not to admire her bluntness and courage. Few, if any, would vote for her, but the lady knew what she was talking about.

It was the first time all three candidates had appeared together, and the first time Tony had watched her under pressure. "She will not be a pushover," he reported to Barry Rinehart. "She knows her stuff and sticks to her guns."

"Yes, but she's broke," Barry said with a laugh. "This is a campaign, and it's all about money."

———

McCarthy wasn't exactly broke, but her campaign was off to a miserable start. She had no campaign manager, no one to coordinate the fifty things that needed to be done immediately while coordinating a thousand details for later. She had offered the job to three people. The first two declined after considering it for twenty-four hours. The third said yes, then a week later said no.

A campaign is a small, frantic business thrown together under great pressure and with the knowledge that it will have a very short life. The full-time staff works brutal hours for low pay. The volunteers are invaluable but not always dependable. A forceful and decisive campaign manager is crucial.

Six weeks after Fisk's announcement, Justice McCarthy had managed to open a campaign office in Jackson, near her condo, and one in Biloxi, near her home. Both were run by longtime friends, volunteers, who stayed busy recruiting more staff and calling potential donors. There were piles of bumper stickers and yard signs, but the campaign had been unable to secure a decent firm to put together the ads, direct mail, and, hopefully, television spots. There was a very basic Web site, but no other Internet activity. Sheila had received $320,000 in contributions, all but $30,000 of it coming from trial lawyers. Bobby Neal and the board had promised her, in writing, that the MTA members would donate at least $1 million, and she did not doubt that they would. But making promises was much easier than writing checks.

Getting organized was made more difficult by the fact that she had a demanding job that could not simply be ignored. The court's docket was backed up for a mile with cases that should have been decided months earlier. There was the constant strain of never catching up. The appeals would never stop. And lives were in the balance: men and women on death row; children pulled back and forth in messy divorces; horribly injured workers waiting on a final ruling that, hopefully, would bring relief. Some of her colleagues were professional enough to detach themselves from the real people behind the cases they considered, but Sheila had never been able to.

But it was summertime, and the schedule was less taxing. She was taking off Fridays and spending long weekends on the road, visiting her district. She worked hard Monday through Thursday, then became the candidate. She planned to spend the month getting her campaign organized and on track.

Her first opponent, Mr. Coley, generally loafed Monday through Friday, resting himself for the rigors of the blackjack table. He gambled only at night, and thus had plenty of time to campaign, if he wanted to. Generally he did not. He showed up at a few county fairs and delivered colorful speeches to enthusiastic crowds. If his volunteers from Jackson were in the mood, they would drive down and erect the Faces of the Dead display, and Clete raised the volume. Every town has a dozen civic clubs, most of which are always looking for speakers. Word spread that candidate Coley could liven up the lunch, and he received an invitation or two each week. Depending on the drive, and the severity of his hangover, he would entertain the idea. By late July, his campaign had received $27,000 in donations, more than enough to cover the costs of his leased SUV and his part-time bodyguards. He'd also spent $6,000 on brochures. Every politician must have something to hand out.

Sheila's second opponent, though, was leading a campaign that ran like a well-tuned engine. Ron Fisk worked hard at his desk on Mondays and Tuesdays, then hit the road with a detailed schedule that left only the tiniest of towns untouched. Using both the Lear 55 and a King Air, he and his traveling staff quickly circled the district. By mid-July, there was an organized committee in each of the twenty-seven counties, and Ron had given at least one speech in all of them. He spoke to civic clubs, volunteer fire departments, library teas, county bar associations, motorcycle clubs, bluegrass festivals, county fairs, and churches, churches, and churches. At least half of his speeches were in pulpits.

On July 18, Josh played his final baseball game of the season, and his father was free to campaign even more. Coach Fisk did not miss a game, though the team fell apart after he announced his candidacy. Most parents agreed that the two were not related.

In the rural areas, Ron's message never varied. Because of liberal judges, our values are under attack from those who support gay marriage, gun control, abortion, and unrestricted access to Internet pornography. Those judges must be replaced. His first loyalty was to the Bible. Laws made by men came next, but as a supreme court justice he would manage to reconcile both when necessary. He began each speech with a short prayer.

In the less rural areas, depending on the audience, he would often move a little from the far right and dwell on the death penalty. Ron found that audiences were captivated by graphic stories of brutal crimes committed by men who were sentenced to die twenty years ago. He worked a couple of these into his routine.

But regardless of where he was, the evil-liberal-judge theme dominated every speech. After a hundred or so, Ron himself believed that Sheila McCarthy was a raging leftist who'd caused many of the state's social problems.

On the money front, with Barry Rinehart quietly pulling the strings, contributions were arriving at a steady rate and managed to keep pace with expenses. By June 30, the first deadline to file financial reports, the Fisk campaign had received $510,000 from twenty-two hundred people. Of his contributors, only thirty-five gave the maximum of $5,000, and every one of these was a Mississippi resident. Ninety percent of donors were from within the state.

Barry knew the trial lawyers would scrutinize the contributors in the hope that out-of-state money was pouring in from big business interests. It had been a troublesome campaign issue before, and he would avoid it in the Fisk race. He was confident he would raise huge sums of money from out of state, but these donations would pour in at the chosen moment, late in the campaign when the state's benign reporting laws protected it from being an issue. In contrast, McCarthy's reports revealed that she was being financed by the trial lawyers, and Barry knew precisely how to wield this as an issue in his favor.

Barry also had the results of his latest poll, one that he would not share with the candidate. As of June 25, half the registered voters were now aware that there was a race. Of that number, 24 percent favored Ron Fisk, 16 percent Sheila McCarthy, and 10 percent Clete Coley. Those numbers were exciting. In less than two months, Barry had packaged an unknown lawyer who'd never worn a black robe and thrust him ahead of an opponent with nine years of experience.

And they had yet to run a single ad on television.

———

On July 1, the Second State Bank was purchased by New Vista Bank, a regional chain based in Dallas. Huffy called Wes Payton with the news and was generally upbeat. The Hattiesburg office had been assured that nothing would change but the name. His loan portfolio had been reviewed by the new owners. They had quizzed him about the Paytons, and seemed content with

Huffy's promises that the loan would eventually be satisfied.

For the fourth straight month, the Paytons sent Huffy a check for $2,000.

CHAPTER 22

In another life, Nathaniel Lester had been a flamboyant criminal defense lawyer with an uncanny knack for winning murder trials. At one point, two decades earlier, he had put together a streak of twelve consecutive not-guilty verdicts, virtually all in small towns throughout Mississippi, the types of places where those accused of heinous crimes are generally presumed guilty the moment they are arrested. His notoriety attracted clients from the civil side, and his country law office in the town of Mendenhall prospered nicely.

Nat won big verdicts and negotiated even larger settlements. His specialty became catastrophic personal injuries on the off-shore oil rigs where many local men went for high-paying jobs. He was active in various trial lawyer groups, gave huge sums to political candidates, built the biggest house in town, went through a series of wives, and began drinking heavily. The booze, along with a string of ethics complaints and legal skirmishes, finally slowed him down, and when he was ultimately boxed in, he surrendered his law license to avoid a prison sentence. He left Mendenhall, found a new wife, sobered up, and resurfaced in Jackson, where he embraced Buddhism, yoga, vegetarianism, and a simpler lifestyle. One of the few smart decisions he'd made during his heyday was to bury some of his money.

During the first week of August, he pestered Sheila McCarthy until she agreed to a quick lunch. Every lawyer in the state knew something of his colorful history, and she was understandably nervous. Over tofu and sprouts, he offered to run her campaign, at no cost. He would devote his considerable energies to nothing else for the next three months. She was apprehensive. His long gray hair fell to his shoulders. He had matching diamond earrings, and though they were quite small, they were still visible. He displayed one tattoo, on his left arm, and she didn't want to think of the others and where they might be. He wore jeans and sandals and a collection of bright leather bracelets on each wrist.

But Nat had not been a successful courtroom lawyer because he was dull and unpersuasive. He most definitely was not. He knew the district, its towns and courthouses and the people who ran them. He had a passionate hatred of big business and the influence it bought, and he was bored and looking for a war.

She caved in and invited him to join hers. Driving away from the restaurant, she questioned her sanity, but she also had a gut feeling that Nathaniel Lester could be the spark her campaign so badly needed. Her own poll showed her trailing Fisk by five points, and a sense of desperation was settling in.

They met again that night at her Jackson headquarters, and in a four-hour meeting Nat assumed control. With a combination of wit, charm, and castigation, he whipped her ragtag staff into a near frenzy of excitement. To prove his mettle, he called three Jackson trial lawyers, at home, and, after a few pleasantries, asked them why in the hell they had not yet sent money to the McCarthy campaign. Using a speakerphone, he shamed them, cajoled them, berated them, and refused to hang up until each had promised significant contributions from themselves and their families, clients, and friends. Don't mail the checks, he said—he would personally drive over before noon tomorrow and get the money himself. The three commitments totaled $70,000. From that moment, Nat was in charge.

The following day he picked up the checks and began the process of calling every trial lawyer in the state. He contacted labor groups and black leaders. He fired one staff member and hired two others. By the end of the week, Sheila was getting a morning printout of Nat's version of her daily schedule. She haggled a little, but not much. He was already working sixteen hours a day and expected that from the candidate and everyone else.

———

In Hattiesburg, Wes stopped by the home of Judge Harrison for a quiet lunch. With thirty Bowmore cases on his docket, it would be unwise to be seen in public. Though they had no intention of discussing pending business, the coziness would seem inappropriate. Tom Harrison had extended the invitation to Wes and Mary Grace, whenever they had the time. Mary Grace was out of town and sent her regrets.

The subject was politics. Tom's circuit court district covered Hattiesburg and Forrest County and the three rural counties of Cary, Lamar, and Perry. Almost 80 percent of the registered voters were in Hattiesburg, his home and also that of Joy Hoover, his opponent. She would do well in certain precincts in the city, but Judge Harrison was confident he would do even better. Nor was he worried about the smaller counties. In fact, he seemed generally unconcerned about losing. Hoover appeared to be well financed, probably with outside money, but Judge Harrison knew his district and enjoyed its politics.

Cary County had the smallest population of the four, and it was continuing to decline with no small measure of help from Krane

Chemical and its toxic history. They avoided that topic and discussed various politicians in and around Bowmore. Wes assured him that the Paytons, as well as their clients, friends, Pastor Denny Ott, and Mary Grace's family, would do everything possible to re-elect Judge Harrison.

Conversation shifted to other races, primarily that of Sheila McCarthy. She had passed through Hattiesburg two weeks earlier and spent half an hour at the Payton firm, where she awkwardly managed to avoid mentioning the Bowmore litigation while rounding up votes. The Paytons admitted they had no money to contribute but promised to work overtime to get her re-elected. A truckload of yard signs and other campaign materials had been delivered to the office the following day.

Judge Harrison lamented the politicization of the supreme court. "It's unseemly," he was saying, "how they are forced to grovel for votes. You, as a lawyer representing a client in a pending case, should have no contact whatsoever with a supreme court justice. But because of the system, one comes to your office seeking money and support. Why? Because some special interests with plenty of money have decided they would like to own her seat on the court. They're spending money to purchase a seat. She responds by raising money from her side of the street. It's a rotten system, Wes."

"How do you fix it?"

"Either take away the private money and finance the races with public funds or switch to appointments. Eleven other states have figured out how to make the appointment system work. I'm not sure their courts are vastly superior to ours in terms of legal talent, but at least the special interests don't control them."

"Do you know Fisk?" Wes asked.

"He's been in my courtroom a couple of times. Nice fella, green as hell. Looks nice in a suit, typical insurance defense routine. Opens his files, files his motions, settles, closes his files, never gets his hands dirty. He's never heard a case, mediated one, tried one, and he's never shown any interest in being a judge. Think about it, Wes. Every small town needs lawyers occasionally to serve as city judges or assistant magistrates or traffic court referees, and we all felt the obligation to step in when we were younger. Not this guy. Every small county needs lawyers to pinch-hit with youth court and drug court and the like, and those of us who aspired to be real judges volunteered. I mean, you gotta start somewhere. Not this guy. I'll bet he's never been to city court in Brookhaven or youth court in Lincoln County. He wakes up one day, decides he's suddenly passionate about the judiciary and, what the hell, he'll just start at the top. It's an insult to those of us who toil in the system and make it work."

"I doubt if running was his idea."

"No, he was recruited. That makes it even more shameful. They look around, pick some greenhorn with a nice smile and no record to attack, and package him with their slick marketing. That's politics. But it shouldn't contaminate the judiciary."

"We beat them two years ago with McElwayne."

"So you're optimistic?"

"No, Judge, I'm terrified. I haven't slept well since Fisk announced, and I won't sleep well until he's defeated. We're broke and in debt, so we can't write a check, but every member of our firm has agreed to spend one hour a day knocking on doors, passing out brochures, putting up yard signs, and making phone calls. We've written letters to our clients. We're leaning on our friends. We've organized Bowmore. We're doing everything possible because if we lose the *Baker* case there is no tomorrow."

"Where is the appeal?"

"All the briefs are in. Everything is nice and tidy and waiting on the court to tell us when, and if, it wants oral argument. Probably early next year."

"No chance of a decision before the election?"

"None whatsoever. It's the most important case on the docket, but then every lawyer feels this way. As you know, the court works on its own schedule. No one can push it."

They had iced coffee as they inspected the judge's small vegetable garden. The temperature was a hundred degrees and Wes was ready to go. They finally shook hands on the front porch. As Wes drove away, he couldn't help but worry about him. Judge Harrison was much more concerned about the McCarthy race than his own.

The hearing was on a motion to dismiss filed by Hinds County. The courtroom belonged to Chancellor Phil Shingleton. It was a small, busy, efficient courtroom with oak walls and the obligatory faded portraits of long-forgotten judges. There was no box for the jurors because jury trials did not occur in chancery court. Crowds were rare, but for this hearing every seat was taken.

Meyerchec and Spano, back from Chicago, sat with their radical lawyer at one table. At the other were two young women representing the county. Chancellor Shingleton called things to order, welcomed the crowd, noted the interest from the media, and looked at the file. Two courtroom artists worked on Meyerchec and Spano. Everyone waited anxiously as Shingleton flipped through paperwork as if he'd never seen it. In fact, he'd read it many times and had already written his ruling.

"Just curious," he said without looking up. "Why did you file this thing in chancery court?"

The radical lawyer stood and said, "It's a matter of equity, Your Honor. And we knew we could expect a fair trial here." If it was intended as humor, it missed its mark.

The reason it was filed in chancery court was to get it dismissed as soon as possible. A hearing in circuit court would take even longer. A federal lawsuit would go off in the wrong direction.

"Proceed," Shingleton said.

The radical lawyer was soon railing against the county and the state and society in general. His words came in short, rapid bursts, much too loud for the small room and much too shrill to listen to for more than ten minutes. He went on and on. The laws of the state were backward and unfair and discriminated against his clients because they couldn't marry each other. Why shouldn't two mature and consenting gay adults who are in love and want all the responsibilities and obligations and commitments and duties of matrimony be allowed the same privileges and legal rights as two heterosexuals? He managed to ask this question at least eight different ways.

The reason, explained one of the young ladies for the county, is that the laws of the state do not permit it. Plain and simple. The state's constitution grants to the legislature the right to make laws regarding marriage, divorce, and so on, and no one else has this authority. If and when the legislature approves same-sex marriage, then Mr. Meyerchec and Mr. Spano will be free to pursue their desires.

"Do you expect the legislature to do this anytime soon?" Shingleton deadpanned.

"No," was the quick reply, and it was good for some light laughter.

The radical lawyer rebutted with the strenuous argument that the legislature, especially "our" legislature, passed laws every year that are struck down by the courts. That is the role of the judiciary! After making this point loud and clear, he devised several ways to present it in slightly different formats.

After an hour, Shingleton was fed up. Without a recess, and glancing at his notes, he gave a ruling that was rather succinct. His job was to follow the laws of the state, and if the laws prohibited marriage between two men or two women, or two men and one woman, or whatever combination, anything other than one man and one woman, then he, as a chancellor, had no choice but to dismiss the case.

Outside the courthouse, with Meyerchec on one side and Spano on the other, the radical lawyer continued his screeching for the press. He was aggrieved. His clients were aggrieved, though it was noted by a few that both looked quite bored with it all.

They were appealing immediately to the Mississippi Supreme Court. That's where they were headed, and that's where they wanted to be. And with the shadowy firm of Troy-Hogan paying the bills from Boca Raton, that's exactly where they were going.

CHAPTER 23

During its first four months, the race between Sheila McCarthy and Ron Fisk had been markedly civil. Clete Coley had thrown his share of mud, but his general appearance and unruly personality made it difficult for voters to see him as a supreme court justice. Though he still received around 10 percent in Rinehart's polls, he was campaigning less and less. Nat Lester's poll gave him 5 percent, but that poll was not as detailed as Rinehart's.

After Labor Day, with the election two months away and the homestretch of the race at hand, Fisk's campaign took its first ugly step toward the gutter. Once on that course, it would not and could not turn back.

The tactic was one Barry Rinehart had perfected in other races. A mass mailing was sent to all registered voters from an outfit called Lawsuit Victims for Truth. It screamed the question "Why Are the Trial Lawyers Financing Sheila McCarthy?" The four-page diatribe that followed did not attempt to answer the question. Instead, it excoriated trial lawyers.

First, it used the family doctor, claiming that trial lawyers and the frivolous lawsuits they bring are responsible for many of the problems in our health-care system. Doctors, laboring under the fear of lawsuit abuse, are forced to perform expensive tests and diagnoses that drive up the cost of medical care. Doctors must pay exorbitant premiums for malpractice insurance to protect themselves from bogus lawsuits. In some states, doctors have been driven out, leaving their patients without care. One doctor (no residence given) was quoted as saying, "I couldn't afford the premiums, and I was tired of spending hours in depositions and trials. So I simply quit. I still worry about my patients." A hospital in West Virginia was forced to close after getting hit with an outrageous verdict. A greedy trial lawyer was at fault.

Next, it hit the checkbook. Rampant litigation costs the average household $1,800 a year, according to one study. This expense is a direct result of higher insurance premiums on automobiles and homes, plus higher prices for a thousand household products whose makers are constantly being sued. Medications, both prescription and over-the-counter, are a perfect example. They would be 15 percent cheaper if the trial lawyers didn't hammer their manufacturers with massive class action cases.

Then it shocked the reader with a collection of some of the country's zaniest verdicts, a well-used and trusted list that always sparked outrage. Three million dollars against a fast-food chain for hot coffee that was spilled; $110 million against a carmaker for a defective paint job; $15 million against the owner of a swimming pool that was fenced and padlocked. The infuriating list went on and on. The world is going crazy and being led by devious trial lawyers.

After breathing fire for three pages, it finished with a bang. Five years earlier, Mississippi had been labeled by a pro-business group as a "judicial hellhole." Only four other states shared this distinction, and the entire process would have been overlooked but for the Commerce Council. It seized the news and splashed it around in newspaper ads. Now the issue was worthy of being used again. According to the Lawsuit Victims for Truth, the trial lawyers have so abused the court system in Mississippi that the state is now a dumping ground for all sorts of major lawsuits. Some of the plaintiffs live elsewhere. Many of the trial lawyers live elsewhere. They forum-shop until they find a friendly county with a friendly judge, and there they file their cases. Huge verdicts are the result. The state has earned a shady reputation, and because of this many businesses avoid Mississippi. Dozens of factories have packed up and left. Thousands of jobs are gone.

All thanks to the trial lawyers, who of course adore Sheila McCarthy and her pro-plaintiff leanings and will spend anything to keep her on the court.

The mailing ended with a plea for sanity. It never mentioned Ron Fisk.

An e-mail blast then sent the ad to sixty-five thousand addresses in the district. Within hours, it had been picked up by the trial lawyers and sent to all of the MTA's eight hundred members.

———

Nat Lester was thrilled with the ad. As campaign manager, he preferred broad-based support from many groups, but the reality was that the only major donors to McCarthy were the trial lawyers. He wanted them angry, spitting nails, frothing at the mouth, ready for an old-fashioned bare-knuckle brawl. So far, they had given just under $600,000. Nat needed twice that, and the only way to get it was by throwing grenades.

He sent an e-mail to every trial lawyer, and in it he explained the urgent necessity of answering the propaganda as quickly as possible. Negative ads, both in print and on television, must be responded to immediately. Direct mail is expensive, but very effective. He estimated the cost of the Lawsuit Victims for Truth mailing at $300,000 (actual cost: $320,000). Since he planned to use direct mail more than once, he demanded an immediate infusion of $500,000, and he insisted on commitments by return e-mail. His coded e-mail address would publish a running total of new contributions from trial lawyers, and until it reached the goal of $500,000, the campaign would remain virtually hamstrung. His tactic bordered on extortion, but then he was still, at heart, a trial lawyer, and he knew the breed. The mailing jolted their blood pressure to near-lethal levels. They loved to fight anyway, and the commitments would pour in.

While he manipulated them, he met with Sheila and tried to calm her. She had never been attacked before in such a manner. She was upset, but also angry. The gloves were off, and Mr. Nathaniel Lester was relishing the fight. Within two hours, he had designed and written a response, met with the printer, and ordered the necessary supplies. Twenty-four hours after the Lawsuit Victims for Truth's plea was sent by e-mail, 330 trial lawyers had committed $515,000.

Nat also went after the Trial Lawyers of America, several of whose members had made fortunes in Mississippi. He e-mailed the Lawsuit Victims for Truth's fulmination to fourteen thousand of its members.

———

Three days later, Sheila McCarthy counterpunched. Refusing to hide behind some silly group organized just to send propaganda, she (Nat) decided to send the correspondence from her own campaign. It was in the form of a letter, with a flattering photo of her at the top. She thanked each voter for his or her support, and quickly ran through her experience and qualifications. She claimed to have nothing but respect for her opponents, but neither had ever worn the black robe. Neither, frankly, had ever shown any interest in the judiciary.

Then she posed the question: "Why Is Big Business Financing Ron Fisk?" Because, she explained in detail, big business is currently in the business of buying seats on supreme courts all over the country. They target justices like herself, compassionate jurists who strive for the common ground and are sympathetic to the rights of workers, consumers, victims injured by the negligence of others, the poor, and the accused. The law's greatest responsibility is to protect the weakest members of our society. Rich people can usually take care of themselves.

Big business, through its myriad support groups and associations, is successfully coordinating a grand conspiracy to drastically change our court system. Why? To protect its own interests. How? By blocking the courthouse door; by limiting liability for companies that make defective products, for negligent doctors, for abusive nursing homes, for arrogant insurance companies. The sad list went on.

She finished with a folksy paragraph asking the voters not to be fooled by slick marketing. The typical campaign run by big business in these races gets very ugly. Mud is their favorite tool. The attack ads would soon begin, and they would be relentless. Big business would spend millions to defeat her, but she had faith in the voters.

———

Barry Rinehart was impressed with the response. He was also delighted to see the trial lawyers rally so quickly and spend so much money. He wanted them to burn money. The high end of his projection was

$2 million for the McCarthy camp, with 90 percent from the trial lawyers.

His boy Fisk could easily double that.

His next ad, again by direct mail, was a sucker punch that would quickly dominate the rest of the campaign. He waited a week, time for the dust to settle from the first exchange of jabs.

The letter came straight from Ron Fisk himself, on his campaign letterhead, with a photo at the top of the handsome Fisk family. Its ominous headline announced: "Mississippi Supreme Court to Rule on Gay Marriage."

After a warm greeting, Ron wasted no time in launching into the issue at hand. The case of *Meyerchec and Spano v. Hinds County* involved two gay men who wanted to get married, and it would be decided the following year by the supreme court. Ron Fisk—Christian, husband, father, lawyer— was adamantly opposed to same-sex marriages, and he would take this unshakable belief to the supreme court. He condemned such unions as abnormal, sinful, against the clear teachings of the Bible, and detrimental to society on many levels.

Halfway through the letter, he introduced

to the fray the well-known voice of the Reverend David Wilfong, a national loudmouth with a huge radio following. Wilfong decried such efforts to pervert our laws and bend, yet again, to the desires of an immoral few. He denounced liberal judges who insert their own beliefs into their rulings. He called upon the decent and God-fearing people of Mississippi, "the heart and soul of the Bible Belt," to embrace men like Ron Fisk and, in doing so, protect their state's sacred laws.

The liberal-judge theme continued to the end of the letter. Fisk signed off with another promise to serve as a conservative, commonsense voice of the people.

———

Sheila McCarthy read the letter with Nat, and neither knew what the next step should be. Her name was never mentioned, but then it really wasn't necessary. Fisk certainly wasn't accusing Clete Coley of being a liberal.

"This is deadly," Nat said, exasperated. "He has claimed this issue as his own, and to take it back, or even to share it, you have to pulverize homosexuals worse than he does."

"I'm not doing that."

"I know you're not."

"It is so improper for a member of the court, or one who aspires to be, to state how he or she will decide a future case. It's horrible."

"This is just the beginning, dear."

They were in the cramped storage room that Nat called his office. The door was shut, no one was listening. A dozen volunteers were busy in the adjacent room. Phones rang constantly.

"I'm not sure we answer this," Nat said.

"Why not?"

"What are you going to say? 'Ron Fisk is being mean.' 'Ron Fisk is saying things he shouldn't.' You'll come off looking bitchy, which is okay for a male candidate, but not for a female."

"That's not fair."

"The only response is a denial of your support for same-sex marriages. You would have to take a position, which—"

"Which I'm not going to do. I'm not in favor of these marriages, but we need some type of civil union arrangement. It's a ridiculous debate, though, because the legislature is in charge of making laws. Not the court."

Nat was on his fourth wife. Sheila was looking for husband number two. "And besides," she said, "how could homosexuals possibly screw up the sanctity of marriage any worse than heterosexuals?"

"Promise me you'll never say that in public. Please."

"You know I won't."

He rubbed his hands together, then ran his fingers through his long gray hair. Indecisiveness was not one of his shortcomings. "We have to make a decision, here and now," he said. "We can't waste time. The smartest route is to answer by direct mail."

"What's the cost?"

"We can scale back some. I'd say two hundred thousand."

"Can we afford it?"

"As of today, I would say no. Let's revisit it in ten days."

"Agreed, but can't we do an e-mail blast and at least respond?"

"I've already written it."

The response was a two-paragraph message sent that day to forty-eight thousand e-mail addresses. Justice McCarthy issued a strong rebuke to Ron Fisk for pledging his vote on a case he was far away from hearing. Had he been a member of the court, he would have been chastised. Dignity demands that the justices keep matters confidential and refrain from any comment whatsoever about pending cases. In the one he mentioned, no briefs had been filed in the appeal. No arguments heard. Nothing was before the court as of this date. Without knowing the facts or the law, how could Mr. Fisk, or anyone else for that matter, possibly decide on a final ruling?

Sadly, it was just another example of Mr. Fisk's woeful inexperience in judicial matters.

———

Clete Coley's losses were piling up at the Lucky Jack, and he confided this to Marlin late one night in a saloon in Under-the-Hill. Marlin was passing through, checking on the candidate, who seemed to have forgotten about the race.

"I have a great idea," Marlin said, warming up to the real reason for his visit. "There are fourteen casinos on the Gulf Coast, big, beautiful, Vegas-style—"

"I've seen them."

"Right. I know the guy who owns Pirate's Cove. He'll put you up three nights a week for the next month, penthouse suite, great view of the Gulf. Meals are on the house. You can play cards all night, and during the day you can do a bit of campaigning. Folks down there need to hear your message. Hell, that's where the votes are. I can line up some audiences. You do the politicking. You've got a great speech and people love it."

Clete was visibly taken with the idea. "Three nights a week, huh?"

"More if you want it. You gotta be tired of this place."

"Only when I'm losing."

"Do it, Clete. Look, the folks who put up the money would like to see more activity. They know it's a long shot, but they are serious about their message."

Clete admitted it was a great idea. He ordered more rum and began thinking of those beautiful new casinos down there.

CHAPTER 24

Mary Grace and Wes stepped off the elevator on the twenty-sixth floor of the tallest building in Mississippi, and into the plush reception suite of the state's largest law firm. She immediately noticed the wallpaper, the fine furniture, the flowers, things that had once mattered.

The well-dressed woman at the desk was sufficiently polite. An associate in the standard-issue navy suit and black shoes escorted them to a conference room, where a secretary asked if they wanted something to drink. No, they did not. The large windows looked down at the rest of Jackson.

The dome of the capitol dominated the view. To its left was the Gartin building, and somewhere in there on someone's desk was the case of *Jeannette Baker v. Krane Chemical.*

The door opened and Alan York appeared with a big smile and warm handshake. He was in his late fifties, short and heavy and a bit sloppy—wrinkled shirt, no jacket, scuffed shoes—unusual for a partner in such a hidebound firm. The same associate was back, carrying two large expandable files. After greetings and small talk they took their places around the table.

The lawsuit the Paytons filed in April on behalf of the family of the deceased pulp-wood cutter had sped through the early rounds of discovery. No trial date was set, and that possibility was at least a year away. Liability was clear—the truck driver who caused the accident had been speeding, at least fifteen miles per hour over the limit. Two eyewitnesses had been deposed and provided detailed and damning testimony about the speed and recklessness of the truck driver. In his deposition, the driver admitted to a long history of moving violations. Before taking to the road, he worked as a pipe fitter but had been fired for smoking pot on the job. Wes had found at least two old DUIs, and the driver thought there might be another one, but he couldn't remember.

In short, the case wouldn't get anywhere near a jury. It would be settled, and after four months of vigorous discovery Mr. Alan York was ready to begin the negotiations. According to him, his client, Littun Casualty, was anxious to close the file.

Wes began by describing the family, a thirty-three-year-old widow and mother with a high school education and no real job skills and three young children, the oldest being twelve. Needless to say, the loss was ruinous in every way.

As he talked, York took notes and kept glancing at Mary Grace. They had spoken on the phone but never met. Wes was handling the case, but York knew she was not there simply because she was pleasant to look at. One of his close friends was Frank Sully, the Hattiesburg lawyer hired by Krane Chemical to add bodies to the defense table. Sully had been pushed to the rear by Jared Kurtin and was still bitter about it. He had passed along to York many stories about the *Baker* trial, and it was Sully's opinion that the Payton tag team worked best when Mary Grace was chatting with the jury. She was tough on cross-examination, very quick on her feet, but her strength was connecting with people. Her closing argument was brilliant, powerful, and, obviously, very persuasive.

York had been defending insurance companies for thirty-one years. He won more than he lost, but there had been a few of those awful moments when juries failed to see the case his way and nailed him for big verdicts. It was part of the business. He had never, though, been in the neighborhood of a $41 million award. It was now a legend in the state's legal circles. Add the drama of the Paytons risking everything, losing their home, office, cars, and borrowing heavily to sustain a four-month trial, and the legend kept growing. Their fate was well-known and much discussed at bar meetings and golf tournaments and cocktail parties. If the verdict stood, they would be primed to rake in huge fees. A reversal, and their survival was seriously in doubt.

As Wes went on, York couldn't help but admire them.

After a brief review of the liability, Wes

summed up the damages, added a chunk for the carelessness of the trucking company, and said, "We think two million is a fair settlement."

"I bet you do," York said, managing the customary defense lawyer reaction of shock and dismay. Eyebrows arched in disbelief. Head shaking slowly in bewilderment. He grabbed his face with his hand and squeezed his cheeks, frowning. His quick smile was long gone.

Wes and Mary Grace managed to convey apathy while their hearts were frozen.

"To get two million," York said, studying his notes, "you have to factor in some element of punitive damages, and, frankly, my client is simply not willing to pay these."

"Oh yes," Mary Grace said coolly. "Your client will pay whatever the jury tells it to pay." Such blustering was also part of the business. York had heard it a thousand times, but it did indeed sound more ominous coming from a woman who, during her last trial, extracted a huge punitive award.

"A trial is at least twelve months away," York said as he looked at his associate for confirmation, as if anyone could project a trial date so far in the future. The associate dutifully confirmed what his boss had already said.

In other words, if this goes to trial, it will be months before you receive a dime in fees. It's no secret that your little firm is drowning in debt and struggling to survive, and everyone knows that you need a big settlement, and quick.

"Your client can't wait that long," York said.

"We've given you a number, Alan," Wes replied. "Do you have a counteroffer?"

York suddenly slapped his file shut, gave a forced grin, and said, "Look, this is really simple. Littun Casualty is very good at cutting its losses, and this case is a loser. My authority to settle is $1 million. Not a penny more. I have a million bucks, and my client told me not to come back for more. One million dollars, take it or leave it."

The referring lawyer would get half of the 30 percent contingency contract. The Paytons would get the other half. Fifteen percent was $150,000, a dream.

They looked at each other, both frowning, both wanting to leap across the table and begin kissing Alan York. Then Wes shook his head, and Mary Grace wrote something on a legal pad.

"We have to call our client," Wes said.

"Of course." York bolted from the room, his associate racing to keep up.

"Well," Wes said softly, as if the room might be bugged.

"I'm trying not to cry," she said.

"Don't cry. Don't laugh. Let's squeeze him a little."

When York was back, Wes said gravely, "We talked to Mrs. Nolan. Her bottom line is one point two million."

York exhaled as his shoulders drooped and his face sagged. "I don't have it, Wes," he said. "I'm being perfectly candid with you."

"You can always ask for more. If your client will pay a million, then they can kick in another $200,000. At trial, this case is worth twice that."

"Littun is a tough bunch, Wes."

"One phone call. Give it a try. What's there to lose?"

York left again, and ten minutes later burst back into the room with a happy face. "You got it! Congratulations."

The shock of the settlement left them numb. Negotiations usually dragged on for weeks or months, with both sides bickering and posturing and playing little games. They had hoped to leave York's office with a general idea of where the settlement might be headed. Instead, they left in a daze and for fifteen minutes roamed the streets of downtown Jackson, saying little. For a moment they stopped in front of the Capitol Grill, a restaurant known more for its clientele than for its food. Lobbyists liked to be seen there, picking up tabs for fine meals with heavyweight politicians. Governors had always favored the place.

Why not splurge and eat with the big boys?

Instead, they ducked into a small deli two doors down and ordered iced tea. Neither had an appetite at the moment. Wes finally addressed the obvious. "Did we just earn $180,000?"

"Uh-huh," she said while sipping tea through a straw.

"I thought so."

"A third goes for taxes," she said.

"Are you trying to kill the party?"

"No, just being practical."

On a white paper napkin, she wrote down the sum of $180,000.

"Are we spending it already?" Wes asked.

"No, we're dividing it. Sixty thousand for taxes?"

"Fifty."

"Income, state and federal. Employee withholding, Social Security, unemployment, I don't know what else but it's at least a third."

"Fifty-five," he said, and she wrote down $60,000.

"Bonuses?"

"What about a new car?" he asked.

"Nope. Bonuses, for all five employees. They have not had a raise in three years."

"Five thousand each."

She wrote down $25,000, then said, "The bank."

"A new car."

"The bank? Half the fee is already gone."

"Two hundred dollars."

"Come on, Wes. We won't have a life until the bank is off our backs."

"I've tried to forget about the loan."

"How much?"

"I don't know. I'm sure you have a figure."

"Fifty thousand for Huffy, and ten thousand for Sheila McCarthy. That leaves us with thirty-five thousand." Which, at that moment, seemed like a fortune. They stared at the napkin, both recasting the numbers and rearranging the priorities, but neither willing to suggest a change. Mary Grace signed her name at the bottom, then Wes did likewise. She put the napkin in her purse.

"Can I at least get a new suit out of the deal?" he asked.

"Depends on what's on sale. I guess we should call the office."

"They're sitting by the phone."

Three hours later, the Paytons walked into their office, and the party started. The front door was locked, the phones were unplugged, the champagne began to flow. Sherman and Rusty, the law clerks, proposed lengthy toasts they had hurriedly put together. Tabby and Vicky, the receptionists, were tipsy after two glasses. Even Olivia, the ancient bookkeeper, kicked up her heels and was soon laughing at everything.

The money was spent, re-spent, overspent, until everyone was rich.

When the champagne was gone, the office closed and everyone left. The Paytons, their cheeks warm from the bubbly, went to their apartment, changed into casual clothes, then drove to the school to fetch Mack and Liza. They had earned a night of fun, though the children were too young to understand the settlement. It would never be mentioned.

Mack and Liza were expecting Ramona, and when they saw both parents in the school pickup line, a long day instantly became brighter. Wes explained that they simply got tired of working and decided to play. The first stop was Baskin-Robbins for ice cream. Next, they went to a shopping mall, where a shoe store attracted their attention. Each Payton picked out a pair, at 50 percent off, with Mack being the boldest with a pair of Marine combat boots. In the center of the mall was a four-screen cinema. They caught the 6:00 p.m. showing of the latest Harry Potter. Dinner was at a family pizzeria with an indoor playground and a rowdy atmosphere. They finally made it home around ten, where Ramona was watching television and enjoying the quiet. The kids handed her leftover pizza, and both talked at once about the movie. They promised to finish their homework in the morning. Mary Grace relented, and the entire family settled onto the sofa and watched a reality rescue show. Bedtime was pushed back to eleven.

When the apartment was quiet and the kids tucked in, Wes and Mary Grace lay on the sofa, heads on opposite ends, legs tangled together, minds drifting far away. For the past four years, as their finances had spiraled downward, with one loss after another, one humiliation following the last, fear had become a daily companion. Fear of losing the home, then the office, then the autos. Fear of not being able to provide for their children. Fear of a serious medical emergency that exceeded their insurance. Fear of losing the *Baker* trial. Fear of bankruptcy if the bank pushed too hard.

Since the verdict, the fear had become more of a nuisance than a constant threat. It was always there, but they had slowly gained control of it. For six straight months now, they had paid the bank $2,000 a month, hard-earned moneys that were left over after all other bills and expenses. It barely covered the interest, and it reminded them of how insurmountable their debt was. But it was symbolic. They were digging out from the rubble and could see the light.

Now, for the first time in years, there was a cushion, a safety net, something to catch them if they fell even deeper. They would take their share of today's settlement and hide it, and when they were afraid again, they would be comforted by their buried treasure.

———

At ten the following morning, Wes dropped by the bank and found Huffy at his desk. He swore him to silence, then whispered the good news. Huffy almost hugged him. Mr. Prickhead was on his back from nine to five, demanding action.

"The money should be here in a couple of weeks," Wes said proudly. "I'll call as soon as it lands."

"Fifty grand, Wes?" Huffy repeated, as if his job had just been saved.

"You got it."

From there Wes drove to his office. Tabby handed him a phone message from Alan

York. Just routine stuff, probably some details to nail down.

But York's voice lacked its usual warmth. "Wes, there's a new wrinkle," he said slowly, as if searching for words.

"What's the matter?" Wes asked. A knot was already forming in his stomach.

"I don't know, Wes, I'm really frustrated, and confused. This has never happened to me, but, well, anyway, Littun Casualty has flipped on the settlement. It's off the table, all of it. They're yanking it. Some tough A-holes. I've been yelling at them all morning. They yell back. This firm has represented the company for eighteen years, never had a problem like this. But, as of one hour ago, they are looking for another firm. I've fired the client. I gave you my word, and now my client has hung me out to dry. I'm sorry, Wes. Don't know what else to say."

Wes pinched the bridge of his nose and tried not to groan. After a false start, he said, "Well, Alan, this is a shock."

"Damned right it is, but in all fairness it does no harm to the lawsuit. I'm just glad this didn't happen the day before the trial or something crazy like that. Some real bad boys up there."

"They won't be so tough at trial."

"Damned right, Wes. I hope you nail these guys for another huge verdict."

"We will."

"I'm sorry, Wes."

"It's not your fault, Alan. We'll survive and push for a trial."

"You do that."

"We'll talk later."

"Sure. Say, Wes, is your cell phone nearby?"

"It's right here."

"Here's my cell number. Hang up and call me back."

When both men were off the landlines, York said, "You didn't hear this from me, okay?"

"Okay."

"The chief in-house lawyer for Littun Casualty is a guy named Ed Larrimore. For twenty years he was a partner in a New York law firm called Bradley & Backstrom. His brother is also a partner at that firm. Bradley & Backstrom does the blue-chip thing, and one of its clients is KDN, the oil exploration firm whose biggest shareholder is Carl Trudeau. That's the connection. I have never talked to Ed Larrimore, there's no reason to.

But the supervising attorney I deal with whispered to me that a decision was made at the very top to stiff this settlement."

"A little retribution, huh?"

"Smells like it. It's nothing illegal or unethical. The insurance company decides not to settle and goes to trial. Happens every day. There's nothing you can do about it, except burn them at trial. Littun Casualty has assets of twenty billion, so they aren't worried about a jury in Pike County, Mississippi. My guess is they'll drag it out until you get to trial, then try to settle."

"I'm not sure what to say, Alan."

"I'm sorry this happened, Wes. I'm out of the picture now, and you didn't get this from me."

"Sure."

Wes stared at the wall for a long time, then mustered the energy to stand, walk, leave his office, and go look for his wife.

CHAPTER 25

Like clockwork, Ron Fisk kissed Doreen goodbye at the front door at six o'clock on a Wednesday morning, then handed his overnight bag and briefcase to Monte. Guy was waiting in the SUV. Both assistants waved to Doreen, then they sped away. It was the last Wednesday in September, week twenty-one of his campaign, and the twenty-first consecutive Wednesday that he had kissed his wife goodbye at 6:00 a.m. Tony Zachary could not have found a more disciplined candidate.

In the rear seat, Monte handed Ron his daily briefing. One of Tony's deputies in

Jackson prepared it during the night and e-mailed it to Monte at exactly five each morning. Page 1 was the schedule. Page 2 was a summary of the three groups he would address that day, along with the names of the important people who would attend.

Page 3 had updates from his opponents' campaigns. It was all mainly gossip but still his favorite part of the briefing. Clete Coley was last seen addressing a small group of sheriffs' deputies in Hancock County, then retiring to the blackjack tables at Pirate's Cove. Today, McCarthy is expected to be at work and has no campaign events.

Page 4 was the financial summary. Contributions so far totaled $1.7 million, with 75 percent coming from within the state. Expenditures of $1.8 million. The deficit was of no concern. Tony Zachary knew the heavy money would arrive in October. McCarthy had received $1.4 million, virtually all from trial lawyers. She had spent half of it. The prevailing thought in the Fisk camp was that the trial lawyers were tapped out.

They were at the airport. The King Air lifted off at 6:30, and at that moment Fisk was on the phone to Tony in Jackson. It was their first chat of the day. Everything was running smoothly. Fisk had already reached the point of believing that all campaigns were so effortless. He was always prompt, fresh, prepared, rested, well financed, and ready to move on to the next event. He had little contact with the two dozen people under Tony's thumb who sweated the details.

———

Justice McCarthy's version of the daily briefing was a glass of fruit juice with Nat Lester at her Jackson headquarters. She aimed for 8:30 each morning, and was fairly prompt. By then, Nat had put in two hours and was yelling at people.

They had no interest in the whereabouts of her two opponents. They spent little time with poll numbers. Their data showed her running even with Fisk, and that was troubling enough. They quickly reviewed the latest fund-raising schemes and talked about potential donors.

"I may have a new problem," she said that morning.

"Only one?"

"Do you remember the Frankie Hightower case?"

"Not at this moment, no."

"State trooper was gunned down in Grenada County five years ago. He stopped a car for speeding. Inside the car were three black men and a black teenager, Frankie Hightower. Someone opened fire with an assault weapon, and the trooper got hit eight times. Left him in the middle of Highway 51."

"Let me guess. The court has reached a decision."

"The court is getting close. Six of my colleagues are ready to affirm the conviction."

"Let me guess. You would like to dissent."

"I'm going to dissent. The kid had inadequate counsel. His defense lawyer was some jackass with no experience and apparently very little intelligence. The trial was a joke. The other three thugs pled for life and pointed the finger at Hightower, who was sixteen years old and sitting in the backseat, without a gun. Yes, I'm going to dissent."

Nat's sandals hit the floor and he began to pace. Arguing the merits of the case was a waste of time. Arguing the politics of it would take some skill. "Coley will go ballistic."

"I don't care about Coley. He's a clown."

"Clowns get votes."

"He's not a factor."

"Fisk will receive it as a wonderful gift from God. More proof that his campaign is divinely inspired. Manna from heaven. I can see the ads now."

"I'm dissenting, Nat. It's that simple."

"It's never that simple. Some of the voters might understand what you're doing and admire your courage. Perhaps three or four of them. The rest will see the Fisk ad with the smiling face of that handsome young state trooper next to the mug shot of Frankie whatever his name is."

"Hightower."

"Thank you. The ad will refer to liberal judges at least ten times, and it will probably show your face. Powerful stuff. You might as well quit now."

His words trailed off but were bitter nonetheless. For a long time they said nothing. Sheila broke the silence by saying, "That's not a bad idea. Quitting. I've caught myself reading the briefs and asking, 'What will the voters think if I rule this way or that?'

I'm not a judge anymore, Nat, I'm a politician."

"You're a great judge, Sheila. One of the three we have left."

"It's all about politics now."

"You're not quitting. Have you written your dissent?"

"I'm working on it."

"Look, Sheila, the election is five weeks away. How slow can you write? Hell, the court is famous for taking its sweet time. Surely to God you can sit on this thing until after the election. What's five weeks? It's nothing. The murder was five years ago." He was stomping around, arms flailing.

"We do have a schedule."

"Bullshit. You can manipulate it."

"For politics."

"Damned right, Sheila. Give me a break here. We're busting our asses for you and you act like you're too good for the dirty work. This is a filthy business, okay?"

"Lower your voice."

He lowered it several octaves but kept pacing. Three steps to one wall, then three steps to the other. "Your dissent is not going to change a damned thing. The court will run over you again 6 to 3, maybe even 7 to 2, perhaps even 8 to 1. The numbers don't really matter. The conviction is affirmed, and Frankie Whoever will stay exactly where he is right now and where he'll be ten years from now. Don't be stupid, Sheila."

She finished her fruit juice and did not respond.

"I don't like that smirk," Nat said. He pointed a long bony finger at her. "Listen to me. If you file a dissent before the election, I'm walking out the door."

"Don't threaten me."

"I'm not threatening. I'm promising. You know ten different ways to sit on that case for another five weeks. Hell, you could bury it for six months."

She stood and said, "I'm going to work."

"I'm not kidding!" he yelled. "I'll quit!"

She yanked open the door and said, "Go find us some money."

———

Three days later, the skillfully coordinated avalanche began. Only a handful of people knew what was coming.

Ron Fisk himself did not comprehend the scope of his own saturation. He had performed for the cameras, changed into various outfits, worked his way through the scripts, dragged in his family and some friends, and he was aware of the budget and the media buys and the market shares of the various television stations in south Mississippi. And, in a normal campaign, he would have worried about financing such expensive marketing.

But the machine that bore his name had many parts he knew nothing about.

The first ads were the soft ones—warm little vignettes to open the doors and let this fine young man into the homes. Ron as a Boy Scout, with the richly accented old voice of an actor playing the role of his scoutmaster in the background. "One of the finest Boy Scouts we ever had. He made it to Eagle in less than three years." Ron in a robe at high school graduation, a star student. Ron with Doreen and the kids and his own voice saying, "Families are our greatest asset." After thirty seconds, the ad signed off with the slogan, in a deep, heavenly voice, "Ron Fisk, a judge with our values."

A second ad, a series of black-and-white still photos, began with Ron on the steps of his church, in a fine dark suit, chatting with his pastor, who narrated, "Ron Fisk was ordained as a deacon in this church twelve years ago." Ron with his jacket off, teaching Sunday school. Ron holding his Bible as he makes a point to a group of teenagers under a shade tree. "Thank God for men like Ron Fisk." Ron and Doreen greeting people at the church's door. And the same farewell: "Ron Fisk, a judge with our values."

There was not the slightest hint of conflict, nothing about the campaign, not a trace of mud, no indication of the savagery that would follow. Just a charming hello from an incredibly wholesome young deacon.

The ads blanketed south Mississippi, and central as well because Tony Zachary was paying the steep prices charged by the Jackson outlets.

———

September 30 was a crucial date on Barry Rinehart's calendar. All contributions made in the month of October would not be reported until November 10, six days after the election. The flood of out-of-state money he was about to unleash would go undetected until it was too late. The losers would scream, but that was all they could do.

On September 30, Rinehart and company kicked into high gear. They began with their A-list: tort-reform groups, right-wing religious organizations, business lobbyists, business PACs, and hundreds of conservative organizations ranging from the well-known American Rifle Association to the obscure Zero Future Tax, a small gang dedicated to abolishing the Internal Revenue Service. Eleven hundred and forty groups in all fifty states. Rinehart sent each a detailed memo and request for an immediate donation to the Fisk campaign in the amount of $2,500, the maximum for an organized entity. From this collection, his goal was $500,000.

For the individuals—$5,000 maximum gift—Rinehart had a list of a thousand corporate executives and senior managers of companies in industries that attracted litigation from trial lawyers. Chief among these were insurance companies, and he would collect a million dollars from his contacts there. Carl Trudeau had given him the names of two hundred executives of companies controlled by the Trudeau Group, though no one from Krane Chemical would write a check. If the Fisk campaign took money from Krane, then a front-page story was likely. Fisk might feel compelled to recuse himself, a disaster Rinehart couldn't begin to contemplate.

He expected $1 million from Carl's boys, though it would not go directly into the Fisk campaign. To keep their names away from nosy reporters, and to make sure no one ever knew of Mr. Trudeau's involvement, Rinehart routed their money into the bank accounts for Lawsuit Victims for Truth and Gunowners United Now (GUN).

His B-list contained a thousand names of donors with proven records of supporting pro-business candidates, though not at the $5,000 level. He expected another $500,000.

Three million dollars was his goal, and he was not at all concerned about reaching it.

CHAPTER 26

In the excitement of the moment, Huffy had made a dreadful mistake. The expectation of a meaningful payment, coupled with the constant pressure from Mr. Prickhead, had caused a lapse in judgment.

Not long after Wes stopped by with the promise of $50,000, Huffy marched into the big office and proudly informed his boss that the Paytons' debt was about to be reduced. When he got the bad news two days later that it was not, he was too afraid to tell anyone.

After losing sleep for almost a week, he finally forced himself to confront the devil again. He stepped in front of the massive desk, swallowed hard, and said, "Some bad news, sir."

"Where's the money?" Mr. Kirkhead demanded.

"It's not going to happen, sir. Their settlement fell through."

Forgoing curse words, Mr. Prickhead said, "We're calling the loan. Do it now."

"What?"

"You heard me."

"We can't do that. They've been paying two thousand a month."

"Super. That doesn't even cover the interest. Call the loan. Now."

"But why?"

"Just a couple of small reasons, Huffy. Number one, it's been in default for at least a year. Number two, it's grossly under-collateralized. As a banker, certainly you can understand these small problems."

"But they're trying."

"Call the loan. Do it now, and if you don't, then you'll be either reassigned or dismissed."

"That's obscene."

"I don't care what you think." Then he relented a bit and said, "It's not my decision,

Huffy. We have new ownership, and I have been ordered to call the loan."

"But why?"

Kirkhead picked up the phone and offered it. "You want to call the man in Dallas?"

"This will bankrupt them."

"They've been bankrupt for a long time. Now they can make it official."

"Son of a bitch."

"Talking to me, son?"

Huffy glared at the fat hairless head, then said, "Not really. More to that son of a bitch in Dallas."

"We'll keep that here, okay?"

Huffy returned to his office, slammed the door, and watched the walls while an hour passed. Prickhead would stop by soon for the follow-up.

———

Wes was in a deposition downtown. Mary Grace was at her desk and took the call.

She admired Huffy for his bravery in extending much more credit than anyone had thought possible, but the sound of his voice always rattled her. "Good morning, Tom," she said pleasantly.

"It's not a good morning, Mary Grace," he began. "It's a bad morning, an awful morning, one of the worst ever."

A heavy pause. "I'm listening."

"The bank, not the bank you've been dealing with but another bank now, one owned by some people I've met only once and never care to see again, has decided that it can no longer wait to be paid. The bank, not me, is calling the loan."

Mary Grace emitted a strange guttural sound that could have passed for an expletive but really wasn't a word at all. Her first thought was of her father. Other than the Paytons' signatures, the only security for the loan was a two-hundred-acre tract of farmland her father had owned for many years. It was near Bowmore, and it did not include the forty acres and family home. The bank would foreclose on the property.

"Any particular reason, Huffy?" she asked coolly.

"None whatsoever. The decision was not made in Hattiesburg. Second State sold out to the devil, if you will recall."

"This doesn't make sense."

"I agree."

"You'll force us into bankruptcy, and the bank will get nothing."

"Except for the farm."

"So you'll foreclose on the farm?"

"Someone will. I hope not me."

"Smart move, Huffy, because when they foreclose on the courthouse steps in Bowmore there might be a killing."

"Maybe they'll get ole Prickhead."

"Are you in your office?"

"Yes, with the door locked."

"Wes is downtown. He'll be there in fifteen minutes. Unlock the door."

"No."

———

Fifteen minutes later, Wes charged into Huffy's office, his cheeks red with anger, his hands ready to strangle. "Where's Prickhead?" he demanded.

Huffy jumped to his feet behind his desk and placed both hands in the air. "Be cool, Wes."

"Where's Prickhead?"

"Right now he's in his car, driving to an urgent meeting, one that suddenly materialized ten minutes ago. Sit down, Wes."

Wes took a deep breath, then slowly

eased into a chair. Huffy watched him, then returned to his own chair. "It's not his fault, Wes," Huffy said. "Technically, the loan has been in default for almost two years. He could have done this months ago, but he didn't. I know you don't like him. I don't like him. His wife doesn't like him. But he's been very patient. This was a decision made in the home office."

"Give me a name at the home office."

Huffy slid across a letter he'd received by fax. It was addressed to the Paytons, on New Vista Bank letterhead, and signed by a Mr. F. Patterson Duvall, vice president. "This arrived thirty minutes ago," Huffy said. "I don't know Mr. Duvall. I've called his office twice, but he's in a very important meeting, one that I'm sure will last until we stop calling. It's a waste of time, Wes."

The letter demanded payment in full of $414,656.22, with daily interest kicking in at $83.50. Pursuant to the terms of the loan agreement, the Paytons had forty-eight hours to pay, or collection and foreclosure proceedings would commence. Of course, the resulting attorneys' fees and court costs would also be tacked on to the amount due.

Wes read it slowly as he continued to cool

down. He placed it back on the desk. "Mary Grace and I talk about this loan every day, Huffy. It's a part of our marriage. We talk about the kids, the office, the debt to the bank, what's for dinner. It's always there, and we've busted our asses to pay off all other obligations so we can bust our asses to pay off the bank. We came very close to giving you fifty thousand last week. We vowed to work ourselves ragged until this bank is out of our lives. Now this stunt. Now some moron in Dallas has decided he's tired of seeing this past-due loan on his daily rap sheet, and he wants to get rid of it. You know what, Huffy—"

"What?"

"The bank just screwed itself. We'll file for bankruptcy, and when you try to foreclose on my father-in-law's property, I'll put him in bankruptcy. And when we work our way out of bankruptcy, and we're back on our feet, guess who ain't getting paid."

"The moron in Dallas?"

"You got it. The bank gets nothing. It'll be wonderful. We can keep the $400,000 when we earn it."

———

Late that afternoon, Wes and Mary Grace called a firm meeting in The Pit. Other than the humiliation of filing for bankruptcy, which seemed to bother no one, there was little to worry about. In fact, the bank's actions would give the firm some breathing room. The $2,000 monthly payments would cease, and the cash could certainly be used elsewhere.

The concern, of course, was the land owned by Mr. Shelby, Mary Grace's father. Wes had a plan. He would find a friendly buyer who would appear at the foreclosure and write a check. Title would pass, and it would be held in "a handshake trust" until the Paytons could buy it back, hopefully within a year. Neither Wes nor Mary Grace could stomach the idea of asking her father to join them at the bankruptcy court.

Forty-eight hours passed with no payment. Sticking to its word, the bank filed suit. Its lawyer, a local gentleman the Paytons knew well, called ahead of time and apologized. He'd represented the bank for years and could not afford to lose it as a client. Mary Grace accepted his apology and gave him her blessing to sue them.

The next day the Paytons filed for bankruptcy, both individually and as Payton & Payton, Attorneys-at-Law. They listed combined assets of $35,000—two old cars, furniture, office equipment—all of which was protected. They listed debts of $420,000. The filing effectively stayed the lawsuit, and would eventually render it useless. The *Hattiesburg American* reported it on its second page the following day.

Carl Trudeau read about it online and laughed out loud. "Sue me again," he said with great satisfaction.

Within a week, three Hattiesburg law firms informed ole Prickhead that they were withdrawing their funds, closing their accounts, and moving their business down the street. There were at least eight other banks in town.

A wealthy trial lawyer named Jim McMay called Wes and offered assistance. The two had been friends for many years and had collaborated twice on product liability cases. McMay represented four Bowmore families in the Krane litigation, but had not pushed the cases aggressively. Like the other trial lawyers suing Krane, he was waiting for the outcome of *Baker* and hoping to

hit the jackpot if and when there was a settlement.

They met for breakfast at Nanny's, and
over biscuits and country ham McMay readily agreed to rescue the two hundred acres
at foreclosure and keep the title until the
Paytons could buy it back. Farmland in
Cancer County wasn't exactly selling at a
premium, and Wes speculated that the
Shelby property would fetch around
$100,000, the only money the bank would
collect from its foolish maneuver.

CHAPTER 27

Sheila McCarthy was enduring the morning's torture on the treadmill when she hit the stop button and gawked at the television in disbelief. The ad ran at 7:29, smack in the middle of the local news. It began with the provocative sight of two well-dressed young men kissing passionately while a minister of some variety smiled behind them. A husky voice-over announced, "Same-sex marriages are sweeping the country. In places like Massachusetts, New York, and California, laws are being challenged. Advocates of gay and lesbian marriages are pushing hard to force their lifestyles on the rest of our society." A still photo of a wedding couple—male and female—at the altar was suddenly desecrated with a bold black X. "Liberal judges are sympathetic to the rights of same-sex marriages." The photo was replaced with a video of a group of happy lesbians waiting to tie the knot in a mass ceremony. "Our families are under attack from homosexual activists and the liberal judges who support them." Next was a quick video of a mob burning an American flag. The voice said, "Liberal judges have approved the burning of our flag." Then a quick shot of a magazine rack lined with copies of *Hustler*. "Liberal judges see nothing wrong with pornography." Then a photo of a smiling family, mother and father and four children. "Will liberal judges destroy our families?" the narrator inquired ominously, leaving little doubt that they would if given half a chance. The family photo was ripped apart into two jagged pieces. Suddenly the handsome but serious face of Ron Fisk appeared. He looked sincerely at the camera and said, "Not in Mississippi. One man. One woman. I'm Ron Fisk, candidate for the supreme court. And I approved this ad."

Dripping with sweat, her heart pounding even faster, Sheila sat on the floor and tried to think. The weatherman was prattling on, but she didn't hear him. She lay down on her back, stretched out her arms and legs, and took deep breaths.

Gay marriage was a dead issue in Mississippi and would remain so forever. No one with an audience or a following had dared to suggest that the laws be changed to allow it. Every member of the state legislature could be expected to rail against it. Only one judge in the entire state—Phil Shingleton—had addressed it, and he had dismissed the Meyerchec/Spano lawsuit in record speed. The supreme court would probably deal with that case in a year or so, but Sheila expected a rather terse review followed by a quick 9–0 vote affirming Judge Shingleton.

How, exactly, had she now been cast as a liberal judge who supported gay marriage?

The room was spinning. At a commercial break, she tensed and waited for another assault, but there was nothing but the squawking of a car dealer and frantic urgings of a discount-furniture retailer.

Fifteen minutes later, though, the ad was

back. She lifted her head and watched in disbelief as the same images followed the same voice.

Her phone was ringing. Caller ID told her not to answer. She showered and dressed in a hurry and at 8:30 walked into her headquarters with a wide smile and warm "Good morning." The four volunteers were subdued. Three televisions were running three different programs. Nat was in his office yelling at someone on the phone. He slammed the phone down, waved her inside, then closed the door behind her.

"You've seen it?" he said.

"Twice," she said softly. On the surface, she seemed unfazed. Everyone else was rattled, and it was important to at least try to appear calm.

"Total saturation," he said. "Jackson, Gulf Coast, Hattiesburg, Laurel, every fifteen minutes on all stations. Plus radio."

"What kind of juice do you have?"

"Carrot," he said and opened his small refrigerator. "They're burning money, which, of course, means they're raking it in by the truckload. Typical ambush. Wait until October 1, then push the button and start printing cash. They did it last year in Illinois and

Alabama. Two years ago in Ohio and Texas." He poured two cups as he spoke.

"Sit down and relax, Nat," she said. He did not.

"Attack ads must be answered in kind," he said. "And quickly."

"I'm not sure this is an attack ad. He never mentions my name."

"He doesn't have to. How many liberal judges are running against Mr. Fisk?"

"None that I know of."

"As of this morning, dear, you are now officially a liberal judge."

"Really? I don't feel any different."

"We have to answer this, Sheila."

"I'm not getting dragged into a mudslinging fight over gay marriage."

Nat finally wiggled himself into his chair and shut up. He drank his juice, stared at the floor, and waited for his breathing to relax.

She took a sip of carrot juice, then said with a smile, "This is deadly, isn't it?"

"The juice?"

"The ad."

"Potentially, yes. But I'm working on something." He reached into a pile of rubble next to his desk and pulled out a thin file. He opened it and lifted three sheets of paper clipped together. "Listen to this. Mr. Meyerchec and Mr. Spano leased an apartment on April 1 of this year. We have a copy of the lease. They waited thirty days, as required by law, then registered to vote. The next day, May 2, they applied for Mississippi driver's licenses, took the exam, and passed. The Department of Public Safety issued licenses on May 4. A couple of months passed, during which there is no record of employment, business licenses, nothing official to indicate they were working here. Remember, they claim to be self-employed illustrators, whatever the hell that is." He was riffling through the papers, checking facts here and there. "A survey of the illustrators who advertise various services in the yellow pages revealed that no one knows Meyerchec or Spano. Their apartment is in a big complex, lots of units, lots of neighbors, none of whom can remember seeing them. In gay circles, not a single person who was contacted has ever met them."

"Contacted by whom?"

"Hang on. Then they try to get a marriage license, and the rest of the story has been in the newspapers."

"Contacted by whom?"

Nat arranged the papers in the file and closed it. "This is where it gets interesting. Last week I received a call from a young man who described himself as a gay law student here in Jackson. He gave me his name and the name of his partner, another law student. They're not in the closet, but not exactly ready for the Gay Pride Parade. They were intrigued by the Meyerchec/Spano case, and when it exploded into a campaign issue, they, like a few other folks with brains, began to get suspicious. They know a lot of the gays here in town, and they began to ask about Meyerchec and Spano. No one knows them. In fact, the gay community was suspicious from the day the lawsuit was filed. Who are these guys? Where did they come from? The law students decided to find the answers. They've called the Meyerchec/Spano phone number five times a day, at different hours, and never gotten an answer. For thirty-six days now, they've made their calls. No answer. They've talked to the neighbors. Never a sighting. No one saw them move in. They've knocked on the door, peeked in the windows. The apartment is barely furnished, nothing on the walls. To make themselves real citizens, Meyerchec and Spano paid $3,000 for a used Saab, titled in both names like a real married couple, then bought Mississippi car tags. The Saab is parked in front of their apartment and hasn't moved in thirty-six days."

"Where might this be going?" she asked.

"I'm getting there. Now, our two law students have found them, in Chicago, where Meyerchec owns a gay bar and Spano works as an interior designer. The students are willing, for a little cash, to fly to Chicago, spend a few days, hang out in the bar, infiltrate, gather information."

"Information for what?"

"Information that, hopefully, will prove that they are not residents of this state; that their presence here was a sham; that someone is using them to exploit the gay marriage issue; and maybe that they are not even a couple in Chicago. If we can prove that, then I'll go to the *Clarion-Ledger*, the Biloxi *Sun Herald*, and every other newspaper in the state and deliver the goods. We can't win a fight on this issue, dear, but we can damned sure fight back."

She drained her glass and shook her

head in disbelief. "Do you think Fisk is this smart?"

"Fisk is a pawn, but, yes, his handlers are this smart. It's a cynical scheme, and it's brilliant. No one thinks about gay marriage here because it will never happen, then, suddenly, everybody's talking about it. Front-page news. Everybody's scared. Mothers are hiding their children. Politicians are blathering."

"But why use two gay men from Chicago?"

"I'm not sure you can find two gay men in Mississippi who want this kind of publicity. Plus, gays here who are committed to tolerance understand the backlash from the straight world. The worst thing they could do is exactly what Meyerchec and Spano have done."

"If Meyerchec and Spano are gay, why would they do something to hurt the cause?"

"Two reasons. First, they don't live here. Second, money. Someone's paying the bills—the apartment lease, the used car, the lawyer, and a few thousand bucks to Meyerchec and Spano for their time and trouble."

Sheila had heard enough. She glanced at her watch and said, "How much do they need?"

"Expense money—airfare, hotel, the basics. Two thousand."

"Do we have it?" she asked with a laugh.

"It's out of my pocket. We'll keep it off the books. I just want you to know what we're doing."

"You have my approval."

"And the Frankie Hightower dissent?"

"I'm hard at work. Should take me another two months."

"Now you're talking like a real supreme court justice."

———

Denny Ott received a left-handed invitation to the meeting when a fellow preacher mentioned it to him over coffee one morning at Babe's. Not every minister in town was invited. Two from the Methodist churches and the Presbyterian pastor were specifically excluded, but it appeared as if all others were welcome. There was no Episcopal church in Bowmore, and if the town had a single Catholic, he or she had yet to come forward.

It was held on a Thursday afternoon in the fellowship hall of a fundamentalist congregation called Harvest Tabernacle. The moderator was the church's pastor, a fiery young man who was generally known as Brother Ted. After a quick prayer, he welcomed his fellow ministers, sixteen in number, including three black ministers. He cast a wary eye at Denny Ott, but said nothing about his presence.

Brother Ted quickly got down to business. He had joined the Brotherhood Coalition, a newly formed collection of fundamentalist preachers throughout south Mississippi. It was their purpose to quietly and methodically do everything possible, within the Lord's will, to elect Ron Fisk and thus kill off any chance of same-sex marriages occurring in Mississippi. He ranted on about the evils of homosexuality and its growing acceptability in American society. He quoted the Bible when appropriate, his voice rising with indignation when necessary. He stressed the urgency of electing godly men to all public positions and promised that the Brotherhood would be a force for years to come.

Denny listened with a straight face but

growing alarm. He'd had several conversations with the Paytons and knew the real issues behind the race. The manipulation and marketing of Fisk made him sick. He glanced at the other ministers and wondered how many funerals they had held for people killed by Krane Chemical. Cary County should be the last place to embrace the candidacy of someone like Ron Fisk.

Brother Ted grew sufficiently pious when he moved to the subject of Sheila McCarthy. She was a Catholic from the Coast, which in rural Christian circles meant she was a woman of loose morals. She was divorced. She liked to party, and there were rumors of boyfriends. She was a hopeless liberal, opposed to the death penalty, and could not be trusted when faced with decisions dealing with gay marriage and illegal immigration and the like.

When he finished his sermon, someone suggested that perhaps churches should not become so involved in politics. This was met with general disapproval. Brother Ted jumped in with a brief lecture about the culture wars and the courage they should have to fight for God. It's time for Christians to get off the sidelines and charge into the arena. This led to a fervent discussion about the erosion of values. Blame was placed on television, Hollywood, the Internet. The list grew long and ugly.

What was their strategy? someone asked.

Organization! Church folk outnumbered the heathen in south Mississippi, and the troops must be mobilized. Campaign workers, door knockers, poll watchers. Spread the message from church to church, house to house. The election was only three weeks away. Their movement was spreading like wildfire.

After an hour, Denny Ott could take no more. He excused himself, drove to his office at the church, and called Mary Grace.

———

The MTA directors met in an emergency session two days after the Fisk campaign launched its waves of anti-gay-marriage ads. The mood was somber. The question was obvious: How did such an issue take center stage? And what could the McCarthy campaign do to counter the attack?

Nat Lester was present and gave a summary of their plans for the final three weeks.

McCarthy had $700,000 to fight with, much less than Fisk. Half of her budget was already committed to television ads that would begin running in twenty-four hours. The remainder was for direct mail and some last-minute radio and TV spots. After that, they were out of money. Small donations were coming from labor, conservationists, good-government groups, and a few of the more moderate lobbying organizations, but 92 percent of McCarthy's funds were mailed in by trial lawyers.

Nat then summarized the latest poll. The race was a dead heat with the two front-runners at 30 percent, with the same number of voters still undecided. Coley remained around 10 percent. However, the poll was conducted the week before and did not reflect any shift due to the gay marriage ads. Because of those ads, Nat would begin polling over the weekend.

Not surprisingly, the trial lawyers had wild and varied opinions about what to do. All of their ideas were expensive, Nat continually reminded them. He listened to them argue. Some had sensible ideas, others were radical. Most assumed they knew more about campaigns than the others, and all of them took for granted that whatever course of action they finally agreed on would be immediately embraced by the McCarthy campaign.

Nat did not share with them some depressing gossip. A reporter from the Biloxi newspaper had called that morning with a few questions. He was exploring a story about the raging new issue of same-sex marriages. During the course of a ten-minute interview, he told Nat that the largest television station on the Coast had sold $1 million in prime airtime to the Fisk campaign for the remaining three weeks. It was believed to be the largest sale ever in a political race.

One million dollars on the Coast meant at least that much for the rest of the markets.

The news was so distressing that Nat was debating whether to tell Sheila. At that moment, he was leaning toward keeping it to himself. And he certainly wouldn't share it with the trial lawyers. Such sums were so staggering that it might demoralize Sheila's base.

The MTA president, Bobby Neal, finally hammered out a plan, one that would cost little. He would send to their eight hundred members an urgent e-mail detailing the dire situation and begging for action. Each trial lawyer would be instructed to (1) make a list of at least ten clients who were willing and able to write a check for $100, and (2) make another list of clients and friends who could be motivated to campaign door-to-door and work the polls on Election Day. Grassroots support was critical.

As the meeting began to break up, Willy Benton stood at the far end of the table and got everyone's attention. He was holding a sheet of paper with small print front and back. "This is a promissory note on a line of credit at the Gulf Bank in Pascagoula," he announced, and more than one lawyer considered diving under the table. Benton was no small thinker, and he was known for drama. "Half a million dollars," he said slowly, the numbers booming around the room. "In favor of the campaign to reelect Sheila McCarthy. I've already signed it, and I'm going to pass it around this table. There are twelve of us here. It requires ten signatures to become effective. Each will be liable for fifty thousand."

Dead silence. Eyes were darting from face to face. Some had already contributed more than $50,000, others much less. Some would spend $50,000 on jet fuel next month, others were bickering with their creditors. Regardless of their bank balances at the moment, each and every one wanted to strangle the little bastard.

Benton handed the note to the unlucky stiff to his left, one without a jet. Fortunately, such moments in a career are rare. Sign it and you're a tough guy who can roll the dice. Pass it along unsigned and you might as well quit and go home and do real estate.

All twelve signed.

CHAPTER 28

The pervert's name was Darrel Sackett. When last seen, he was thirty-seven years old and housed in a county jail awaiting a new trial on charges of molesting small children. He certainly looked guilty: long sloping forehead, vapid bug eyes enlarged by thick glasses, splotchy stubble from a week's growth, a thick scar stuck to his chin—the type of face that would alarm any parent, or anyone else for that matter. A career pedophile, he was first arrested at age sixteen. Many other arrests followed, and he'd been convicted at least four times in four different states.

Sackett, with his frightening face and disgusting rap sheet, was introduced to the registered voters of south Mississippi in a snazzy direct mailing from another new organization, this one calling itself Victims Rising. The two-page letter was both a bio of a pathetic criminal and a summary of the miserable failures of the judicial system.

"Why Is This Man Free?" the letter screamed. Answer: Because Justice Sheila McCarthy overturned his conviction on sixteen counts of child molestation. Eight years earlier, a jury convicted Sackett, and the judge sentenced him to life without parole. His lawyer—one paid by taxpayers—appealed his case to the supreme court, and "there Darrel Sackett found the sympathetic embrace of Justice Sheila McCarthy." McCarthy condemned the honest and hardworking detectives who extracted a full confession from Sackett. She chastised them for what she saw as their faulty search-and-seizure methods. She hammered the trial judge, who was highly respected and tough on crime, for admitting into evidence the confession and materials taken from Sackett's apartment. (The jury was visibly shaken when forced to view

Sackett's stash of child porn, seized by the cops during a "valid" search.) She claimed distaste for the defendant, but begged off by saying that she had no choice but to reverse his conviction and send his case back for a new trial.

Sackett was moved from the state prison back to the Lauderdale County jail, where he escaped one week later. He had not been heard from since. He was out there, "a free man," no doubt continuing his violence against innocent children.

The last paragraph ended with the usual rant against liberal judges. The fine print gave the standard approval by Ron Fisk.

Certain relevant facts were conveniently omitted. First, the court voted 8 to 1 to reverse the Sackett conviction and send it back for a new trial. The actions of the police were so egregious that four other justices wrote concurring opinions that were even more scathing in their condemnation of the forced confession and warrantless, unconstitutional search. The lone dissenter, Justice Romano, was a misguided soul who had never voted to reverse a criminal conviction, and privately vowed that he would never do so.

Second, Sackett was dead. Four years earlier he'd been killed in a bar fight in Alaska. The news of his passing barely made it to Mississippi, and when his file was retired in Lauderdale County, not a single reporter noticed. Barry Rinehart's exhaustive research discovered the truth, for what little it mattered.

The Fisk campaign was far beyond the truth now. The candidate was too busy to sweat the details, and he had placed his complete trust in Tony Zachary. The race had become a crusade, a calling of the highest order, and if facts were slightly bent or even ignored, then it was justified because of the importance of his candidacy. Besides, it was politics, a dirty game, and you could rest assured the other side wasn't playing fair, either.

Barry Rinehart had never been shackled by the truth. His only concern was not getting caught in his lies. If a madman like Darrel Sackett was out there, on the loose, very much alive and doing his filthy deeds, then his story was more shocking. A dead Sackett was a pleasant thought, but Rinehart preferred the power of fear. And he knew that McCarthy couldn't respond. She had reversed his conviction, plain and simple. Any effort to explain why would be futile in the world of thirty-second ads and snappy sound bites.

After the shock of the ad, she would try to erase Sackett from her mind.

———

After the shock, though, she had to at least revisit the case. She saw the ad online, at the Victims Rising Web site, after receiving a frantic call from Nat Lester. Paul, her clerk, found the reported case, and they read it in silence. She vaguely remembered it. In the eight years since, she had read a thousand briefs and written hundreds of opinions.

"You got it right," Paul said when he finished.

"Yes, but why does it look so wrong now?" she said. She'd been hard at work, her desk covered with memos from half a dozen cases. She was stunned, bewildered.

He didn't answer.

"I wonder what's next," she said, closing her eyes.

"Probably a death penalty case. And they'll cherry-pick the facts again."

"Thanks. Anything else?"

"Sure. There's lots of material in these books. You're a judge. Every time you make a decision someone loses. These guys don't care about the truth, so they can make anything sound bad."

"Please shut up."

———

Her first ads began, and they lightened the mood somewhat. Nat chose to begin with a straightforward piece with Sheila in a black robe sitting at the bench, smiling earnestly at the camera. She talked about her experience—eight years as a trial judge in Harrison County, nine years on the supreme court. She hated to pat her own back, but twice in the past five years she had received the highest rating in the state bar's annual review of all appellate judges. She was not a liberal judge, nor a conservative one. She refused to be labeled. Her commitment was simply to follow the laws of Mississippi, not to make new ones. The best judges are those without agendas, without preconceived notions of how they might rule. The best judges are those with experience. Neither of her opponents had ever presided over a trial, or issued a ruling, or studied complicated briefs, or listened to oral arguments, or written a final opinion. Until now, neither of her opponents had shown the slightest interest in sitting as a judge. Yet they are asking the voters to jump-start their judicial careers at the very top. She finished by saying, without the smile, "I was appointed to this position by the governor nine years ago, then I was reelected by you, the people. I am a judge, not a politician, and I don't have the money that some are spending to purchase this seat. I ask you, the voters, to help send the message that a seat on the Mississippi Supreme Court cannot be bought by big business. Thank you."

Nat spent little money at the Jackson stations and much more on the Coast. McCarthy would never be able to saturate like Fisk. Nat speculated that Fisk and all those wealthy folks behind him were burning $200,000 a week on the anti-gay-marriage ads alone.

Sheila's first round was about half of that, and the response was lukewarm. The ad was called "uncreative" by her coordinator in Jackson County. A noisy trial lawyer, no doubt an expert in all things political, sent an angry e-mail in which he blasted Nat for such a soft approach. You gotta fight fire with fire and answer the attack ads with more of the same. He reminded Nat that his firm had contributed $30,000 and might forgo any more if McCarthy didn't take off the gloves.

Women seemed to like the ad. Men were more critical. After reading a few dozen e-mails, Nat realized he was wasting his time.

———

Barry Rinehart had been waiting impatiently for some television from the McCarthy strategists. When he finally saw her first ad, he laughed out loud. What an old-fashioned, out-of-date, pathetically lame effort—judge in black robe, at a bench, thick law books as props, even a gavel for good measure. She looked sincere, but she was a judge, not a television presence. Her eyes moved as she read from the teleprompter. Her head was as rigid as a deer in headlights.

A weak response indeed, but it had to be answered. It had to be buried. Rinehart reached into his video library, his arsenal, and selected his next grenade.

Ten hours after McCarthy began running her ad, she was blown off the television by an attack ad that stunned even the most jaded political junkies. It began with the sharp crack of a rifle shot, then a black-and-white photo of Justice McCarthy, one from the court's official Web site. A powerful, barbed voice announced, "Justice Sheila McCarthy does not like hunters. Seven years ago she wrote, 'The hunters of this state have a poor record on safety.' " This quote was splashed across her face. The photo changed to one from a newspaper story with Sheila shaking hands at a rally. The voice continued, "And Justice Sheila McCarthy does not like gun owners. Five years ago she wrote, 'The ever vigilant gun lobby can always be expected to attack any statute that might in any way restrict the use of handguns in vulnerable areas. Regardless of how sensible a proposed statute might be, the gun lobby will descend upon it with a vengeance.' " This, too, was printed rapidly, word for word, across the screen. Then there was another blast, this one from a shotgun firing at a blue sky. Ron Fisk appeared, decked out like the real hunter he was. He lowered his shotgun and chatted with the voters for a few seconds. Memories of his grandfather, hunting in these woods as a child, love of nature, a vow to protect the sacred rights of hunters and gun owners. It ended with Ron walking along the edge of the woods, a pack of frisky dogs behind him.

Some small, quick print at the end of the ad gave credit to an organization called Gunowners United Now (GUN).

The truth: The first case mentioned in the ad involved the accidental shooting death of a deer hunter. His widow sued the man who shot him, a nasty trial ensued, and the jury in Calhoun County awarded her $600,000, the highest ever in that courtroom. The trial was as sordid as a divorce, with allegations of drinking and pot smoking and bad behavior. The two men were members of a hunting club and had been at deer camp for a week. During the trial, a contentious issue was safety, and several experts testified about gun laws and hunter education. Though the evidence was hotly disputed, it appeared, from the record, that the bulk of the testimony proved that the state's record on safety lagged behind others'.

In the second case, the City of Tupelo, in response to a schoolyard shooting that killed none but injured four, passed an ordinance banning the possession of a firearm within a hundred yards of any public school. Gun advocates sued, and the American Rifle Association wedged itself into the picture by filing a portentous and overblown friend-of-the-court brief. The court struck down the ordinance on Second Amendment grounds, but Sheila dissented. In doing so, she couldn't resist the temptation to take a swipe at the ARA.

Now the swipe was back. She watched Fisk's latest ad in her office, alone and with the sinking feeling that her chances were fading. On the stump, she had the time to explain her votes and point out the unfairness of taking her words out of context. But on television, she had thirty seconds. It was impossible, and the clever handlers of Ron Fisk knew it.

———

After a month at Pirate's Cove, Clete Coley had overstayed his welcome. The owner was fed up with giving away a penthouse suite, and he was fed up with feeding Coley's astounding appetite. The candidate was getting three meals a day, many of them sent to his room. At the blackjack tables, he drank rum like it was water and got hammered every night. He badgered the dealers, insulted the other players, and groped the cocktail waitresses. The casino had pocketed about $20,000 from Coley, but his expenses were at least that much.

Marlin found him at the bar early one evening, having a drink and limbering up for another long night at the tables. After small talk, Marlin cut to the chase. "We'd like for you to drop out of the race," he said. "And while you're leaving, endorse Ron Fisk."

Clete's eyes narrowed. Deep wrinkles tightened around his forehead. "Say what?"

"You heard me."

"I'm not so sure I did."

"We're asking you to withdraw and endorse Fisk. It's simple."

Coley gulped the rum without taking his eyes off Marlin. "Keep talking," he said.

"There's not much to say. You're a long shot, to put it mildly. You've done a good job of stirring things up, attacking McCarthy, but it's time to bail out and help elect Fisk."

"What if I don't like Fisk?"

"I'm sure he doesn't like you. It's immaterial. The party's over. You've had your jollies, gotten some headlines, met lots of interesting folks along the way, but you've made your last speech."

"The ballots have been printed. My name is on them."

"That means that a handful of your fans won't hear the news. Big deal."

Another long pull on the rum, and Coley said, "Okay, a hundred thousand to get in, how much to get out?"

"Fifty."

He shook his head and glanced at the blackjack tables in the distance. "That's not enough."

"I'm not here to negotiate. It's fifty thousand cash. Same suitcase as before, just not as heavy."

"Sorry. My figure is a hundred."

"I'll be here tomorrow, same time, same place." And with that, Marlin disappeared.

At nine the next morning, two FBI agents banged on the door to the penthouse suite. Eventually, Clete staggered to the door and demanded, "Who the hell is it?"

"FBI. Open up."

Clete cracked the door and peered over the chain. Twins. Dark suits. Same barber. "What do you want?"

"We'd like to ask you some questions, and we prefer not to do it from this side of the door."

Clete opened it and waved them in. He was wearing a T-shirt and a pair of NBA-style shorts that fell to his knees and sagged halfway down his ass. As he watched them sit at the small dining table, he racked his muddled brain for some recollection of which law he'd broken. Nothing recent sprang to mind, but then nothing would at this miserable time of the day. He maneuvered his cumbersome stomach— how much weight had he gained in the last month?—into a chair and glanced at their badges.

"Does the name Mick Runyun ring a bell?" one asked.

It did, but he wasn't ready to admit anything. "Maybe."

"Meth dealer. You represented him three years ago in federal court. Pled to ten years, cooperated with the government, real nice boy."

"Oh, that Mick Runyun."

"Yes, that one. Did he pay you a fee?"

"My records are at the office in Natchez."

"Great. We have a warrant for them. Can we meet there tomorrow?"

"Love to."

"Anyway, we're betting that your records don't tell us too much about the fees paid by Mr. Runyun. We have a real good source telling us that he paid you in cash, twenty thousand bucks, and that this was never reported."

"Do tell."

"And if this is true, then it's a violation of RICO and a few other federal statutes."

"Good ole RICO. You boys wouldn't be in business without it."

"What time tomorrow?"

"I was planning on campaigning tomorrow. The election is in two weeks."

They looked at this bleary-eyed, wild-haired, hungover beast and found it comical that he was a candidate for the supreme court.

"We'll be at your office in Natchez at noon tomorrow. If you don't show, then we'll have a warrant for your arrest. That should impress the voters."

They marched out of the room and slammed the door behind them.

Late that afternoon, Marlin appeared, as promised. He ordered coffee, which he didn't touch. Clete ordered rum and soda and smelled as though it was not the first one of the day.

"Can we agree on fifty, Clete?" Marlin asked after a long spell of gazing at the cocktail waitresses scurrying about.

"I'm still thinking."

"Were those two Fibbies nice to you this morning?"

Clete absorbed this without a flinch, without the slightest twitch to indicate his surprise. In fact, he wasn't surprised at all. "Nice boys," he said. "The way I figure it, Senator Rudd is meddling again. He wants Fisk to win because they're from the same tribe. Of course we know that Rudd is the uncle of the U.S. attorney down here, a real imbecile who got the job only because of his connections. Damned sure couldn't find a job anywhere else. Rudd leans on his nephew, who brings in the FBI to twist my arm. I drop out while singing the praises of Ron Fisk, and he squeaks out a great victory. He's happy. Rudd's happy. Big business is happy. Ain't life grand?"

"You're very close," Marlin said. "And you also took a $20,000 cash fee from a drug dealer and didn't report it. Pretty stupid, but not the end of the world. Nothing that can't be fixed by The Senator. You play along now, take your cash, bow out gracefully, and you'll never hear from the Fibbies again. Case closed."

Clete's red eyes settled on Marlin's blue ones. "You swear?"

"I swear. We shake hands now, you can forget the meeting at noon tomorrow in Natchez."

"Where's the money?"

"Outside, to the right. Same green Mustang." Marlin gently laid his keys on the bar. Clete grabbed them and disappeared.

CHAPTER 29

With only fifteen days left before the election, Barry Rinehart was invited to dinner at the Vietnamese hole-in-the-wall on Bleecker Street. Mr. Trudeau wanted an update.

On the flight from Boca, Barry gloated over his latest poll. Fisk was sixteen points ahead, a lead that could not be lost. The gay marriage issue had bumped him four points. The GUN attacks on McCarthy added three more. Clete Coley's rather lame farewell added another three. The campaign itself was running smoothly. Ron Fisk was a workhorse who did exactly what Tony

Zachary told him to do. There was plenty of money. Their television ads were hitting all markets with perfect regularity. The responses from their direct mail were nothing short of astonishing. The campaign had raised $320,000 from small donors who were upset about gays and guns. McCarthy was running hard to catch up and falling further behind.

Mr. Trudeau looked lean and tanned, and he was thrilled with the latest summaries. The sixteen-point lead dominated the dinner conversation. Carl quizzed Rinehart relentlessly about the numbers. Could they be trusted? How were they arrived at? How did they compare with Barry's other races? What would it take to blow the lead? Had Barry ever seen such a big lead evaporate?

Barry all but guaranteed a win.

———

For the first three quarters of the year, Krane Chemical reported dismal sales and weak earnings. The company was racked with production problems in Texas and Indonesia. Three plants shut down for major, unscheduled repairs. A plant in Brazil closed for undisclosed reasons, leaving its two thousand employees out of work. Huge orders were unfilled. Longtime customers left in frustration. The sales force could not get product. Competitors cut prices and poached business. Morale was down and there were rumors of major cutbacks and layoffs.

Behind the chaos, Carl Trudeau was skillfully pulling all the strings. He did nothing illegal, but cooking the books was an art he'd mastered many years ago. When one of his companies needed bad numbers, Carl could deliver them. During the year, Krane wrote off huge chunks of research and development, shifted unusually large sums of money into legal reserves, borrowed heavily on its credit lines, stifled sales by sabotaging production, bloated expenses, sold two profitable divisions, and managed to alienate many of its customers. Through it all, Carl coordinated enough leaks to float a printing press. Since the verdict, Krane had been on the radar of business reporters, and all bad news got plenty of ink. Of course, every story referred to the massive legal problems the company was facing. The possibility of bankruptcy had been mentioned several times, after careful plants by Carl.

The stock began the year at $17.00. Nine months later, it was $12.50. With the election just two weeks away, Carl was ready for one last assault on the battered common shares of Krane Chemical Corporation.

The phone call from Jared Kurtin seemed like a dream. Wes listened to the words and closed his eyes. It could not be true.

Kurtin explained that he had been instructed by his client to explore the possibilities of settling the Bowmore litigation. Krane Chemical was a mess, and until the lawsuits went away, it could not regain its focus and compete effectively. His proposal was to gather all the attorneys in one room at one time and start the process. It would be complicated because there were so many plaintiffs with so many issues. It would be difficult because there were so many lawyers to control. He insisted that Wes and Mary Grace act as lead counsel for the plaintiffs' lawyers, but they could work out those details at the first meeting. Time was suddenly crucial. Kurtin had already reserved a convention room at a hotel in Hattiesburg, and he wanted the meeting to begin on Friday and run through the weekend, if necessary.

"Today is Tuesday," Wes said, gripping the phone with white knuckles.

"Yes, I know. As I said, my client is anxious to begin this process. It could take weeks or months to complete, but we're ready to sit down."

Wes was ready, too. He had a deposition set for Friday, something that was easily postponed. "What are the rules?" he asked.

Kurtin had the benefit of hours of planning. Wes was reacting out of shock and excitement. Plus, Kurtin had been around the block a few more times than Wes. He had negotiated mass settlements on several occasions. Wes could only dream of one.

"I'm sending a letter to all known plaintiffs' attorneys," Kurtin said. "Look over the list and see if I'm missing anyone. As you know, they're still popping up. All lawyers are invited, but the easiest way to screw up a settlement conference like this is to give the trial lawyers the microphones. You and Mary Grace will talk for the plaintiffs. I'll talk for Krane. The first challenge is to identify all persons who are making any sort of claim. Our records show about six hundred, and these range from dead bodies to nose-bleeds. In my letters, I'm asking the lawyers to submit the names of clients, whether they have filed suit or not. Once we know who expects a piece of the pie, the next challenge will be to classify the claims. Un-like some mass tort settlements with ten thousand plaintiffs, this one will be manage-able in that we can talk about individual claims. Our current numbers show 68 dead, 143 wounded and probably dying, and the rest with various afflictions that, in all prob-ability, are not life threatening."

Kurtin ticked off the numbers like a war correspondent reporting from battle. Wes couldn't help but grimace, nor could he suppress another vile thought about Krane Chemical.

"Anyway, we'll start the process of going through these numbers. The goal is to arrive at one figure, then compare it with the cash my client is willing to spend."

"And what might that number be?" Wes asked with a desperate laugh.

"Not now, Wes, maybe later. I'm asking each lawyer to fill out a standardized form

for each client. If we can get these back before Friday, we'll have a head start. I'm
bringing a full team, Wes. My litigators, support staff, experts, number crunchers, and
I'll even have a guy with some spine from
Krane. Plus, of course, the usual crew from
the insurance companies. You might want
to reserve a large room for your support
people."

Reserve with what? Wes almost asked.
Surely Kurtin knew about the bankruptcy.

"Good idea," he said.

"And, Wes, my client is really concerned
about secrecy. There is no reason for this to
be publicized. If word gets out, then the
plaintiffs and their lawyers and the whole
town of Bowmore will get excited. What
happens then if the negotiations go nowhere? Let's keep a lid on this."

"Sure." How ridiculous. Kurtin was about
to send his letter to no fewer than twenty
law firms. Babe at the coffee shop in Bowmore would know about the settlement
conference before she began serving lunch.

––––––

The following morning the *Wall Street Journal* ran a front-page story about Krane

Chemical's settlement overtures. An anonymous source who worked for the company confirmed the truth of the rumors. Experts chimed in with varying opinions, but it was generally regarded as a positive step for the company. Large settlements can be calculated. Liabilities can be contained. Wall Street understands hard numbers, and it hates unpredictability. There is a long history of battered companies shoring up their financial futures with massive settlements that, while costly, were effective in cleaning up litigation.

Krane opened at $12.75 and advanced $2.75 in heavy trading.

By midafternoon Wednesday, the phones were ringing nonstop at Payton & Payton, and many other law firms as well. Word of a settlement was out there, on the street and flying around the Internet.

Denny Ott called and talked to Mary Grace. A group of Pine Grove residents had gathered at the church to offer prayers, exchange gossip, and wait for a miracle. It was like a vigil, he said. Not surprisingly, there were different versions of the truth. A settlement had already been negotiated, and money was on the way. No, the settlement would take place on Friday, but there was no doubt that it would happen. No, there was no settlement at all, just a meeting of the lawyers. Mary Grace explained what was happening and asked Denny to pass along the truth. It quickly became apparent that either she or Wes would need to hustle over to the church and meet with their clients.

Babe's was packed with spirited coffee drinkers, all looking for the latest word. Would Krane be required to clean up its toxic dump? Someone claiming authority answered yes, that would be a condition of the settlement. How much would the death claims be worth? Someone else had heard the figure of $5 million each. Arguments raged. Experts rose up and were soon shouted down.

F. Clyde Hardin walked over from his law office and immediately took center stage. His class action had been ridiculed by many of the locals who felt he was just riding the Paytons' coattails with a bunch of opportunistic clients. He and his good pal Sterling Bintz from Philadelphia were claiming almost three hundred "severely and permanently injured" members of their class action. Since its filing in January, it had gone nowhere. Now, however, F. Clyde had instantly gained stature. Any settlement had to include "his people." He would have a seat at the table on Friday, he explained to the silent crowd. He would be sitting there alongside Wes and Mary Grace Payton.

Jeannette Baker was behind the counter of a convenience store at the south edge of Bowmore when she received the call from Mary Grace. "Do not get excited," her lawyer warned, rather sternly. "This could be a lengthy process, and the possibility of a settlement is remote." Jeannette had questions but did not know where to begin. Mary Grace would be at the Pine Grove Church at 7:00 p.m. for a full discussion with all of her clients. Jeannette promised to be there.

With a $41 million verdict attached to it, Jeannette Baker's case would be the first one on the table.

The settlement news was too much for Bowmore to handle. In the small offices downtown the secretaries and Realtors and insurance agents talked of nothing else. The languid human commerce along Main Street stopped dead as friends and neighbors found it impossible to pass one another without comparing gossip. The clerks in the Cary County Courthouse collected rumors, amended them, embellished some, and reduced some, then passed them along. In the schools the teachers gathered in their coffee rooms and exchanged the latest news. Pine Grove wasn't the only church where the faithful and the hopeful met for prayer and counseling. Many of the town's pastors spent the afternoon on the phone listening to the victims of Krane Chemical.

A settlement would close the town's ugliest chapter, and allow it to begin again. The infusion of money would compensate those who had suffered. The cash would be spent and re-spent and boost the dying economy. Krane would certainly be required to clean up its pollution, and once it was finally gone, perhaps the water would become safe again. Bowmore with clean water—a dream almost impossible to believe. The community could finally shake off the nickname Cancer County.

A settlement was a fast and final end to the nightmare. No one in the town wanted litigation that would be prolonged and ugly.

No one wanted another trial like Jeannette Baker's.

———

Nat Lester had been pestering newspaper editors and reporters for a month. He was furious at the misleading advertising that had drenched south Mississippi, and even angrier at the editors for not railing against it. He put together a report in which he took the Fisk ads—print, direct mail, radio, Internet, and television—and dissected them, pointing out every lie, half-truth, and manipulated word. He also estimated, based on direct mail media buys, the amount of cash that was pouring into the Fisk campaign. His figure was at least $3 million, and he predicted that the vast majority was coming from out of state. There was no way to verify this until after the election. His report was e-mailed and sent overnight to every newspaper in the district, then followed up with aggressive phone calls. He updated it every day, then re-sent it and grew even more obnoxious on the phone. It finally paid off.

To his amazement, and great satisfaction, the three largest papers in the district informed him, separately and off the record of course, that they planned to run stinging editorials on the Fisk campaign in the upcoming Sunday editions.

And Nat's luck continued. The same-sex marriage issue caught the attention of the *New York Times*, and a reporter arrived in Jackson to poke around. His name was Gilbert, and he soon made his way to the McCarthy campaign office, where Nat gave him an earful, off the record. He also gave Gilbert the phone numbers of the two gay law students who were stalking Meyerchec and Spano.

Speaking off the record, they told Gilbert everything and showed him their file. They had spent four days in Chicago and learned a lot. They met Meyerchec in his bar near Evanston, told him they were new to the city and looking for friends. They spent hours in the place, got roaring drunk with the regulars, and never once heard anyone mention anything about a lawsuit in Mississippi. In the photos in the Jackson paper, Meyerchec had blond hair and funky eyeglasses. In Chicago, the hair was darker and there was no eyewear. His smiling face was in one of the group photos they had taken at the bar. As for Spano, they visited the design center where he worked as a consultant for lower-end home buyers. They pretended to be new residents in an old building nearby, and they spent two hours with him. Noticing their accents, Spano at one point asked where they were from. When they answered Jackson, Mississippi, he had no reaction to the place.

"Ever been there?" one of them asked.

"I've passed through a couple of times," Spano said. This, from a registered voter, a licensed driver, and a current appellant before the state's supreme court. Though Spano was never seen at Meyerchec's bar, it appeared as if the two men were indeed a couple. They shared the same address, a bungalow on Clark Street.

The law students had continued to call and visit the near empty apartment in Jackson, with no response. Forty-one days earlier, while knocking on the door, they stuck a piece of junk mail into a small gap near the doorknob. It was still there; the door had not been opened. The old Saab had not been moved. One tire was flat.

Gilbert became captivated by the story and pursued it doggedly. The attempt to get married in Mississippi smelled like a cynical ploy to thrust the same-sex marriage issue to the forefront of the McCarthy-Fisk race. And only McCarthy was getting hurt.

Gilbert badgered the radical lawyer who represented Meyerchec and Spano, but got nowhere. He dogged Tony Zachary for two days but couldn't get a word. His phone calls to Ron Fisk and his campaign head-quarters went unanswered. He spoke to both Meyerchec and Spano by phone, but was quickly cut off when he pressed them on their ties to Mississippi. He gathered a few choice quotes from Nat Lester, and he verified the facts dug up by the law students.

Gilbert finished his report and sent it in.

CHAPTER 30

The first fight was over the question of who would be allowed in the room. On the defense side, Jared Kurtin had full command of his battalion and there were no problems. The brawl was on the other side.

Sterling Bintz arrived early and loudly with an entourage that included young men who appeared to be lawyers and others who appeared to be leg breakers. He claimed to represent over half of the Bowmore victims, and therefore deserved a lead role in the negotiations. He spoke with a clipped nasal voice and in an accent quite foreign to south Mississippi, and he was instantly despised by everyone there. Wes settled him down, but only for a moment. F. Clyde Hardin watched from the safety of a corner, crunching a biscuit, enjoying the argument, and praying for a quick settlement. The IRS was now sending registered letters.

A national toxic tort star from Melbourne Beach, Florida, arrived with his support staff and joined in the debate. He, too, claimed to represent hundreds of injured people, and, since he was a veteran of mass tort settlement, he figured he should handle things from the plaintiffs' side.

The two class action lawyers were soon bickering over stolen clients.

There were seventeen other law firms jockeying for position. A few were reputable personal injury firms, but most were small-town car-wreck lawyers who had picked up a case or two while sniffing around Bowmore.

Tensions were high hours before the meeting began, and once the yelling started, there was the real possibility of a punch being thrown. When the voices were sharpest, Jared Kurtin calmly got their attention and announced that Wes and Mary Grace Payton would decide who sat where. If anyone had a problem with that, then he and his client and its insurance company would walk out the door with all the money. This calmed things down.

Then there was the issue of the press. At least three reporters were on hand to cover this "secret" meeting, and when asked to leave, they were quite reluctant. Fortunately, Kurtin had arranged for some armed security. The reporters were eventually escorted out of the hotel.

Kurtin had also suggested, and offered to pay for, a referee, a disinterested person well versed in litigation and settlements. Wes had agreed, and Kurtin found a retired federal judge in Fort Worth who worked part-time as a mediator. Judge Rosenthal quietly assumed control after the trial lawyers had settled down. It took him an hour to negotiate the seating. He would have the chair at the end of the long table. To his right, halfway down and in the center, would be Mr. Kurtin, flanked by his partners, associates, Frank Sully from Hattiesburg, two suits from Krane, and one from its liability insurance carrier. A total of eleven at the table for the defense, with another twenty packed behind them.

To his left, the Paytons sat in the center, opposite Jared Kurtin. They were flanked by Jim McMay, the Hattiesburg trial lawyer with four death cases out of Bowmore. McMay had made a fortune on the fen-phen diet pill litigation and had participated in several mass settlement conferences. He was joined by a lawyer from Gulfport who had similar experience. The other chairs were taken by Mississippi lawyers who had legitimate cases from Bowmore. The class action boys were shoved into the background. Sterling Bintz voiced his objection to his placement in the room, and Wes angrily told him to shut up. When the leg breakers reacted badly, Jared Kurtin announced that the class actions were the lowest priority on Krane's list, and if he, Bintz, hoped to collect a dime, then he should keep quiet and stay out of the way.

"This ain't Philadelphia," Judge Rosenthal said. "Are those bodyguards or lawyers?"

"Both," Bintz snapped back.

"Keep them under control."

Bintz sat down, mumbling and cursing.

It was 10:00 a.m., and Wes was already exhausted. His wife, though, was ready to begin.

———

For three hours nonstop they shuffled papers. Judge Rosenthal directed traffic as client summaries were produced, copied next door, reviewed, then classified according to the judge's arbitrary rating system: death was Class One, confirmed cancer was Class Two, all others were Class Three.

A stalemate occurred when Mary Grace suggested that Jeannette Baker be given first priority, and thus more money, because she had actually gone to trial. Why is her case worth more than the other death cases? a trial lawyer asked.

"Because she went to trial," Mary Grace shot back with a hard gaze. In other words, Baker's lawyers had the guts to take on Krane while the other lawyers chose to sit back and watch. In the months before the trial, the Paytons had approached at least five of the other trial lawyers present, including Jim McMay, and practically begged them for help. All declined.

"We will concede that the *Baker* case is worth more," Jared Kurtin said. "Frankly, I'm unable to ignore a $41 million verdict." And for the first time in years, Mary Grace actually smiled at the man. She could have hugged him.

At one, they broke for a two-hour lunch. The Paytons and Jim McMay hid away in a corner of the hotel restaurant and tried to analyze the meeting so far. Going in, they were consumed with the question of Krane's intent. Was it serious about a settlement? Or was it a stunt to push along the company's agenda? The fact that the national business papers knew so much about the secret settlement talks made the lawyers suspicious. But so far Mr. Kurtin had given every indication that he was a man on a mission. There had been no smiles from the Krane suits or the insurance boys, perhaps a sign that they were about to part with their money.

———

At 3:00 p.m. in New York, Carl Trudeau leaked the word that the negotiations were progressing nicely down in Mississippi. Krane was optimistic about a settlement.

Its stock closed the week at $16.50, up $4.00.

At 3:00 p.m. in Hattiesburg, the negotiators reassumed their positions, and Judge Rosenthal started the paper mill again. Three hours later, the initial accounting was complete. On the table were the claims of 704 people. Sixty-eight had died of cancer, and their families were blaming Krane. A hundred and forty-three were now suffering from cancer. The rest had a wide range of lesser illnesses and afflictions that were allegedly caused by the contaminated drinking water from the Bowmore pumping station.

Judge Rosenthal congratulated both sides on a hard and productive day, and adjourned the meeting until nine o'clock Saturday morning.

Wes and Mary Grace drove straight to the office and reported to the firm. Sherman had been in the negotiating room all day and shared his observations. They agreed that Jared Kurtin had returned to Hattiesburg with the goal of settling the Bowmore litigation and that his client seemed committed to that end. Wes cautioned that it was much too early to celebrate. They had managed only to identify the parties. The first dollar was nowhere near the table.

Mack and Liza begged them to go to the movies. Halfway through the eight o'clock show, Wes began to nod off. Mary Grace stared blankly at the screen, munching on popcorn and mentally crunching numbers related to medical expenses, pain and suffering, loss of companionship, loss of wages, loss of everything. She did not dare entertain thoughts of calculating attorneys' fees.

———

There were fewer suits and ties at the table Saturday morning. Even Judge Rosenthal looked quite casual in a black polo shirt under a sport coat. When the restless lawyers were in place and things were quiet, he said, with a great old voice that must have dominated many trials, "I suggest we start with the death cases and walk through them all."

No two death cases were the same from a settlement standpoint. Children were worth much less than adults because they have no record of earning power. Young fathers were worth more because of the loss of future wages. Some of the dead folks suffered for years, others went quickly. Everyone had a different figure for medical bills. Judge Rosenthal presented another scale, arbitrary but at least a starting point, in which each case would be rated based on its value. The highest cases would get a 5, and the cheapest (children) would get a 1. Time-out was called several times as the plaintiffs' lawyers haggled over this. When it was finally agreed upon, they began with Jeannette Baker. She was given a 10. The next case involved a fifty-four-year-old woman who worked part-time in a bakery and died after a three-year battle with leukemia. She was given a 3.

As they plowed through the list, each lawyer was allowed to present his particular case and plead for a higher rating. Through it all, there was no indication from Jared Kurtin of how much he was willing to pay for any of the death cases. Mary Grace watched him carefully when the other lawyers were talking. His face and actions revealed nothing but deep concentration.

At 2:30, they finished with Class One and moved to the longer list of those claimants who were still alive but battling cancer. Rating their cases was trickier. No one could know how long each would survive or how much each would suffer. No one could predict the likelihood of death. The lucky ones would live and become cancer-free. The discussion disintegrated into several heated arguments, and at times Judge Rosenthal was flustered and unable to suggest a compromise. Late in the day, Jared Kurtin began to show signs of strain and frustration.

As 7:00 p.m. approached and the session was mercifully winding down, Sterling Bintz could not restrain himself. "I'm not sure how much longer I can sit here and watch this little exercise," he announced rudely as he approached the table at the far end, away from Judge Rosenthal. "I mean, I've been here for two days and I haven't been allowed to speak. Which, of course, means my clients have been ignored. Enough is enough. I represent a class action of over three hundred injured people, and you all seem determined to screw them."

Wes started a rebuke, but thought better of it. Let him ramble. They were about to adjourn anyway.

"My clients are not going to be ignored," he practically shouted, and everyone grew still. There was a hint of madness in his voice and certainly in his eyes, and perhaps it was best to let him rant a little. "My clients have suffered greatly, and are still suffering. And you people are not concerned with them. I can't hang around here forever. I'm due in San Francisco tomorrow afternoon for another settlement. I got eight thousand cases against Schmeltzer for their laxative pills. So, since everyone here seems quite content to chat about everything but money, let me tell you where I am."

He had their attention. Jared Kurtin and the money boys perked up and stiffened a bit. Mary Grace watched every wrinkle in Kurtin's face. If this nut was about to throw a figure on the table, she wanted her adversary's reaction.

"I'm not settling my cases for less than a hundred thousand each," Bintz said with a sneer. "Maybe more, depending on each client."

Kurtin's face was frozen, but then it usually was. One of his associates shook his head, another one smiled a silly smile of amusement. The two Krane executives frowned and shifted as they dismissed this as absurd.

As the notion of $30 million floated around the room, Wes did the simple math. Bintz would probably take a third, throw a few crumbs at F. Clyde Hardin, then quickly move on to the next mass tort bonanza.

F. Clyde was cowering in a far corner, the same spot he'd occupied for many hours now. The paper cup in his hand was filled with orange juice, crushed ice, and four ounces of vodka. It was, after all, almost 7:00 p.m. on a Saturday. The math was so simple he could do it in his sleep. His cut was 5 percent of the total fees, or $500,000 under the rather reasonable scheme being so boldly suggested by his co-counsel. Their arrangement also paid F. Clyde $500 per client, and with three hundred clients he should have already received $150,000. He had not. Bintz had passed along about a third of that, but seemed disinclined to discuss the rest. He was a very busy lawyer and hard to get on the phone. Surely, he would come through as promised.

F. Clyde gulped his drink as Bintz's declaration rattled around the room.

Bintz continued. "We're not taking peanuts and going home," he threatened. "At some point in these negotiations, and the sooner the better, I want my clients' cases on the table."

"Tomorrow morning at nine," Judge Rosenthal suddenly barked. "As for now, we are adjourned."

———

"A Pathetic Campaign" was the title of the lead editorial in Sunday's *Clarion-Ledger* out of Jackson. Using a page out of Nat Lester's report, the editors damned the Ron Fisk campaign for its sleazy advertising. They accused Fisk of taking millions from big business and using it to mislead the public. His ads were filled with half-truths and statements taken wholly out of context. Fear was his weapon—fear of homosexuals, fear of gun control, fear of sexual predators. He was condemned for labeling Sheila McCarthy a "liberal" when in fact her body of work, which the editors had studied, could only be considered quite moderate. They blasted Fisk for promising to vote this way or that on cases he had yet to review as a member of the court.

The editorial also decried the entire process. So much money was being raised and spent, by both candidates, that fair and unbiased decision making was in jeopardy. How could Sheila McCarthy, who had so far received over $1.5 million from trial lawyers, be expected to ignore this money when those same lawyers appeared before the supreme court?

It finished with a call to abolish judicial elections and have the judges appointed based on merit by a nonpartisan panel.

The *Sun Herald* from Biloxi was even nastier. It accused the Fisk campaign of outright deceit and used the Darrel Sackett mailing as its prime example. Sackett was dead, not loose and on the prowl. He'd been dead for four years, something Nat Lester had learned with a couple of quick phone calls.

The *Hattiesburg American* challenged the Fisk campaign to retract its negative and misleading ads and to disclose, before Election Day, its contributions from big donors outside the state. It urged both candidates to clean up the race and honor the dignity of the supreme court.

On page 3 of section A of the *New York Times*, Gilbert's exposé ran with photos of Meyerchec and Spano, as well as Fisk and McCarthy. It covered the race in general, then focused on the gay marriage issue created and injected into the race by the two men from Illinois. Gilbert did a thorough job of accumulating evidence that the two men were longtime residents of Chicago and had virtually no ties to Mississippi. He did not speculate that they were being used by conservative political operatives to sabotage McCarthy. He didn't have to. The punch line was delivered in the final paragraph. Nat Lester was quoted as saying: "These guys are a couple of stooges being used by Ron Fisk and his backers to create an issue that does not exist. Their goal is to fire up the right-wing Christians and march them down to the polls."

Ron and Doreen Fisk were at the kitchen table, ignoring their early coffee, rereading the Jackson editorial, and fuming. The campaign had gone so smoothly. They were ahead in all the polls. Nine days to go and they could see the victory. Why, then, was Ron suddenly being described as "deceitful" and "dishonest" by the state's largest newspaper? It was a painful, humiliating slap, one that they had no idea was coming.

And it was certainly not deserved. They were honest, upstanding, clean-cut Christian people. Why this?

The phone rang and Ron grabbed it. Tony's tired voice said, "Have you seen the Jackson paper?"

"Yes, we're looking at it now."

"Have you seen the one from Hattiesburg and the *Sun Herald*?"

"No. Why?"

"Do you read the *New York Times*?"

"No."

"Check them out online. Call me in an hour."

"Is it bad?"

"Yes."

They read and fumed for another hour, then decided to skip church. Ron felt betrayed and embarrassed and was in no mood to leave the house. According to the latest numbers from his pollster in Atlanta, he had a comfortable lead. Now, though, he felt defeat was certain. No candidate could survive such a thrashing. He blamed the liberal press. He blamed Tony Zachary and those who controlled the campaign. And he blamed himself for being so naive. Why did he place so much trust in people he barely knew?

Doreen assured him it was not his fault. He had thrown himself so completely into the campaigning that he'd had little time to watch everything else. Any campaign is chaotic. No one can monitor the actions of all the workers and volunteers.

Ron unloaded on Tony during a lengthy and tense phone conversation. "You've embarrassed me," Ron said. "You've humiliated me and my family to the point that I really don't want to leave the house. I'm thinking about quitting."

"You can't quit, Ron, you have too much invested," Tony replied, trying to control his panic and reassure his boy.

"That's the problem, Tony. I've allowed you guys to generate too much cash, and you cannot handle it. Stop all television ads right now."

"That's impossible, Ron. They're already in the pipeline."

"So I'm not in control of my own campaign, is that what you're telling me, Tony?"

"It's not that simple."

"I'm not leaving the house, Tony. Pull all the ads right now. Stop everything, and I'm calling the editors of these newspapers. I'm admitting my mistakes."

"Ron, come on."

"I'm the boss, Tony, it's my campaign."

"Yes, and you've got the race won. Don't screw it up with only nine days to go."

"Did you know that Darrel Sackett was dead?"

"Well, I really can't—"

"Answer the question, Tony. Did you know he was dead?"

"I'm not sure."

"You knew he was dead and you deliberately ran a false ad, didn't you?"

"No, I—"

"You're fired, Tony. You're fired and I quit."

"Don't overreact, Ron. Settle down."

"You're fired."

"I'll be down in an hour."

"You do that, Tony. You get down here as quick as possible, and until then you're fired."

"I'm leaving now. Don't do anything until I get there."

"I'm calling the editors right now."

"Don't do that, Ron. Please. Wait until I get there."

The lawyers had little time for newspapers on Sunday morning. By eight o'clock they were gathering at the hotel for what would surely be the most important day yet. There had been no indication from Jared Kurtin as to how long he might negotiate before heading back to Atlanta, but it was assumed that round one would be over on Sunday afternoon. Other than the $30 million suggestion made by Sterling Bintz the evening before, there had been no talk of money. That had to change on Sunday. Wes and Mary Grace were determined to leave that day with a general idea of how much the Class One and Class Two cases were worth.

By 8:30 all the plaintiffs' lawyers were in place, most of them huddled in serious conversations, all of them ignoring Sterling Bintz, who in turn ignored them. His entourage was still intact. He was not speaking to the other class action lawyer from Melbourne Beach. Judge Rosenthal arrived at 8:45 and commented on the absence of everyone on the defense side. The trial lawyers finally noticed this. There was not a soul sitting opposite them. Wes punched in the number of Jared Kurtin's cell phone, but listened to his recording.

"We did agree on 9:00 a.m., didn't we?" asked Rosenthal, five minutes before the hour. It was unanimously agreed that nine was the magic hour. They waited, and time suddenly moved much slower.

At 9:02, Frank Sully, local counsel for Krane, walked into the room and said, somewhat sheepishly, almost in embarrassment, "My client has decided to recess these negotiations until further notice. I'm very sorry for the inconvenience."

"Where's Jared Kurtin?" Judge Rosenthal demanded.

"He's flying back to Atlanta right now."

"When did your client make this decision?"

"I don't know. I was informed about an hour ago. I'm very sorry, Judge. I apologize to everyone here."

The room seemed to tilt as one side sank under the weight of this sudden turn of events. Lawyers giddy in anticipation of finally slicing up the pie dropped their pens and pencils and gaped at one another in shock. Great gasps of air were discharged.

Curses were mumbled just loud enough to be heard. Shoulders sagged. They wanted to throw something at Sully, but he was just the local and they had learned a long time ago that he had no clout.

F. Clyde Hardin wiped sweat from his wet face and tried valiantly not to throw up.

There was a sudden rush to leave, to clear out. It was maddening to sit there and stare at the empty chairs, chairs once occupied by men who just might have made them rich. The trial lawyers quickly gathered stacks of papers, restuffed their briefcases, and offered brusque goodbyes.

Wes and Mary Grace said nothing as they drove to their apartment.

CHAPTER 31

Monday morning, the *Wall Street Journal* broke the news of the collapse of the settlement negotiations down in Hattiesburg. The story, on page 2, was written by a reporter with some very good sources inside Krane Chemical, one of whom blamed the plaintiffs' lawyers. "Their demands were just too unrealistic. We went in in good faith, and got nowhere." Another anonymous source said, "It's hopeless. Because of the verdict, every trial lawyer thinks his case is worth forty million bucks." Mr. Watts, Krane's CEO, said, "We are very disappointed. We wanted to get this litigation behind us and move on. Now our future is quite uncertain."

Carl Trudeau read the story online at 4:30 in the morning in his penthouse. He laughed and rubbed his hands together in anticipation of a very profitable week.

Wes called Jared Kurtin throughout the morning, but the great man was traveling and could not be reached. His cell phone was stuck on voice mail. His secretary eventually became rude, but then so was Wes. He and Mary Grace seriously doubted if the wild demands by Sterling Bintz had frightened Krane away. In relative terms, his suggestion of $30 million would be a fraction of any workable settlement.

When the news finally arrived in Bowmore, it was received like another plague.

————

At McCarthy headquarters, Nat Lester had worked through the night and was still wired when Sheila arrived at 8:30, her usual time. He had e-mailed the *Times* story to every newspaper in the district and was calling reporters and editors when she walked in with a well-rested smile and asked for a pineapple juice.

"We've got these clowns on the run!" he announced jubilantly. "Their dirty tricks have caught up with them."

"Congratulations. It's beautiful."

"We're sending the editorials and the *Times* story to every registered voter."

"How much does that cost?"

"Who cares? With a week to go, we can't pinch pennies. Are you ready?"

"I leave in an hour."

The next seven days would take her to thirty-four stops in twenty counties, all made possible by the use of a King Air on loan from one trial lawyer and a small jet from another. The blitz had been coordinated by Nat and would take place with the help of school-teachers, labor bosses, black leaders, and, of course, trial lawyers. She would not return to Jackson until after the election. While she was on the stump, her last round of television ads would flood the district.

By the time the votes were counted, her campaign would not have one dime. She was praying that it would not be in debt.

———

Ron Fisk finally left the house on Monday morning, but he did not make his usual trip to the office. Instead, he and Doreen drove to Jackson, to the offices of Judicial Vision for another long and stressful meeting with Tony Zachary. They had slugged their way through a four-hour ordeal on Sunday afternoon in the den of the Fisk home, and they had resolved little. Ron was suspending all campaign activities until he could repair his good name. He had fired Tony at least four times, but they were still talking.

Throughout the day and into Sunday night, Tedford in Atlanta had been polling furiously, and by late Monday morning there were some results. In spite of the barrage of condemnation, Ron Fisk was still three points ahead of Sheila McCarthy. The gay marriage issue had captivated the voters, most of whom still favored the more conservative candidate.

Ron wasn't sure if he could believe anyone who worked for his campaign, but the new poll did lighten his mood somewhat. "You've got this thing won, Ron," Tony said again and again. "Don't blow it."

They finally reached an understanding, one that Ron insisted they sign as if they had negotiated a contract. First, Ron would stay in the race. Second, Tony would keep his job as campaign manager. Third, Ron would meet with the newspaper editors, admit his mistakes, and promise a clean race for the remaining eight days. Fourth, no campaign literature, ads, TV spots, direct mail, radio commercials, nothing would be used until it was first approved by Ron.

When they were pals again, they enjoyed a quick lunch at the Capitol Grill, then Ron and Doreen drove home. They were proud that they had held their ground, and anxious to resume the campaign. They could smell the victory.

Barry Rinehart arrived in Jackson at noon on Monday and established his base in the largest suite of a downtown hotel. He would not leave Mississippi until after the election.

He waited impatiently for Tony to arrive with the news that they still had a horse in the race. For a man who took great pride in staying cool regardless of the pressure, the past twenty-four hours had been nerve-racking. Barry had slept little. If Fisk quit, then Rinehart's career would be severely damaged, if not outright ruined.

Tony walked into the suite with a huge smile, and both men were able to laugh. They were soon reviewing their media buys and advertising plans. They had the cash to saturate the district with TV ads, and if Mr. Fisk wanted only positive ones, then so be it.

———

The market's reaction to the settlement news was swift and ugly. Krane opened at $15.25 and by noon was trading at $12.75. Carl Trudeau watched the fall gleefully, his net worth shrinking by the minute. To add to the fear and frenzy, he organized a meeting between the top Krane executives and the company's bankruptcy attorneys, then leaked this news to a reporter.

On Tuesday morning, the Business section of the *New York Times* ran a story in which an in-house lawyer for the company said, "We'll probably file for bankruptcy protection this week." For the first time in twenty years, the stock fell through the $10.00 floor and traded around $9.50.

At midday on Tuesday, Meyerchec and Spano arrived in Jackson by private jet. They were picked up by a car with a driver and taken to the office of their attorney, where they met a reporter with the Jackson *Clarion-Ledger*. In a one-hour interview, they rebuked the story by Gilbert, reaffirmed their citizenship in their new state, and talked at length about the importance of their lawsuit now pending before the Mississippi Supreme Court. They held hands throughout the entire interview and posed for a photographer from the newspaper.

While this was happening, Barry Rinehart and Tony Zachary pored over the findings from their latest poll. Fisk's sixteen-point lead had been reduced to five, the most dramatic seventy-two-hour drop Barry had ever seen. But he was too seasoned to panic. Tony, however, was a nervous wreck.

They decided to reshuffle the television ads. They discarded the Darrel Sackett attack piece and one showing illegal aliens crossing the border. For the next three days, they would stick to gay marriage and the glory of guns. Over the weekend, they would shift to the comfort ads and leave the voters with warm and fuzzy feelings about Ron Fisk and his wholesomeness.

Meanwhile, the weary mail carriers in south Mississippi would deliver several tons of Fisk propaganda each day until the campaign was mercifully over.

All to be done with Mr. Fisk's approval, of course.

————

Denny Ott finished his letter after several drafts and asked his wife to read it. When she approved, he took it to the post office. It read:

Dear Brother Ted:

I have listened to a recording of your sermon last Sunday, broadcast on radio station WBMR during your worship hour. I hesitate to call it a sermon. It was more along the lines of a stump speech. I'm sure your condemnation of homosexuals is standard fare from your pulpit, and I will not comment on it. However, your attack on liberal judges, nine days before the election, was nothing but a diatribe against Sheila McCarthy, who, of course, was never called by name. By attacking her, you obviously endorsed her opponent.

Such political speech is expressly forbidden by law, and specifically forbidden by Internal Revenue Service regulations. As a 501 (C) (3) nonprofit organization, Harvest Tabernacle cannot engage in political activity. To do so is to risk losing its nonprofit status, a catastrophic event for any church.

I have heard from good sources that other local pastors, all members of your Brotherhood Coalition, are involving themselves and their churches in this campaign. I'm sure this is part of a well-coordinated effort to help elect Ron Fisk, and I have no doubt that this Sunday you and the others will use the pulpit to urge your members to vote for him.

Mr. Fisk is being used by a conspiracy of big business interests to stack our supreme court with judges who will protect corporate wrongdoers

by limiting their liability. Only the little
folks will suffer—your people and mine.
Be warned that I will be watching
and listening this Sunday. And I will not
hesitate to notify the Internal Revenue
Service if you continue your illegal
activities.
Yours in Christ,
Denny Ott

———

At noon Thursday, the Payton law firm met for a quick lunch and final review of its last-minute campaigning. On a Sheetrock wall in The Pit, Sherman had arranged, in chronological order, the print ads used so far by Ron Fisk. There were six full-page solicitations from newspapers and five direct mailings. The collection was now being updated daily because the Fisk printing presses were working overtime.

It was an impressive, and quite depressing, lineup.

Using a street map of Hattiesburg and a list of registered voters, Sherman assigned neighborhoods near the university. Walking door-to-door, he would go with Tabby, Rusty with Vicky, Wes with Mary Grace.

They had two thousand doors to cover during the next five days. Olivia agreed to stay behind and answer the phone. She was a bit too arthritic to hit the streets.

Other teams, many of them from the offices of local trial lawyers, would canvass the rest of Hattiesburg and its outlying suburbs. In addition to handing out McCarthy materials, most of these volunteers would distribute brochures for Judge Thomas Harrison.

The prospect of knocking on hundreds of doors was actually quite welcome, at least to Wes and Mary Grace. The mood at the office had been funereal since Monday. The settlement fiasco had drained their spirits. The constant chatter about Krane filing Chapter 11 frightened them. They were distracted and edgy, and both needed a few days off.

The final push was orchestrated by Nat Lester. Every precinct in all twenty-seven counties had someone assigned to it, and Nat had the cell phone number of every volunteer. He started calling them Thursday afternoon, and he would hound them until late Monday night.

The letter from Brother Ted was hand delivered to Pine Grove Church. It read:

Dear Pastor Ott:

I'm touched by your concern, and I'm also delighted you have taken an interest in my sermons. Listen to them carefully, and one day you may come to know Jesus Christ as your personal savior. Until then, I will continue to pray for you and all those you are leading astray.

God built our house of worship fourteen years ago, then He paid off the mortgage. He led me to the pulpit there, and each week He speaks to His beloved flock through my words.

When preparing my sermons, I listen to no one but Him. He condemns homosexuality, those who practice it, and those who support it. It's in the Bible, which I suggest you spend more time reading.

And you can stop wasting your time worrying about me and my church.

Surely, you have enough on your plate in Pine Grove.

I shall preach whatever I choose. Send in the federal government. With God on my side, I have nothing to fear.

Praise be to Him,
Brother Ted

CHAPTER 32

By noon Friday, Barry Rinehart had propped up his poll numbers to the point where he felt confident enough to call Mr. Trudeau. Fisk was seven points ahead and seemed to have regained momentum. Barry had no qualms about rounding the numbers up a bit to make the great man feel better. He'd been lying all week anyway. Mr. Trudeau would never know they had almost blown a sixteen-point lead.

"We're up by ten points," Barry said confidently from his hotel suite.

"Then it's over?"

"I know of no election in which the front-runner has dropped ten points over the last weekend. And, with all the money we're spending on media, I think we're gaining."

"Nice job, Barry," Carl said, and closed his phone.

As Wall Street waited for the news that Krane Chemical would file for bankruptcy, Carl Trudeau purchased five million shares of the company's stock in a private transaction. The seller was a fund manager who handled the retirement portfolio of the public employees of Minnesota. Carl had been stalking the stock for months, and the manager was finally convinced that Krane was hopeless. He dumped the stock for $11 a share and considered himself lucky.

Carl then launched a plan to purchase another five million shares as soon as the market opened. His identity as the buyer would not be disclosed until he filed with the SEC ten days later.

By then, of course, the election would be over.

In the year since the verdict, he had secretly and methodically increased his stake in the company. Using offshore trusts, Panamanian banks, two dummy corporations based in Singapore, and the expert advice of a Swiss banker, the Trudeau Group now owned 60 percent of Krane. The sudden grab for ten million more shares would raise Carl's ownership to 77 percent.

At 2:30 p.m. Friday, Krane issued a brief press release announcing that "a bankruptcy filing has been indefinitely postponed."

———

Barry Rinehart was not following the news on Wall Street. He had little interest in Krane Chemical and its financial dealings. There were at least three dozen important matters to monitor during the next seventy-two hours, and none could be overlooked. However, after five days in the hotel suite, he needed to move.

With Tony driving, they left Jackson and went to Hattiesburg, where Barry got a quick tour of the important sights: the Forrest County Circuit Court building, where the verdict started it all, the semi-abandoned shopping center that the Paytons called their office—Kenny's Karate on one side and a whiskey store on the other—and a couple of neighborhoods where Ron Fisk yard signs outnumbered Sheila Mc-

Carthy's two to one. They had dinner in a downtown restaurant called 206 Front Street and at 7:00 p.m. parked outside Reed Green Coliseum on the campus of Southern Miss. They sat in the car for thirty minutes and watched the crowd arrive, in vans and converted school buses and fancy coaches, each one with the name of its church painted boldly along the sides. They were from Purvis, Poplarville, Lumberton, Bowmore, Collins, Mount Olive, Brooklyn, and Sand Hill.

"Some of those towns are an hour from here," Tony said with satisfaction.

The worshippers poured into the parking lots around the coliseum and hurried inside. Many carried identical blue and white signs that said, "Save the Family."

"Where did you get the signs?" Tony asked.

"Vietnam."

"Vietnam?"

"Got 'em for a buck ten, fifty thousand total. The Chinese company wanted a buck thirty."

"So nice to hear we're saving money."

At 7:30, Rinehart and Zachary entered the coliseum and hustled up to the nosebleed

seats, as far away as possible from the excited mob below. A stage was set up at one
end, with huge "Save the Family" banners
hanging behind it. A well-known white
gospel quartet ($4,500 for the night,
$15,000 for the weekend) was warming up
the crowd. The floor was covered with neat
rows of folding chairs, thousands of them,
all filled with folks in a joyous mood.

"What's the seating capacity?" Barry
asked.

"Eight thousand for basketball," Tony said
glancing around the arena. A few sections
behind the stage were empty. "With the
seats on the floor, I'd say we're close to nine
thousand."

Barry seemed satisfied.

The master of ceremonies was a local
preacher who quieted the crowd with a long
prayer, toward the end of which many of his
people began waving their hands upward,
as if reaching for heaven. There was a fair
amount of mumbling and whispering as
they prayed fervently. Barry and Tony just
watched, content in their prayerlessness.

The quartet fired them up with another
song, then a black gospel group ($500 for
the night) rocked the place with a rowdy

rendition of "Born to Worship." The first speaker was Walter Utley, from the American Family Alliance in Washington, and when he assumed the podium, Tony recalled their first meeting ten months earlier when Ron Fisk made the rounds. It seemed like years ago. Utley was not a preacher, nor was he much of a speaker. He dulled the crowd with a frightening list of all the evils being proposed in Washington. He railed against the courts and politicians and a host of other bad people. When he finished, the crowd applauded and waved their signs.

More music. Another prayer. The star of the rally was David Wilfong, a Christian activist with a knack for wedging himself into every high-profile dispute involving God. Twenty million people listened to his radio show every day. Many sent him money. Many bought his books and tapes. He was an educated, ordained minister with a fiery, frantic voice, and within five minutes he had the crowd jumping up in a standing ovation. He condemned immorality on every front, but he saved his heavy stuff for gays and lesbians who wanted to get married. The crowd could not sit still or remain quiet. It was their chance to verbally express their opposition, and to do so in a very public manner. After every third sentence, Wilfong had to wait for the applause to die down.

He was being paid $50,000 for the weekend, money that had originated months earlier from somewhere in the mysterious depths of the Trudeau Group. But no human could trace it.

Twenty minutes into his performance, Wilfong stopped for a special introduction. When Ron and Doreen Fisk stepped onto the stage, the arena seemed to shake. Ron spoke for five minutes. He asked for their votes come Tuesday, and for their prayers. He and Doreen walked across the stage to a thunderous standing ovation. They waved and shook their fists in triumph, then walked to the other side of the stage as the mob stomped its feet.

Barry Rinehart managed to contain his amusement. Of all his creations, Ron Fisk was the most perfect.

———

Families were saved throughout south Mississippi the following day and into Sunday. Utley and Wilfong drew huge crowds, and of course the crowds adored Ron and Doreen Fisk.

Those who chose not to take a church bus to a rally were bombarded with relentless advertising on television. And the mailman was always close by, hauling to the besieged homes yet more campaign propaganda.

While publicly the campaign raced on in a numbing frenzy, a darker side came together over the weekend. Under Marlin's direction, a dozen operatives fanned out through the district and hooked up with old contacts. They visited rural supervisors on their farms, and black preachers in their churches, and county ward bosses in their hunting cabins. Voter registration rolls were reviewed. Numbers were agreed upon. Sacks of cash changed hands. The tariff was $25 per vote. Some called it "gas money," as if it could be justified as a legitimate expense.

The operatives were working for Ron Fisk, though he would never know of their activities. Suspicions would be raised after the votes were counted, after Fisk received an astounding number of votes in black precincts, but Tony would assure him that it was simply a case of some wise people understanding the issues.

———

On November 4, two-thirds of those registered in the southern district cast their votes.

When the polls closed at 7:00 p.m., Sheila McCarthy drove straight to the Biloxi Riviera Casino, where her volunteers were preparing for a party. No reporters were allowed. The first results were somewhat satisfying. She carried Harrison County, her home, with 55 percent of the vote.

When Nat Lester saw this figure in Jackson, at the McCarthy headquarters, he knew they were dead. Fisk got almost half the votes in the most laid-back county in the district. It soon got much worse.

Ron and Doreen were eating pizza at the crowded campaign office in downtown Brookhaven. The Lincoln County votes were being tallied just down the street, and when the news came that his neighbors had turned out in big numbers and given him 75 percent of the vote, the party began. In Pike County, next door, Fisk received 64 percent.

When Sheila lost Hancock County on the

Coast, her night was over, as was her career on the supreme court. In one ten-minute span, she then lost Forrest County (Hattiesburg), Jones County (Laurel), and Adams County (Natchez).

All precincts were in by 11:00 p.m. Ron Fisk won easily with 53 percent of the vote. Sheila McCarthy received 44 percent, and Clete Coley retained enough admirers to give him the remaining 3 percent. It was a solid thrashing, with Fisk losing only Harrison and Stone counties.

He even beat McCarthy in Cancer County, though not in the four precincts within the city limits of Bowmore. In the rural areas, though, where the Brotherhood ministers toiled in the fields, Ron Fisk took almost 80 percent of the vote.

Mary Grace wept when she saw the final numbers from Cary County: Fisk, 2,238; McCarthy, 1,870; Coley, 55.

The only good news was that Judge Thomas Harrison had survived, but barely.

———

The dust settled in the week that followed. In several interviews, Sheila McCarthy presented the face of a graceful loser. She did, however, say, "It will be interesting to see how much money Mr. Fisk raised and spent."

Justice Jimmy McElwayne was less gracious. In several articles, he was quoted as saying, "I'm not too keen to serve with a man who paid three million for a seat on the court."

When the reports were filed, though, three million looked rather cheap. The Fisk campaign reported total receipts of $4.1 million, with a staggering $2.9 million collected in the thirty-one days of October. Ninety-one percent of this money flooded in from out of state. The report did not list any contributions from or expenses paid to such groups as Lawsuit Victims for Truth, Victims Rising, and GUN. Ron Fisk signed the report, as required by law, but had many questions about the financing. He pressed Tony for answers about his fund-raising methods, and when the answers were vague, they exchanged heated words. Fisk accused him of hiding money and of taking advantage of his inexperience. Tony responded hotly that Fisk had been promised unlimited funds, and it wasn't fair to complain after the fact. "You should be thanking me, not bitching about the money," he yelled during a long, contentious meeting.

Soon, though, they would be attacked by reporters and forced to present a united front.

The McCarthy campaign raised $1.9 million and spent every penny of it. The $500,000 note produced by Willy Benton and signed by twelve of the MTA directors would take years to satisfy.

Once the final numbers were available, a storm erupted in the media. A team of investigative journalists with the *Clarion-Ledger* went after Tony Zachary, Judicial Vision, Ron Fisk, and many of the out-of-state donors who'd sent $5,000 checks. The business groups and the trial lawyers exchanged heated words through the various newspaper stories. Editorials raged about the need for reform. The secretary of state pursued Lawsuit Victims for Truth, Victims Rising, and GUN for such details as the names of members and total amounts spent on advertising. But the inquiries were met with stiff resistance by Washington lawyers with wide experience in election issues.

Barry Rinehart watched it from the safety

of his splendid office in Boca Raton. Such postgame antics were the rule, not the exception. The losers always squawked about the lack of fairness. In a couple of months, Justice Fisk would be on the big bench and most folks would forget the campaign that put him there.

Barry was moving on, negotiating with other clients. An appellate judge in Illinois had been ruling against the insurance industry for many years, and it was time to take him out. But they were haggling over Barry's fees, which had jumped dramatically after the Fisk victory.

Of the $8 million funneled through various routes by Carl Trudeau to Barry and his related "units," almost $7 million was still intact, still hidden.

Thank God for democracy, Barry said to himself many times a day. "Let the people vote!"

PART THREE

THE OPINION

CHAPTER 33

Ron Fisk was sworn in as associate justice of the Supreme Court of Mississippi during the first week of January. It was a short, quiet ceremony attended by Doreen and the three children, a few friends from Brookhaven, Tony Zachary, and the other eight members of the court and some of the staff. The chief justice, the most senior member, gave a short welcoming speech, then everybody had punch and cookies. Justice Jimmy McElwayne skipped the refreshments and returned to his office. He had not expected to like Ron Fisk, and so far he had not been disappointed. Fisk stumbled badly when he summarily fired Sheila's law clerks and secretary without the courtesy of first meeting them. He stumbled again when he showed up in early December and began pestering the chief justice to see the docket and have a look at some of the upcoming cases. At forty years of age, Fisk was by far the youngest member of the court, and his eager-beaver enthusiasm had already rankled some of his brethren.

Once sworn in, Fisk had the right to participate in every case not yet decided, regardless of how long the matter had been before the court. He plunged into the work and was soon putting in long hours. Ten days after arriving, he voted with a seven-member majority (including McElwayne) to reverse a zoning case out of DeSoto County, and he dissented with three others in a wetlands dispute in Pearl River County. He just voted, without comment.

In each case, every judge can write his own opinion, either concurring with the majority or dissenting from it. Ron was itching to write something, but he wisely kept quiet. It was best not to rush things.

The people of Mississippi got their first glimpse of the new, post-McCarthy court in late January. The case involved an eighty-year-old woman with Alzheimer's who was found under her nursing home bed, naked and filthy. She was found there by her son, who went ballistic and eventually sued the nursing home on her behalf. Though accounts varied and records were incomplete, testimony at trial proved that the woman had been completely neglected for at least six hours. She had not been fed for nine. The nursing home was a low-end facility, one of many owned by a company from Florida, and its history of safety and sanitation violations was long and pathetic. The jury, in the rural county of Covington, awarded actual damages of $250,000, though it was difficult to gauge the extent of the physical injuries. There were bruises on her forehead, but the poor lady had lost her mind a decade earlier. The interesting part of the case was the punitive award of $2 million, a record for Covington County.

Justice Calligan had been assigned the case. He rounded up his other three votes and wrote an opinion that reversed the $250,000 and sent it back for another trial. More proof was needed on the issue of damages. As for the punitive award, it "shocked the conscience of the court" and was reversed and rendered—thrown out once and for all. Judge McElwayne wrote an opinion in which he upheld the entire verdict. He went to great lengths to spell out the wretched history of the nursing home— lack of staff, untrained staff, unsanitary rooms and bed linens and towels, poisonous food, inadequate air-conditioning, overcrowded rooms, and so on. His opinion was joined by three others, so the old court was equally divided. The new man would be the swing vote.

Justice Fisk did not hesitate. He, too, found the medical proof inadequate, and claimed to be shocked by the punitive award. As an insurance defense lawyer, he had spent fourteen years fighting off the wild claims of punitive damages so carelessly thrown about by the plaintiffs' bar. At least half the lawsuits he defended had included a bogus plea for an exorbitant sum of money because of the defendant's "outrageous and reckless conduct."

By a vote of 5–4, the court announced its new course and sent the case back to Covington County in much worse shape than when it left.

The elderly victim's son was a fifty-six-year-old cattle farmer. He was also a deacon in a country church a few miles outside the town of Mount Olive. He and his wife had been strong supporters of Ron Fisk because they viewed him as a godly man who shared their values and would protect their grandchildren.

Why would Mr. Fisk now rule in favor of some outlaw corporation from another state?

———

Each case accepted for review by the supreme court is assigned by the clerk to one of the nine judges, who have no control over the process. Each one knows that every ninth case will land on his or her desk. They work on three-judge panels for six weeks, then the little teams are reshuffled.

In almost all cases before the supreme court, the lawyers request an oral argument, but these are rarely granted. The panels listen to the lawyers in less than 5 percent of the appeals.

Because of the size of the verdict, the case of *Jeannette Baker v. Krane Chemical Corporation* was deemed important enough to allow the attorneys an audience with its three-judge panel. On February 7, they gathered—Jared Kurtin and his mob, and the entire firm of Payton & Payton.

The case had been assigned to Justice Albritton months earlier. Ron Fisk had no business in the courtroom that day and was not there. Tony Zachary stopped by out of curiosity, but sat in the back row and did not speak to anyone. He took notes and would call Barry Rinehart as soon as the hearing ended. A vice president for Krane also sat in the back row and took notes.

Each side was allowed twenty minutes, and a digital timer clicked off the seconds. Warnings were given by a clerk. Long-winded lawyers were not tolerated. Jared Kurtin went first and quickly cut to the heart of his client's appeal. Krane had always argued that there was no credible, reasonable medical link between the BCL and cartolyx found on its property and the cancers that afflicted so many of Bowmore's residents. Krane would never concede that illegal dumping had occurred, but, hypothetically speaking, even if you assumed toxic wastes were emitted into the soil and found their way into the water, there was "no medically causal connection" between the chemicals and the cancers. Oh, there was lots of speculation all right. Look at the rate of cancer in Bowmore. Look at the cancer clusters. But cancer rates vary widely from region to region. And, most important, there are thousands of carcinogens in the air, food, beverages, household products, the list goes on and on. Who can say that the cancer that killed little Chad Baker came from the water, and not the air? How do you rule out the carcinogens found in the highly processed foods Ms. Baker admitted they had eaten for years? It's impossible.

Kurtin was on his game, and the three judges left him alone for ten minutes. Two were already with him. Justice Albritton was not, and he finally asked, "Mr. Kurtin, excuse me, but were there any other factories or plants in this general area that manufactured pesticides or insecticides?"

"Not to my knowledge, Your Honor."

"Does that mean something other than 'No'?"

"The answer is no, Your Honor. There were no other manufacturers in Cary County."

"Thank you. And with all of your experts

did you find any other factory or plant where bichloronylene, cartolyx, or aklar was processed and/or disposed of?"

"No, Your Honor."

"Thank you. And when you argue that other areas of the country have seen very high rates of cancer, you're not suggesting that any of these other places are fifteen times above the national average, are you?"

"No, I'm not suggesting that, but we do dispute the ratio of fifteen."

"Fine, then will you stipulate to a rate of cancer twelve times the national average?"

"I'm not sure—"

"That was what your expert said at trial, Mr. Kurtin. Bowmore's rate is twelve times the national average."

"Yes, I believe you are correct, Your Honor."

"Thank you."

There were no more interruptions, and Kurtin finished a few seconds after his buzzer.

Mary Grace looked spectacular. The boys might be limited by their black and navy suits, white shirts, dull ties, and black wing tips, the usual boring everyday getup, but the girls had no rules. Mary Grace wore a bright dress that fell just above the knees and a matching jacket with sleeves that stopped at the elbows. Black stiletto heels. Plenty of leg, though none visible to the three justices once she assumed the podium.

Picking up where Justice Albritton left off, she launched into an attack on Krane's defense. For at least twenty years the company had illegally dumped tons of class-1 carcinogens into the ground. As a direct cause of this dumping, Bowmore's drinking water was polluted with these same carcinogens, none of which were produced or dumped or even found in significant quantities anywhere else in the county. The people of Bowmore drank the water, the same way that each member of the panel had drunk water that very morning. "You shaved, brushed your teeth, showered, used the city's water in your coffee or tea. You drank it at home and you drank it here at work. Did you question the water? Where did it come from? Is it safe? Did you for one second this morning ask yourself if your water contained carcinogens? Probably not. The people of Bowmore were no different."

As a direct result of drinking the water, the

people got sick. The town was hit with a wave of cancer never before seen in this country.

And, as always, this fine, upstanding New York corporation—and here she turned and waved a hand at Jared Kurtin—denied everything. Denied the dumping, the cover-up, denied the lying, even denied its own denials. And, most important, denied any causation between its carcinogens and the cancer. Instead, as we've heard here today, Krane Chemical blames it on the air, the sun, the environment, even the peanut butter and sliced turkey Jeannette Baker used to feed her family. "The jury really loved that part of the trial," she said to a hushed crowd. "Krane dumped tons of toxic chemicals into our ground and our water, but, hey, let's blame it on Jif peanut butter."

Maybe it was out of respect for the lady, or maybe it was their reluctance to interrupt such an impassioned plea, but, whatever the reason, the three judges said nothing.

Mary Grace finished with a quick lecture on the law. The law did not require them to prove that the BCL found in the tissue cells of Pete Baker came directly from the Krane facility. To do so would elevate the standard of proof to clear and convincing evidence. The law only required proof by a preponderance of the evidence, a lower standard.

When her time was up, she sat down next to her husband. The judges thanked the lawyers, then called the next case.

———

The midwinter meeting of the MTA was a somber affair. Attendance was up sharply. The trial lawyers were anxious, deeply concerned, even frightened. The new court had reversed the first two plaintiffs' verdicts on its docket for the year. Could this be the beginning of some horrible streak? Was it time to panic, or was it already too late?

A lawyer from Georgia helped darken the mood with a summary of the sorry state of things in his state. The Supreme Court of Georgia also had nine members, eight of whom were loyal to big business and consistently rejected verdicts for injured or dead plaintiffs. Twenty-two of the last twenty-five verdicts had been reversed. As a result, insurance companies were no longer willing to settle, and why should they? They were not afraid of juries anymore, because they owned the supreme court. Once upon a time, most cases were settled before trial. For a trial lawyer, this meant a caseload that was manageable. Now nothing got settled, and the plaintiff's lawyer had to take every case to trial. And even if he got a verdict, it wouldn't stand on appeal. The fallout is that lawyers are taking fewer cases and fewer injured folks with legitimate claims are being compensated. "The courthouse doors are closing rapidly," he said as he finished.

Though it was only 10:00 a.m., many in the crowd were looking for a bar.

The next speaker lightened the mood, if only a little. Former Justice Sheila McCarthy was introduced and greeted warmly. She thanked the trial lawyers for their unwavering support and hinted that she might not be finished with politics. She railed against those who had conspired to defeat her. And as she was winding down, she brought them to their feet when she announced that since she was now in private practice, she had paid her dues and was a proud member of the Mississippi Trial Advocates.

The Mississippi Supreme Court decides, on average, about 250 cases each year. Most are uncomplicated, fairly routine disputes. Some involve novel issues the court has never seen before. Virtually all are disposed of in an orderly, almost genteel fashion. Occasionally, though, one starts a war.

The case involved a large commercial grass cutter commonly known as a bush hog. The one in question was being pulled behind a John Deere tractor when it struck an abandoned manhole cover hidden in the weeds of a vacant lot. A four-inch piece of jagged steel was launched from the swirling blades of the bush hog. Once airborne, it traveled 238 feet before striking a six-year-old boy in the left temple. The boy's name was Aaron, and he was holding his mother's hand as they walked into a branch bank office in the town of Horn Lake. Aaron was grievously injured, almost died on several occasions, and in the four years since the accident had undergone eleven operations. His medical bills were well over the cap of $500,000 on the family's health insurance policy. Expenses for his future care were estimated at $750,000.

Aaron's lawyers had determined that the

bush hog was fifteen years old and not equipped with side rail guards, debris chains, or any other safety feature used by most of the industry for at least thirty years. They sued. A jury in DeSoto County awarded Aaron $750,000. Afterward, the trial judge increased the award to include the medical expenses. He reasoned that if the jury found liability, then Aaron should be entitled to more damages.

The supreme court was faced with several options: (1) affirm the jury's award of $750,000; (2) affirm the judge's increased award of $1.3 million; (3) reverse on either liability or damages and send it back for a new trial; or (4) reverse and render and kill the lawsuit. Liability appeared to be clear, so the question was more about the money.

The case was assigned to Judge McElwayne. His preliminary memo agreed with the trial judge and pushed for the higher award. If given the chance, he would have advocated for even more money. There was nothing in either amount to compensate the child for the excruciating pain he had endured and would continue to face in the future. Nor was there any award for the loss of future earning capacity. The child, while actually holding hands with his mother, had been crippled for life by an inherently dangerous product that was carelessly manufactured.

Justice Romano from the central district saw it differently. He rarely saw a big verdict he couldn't attack, but this one proved to be a challenge. He decided that the bush hog was, in fact, reasonably designed and properly assembled at the factory, but in the intervening years its safety features and devices had been removed by its various owners. Indeed, the chain of ownership was not clear. Such is the nature of products like bush hogs. They are not clean, neat, safe products. Instead, they are designed to do one thing—cut down thick grass and brush through the use of a series of sharp blades rotating at high speeds. They are extremely dangerous products, but they are nonetheless efficient and necessary.

Justice McElwayne eventually picked up three votes. Justice Romano worked on his brethren for several weeks before getting his three. Once again, it would be decided by the new guy.

Justice Fisk wrestled with the case. He

read the briefs shortly after being sworn in, and changed his mind from day to day. He found it easy to believe that the manufacturer could reasonably expect its product to be modified over time, especially in light of the violent nature of a bush hog. But the record wasn't entirely clear as to whether the manufacturer had complied with all federal regulations at the factory. Ron had great sympathy for the child, but would not allow his emotions to become a factor.

On the other hand, he had been elected on a platform of limiting liability. He had been attacked by trial lawyers and supported by the people they loved to sue.

The court was waiting; a decision was needed. Ron flip-flopped so many times he became hopelessly confused. When he finally cast his vote with Romano, he had no appetite and left the office early.

Justice McElwayne revised his opinion, and in a scathing dissent accused the majority of rewriting facts, changing legal standards, and circumventing the jury process, all in an effort to impose its own brand of tort reform. Several in the majority fired back (Ron did not), and when the opinion was finally published, it spoke more to the internal upheaval in the supreme court than to the plight of little Aaron.

Such nastiness among civilized jurists was extremely rare, but the bruised egos and hurt feelings only deepened the rift between the two sides. There was no middle ground, no room for compromise.

When a case involved a substantial verdict, the insurance companies could now relax.

CHAPTER 34

Justice McElwayne's bitter dissents continued into the spring. But after the sixth loss
in a row, another 5–4 split, he lost some of
his spunk. The case involved gross negligence on the part of an incompetent doctor,
and when the court took away the verdict,
McElwayne knew that his brethren had
shifted so far to the right that they would
never return.

An orthopedic surgeon in Jackson
botched a routine surgery to repair a herni-
ated disk. His patient was rendered a paraplegic, and eventually filed suit. The doctor
had been sued five times previously, had

lost his medical license in two other states, and had been treated on at least three occasions for addiction to painkillers. The jury awarded the paraplegic $1.8 million for actual damages, then slapped the doctor and the hospital with $5 million in punitive damages.

Justice Fisk, in his first written opinion for the majority, declared the actual damages to be excessive and the punitive award unconscionable. The decision sent the case back for a new trial on actual damages only. Forget punitive.

Justice McElwayne was apoplectic. His dissent bristled with vague allegations that special interests of the state now had more influence on the supreme court than did four of its own members. The final sentence of his initial draft was almost libelous: "The author of the majority opinion feigns shock at the amount of the punitive award. However, he should be rather comfortable with the sum of $5 million. That was the price of the seat he now occupies." To get a laugh, he e-mailed a copy of the draft to Sheila McCarthy. She indeed laughed, then begged him to remove the last sentence. Eventually, he did.

McElwayne's dissent raged for four pages. Albritton concurred with another three. They wondered privately if they could find happiness in writing useless dissents for the rest of their careers.

———

Their useless dissents were beautiful music to Barry Rinehart. He was carefully reading every decision out of Mississippi. His staff was analyzing the opinions, the pending cases, and the recent jury trials that might one day send a verdict to the high court. As always, Barry was watching closely.

Electing a friendly judge was indeed a victory, but it wasn't complete until the pay-off. So far, Justice Fisk had a perfect voting record. *Baker v. Krane Chemical* was ripe for a decision.

On a flight to New York to see Mr. Trudeau, Barry decided that their boy needed some reassurance.

———

The dinner was at the University Club, on the top floor of Jackson's tallest building. It was a quiet event, almost secret, by invitation only and the invitations were not printed. A phone network had rounded up the eighty or so guests. The evening was in honor of Justice Ron Fisk. Doreen was there and had the high honor of sitting next to Senator Myers Rudd, who'd just flown in from Washington. Steak and lobster were served. The first speaker was the president of the state medical association, a dignified surgeon from Natchez who at times seemed near tears as he talked about the enormous sense of relief in the medical community. For years, the doctors had labored under the fear of litigation. They had paid enormous insurance premiums. They had been subjected to frivolous lawsuits. They had been abused in depositions and during trials. But now everything had changed. Because of the new direction of the supreme court, they could properly treat their patients without looking over their shoulders. He thanked Ron Fisk for his courage, his wisdom, and his commitment to protecting the doctors and nurses and hospitals of the state of Mississippi.

Senator Rudd was on his third scotch, and the host knew from experience that the fourth one meant trouble. He called on The Senator to say a few words. Thirty minutes later, after fighting battles around the world and settling everything but the conflict in the Middle East, Rudd finally remembered why he was there. He never used notes, never planned a speech, never wasted time on forethought. His presence alone was enough to thrill everyone. Oh yes, Ron Fisk. He recounted their first meeting in Washington a year earlier. He called him "Ronny" at least three times. When he saw the host point at his watch, he finally sat down and demanded scotch number four.

The next speaker was the executive director of the Commerce Council, a veteran of many bruising battles with the trial lawyers. He spoke eloquently about the drastic change in the state's economic development environment. Companies young and old were suddenly making bold plans, no longer afraid to take risks that might lead to litigation. Foreign firms were now interested in locating facilities in the state. Thank you, Ron Fisk.

Mississippi's reputation as a judicial hellhole, as a dumping ground for thousands of frivolous lawsuits, as a haven for reckless trial lawyers, had changed almost overnight. Thank you, Ron Fisk.

Many firms were beginning to see the first signs of stabilized rates for liability insurance protection. Nothing definite yet, but things looked promising. Thank you, Ron Fisk.

After Justice Fisk had been showered with praise, almost to the point of embarrassment, he was asked to say a few words himself. He thanked everyone for their support during his campaign. He was pleased with his first three months on the court, and he was certain that the majority there would hold together on the issues of liability and damages. (Heavy applause.) His colleagues were bright and hardworking, and he claimed to be enamored with the intellectual challenge of the cases. He did not feel the least bit disadvantaged because of his inexperience.

On behalf of Doreen, he thanked them for a wonderful evening.

————

It was a Friday night, and they drove home to Brookhaven still floating on the accolades and admiration. The kids were asleep when they arrived at midnight.

Ron slept six hours and awoke in a panic

over where to find a catcher. Baseball season was beginning. Tryouts were at 9:00 a.m. for the eleven- and twelve-year-olds. Josh, eleven, was moving up and would be one of the highest-ranked newcomers to the league. Because of his demanding job, Ron could not commit to a head coaching position. He could not make all the practices, but he was determined not to miss a single game. He would handle the pitchers and catchers. One of his former law partners would handle the rest and call himself the head coach. Another father would organize the practices.

It was the first Saturday in April, a chilly morning throughout the state. A nervous bunch of players and parents and especially coaches gathered at the city park for the beginning of the season. The nine- and ten-year-olds were sent to one field, the elevens and twelves to another. All players would be evaluated, then ranked, then placed in the draft.

The coaches met behind home plate to get organized. There was the usual nervous chatter and cheap shots and lighthearted insults. Most of them had coached in the same league the year before. Ron, back then, had been a popular coach, just another young father who would spend hours on the field from April to July. Now, though, he felt a bit elevated. He had put together a brilliant campaign and won an important political race with a record vote. That made him unique among his peers. There was, after all, only one supreme court justice in the town of Brookhaven. There was a certain detachment that he did not particularly like, though he wasn't sure if he disliked it, either.

There were already calling him "Judge."

Judge Fisk pulled a name out of the hat. His team was the Rockies.

———

The apartment was so cramped during the week they had to escape on Saturdays.

The Paytons coaxed Mack and Liza out of bed with the suggestion of breakfast at a nearby pancake house. Afterward, they left Hattiesburg and arrived in Bowmore before 10:00 a.m. Mrs. Shelby, Mary Grace's mother, had promised a long lunch under an oak tree—catfish followed by homemade ice cream. Mr. Shelby had the boat ready.

He and Wes took the kids to a small lake where the crappie were biting.

Mary Grace and her mother sat on the porch for an hour, covering the usual topics, avoiding anything remotely related to the law. Family news, church gossip, weddings, and funerals, but they stayed away from cancer, which for years had dominated the chatter in Cary County.

Long before lunch, Mary Grace drove to town, to Pine Grove, where she met with Denny Ott. She passed along her latest thoughts on the new supreme court, a rather sad summary. Not for the first time she warned Denny that they would probably lose. He was preparing his people. He knew they would survive. They had lost everything else.

She drove two blocks and parked in the gravel driveway of Jeannette's trailer. They sat outside, under a shade tree, sipping bottled water and talking about men. Jeannette's current boyfriend was a fifty-five-year-old widower with a nice job and a nice home and little interest in her lawsuit—not that the lawsuit was attracting the attention it once commanded. The verdict was now seventeen months old. Not a dime had changed hands, and none was anticipated.

"We expect a ruling this month," Mary Grace said. "And it will be a miracle if we win."

"I'm praying for a miracle," Jeannette said, "but I'm ready for whatever happens. I just want it to be over."

After a long chat and a quick hug, Mary Grace left. She drove the streets of her hometown, past the high school and the homes of childhood friends, past the stores on Main Street, then into the countryside. She stopped at Treadway's Grocery, where she bought a soda and said hello to a lady she had known her entire life.

Driving back to her parents' home, she passed the Barrysville Volunteer Fire Department, a small metal building with an old pumper that the boys rolled out and washed on election days. The station also served as a precinct, where, five months earlier, 74 percent of the fine folks of Barrysville voted for God and guns and against gays and liberals. Barely five miles from the Bowmore town limits, Ron Fisk had convinced these people that he was their protector.

Perhaps he was. Perhaps his mere presence on the court was too intimidating for some.

The Meyerchec and Spano appeal was dismissed by the clerk for a lack of prosecution. They failed to file the required briefs, and after the usual warnings from the clerk their lawyer said they had no desire to go forward. They were not available for comment, and their lawyer did not return phone calls from reporters.

On the day of the dismissal, the supreme court reached a new low in its movement to drastically limit corporate exposure. A privately held pharmaceutical company called Bosk had made and widely marketed a strong painkiller called Rybadell. It proved to be horribly addictive, and within a few years Bosk was getting hammered with lawsuits. During one of the first trials, Bosk executives were caught lying. A U.S. attorney in Pennsylvania opened an investigation, and there were allegations that the company had known about Rybadell's addictive propensities but had tried to bury this information. The drug was extremely profitable.

A former Jackson cop named Dillman was injured in a motorcycle accident, and in the course of his recovery became addicted to Rybadell. He battled the addiction for two years, during which time his health and the rest of his life disintegrated. He was arrested twice for shoplifting. He eventually sued Bosk in the Circuit Court of Rankin County. The jury found the company liable and awarded Dillman $275,000, the lowest Rybadell verdict in the country.

On appeal, the supreme court reversed, 5–4. The principal reason, set forth in the majority opinion by Justice Romano, was that Dillman should not be awarded damages because he was a drug addict.

In a rancorous dissent, Justice Albritton begged the majority to step forward and produce any scintilla of proof that the plaintiff was a drug addict "before his introduction to Rybadell."

Three days after the decision, four Bosk executives pled guilty to withholding information from the Food and Drug Administration, and to lying to federal investigators.

CHAPTER 35

Krane Chemical's first-quarter earnings were much better than expected. In fact, they astounded the analysts, who had been expecting about $1.25 per share on the high end. When Krane reported $2.05 per share, the company and its amazing comeback attracted even more interest from financial publications.

All fourteen plants were running at full throttle. Prices had been cut to recapture market share. The sales force was working overtime to fill orders. Debt had been slashed. Most of the problems that had

dogged the company throughout the preceding year were suddenly gone.

The stock had made a steady and impressive climb from single digits, and was
trading around $24 when the earnings news
hit. It jumped to $30. When last seen at that
price, the stock was free-falling the day after the verdict in Hattiesburg.

The Trudeau Group now owned 80 percent of Krane, or around forty-eight million
shares. Since the rumors of bankruptcy just
before the election back in November, Mr.
Trudeau's net worth had increased by $800
million. And he was quite anxious to double
that.

———

Before a final decision is handed down by
the supreme court, the justices spend
weeks reading one another's memos and
preliminary opinions. They sometimes argue, privately. They lobby for votes to support their positions. They lean on their
clerks for useful gossip from down the hall.
Occasionally, there are deadlocks that take
months to resolve.

The last thing Justice Fisk read late Friday
afternoon was McElwayne's dissent in the

case of *Jeannette Baker v. Krane Chemical Corporation.* It was widely assumed to be a dissent with three others concurring. The majority opinion was written by Justice Calligan. Romano was working on a concurring opinion, and there was a chance that Albritton would write a dissent of his own. Though the details were not complete, there was little doubt that the final decision would be a 5–4 reversal of the verdict.

Fisk read the dissent, scoffed at it, and decided to concur with Calligan first thing Monday morning. Then Justice Fisk changed clothes and became Coach Fisk. It was time for a game.

The Rockies opened their season with a weekend jamboree in the delta town of Russburg, an hour northwest of Jackson. They would play one game on Friday night, at least two on Saturday, and maybe one on Sunday. The games were only four innings long, and every player was encouraged to pitch and play different positions. There were no trophies and no championships—just a loosely competitive round-robin to start the season. Thirty teams signed up in the eleven- and twelve-year-old division, including two others from Brookhaven.

The Rockies' first opponent was a team from the small town of Rolling Fork. The night was cool, the air clear, the sports complex filled with players and parents and the excitement of five games going at once.

Doreen was in Brookhaven with Clarissa and Zeke, who had a game at nine on Saturday morning.

In the first inning, Josh played second base, and when he came to bat, his father was coaching at third. When he struck out on four pitches, his father yelled encouragement and reminded him that he could not hit the ball if he kept the bat on his shoulder. In the second inning, Josh went to the mound and promptly struck out the first two batters he faced. The third hitter was a stocky twelve-year-old, the catcher, batting in the seven hole. He yanked the first pitch foul but very hard.

"Keep it low and away," Ron yelled from the dugout.

The second pitch was not low and away. It was a fastball right down the middle of the plate, and the hitter ripped it hard. The ball shot off the barrel of the aluminum bat and left the plate much faster than it had arrived. For a split second, Josh was frozen, and by the time he began to react, the ball was in his face. He jerked just slightly as the ball hit him square in the right temple. The ball then careened over the shortstop and rolled into left field.

Josh's eyes were open when his father reached him. He was lying in a heap at the base of the mound, stunned and groaning.

"Say something, Josh," Ron said as he gently touched the wound.

"Where's the ball?" Josh asked.

"Don't worry about it. Can you see me all right?"

"I think so." Tears were leaking from his eyes, and he clenched his teeth to keep from crying. The skin had been scraped, and there was a little blood in his hair. The swelling had already started.

"Get some ice," someone said.

"Call the EMTs."

The other coaches and umpires hovered around. The kid who hit the line drive stood nearby, ready to cry himself.

"Don't close your eyes," Ron said.

"Okay, okay," Josh said, still breathing rapidly.

"Who plays third base for the Braves?"

"Chipper."

"And center field?"

"Andruw."

"Attaboy."

After a few minutes, Josh sat up and the fans applauded. Then he stood and walked with his father's help to the dugout, where he stretched out on the bench. Ron, his heart still hammering away, gently placed a bag of ice on the knot on Josh's temple. The game slowly picked up again.

A medic arrived and examined Josh, who seemed perfectly responsive. He could see, hear, remember details, and even mentioned returning to the game. The medic said no, as did Coach Fisk. "Maybe tomorrow," Ron said, but only to comfort his son. Ron had a knot of his own, stuck firmly in his throat, and he was just beginning to calm down. He planned to take him home after the game.

"He looks fine," the medic said. "But you might want to get him x-rayed."

"Now?" Ron asked.

"No rush, but I'd do it tonight."

By the end of the third inning, Josh was sitting up and joking with his teammates. Ron returned to the third-base coach's box and was whispering to a runner when one of the Rockies yelled from the dugout, "Josh is throwing up!"

The umpires stopped the game again, and the coaches cleared the Rockies' dugout. Josh was dizzy, sweating profusely, and violently nauseous. The medic was nearby, and within minutes a stretcher arrived with two emergency medical technicians. Ron held his son's hand as they rolled him to the parking lot. "Don't close your eyes," Ron said over and over. And, "Talk to me, Josh."

"My head hurts, Dad."

"You're okay. Just don't close your eyes."

They lifted the stretcher into the ambulance, locked it down, and allowed Ron to squat beside his son. Five minutes later, they wheeled him into the emergency room entrance at Henry County General Hospital. Josh was alert and had not vomited since leaving the ballpark.

A three-car smashup had occurred an hour earlier, and the emergency room was in a frenzy. The first doctor to examine Josh ordered a CT scan and explained to Ron that he would not be allowed to go farther into the hospital. "I think he's fine," the doctor said, and Ron found a chair in the cluttered waiting room. He called Doreen and managed to get through that difficult conversation. Time virtually stopped as the minutes dragged on.

The Rockies' head coach, Ron's former law partner, arrived in a rush and coaxed Ron outside. He had something to show him. From the backseat of his car he produced an aluminum bat. "This is it," he said gravely. It was a Screamer, a popular bat manufactured by Win Rite Sporting Goods, one of a dozen to be found in any ballpark in the country.

"Look at this," the coach said, rubbing the barrel where someone had tried to sand off part of the label. "It's a minus seven, outlawed years ago."

Minus seven referred to the differential between the weight and the length of the bat. It was twenty-nine inches long but weighed only twenty-two ounces, much easier to swing without yielding any of the force upon contact with the ball. Current rules prohibited a differential greater than four. The bat was at least five years old.

Ron gawked at it as if it were a smoking gun. "How'd you get it?"

"I checked it when the kid came to the

plate again. I showed it to the ump, who threw it out and went after the coach. I went after him, too, but, to be honest, he didn't have a clue. He gave me the damned thing."

More of the Rockies' parents arrived, then some of the players. They huddled around a bench near the emergency exit and waited. An hour passed before the doctor returned to brief Ron.

"CT scan's negative," the doctor said. "I think he's okay, just a mild concussion."

"Thank God."

"Where do you live?"

"Brookhaven."

"You can take him home, but he needs to be very still for the next few days. No sports of any kind. If he experiences dizziness, headaches, double vision, blurred vision, dilated pupils, ringing in his ears, bad taste in his mouth, moodiness, or drowsiness, then you get him to your local doctor."

Ron nodded and wanted to take notes.

"I'll put all this in a discharge report, along with the CT scan."

"Fine, sure."

The doctor paused, looked at Ron a bit closer, then said, "What do you do for a living?"

"I'm a judge, supreme court."

The doctor smiled, offered a hand to shake. "I sent you a check last year. Thank you for what you're doing down there."

"Thanks, Doc."

An hour later, ten minutes before midnight, they left Russburg. Josh sat in the front seat with an ice pack stuck to his head and listened to the Braves-Dodgers game on the radio. Ron glanced at him every ten seconds, ready to pounce on the first warning sign. There were none, until they entered the outskirts of Brookhaven and Josh said, "Dad, my head hurts a little."

"The nurse said a small headache is okay. But a bad one means trouble. On a scale of one to ten, where is it?"

"Three."

"Okay, when it gets to five, I want to know."

Doreen was waiting at the door with a dozen questions. She read the discharge summary at the kitchen table while Ron and Josh ate a sandwich. After two bites, Josh said he was not hungry. He'd been starving when they left Russburg. He was suddenly irritable, but it was hours past his bedtime. When Doreen began her version of a physical exam, he barked at her and went to use the bathroom.

"What do you think?" Ron asked.

"He appears to be fine," she replied. "Just a little cranky and sleepy."

They had a huge fight over the sleeping arrangements. Josh was eleven years old and wasn't about to sleep with his mother. Ron explained to him, rather firmly, that on this particular night, and under these unusual circumstances, he would indeed go to sleep with his mother at his side. Ron would be napping in a chair next to the bed.

Under the steady gaze of both parents, he fell asleep quickly. Then Ron nodded off in the chair, and at some point around 3:30 a.m. Doreen finally closed her eyes.

She opened them an hour later when Josh screamed. He had vomited again, and his head was splitting. He was dizzy, incoherent, and crying and said everything looked blurry.

The family doctor was a close friend named Calvin Treet. Ron called him while Doreen ran next door to fetch a neighbor. In less than ten minutes, they were walking into the ER at the Brookhaven hospital. Ron was carrying Josh, and Doreen had the discharge papers and the CT scan. The ER physician did a quick exam, and everything was wrong—slow heart rate, unequal pupils, drowsiness. Dr. Treet arrived and took over while the ER physician examined the discharge summary.

"Who read the scan?" Treet asked.

"The doctor in Russburg," Ron said.

"When?"

"About eight o'clock last night."

"Eight hours ago?"

"Something like that."

"It doesn't show much," he said. "Let's do a scan here."

The ER doctor and a nurse took Josh to an exam room. Treet said to the Fisks, "You need to wait out there. I'll be right back."

They sleepwalked to the ER waiting room, too numb and too terrified to say anything for a few moments. The room was empty but gave the impression of having survived a rough night—empty soda cans, newspapers on the floor, candy wrappers on the tables. How many others had sat here in a daze waiting for the doctors to appear and deliver bad news?

They held hands and prayed for a long time, silently at first, then back and forth in short soft sentences, and when the praying was over, they felt some relief. Doreen called home, talked to the neighbor who was babysitting, and promised to call again when they knew something.

When Calvin Treet walked into the room, they knew things were not going well. He sat down and faced them. "Josh has a fracture of the skull, according to our CT scan. The scan you brought from Russburg is not very helpful because it belongs to another patient."

"What the hell!" Ron said.

"The doctor there looked at the wrong CT scan. The patient's name is barely readable at the bottom, but it ain't Josh Fisk."

"This can't be true," Doreen said.

"It is, but we'll worry about it later. Listen carefully; here's where we are. The ball hit Josh right here," he said, pointing to his right temple. "It's the thinnest part of the skull, known as the temporal bone. The crack is called a linear fracture, and it's about two inches long. Just inside the skull is a membrane that encases the brain, and feeding it is the middle meningeal artery. This artery goes through the bone, and when the bone was cracked, the artery was lacerated, causing blood to accumulate between the bone and the membrane. This compressed the brain. The blood clot, known as an epidural hematoma, grew and increased the pressure inside the skull. The only treatment now is a craniotomy, which is a removal of the hematoma by opening the brain."

"Oh, my God," Doreen said and covered her eyes.

"Please listen," Treet went on. "We need to get him to Jackson, to the trauma unit at University Medical Center. I suggest we call their air ambulance and get him there in a helicopter."

The ER physician arrived in a hurry and said to Dr. Treet, "The patient is deteriorating. You need to take a look."

As Dr. Treet started to walk away, Ron stood, grabbed his arm, and said, "Talk to me, Calvin. How serious is this?"

"It's very serious, Ron. It could be life threatening."

———

Josh was boarded onto the helicopter and whisked away. Doreen and Calvin Treet rode with him while Ron raced home, checked on Zeke and Clarissa, and threw a few necessities in an overnight bag. Then he sped north on Interstate 55, driving a hundred miles per hour and daring any cop to stop him. When he wasn't plea-bargaining with God, he was cursing the doctor in Russburg who studied the wrong CT scan. And occasionally, he turned around and glanced at the defectively designed and unreasonably dangerous product in the rear seat.

He had never liked aluminum bats.

CHAPTER 36

At ten minutes after eight on Saturday morning, some thirteen hours after being struck by the baseball, Josh underwent surgery at the University of Mississippi Medical Center in Jackson.

Ron and Doreen waited in the hospital's chapel with friends who were arriving from Brookhaven. Their pastor was with them. Back at St. Luke's, a prayer vigil was under way in the church's sanctuary. Ron's brother arrived at noon with Zeke and Clarissa, both as frightened and shell-shocked as their parents. Hours passed with no word from the surgeons. Dr. Treet disappeared from time to time to check on things, but seldom brought back any useful news. As some of their friends left, others came to replace them. Grandparents and uncles and aunts and cousins arrived, and waited, and prayed, and then left to roam around the sprawling hospital.

Four hours after the Fisks last saw their son, the chief surgeon appeared and motioned for them to follow him. Dr. Treet joined the conversation as they walked down a hallway, away from the crowd. They stopped near a door to a restroom. Ron and Doreen clutched each other, bracing for the worst. The surgeon spoke in a grave and weary voice: "He has survived the surgery and is doing as well as can be expected. We removed a large hematoma compressing the brain. The pressure inside the skull has been reduced. But there was a lot of brain swelling, an extraordinary amount to be honest. There will likely be some permanent damage."

"Life" and "death" are easily understood, but "damage" conveys fears that are not readily defined.

"He's not going to die," Doreen said.

"As of right now, he's alive and his vital

signs are good. He has a 90 percent chance of survival. The next seventy-two hours will be crucial."

"How much damage?" Ron asked, getting to the point.

"There's no way to tell right now. Some of the damage might be reversible with time and therapy, but that's really a conversation for another day. Right now, let's just continue to pray that he improves over the next three days."

———

Late Saturday night, Josh was in the ICU. Ron and Doreen were allowed to see him for ten minutes, though he was in a drug-induced coma. They didn't manage to maintain their composure when they first saw him. His head was wrapped like a mummy, and a breathing tube ran from his mouth. He was hooked to a ventilator. Doreen was afraid to touch any part of his body, even his foot.

A sympathetic nurse agreed to move a chair to a spot outside his room and allow one parent to sit there throughout the night. Ron and Doreen sent their support team back to Brookhaven, then began alternating between the ICU and the waiting room. Sleep was out of the question, and they walked the halls until sunrise Sunday morning.

The doctors were pleased with Josh's first night. After an early morning review, Ron and Doreen found a motel nearby. They showered and managed a quick nap before reassuming their positions at the hospital. The waiting rituals began again, as did the prayer vigils at home. The flow of visitors coming and going soon became an ordeal in itself. Ron and Doreen just wanted to be alone in the room with their son.

Late Sunday night, when Doreen was in the ICU and the crowd had left, Ron strolled the corridors of the hospital, stretching his legs and trying to stay awake. He found another waiting room, one for the families of noncritical patients. It was much more inviting, with nicer furniture and a wider selection of vending machines. Dinner was a diet soda and a bag of pretzels, and as he crunched on them mindlessly, a small boy walked by and seemed ready to touch his knee.

"Aaron," his mother barked from across the room. "Come here."

"He's fine," Ron said, smiling at the child, who quickly drifted away.

Aaron. The name brought back a memory. Aaron was the boy struck in the head by the piece of metal thrown by the bush hog. A brain injury, permanent disability, financial ruin for the family. The jury found the manufacturer liable. The trial had a clean record. At that moment, Justice Fisk could not remember why he had so easily voted with the majority in reversing the verdict.

Back then, barely two months ago, he had never felt the pain of a parent with a severely injured child. Or the fear of losing the child.

Now, in the middle of this nightmare, he remembered Aaron in a different way. When he read the medical summaries in the case, he had done so in the comfort of his office, far removed from reality. The kid was severely injured, which was a pity, but accidents happen in everyday life. Could the accident have been prevented? He thought so then, and he certainly thought so now.

Little Aaron was back, staring at the bag of pretzels. It was shaking.

"Aaron, leave that man alone," the mother yelled.

Ron stared at the shaking pretzels.

The accident could have been prevented, and should have been. If the manufacturer had followed established regulations, then the bush hog would have been much safer. Why had he been so eager to protect its manufacturer?

The case was gone, forever dismissed by five supposedly wise men, none of whom had ever shown much sympathy for those who suffer. He had to wonder if the other four—Calligan, Romano, Bateman, and Ross—had ever roamed the tomb-like halls of a hospital at all hours of the day and night waiting for a child to live or die.

No, they had not. Otherwise, they wouldn't be what they are today.

———

Sunday slowly yielded to Monday. Another week began, though it was far different from any one before. Ron and Doreen refused to leave the hospital for more than an hour or two. Josh was not responding well, and they were afraid that each visit to his bed might be their last glimpse of him alive. Friends brought clothes and food and newspapers, and they offered to sit and wait if the Fisks would like to go home for a few hours. But Ron and Doreen stood fast and plowed on with a fixed determination, zombielike in their belief that Josh would do better if they stayed close by. Tired and haggard, they lost patience with the parade of visitors from home and began to hide in various places around the hospital.

Ron called his office and told his secretary he had no idea when he might return. Doreen told her boss she was taking a leave of absence. When the boss explained, delicately, that their policies did not grant such leaves, she politely informed him it was time to change said policies. He agreed to do so immediately.

The hospital was fifteen minutes from the Gartin building, and early Tuesday Ron stopped by for a quick look at his desk. It had accumulated several new piles of paperwork. His chief clerk ran down the list of all pending cases, but Ron was distracted. "I'm thinking about a leave of absence. Run it by the chief," he instructed the clerk. "For thirty days, maybe sixty. I can't concentrate on this stuff right now."

"Sure, will do. You were planning to concur this morning on *Baker versus Krane*."

"It can wait. Everything can wait."

He managed to leave the building without seeing another member of the court.

———

Tuesday's edition of the *Clarion-Ledger* ran a story about Josh and his injury. Justice Fisk could not be reached for comment, but an unidentified source got most of the facts right. The doctors had removed a large blood clot that had been pressing on his brain. His life was no longer in danger. It was too soon to speculate about long-term problems. There was no mention of the doctor who read the wrong CT scan.

However, the online chatter soon filled in the gaps. There was gossip about an illegal baseball bat involved in the accident, and speculation about severe brain damage, and an account from someone inside the Henry County General Hospital who claimed to know that the doctors there had screwed up. There were a couple of wild theories that Justice Fisk had undergone a dramatic conversion in his judicial philosophy. One rumor declared that he was about to resign.

Wes Payton watched it carefully from his

office. His wife did not. She was working hard to distract herself with other cases, but Wes was consumed with the story about Josh. As the father of young children, he could not imagine the horror the Fisks were enduring. And he could not avoid wondering how the tragedy might affect the *Baker* case. He did not expect a sudden about-face by Ron Fisk, but the possibility was there.

They had only one prayer left, and that was for a miracle. Could this be it?

They waited. The decision was due any day now.

———

By early Tuesday afternoon, Josh was beginning to show signs of improvement. He was awake, alert, and following commands. He couldn't talk, because of the breathing tube, but he seemed fidgety, which was a good sign. The pressure on his brain had been reduced to almost normal levels. The doctors had explained several times that it would take days, maybe weeks to determine a long-term prognosis.

With Josh awake, the Fisks decided to spend the night at home. This was greatly encouraged by the doctors and nurses. Doreen's sister agreed to sit in the ICU, within fifteen feet of her nephew's bed.

They left Jackson, relieved to be away from the hospital and anxious to see Zeke and Clarissa. Their conversation was about home-cooked food, long showers, and their comfortable bed. They vowed to savor the next ten hours, because their ordeal was just beginning.

But it would be difficult to relax. On the outskirts of Jackson, Ron's cell phone rang. It was Justice Calligan, and he began the conversation with a long-winded inquiry into Josh's condition. He conveyed condolences from everyone at the court. He promised to stop by the hospital as soon as possible. Ron was thankful, but soon had the feeling there was a business angle to the call.

"Just a couple of matters, Ron," Calligan said, "and I know you're preoccupied right now."

"I am indeed."

"There's nothing terribly urgent here, except for two cases. It looks as though that Bowmore toxic case is split 4 to 4. No surprise there, I guess. I was hoping you would concur with me on this one."

"I thought Romano was writing, too."

"He is, and he's finished, as is Albritton. All opinions are ready, and we need your concurrence."

"Let me sleep on it."

"Fine. The other is that nursing home case out of Webster County. Another 4–4 split."

"That's a very ugly case," Ron said, almost in disgust. In yet another nursing home case, a patient was basically abandoned by the staff and eventually found unfed, lying in his own waste, covered in bedsores, unmedicated, and delirious. The company that owned the facility had reported huge profits, which came as a surprise to the jury when it was proven just how little was spent on patient care. Nursing home abuse was so rampant Ron was already sick of reading about it.

"Yes, it is. Very tragic," Calligan said, as if he were capable of sympathy.

"And I guess you want to reverse?"

"I don't see the liability, and the damages are exorbitant."

In the three and a half months Ron had

been on the court, Justice Calligan had never managed to see liability in any death or injury case. He believed jurors were stupid and easily led astray by slick trial lawyers. And he believed that it was his solemn responsibility to correct every miscarriage of justice (plaintiff's verdict) from the comfort of his detached environment.

"Let me sleep on it," Ron said again. Doreen was becoming irritated with the phone call.

"Yes, always a good idea. If we could finish these two cases, Ron, then a short leave of absence might work."

A short leave of absence, or a long one for that matter, was solely within the discretion of each justice. Ron did not need Calligan to approve it. He thanked him anyway and hung up.

The Fisks' kitchen was filled with food from friends, mainly cakes and pies and casseroles. A buffet was arranged on one counter, and they ate with Zeke, Clarissa, two neighbors, and Doreen's parents. They slept six hours, then drove back to the hospital.

When they arrived, Josh was in the midst of a prolonged seizure, the second in the past hour. It passed and his vital signs improved, but it was a setback in his slow recovery. Thursday morning, he was alert again, but irritable, restless, unable to concentrate, unable to remember anything about the accident, and highly agitated. One of the doctors explained that his condition was symptomatic of post-concussion syndrome.

Thursday night, the Rockies' coach, Ron's former law partner, drove to Jackson for another visit. He and Ron had dinner in the hospital canteen, and over soup and salad he pulled out his notes. "I've done some research," the coach said. "Win Rite stopped making the lighter bats six years ago, probably in response to complaints about injuries. In fact, the entire industry went to minus four and nothing higher. Over the years, the aluminum alloys got lighter but also stronger. The barrel of the bat wall actually absorbs the ball upon contact, then launches it when the wall pops back into its original position. The result is a lighter bat, but also a much more dangerous one. Safety advocates have been bitching about these bats for a decade, and lots of studies have been done. In one test, a pitching machine threw a fastball at 90 miles an hour, and the ball came off the bat at 120. Two fatalities on record, one in high school, one in college, but hundreds of injuries in all age-groups. So, Little League and some of the other youth organizations got together and banned anything above a minus four.

"But the problem is obvious. Win Rite and the other bat makers have a million of the old bats still out there, still being used, and we finally saw one in the game last Friday."

"There was never a recall?" Ron asked.

"None whatsoever. And they know the damned things are dangerous. Their own tests prove it."

Ron was nibbling on a saltine, certain of where this was going and unwilling to help it get there.

"The Rolling Fork team is probably liable, but it's not worth the trouble. The City of Russburg could be held liable because the umpire, a city employee by the way, failed to check the equipment. And the big tuna is, of course, Win Rite. Assets of two billion. Tons of insurance coverage. Very good case of liability. Damages undetermined but substantial. All in all a strong case, except for one small problem. Our supreme court."

"You sound like a trial lawyer."

"They're not always wrong. If you ask me, I say you should consider filing a product case."

"I don't recall asking you, and I can't file a lawsuit. I'd be laughed out of the state."

"What about the next kid, Ron? What about the next family that will go through the same nightmare? Litigation has cleaned up a lot of bad products and protected a lot of people."

"There's no way."

"And why should you and the State of Mississippi get stuck with a million bucks in medical bills? Win Rite is worth billions. They made a lousy product; make them pay."

"You are a trial lawyer."

"No. I'm your former partner. We practiced together for fourteen years, and the Ron Fisk I remember had great respect for the law. Justice Fisk seems determined to change all of it."

"Okay, okay. I've heard enough."

"I'm sorry, Ron. I shouldn't have—"

"It's okay. Let's go check on Josh."

Tony Zachary returned to Jackson on Friday and heard the news about Josh Fisk. He went straight to the hospital and eventually found Ron napping on a waiting room sofa. They talked for an hour about the accident, about the surgery, and also about Tony's fishing expedition down in Belize.

Tony was deeply concerned about young Josh. He certainly hoped the child would make a quick and complete recovery. But what he wanted to know, but couldn't bring himself to ask, was, "When might you finish up with the *Krane* appeal?"

As soon as he was in his car, he called Barry Rinehart with the disturbing news.

———

A week after he arrived at the hospital, Josh was moved from the ICU to a private room, one that was immediately inundated with flowers, stuffed animals, cards from his fifth-grade classmates, balloons, and enough candy to feed an entire elementary school. A cot was arranged so that one of his parents could sleep next to his bed.

While the room at first gave the impression of a lighter mood, things turned gloomy almost immediately. The team of neurologists began extensive evaluations. There was no paralysis, but a definite decline in motor skills and coordination, along with severe memory loss and an inability to concentrate. Josh was easily distracted and slow to recognize objects. The tubes were gone, but his speech was noticeably slower. Some recovery was likely in the months to come, but there was a good chance of permanent damage.

The thick head bandages were replaced with much smaller ones. Josh was allowed to walk to the restroom, a heartbreaking sight as he shuffled awkwardly forward, one clumsy step after another. Ron helped him, and fought back tears.

His little baseball star had played his final game.

Chapter 37

Dr. Calvin Treet drove to Russburg and arranged a meeting with the ER physician who had read the wrong CT scan. After they examined the two scans, Josh's and the other patient's, they argued briefly before the doctor admitted that the emergency room that night had been chaotic and understaffed, and, yes, mistakes were made. The fact that he'd botched the treatment of the son of a supreme court justice was overwhelming. "Will the family file suit?" he asked, clearly shaken.

"I don't know, but you should notify your insurance company."

Treet took the file to Jackson and discussed it with Ron and Doreen. He walked them through standard CT scan procedure, then recounted his conversation with the ER doctor.

"What should've been done?" Doreen asked.

Treet knew the question was coming. He knew he would be asked by his friends to pass judgment on the performance of another doctor. He had decided days ago to be as honest as possible. "They should've brought him here immediately and removed the blood clot. It's brain surgery, but it's not a complicated procedure. Josh would have been home two days after surgery, completely healed with no damage whatsoever."

"This CT scan was taken at eight o'clock Friday night," Ron said. "You saw Josh in Brookhaven about nine hours later, right?"

"Something like that."

"So for nine hours the pressure continued to build inside his skull?"

"Yes."

"And the compression of the brain by the blood clot damages the brain?"

"Yes."

There was a long silence as they danced

around the obvious conclusion. Ron finally asked, "Calvin, what would you do if it were your kid?"

"Sue the bastard. It's gross negligence."

"I can't sue, Calvin. I'd make a mockery out of myself."

———

After a game of squash, a shower, and a massage in the Senate gym, Myers Rudd ducked into a limo and suffered through the late afternoon traffic like everyone else. An hour later, he arrived at the general aviation terminal at Dulles, and there he boarded a Gulfstream 5, the newest in the fleet owned by Mr. Carl Trudeau. The Senator did not know who owned the jet, nor had he ever met Mr. Trudeau, which in most cultures would seem odd since Rudd had taken so much money from the man. But in Washington, money arrives through a myriad of strange and nebulous conduits. Often those taking it have only a vague idea of where it's coming from; often they have no clue. In most democracies, the transference of so much cash would be considered outright corruption, but in Washington the corruption has been legalized. Senator Rudd didn't know and didn't care that he was owned by other people. He had over $11 million in the bank, money he could eventually keep if not forced to waste it on some frivolous campaign. In return for such an investment, Rudd had a perfect voting record on all matters dealing with pharmaceuticals, chemicals, oil, energy, insurance, banks, and on and on.

But he was a man of the people.

He traveled alone on this night. The two flight attendants served him cocktails, lobster, and wine, and the meal was hardly over when the Gulfstream began its descent into Jackson International. Another limo was waiting, and twenty minutes after landing, The Senator was dropped off at a side entrance of the University Medical Center. In a room on the third floor, he found Ron and Doreen staring blankly at a television while their son slept. "How's the boy?" he asked with great warmth as they scrambled to get to their feet and look somewhat presentable. They were stunned to see the great man himself suddenly appearing from nowhere at 9:30 on a Tuesday night. Doreen couldn't find her shoes.

They chatted softly about Josh and his progress. The Senator claimed to be in town on business, just passing through on his way back to Washington, but he'd heard the news and felt compelled to drop in for a quick hello. They were touched by his presence. In fact, they were rattled and found it hard to believe.

A nurse broke things up and declared it was time to turn off the lights. The Senator hugged Doreen, pecked her cheek, squeezed her hands, promised to do anything within his power to help, then left the room with Ron, who was startled to see no signs of an entourage hovering in the hallway. Not a single staffer, gofer, bodyguard, driver. No one.

The Senator had come to visit, all by himself. The gesture meant even more to Ron.

As they walked down the hall, Rudd offered the same quick "Howdy" and the same plastic grin to everyone they passed. These were his people, and he knew that they adored him. He was blathering on about some mundane fight in Congress, and Ron was trying to appear captivated while suddenly wishing the man would just wrap things up and leave. At the exit doors, Rudd wished him well, promised to pray for the family, and extended offers to help on any front.

As they shook hands, The Senator, almost as an afterthought, said, "By the way, Judge, it'd be nice to finish that *Krane* appeal."

Ron's hand went limp and his jaw dropped. He tried to think of a response. As he treaded water, The Senator gave his parting shot. "I know you'll do the right thing. These verdicts are killing our state."

Rudd grabbed his shoulder, blessed him with another plastic grin, then walked through the doors and disappeared.

Back in the limo, Rudd ordered the driver to the suburbs north of town. There he would spend the night with his Jackson mistress, then hustle back to D.C. on the Gulfstream early in the morning.

———

Ron lay on the cot and tried to settle himself in for another long night. Josh's sleep patterns had become so erratic that every night was a new adventure. When the nurse made the rounds at midnight, both father and son were wide awake. Doreen, thankfully, was at the motel, fast asleep thanks to little green pills the nurses were sneaking to them. Ron took another one, and the nurse gave Josh his own sedative.

In the awful darkness of the room, Ron grappled with the visit by Senator Rudd. Was it a simple matter of an arrogant politician stepping over the line to help a big donor? Rudd relentlessly took money from anyone who wanted to hand it out, legally, so it would be no surprise if he'd taken a bundle from Krane.

Or was it more complicated than that? Krane had not contributed one dime to the Fisk campaign. Ron had combed through the records after the election when he, too, had been shocked at the cash raised and spent. He had argued and fought with Tony Zachary about where the money came from. It's all right there in the reports, Tony said over and over. And Ron had studied the reports. His donors were corporate executives and doctors and defense lawyers and lobbying groups, all dedicated to limiting liability. He knew that when his campaign began.

He smelled a conspiracy, but fatigue finally engulfed him.

———

Somewhere in the deep murkiness of a chemical-induced sleep, Ron heard the steady clicking of something he couldn't identify. Click, click, click, click, the same sound over and over and very rapid. It was near him.

He reached through the darkness and felt Josh's bed, then he bolted to his feet. In the dim light from the bathroom, he could see his son in the grips of a grotesque seizure. His entire body was shaking violently. His face contorted, his mouth open, his eyes wild. The clicking and rattling got louder. Ron pushed the button to call the nurses, then he grabbed Josh by the shoulders and tried to settle him. He was astounded at the ferocity of the attack. Two nurses swept in and took charge. A third was right behind them, then a doctor. There was little to be done except stick a depressor in Josh's mouth to prevent an injury to his tongue.

When Ron couldn't watch any longer, he backed away, into a corner, and looked at the surreal image of his badly damaged son lost in a crowd of helping hands while the bed still shook and rails still clicked. The seizure finally relented, and the nurses were soon washing his face with cool water and speaking in childlike voices. Ron eased from the room for another mindless hike through the corridors.

The seizures continued off and on for twenty-four hours, then abruptly stopped. By that time, Ron and Doreen were too weary and frazzled to do anything but stare at their son and pray that he remained still and calm. Other doctors arrived, all grim faced and uttering incomprehensible words among themselves. More tests were ordered, and Josh was taken away for hours, then brought back.

Days passed and blurred together. Time meant nothing.

———

On a Saturday morning, Ron sneaked into his office at the Gartin building. Both clerks were there, at his request. There were twelve cases to decide, and Ron had read their brief summaries and recommendations. The clerks had their own little docket prepared and were ready for the roll call.

A rape conviction from Rankin County. Affirmed, with a unanimous court.

An election dispute from Bolivar County. Affirmed, with seven others.

An extremely dull secured-transaction brouhaha from Panola County. Affirmed, with a unanimous court.

And so on. With Ron preoccupied and showing little interest in the work, the first ten cases were disposed of in twenty minutes.

"*Baker versus Krane Chemical*," a clerk said.

"What's the buzz?" Ron asked.

"Four–four split, with everybody throwing knives. Calligan and company are quite nervous about you. McElwayne and his side are curious. Everybody's watching, waiting."

"They think I've cracked up?"

"No one's sure. They think you're under a great deal of stress, and there's speculation about some great cathartic flip-flop because of what's happened."

"Let 'em speculate. I'll wait on *Baker* and that nursing home case."

"Are you considering a vote to uphold the verdicts?" the other clerk asked.

Ron had already learned that most of the court's gossip was created and spread by the network of clerks, all of them.

"I don't know," he said. Thirty minutes later, he was back at the hospital.

CHAPTER 38

Eight days later, on a rainy Sunday morning, Josh Fisk was loaded into an ambulance for the drive to Brookhaven. Once there, he would be placed in a room at the hospital five minutes from home. He would be watched closely for a week or so, then, hopefully, released.

Doreen rode with him in the ambulance.

Ron drove to the Gartin building and went to his office on the fourth floor. There was no sign of anyone there, which was precisely what he wanted. For the third or fourth time, he read Calligan's opinion reversing the verdict in *Baker v. Krane Chem-*

ical, and though he had once agreed with it completely, he now had doubts. It could have been written by Jared Kurtin himself. Calligan found fault with virtually all of *Baker*'s expert testimony. He criticized Judge Harrison for admitting most of it. His sharpest language condemned the expert who linked the carcinogenic by-products to the actual cancers, calling it "speculative at best." He imposed an impossible standard that would require clear proof that the toxins in the Bowmore water caused the cancers that killed Pete and Chad Baker. As always, he caterwauled at the sheer size of the shocking verdict, and blamed it on the undue passion created by Baker's attorneys that inflamed the jurors.

Ron read again the opinion by McElwayne, and it, too, sounded much different.

It was time to vote, to make his decision, and he simply had no stomach for it. He was tired of the case, tired of the pressure, tired of the anger at being used like a pawn by powerful forces he should have recognized. He was exhausted from Josh's ordeal and just wanted to go home. He had no confidence in his ability to do what was right, and he wasn't sure what that was anymore. He had prayed until he was tired of praying. He had tried to explain his misgivings to Doreen, but she was as distracted and unstable as he was.

If he reversed the verdict, he would betray his true feelings. But his feelings were changing, were they not? How could he, as a detached jurist, suddenly swap sides because of his family's tragedy?

If he upheld the verdict, he would betray those who had elected him. Fifty-three percent of the people had voted for Ron Fisk because they believed in his platform. Or did they? Perhaps they had voted for him because he was so well marketed.

Would it be fair to all the Aarons out there for Ron to selfishly change his judicial philosophy because of his own son?

He hated these questions. They exhausted him even more. He paced around his office, more confused than ever, and he thought of leaving again. Just run, he told himself. But he was tired of running and pacing and talking to the walls.

He typed his opinion: "I concur and agree with Justice Calligan, but I do so with grave misgivings. This court, with my complicity and especially because of my presence, has rapidly become a blind protector of those who wish to severely restrict liability in all areas of personal injury law. It is a dangerous course."

In the nursing home case, he typed his second opinion: "I concur with Justice Albritton and uphold the verdict rendered in the Circuit Court of Webster County. The actions of the nursing home fall far short of the standard of care our laws require."

Then he typed a memo to the court that read: "For the next thirty days, I will be on a leave of absence from the court's business. I am needed at home."

The Supreme Court of Mississippi posts its rulings on its Web site each Thursday at noon.

And each Thursday at noon quite a few lawyers either sat before their computers in nervous anticipation or made sure someone did so for them. Jared Kurtin kept an associate on guard. Sterling Bintz watched his smart phone at that precise hour, regardless of where in the world he happened to be. F. Clyde Hardin, still a caveman with technology, sat in the darkness of his locked office, drank his lunch, and waited. Every trial lawyer with a Bowmore case kept watch.

The anticipation was shared by a few nonlawyers as well. Tony Zachary and Barry Rinehart made it a point to be on the phone with each other when the opinions came down. Carl Trudeau counted the minutes each week. In lower and mid-Manhattan dozens of securities analysts monitored the Web site. Denny Ott had a sandwich with his wife in the office at the church. The parsonage next door did not have a computer.

And nowhere was the magical hour more dreaded and anticipated than within the shabby confines of Payton & Payton. The entire firm gathered in The Pit, at the always cluttered worktable, and had lunch as Sherman stared at his laptop. On the first Thursday in May, at 12:15, he announced, "Here it is." Food was shoved aside. The air grew thinner, and breathing became more difficult. Wes refused to look at Mary Grace, and she refused to look at him. Indeed, no one in the room made eye contact with anyone else.

"The opinion is written by Justice Arlon Calligan," Sherman continued. "I'll just skim along here. Five pages, ten pages, fifteen pages, let's see, a majority opinion that's twenty-one pages long, joined by Romano, Bateman, Ross, Fisk. Reversed and rendered. Final judgment entered for the defendant, Krane Chemical."

Sherman continued: "Romano concurs with four pages of his usual drivel. Fisk concurs briefly." A pause as he kept scrolling. "And then a twelve-page dissent by McElwayne with Albritton concurring. That's all I need to know. I won't read this piece of shit for at least a month." He stood and left the room.

"It's not exactly a surprise," Wes said. No one responded.

———

F. Clyde Hardin wept at his desk. This disaster had been looming for months, but it still crushed him. His one chance to strike it rich was gone, and with it all of his dreams. He cursed Sterling Bintz and his harebrained class action. He cursed Ron Fisk and the other four clowns in his majority. He cursed the blind sheep in Cary County and throughout the rest of south Mississippi who had been hoodwinked into voting against Sheila McCarthy. He fixed another vodka, then cursed and drank and cursed and drank until he passed out with his head on his desk.

Seven doors down, Babe took a phone call and got the news. Her coffee shop was soon packed with the Main Street crowd looking for answers and gossip and support. For many, the news was incomprehensible. There would be no cleanup, no recovery, no compensation, no apologies. Krane Chemical was walking free and thumbing its nose at the town and its victims.

Denny Ott received a call from Mary Grace. She gave a quick summary and stressed that the litigation was over. They had no viable options. The only avenue left was an appeal to the U.S. Supreme Court, and they would, of course, file the obligatory paperwork. But there was no chance that the Court would agree to consider such a case. She and Wes would be down in a few days to meet with their clients.

Denny and his wife opened the fellowship hall, pulled out some cookies and bottled water, and waited for their people to arrive for consoling.

Late in the afternoon, Mary Grace walked into Wes's office and closed the door. She had two sheets of paper, and she handed one to him. It was a letter to their Bowmore clients. "Take a look," she said, and sat down to read it herself. It read:

Dear Client:
Today the Supreme Court of Mississippi ruled in favor of Krane Chemical. Jeannette Baker's appeal was reversed and rendered, which means that it cannot be retried or re-filed. We intend to ask the court for a rehearing, which is customary, but also a waste of time. We will also appeal her case to the U.S. Supreme Court, but this, too, is a mere formality. That Court rarely considers state court cases such as this.
Today's ruling, and we will send you a full copy next week, makes it impossible to proceed with your case against Krane. The court applied a standard of proof that makes it impossible to pin liability on the company. And it's painfully obvious

what would happen to another verdict when presented to the same court.

Words cannot express our disappointment and frustration. We have fought this battle for five years against enormous odds, and we have lost in many ways.

But our losses are nothing compared to yours. We will continue to think of you, pray for you, and talk to you whenever you need us. We have been honored by your trust. God bless you.

"Very nice," Wes said. "Let's get 'em in the mail."

———

Krane Chemical roared to life in the afternoon's trading. It gained $4.75 a share and closed at $38.50. Mr. Trudeau had now regained the billion he lost, and more was on the way.

He gathered Bobby Ratzlaff, Felix Bard, and two other confidants in his office for a little party. They sipped Cristal champagne, smoked Cuban cigars, and congratulated themselves on their stunning turnaround. They now considered Carl a true genius, a visionary. Even in the darkest days, he never wavered. His mantra had been "Buy the stock. Buy the stock."

He reminded Bobby of his promise on the day of the verdict. Not one dime of his hard-earned profits would ever be handed over to those ignorant people and their slimy lawyers.

CHAPTER 39

The guests ranged from hard-core Wall Street types like Carl himself all the way down to Brianna's hair colorist and two semi-employed Broadway actors. There were bankers with their aging though nicely sculpted wives, and moguls with their superbly starved trophies. There were Trudeau Group executives who would rather have been anywhere else, and struggling painters from the MuAb crowd who were thrilled at the rare chance to mingle with the jet set. There were a few models, number 388 on the Forbes 400 list, a running back who played for the Jets, a reporter from the

Times along with a photographer to record it all, and a reporter from the *Journal* who would report none of it but didn't want to miss the party. About a hundred guests, all in all a very rich crowd, but no one at the party had ever seen a yacht like the *Brianna.*

It was docked on the Hudson at the Chelsea Piers, and the only vessel larger at that moment was a mothballed aircraft carrier a quarter of a mile to the north. In the rarefied world of obscenely expensive boating, the *Brianna* was classified as a mega-yacht, which was larger than a super-yacht but not in the same league as a giga-yacht. The latter, so far, had been the exclusive domain of a handful of software zillionaires, Saudi princes, and Russian oil thugs.

The invitation read: "Please join Mr. and Mrs. Carl Trudeau on the maiden voyage of their mega-yacht, *Brianna*, on Wednesday, May 26, at 6 p.m., at Pier 60."

It was 192 feet long, which ranked it number twenty-one on the list of the largest yachts registered in America. Carl paid $60 million for it two weeks after Ron Fisk was elected, then spent another $15 million on renovations, upgrades, and toys.

Now it was time to show it off, and to display one of the more dramatic comebacks in recent corporate history. The crew of eighteen gave tours as the guests arrived and took their glasses of champagne. With four decks above water, the ship could comfortably accommodate thirty pampered friends for a month at sea, not that Carl ever intended to have that many people living so close to him. Those lucky enough to be chosen for an extended cruise would have access to a gym with a trainer, a spa with a masseuse, six Jacuzzis, and a chef on call around the clock. They would dine at one of four tables scattered throughout the boat, the smallest with ten seats and the largest with forty. When they felt like playing, there was scuba gear, clear-bottom kayaks, a thirty-foot catamaran, Jet Skis, and fishing gear, and, of course, no mega-yacht is complete without a helicopter. Other luxuries included a movie theater, four fireplaces, a sky lounge, heated tile floors in the bathrooms, a private pool for nude sunbathing, and miles of mahogany and brass and Italian marble. The Trudeaus' stateroom was larger than their bedroom back on land. And, in the formal dining room on the third level, Carl had finally found the permanent place for *Abused Imelda*.

Never again would she greet him in the foyer of his penthouse after a hard day at the office.

As a string quartet played on the main deck, the *Brianna* shoved off and turned south on the Hudson. It was dusk, a beautiful sunset, and the view of lower Manhattan from the river was breathtaking. The city shook with its frenetic energy, which was fascinating to watch from the deck of such a fine boat. The champagne and caviar also helped the view. Those on ferries and smaller vessels couldn't help but gawk as *Brianna* moved by, her twin 2,000-horsepower Caterpillar diesels churning a quiet wake.

A small army of black-tied waiters moved deftly about the decks, hauling drinks on silver trays and finger food too pretty to eat. Carl ignored most of his guests and spent his time with those he controlled, one way or another. Brianna was the perfect hostess, gliding from group to group, kissing all the men and all the women, making sure everyone got the chance to see her.

The captain circled wide so the guests

could have a nice view of Ellis Island and the Statue of Liberty, then turned north in the direction of the Battery, at the southern tip of Manhattan. It was dark now, and the rows of skyscrapers lit up the financial district. Under the Brooklyn Bridge, under the Manhattan Bridge, under the Williamsburg Bridge, the *Brianna* sailed up the East River in all its majesty. The string quartet retired, and the best of Billy Joel boomed through the ship's elaborate sound system. Dancing erupted on the second-level deck. Someone got shoved into a pool. Others followed, and clothing soon became optional. It was the younger crowd.

As per Carl's instructions, the captain turned around at the United Nations building and increased speed, though it was not noticed. Carl, at that moment, was giving an interview in his sweeping office on the third deck.

At precisely 10:30, on schedule, the *Brianna* docked at Pier 60, and the guests began their slow departures. Mr. and Mrs. Trudeau saw them off, hugging, kissing, waving, wishing they would all hurry along now. A midnight dinner was waiting. Fourteen remained behind, seven lucky couples who would cruise south to Palm Beach for a few days. They changed into more casual clothing and met in the formal dining room for yet another drink while the chef finalized the first course.

Carl whispered to the first mate that it was now time to leave, and fifteen minutes later the *Brianna* pushed off again from Pier 60. While the guests were being charmed by his wife, he excused himself for a few minutes. He climbed the steps to the fourth level, and on a small elevated deck found his favorite spot on this fabulous new toy of his. It was an observation post, the ship's highest point above the water.

As the cool wind blew his hair, he gripped the brass railing and stared at the mammoth towers in the financial district. He caught a glimpse of his building, and his office, forty-five floors up.

Everything was up. Krane common stock was just under $50 a share. Its earnings were through the roof. His net worth was over $3 billion and rising steadily.

Some of those idiots out there had been laughing eighteen months earlier. Krane is finished. Trudeau is a fool. How can a man lose a billion dollars in one day? they howled.

Where was their laughter now?

Where were all those experts now?

The great Carl Trudeau had outfoxed them again. He'd cleaned up the Bowmore mess and saved his company. He'd driven its stock into the ground, bought it cheap at a fire sale, and now owned virtually all of it. It was making him even richer.

He was destined to move up the Forbes 400 list, and as Carl sailed along the Hudson at the very top of his extraordinary ship, and gazed with smug satisfaction at the gleaming towers packed around Wall Street, he admitted to himself that nothing else mattered.

Now that he had three billion, he really wanted six.

Author's Note

I am compelled to defend my native state, and do so with this flurry of disclaimers. All characters herein are purely fictional. Any similarity to a real person is coincidental. There is no Cary County, no town of Bowmore, no Krane Chemical, and no product such as pillamar 5. Bichloronylene, aklar, and cartolyx do not exist, as far as I know. The Mississippi Supreme Court has nine elected members, none of whom were used as models or inspiration for anyone mentioned or described in the preceding pages. None of the organizations, associations, groups, nonprofits, think tanks, churches, casinos, or corporations are real. I just made them up. Some of the towns and cities can be found on a map, others cannot. The campaign is a figment of my imagination. The lawsuit is borrowed from several actual cases. A few of the buildings really do exist, but I'm not altogether sure which ones.

In another life, I served as a member of the Mississippi House of Representatives, and in that capacity had a role in making laws. In this book, some of those laws have been amended, modified, ignored, and even outright butchered. Writing fiction sometimes requires this.

A few of the laws, especially those dealing with casino gambling, survive without tampering on my part.

Now that I have impugned my own work, I must say that there is a lot of truth in this story. As long as private money is allowed in judicial elections we will see competing interests fight for seats on the bench. The issues are fairly common. Most of the warring factions are adequately described. The tactics are all too familiar. The results are not far off the mark.

As always, I leaned on others for advice

and expertise. Thanks to Mark Lee, Jim Craig, Neal Kassell, Bobby Moak, David Gernert, Mike Ratliff, Ty, Bert Colley, and John Sherman. Stephen Rubin published this book, Doubleday's twentieth, and the gang there—John Fontana, Rebecca Holland, John Pitts, Kathy Trager, Alison Rich, and Suzanne Herz—again made it happen.

And thanks to Renee for her usual patience and abundance of editorial comments.

John Grisham
October 1, 2007